# Sacred Bond

## Splintered Empire Book Two

Erin Robinson

Editing by Yvette Rebello at yreditor.com

Proofreading by Ebb and Flow Editing

Cover by Maria at Steamy Designs

# Dedication

*For the girls who need to be loud and take up space without any guilt or shame—you deserve it regardless of what anyone else says.*

# Contents

# Author's Note

This is an adult dark mafia romance. It contains on-page violence, murder, as well as graphic depictions of abuse. For the full list of content warnings, please visit the author's website at authorerinrobinson.com/content-warnings

# CHAPTER 1

# Emiliya

C haos is just as likely to be a blight as it is an asset, but if I've
learned anything over a lifetime of being beaten down
and tossed aside, it's that if you see an opportunity, you need to
grab it with both hands and hold on like your life depends on
it.

I toss my hair over my shoulder as I move to the pulsing beat
of the music, flashing a flirty smile at the man who's pulling me
against him, pulling me closer so he can grind against my ass.

His grip is on the wrong side of too tight, fingers digging in
until I have to fight the urge to pull away.

I spent way too long styling my hair to let this moron stop me
from enjoying myself.

Enclave is Bratva-owned, but either this guy doesn't know
that, or he has no clue who I am. I force myself not to flinch
when he puts his face next to mine. His breath reeks of cheap
liquor, making me cringe as he smiles in a way I'm sure he
thinks is charming, but instead makes him come across as an
overconfident dick.

"Want to get out of here?"

No. Not only no, but *absolutely the fuck not*.

It's been one dance—one that I didn't even ask for—and the smirk on his face tells me he thinks he's *entitled* to my time. He slips his hands to the small of my back, pressing me so tight against him I have no choice but to contend with the smell of stale cigarettes clinging to his clothes.

I swallow hard to trap my gag in my throat.

The last thing I want is to spend more time with this guy, but when I try to wiggle free from his pawing hands, his fingers dig in, like he can keep me here out of sheer force of will.

*Fantastic.*

Security is dotted around the club, both hired men and Bratva men who won't hesitate to handle this guy if I manage to get their attention, but the whole point of tonight was to be anonymous, to cut loose.

I flutter my eyelashes, putting on a practiced expression, and keep my limbs loose, pretending the way his fingers are playing with the hem of my dress isn't making my skin crawl.

"Sure, handsome," I reply. His answering grin shows far too many teeth for him to look friendly. "Let me freshen up, and we can head out." My tone is so sickly sweet it makes me nauseous, but if it gets me away from this creep without making a scene, it'll be worth it.

He takes a step back with a nod. It takes more effort than I'm willing to admit to hold back a sigh of relief.

"Meet you at the bar." He grins with an uncoordinated wink. It looks more like he's having a muscle spasm than anything else.

God help the next woman he subjects himself to, but it isn't going to be me.

I make my way toward the bathrooms, putting an extra sway in my hips as I move, the easy smile dropping as soon as I turn around.

What a creep.

I figured Alexei Trenin's club would be safer than going somewhere that wasn't affiliated with the Bratva. But the downside of it is knowing that if I have to ask for help, it'll inevitably get back to my father, and I don't need another one of his lectures any time soon.

When I turn toward the back exit, the shape of firm shoulders encased in a suit so perfectly tailored it would be a crime to look away catches my eye, snatching my attention and crumpling up my plans to slip out the back door like a piece of scrap paper. I pause, silently begging the crowd to conceal me as I watch Alexei slip out of a hidden door, taking care to lock it behind him.

Of all his clubs, why'd he have to be at this one? Enclave is his oldest business. Wouldn't his time be better spent at Savage, which only opened a few months ago? Why is he *here*?

From what I've gathered, his clubs practically print money, but the newest one is raking in cash hand over hand.

Given the shitshow that losing Maksim, the former pakhan, has been, I figured Alexei would be locked away with the rest of the loud, angry men who want to find a quick end to the brewing war with The Outfit—not working in his oldest club.

Alexei's blond hair is messy, his waves a riot like he's been running his hands through them, and his normally clean-shaven cheeks have a shadow of scruff that only appears after a long day.

We've never been properly introduced, and I'm banking on him being so caught up in his own work that he has no idea who I am. Father likes to trot me out and show me off on occasion, but I do a decent job of staying away from most of the men who grace our halls for business.

Whether or not he knows me, I know Alexei. At least in theory.

His existence has been a thorn in my side for months, and even though this is so far from what I was planning, I know an opportunity when I see one.

My shoulders relax as I walk toward him, my hips moving with the beat. I can only hope that sweating on the dance floor smeared my makeup in that perfect just-got-fucked way men lose their minds over, because I'm not going to waste time detouring to check in the bathroom.

Not when Alexei's such a difficult man to catch alone.

I teeter on my heels, nearly falling flat when I see who's standing next at the bar, right in the direction Alexei's walking.

Just my fucking luck.

The handsy asshole is still there, scanning the room as he looks for me, and Alexei's heading right for him.

Well, there goes my chance of not making a scene. I need to find a way to spin this in my favor, because if I blow this chance, I have no clue when—or if—I'll be able to engineer another one.

Abandoning my attempts to remain unseen, I shuffle toward the bar just like any other patron would, making sure to look both surprised and confused when the asshole saunters up to me, wrapping an overbearing arm around my shoulders.

"There you are, babe." He smirks, and when I try to duck out from under him, he grabs my shoulder, pulling me against his side. "What took you so long?" He tries to maneuver me to face the door, but I dig my heels in, pressing my hands against his chest.

"What're you talking about?" My voice is louder than it needs to be, pulling the attention of the people around us as I twist free. "Who are you?"

His brows draw together, his eyes glinting with poorly concealed anger.

"Very funny, babe." He chuckles, but it doesn't reach his eyes. "C'mon, let's get out of here." He grabs my bicep, trying to drag me toward the entrance with a clenched jaw.

"Let go of me!"

If he weren't such an entitled ass, and Alexei weren't here, maybe I would've been content to spend the night with this guy. Too bad he doesn't have the charm to pull off his arrogant attitude.

More heads turn in our direction, but I only need one.

As if on cue, someone steps up behind me, the air practically vibrating with his anger. The creep's grip tightens, but when he looks up, his face pales. His reaction is all I need to confirm what I already knew.

This creep knows exactly who this nightclub belongs to, and he knows exactly what sort of consequences he was inviting by pushing himself on someone here.

*Mudak.*

"Is there a problem here?" Alexei's voice is gravely, a low rumble that sends a shiver down my spine. The grip on my arm drops away as the guy puts his hands up in front of him in an effort to look as harmless as possible. Sweat dots his brow, and if I were a better person, I might feel bad for him.

Unfortunately for him, I'm nothing but my father's daughter. Besides my mother, no one would ever accuse me of being a good person.

I rub the place where he held me, trying to stave off the red marks that are already appearing. He's lucky that his claws weren't tight enough to leave bruises, but I hope the dim lights are enough to hide the marks.

Talk about a turnoff.

"No problem," he says with a grin. His hands are shaking as he lowers them to his sides. "My girl here is just playing a little game. You know how it is, right?"

A chill sweeps over me at the vicious glint in his eye as he calls me *his girl*.

Alexei's nostrils flare as he looks at this guy like he's less than the gum on the bottom of his shoe, his strong jaw clenched so hard the muscles flex with the effort. His eyes radiate pure malice, and I bite my lip.

Alexei snaps his fingers, holding out his hand.

"Give me your ID."

The creep takes a half step back, only to bump into another man as a hand clamps down on his shoulder, holding him in place. His eyes dart around the room, wide and wild as he looks for any sort of lifeline, but everyone else has gone back to studiously minding their own business.

Most people have enough self-preservation to ignore trouble when they see it, and no one's stupid enough to walk into a Bratva club and stand up to the owner.

"Hey, man, I'm not looking for any trouble." The creep tries to pry himself loose, but freezes when the man holding him leans forward, saying something into his ear that I can't hear over the music.

"Do you know this man?" Alexei asks me, his hazel eyes probing.

I've never been this close to him before. I've only ever seen Alexei from a distance, but this close, I'm pinned in place by the gold flecks in his eyes, fiery and hypnotizing. It's almost painful to tear my gaze away from them.

Mutely, I shake my head.

I don't need to be looking at him to feel the moment he looks away when his guard holds out the guy's driver's license, his wallet in the other hand. I don't want to find out what he did to get it so easily. With his buzzed hair and shadowed eyes, he looks exactly like the type of person I'd hate to be caught alone in a room with.

"Nathaniel Elijah Cohen," Alexei reads, sounding bored. "2118 Blue Spring Road. Not an organ donor," he remarks, tucking the ID into his back pocket. "I'm shocked." His dry tone almost startles a laugh out of me, but the smirk on his guard's face tells me that he sees me clear as day.

"Now, I've been under the impression that the sort of game where you pretend you're not interested requires previous discussion. It isn't the kind of thing you spring on someone who claims to have never met you." Alexei leans forward, his voice a cold steel blade. "Tell me, Nathaniel, do you even know this woman's name?"

"Y-yeah. Of course I do." The asshole's eyes cut to mine, like he expects me to be the one to throw him a rope. "That's Katie. We've been dating for three weeks. Right?" His Adam's apple bobs as he swallows thickly. "Babe?"

I sway where I stand, pulling on the hem of my dress so it shows off less of my thighs as I meet Alexei's eyes. He has one brow raised in question, his hands held casually in his pockets.

"I've never met this man before."

Not technically a lie. Nathaniel didn't bother to introduce himself. Then again, with a name like that, I'd probably skip introductions, too.

Alexei nods, humming to himself.

His skin is a warm shock to my system as he cups my elbow. "In that case, Mr. Cohen," he says, looking deadly, "Lev here is going to escort you out. If, by some miracle, he leaves you with enough brainpower to even *think* about entering one of my establishments again, rest assured that he won't make the same mistake twice."

I flush at how casually he's able to command attention, and I can only hope no one notices.

Without another word, his guard—*Lev*—effortlessly maneuvers the asshole through the crowd, ignoring Nathaniel's blubbering and panicked, desperate protests.

"Are you alright?" Alexei asks, his voice no less commanding, but without the edge it had.

I smile shyly, tucking my hair behind my ear. I don't miss the way his eyes trace down the length of my body, lingering briefly on my cleavage.

"Better now, thank you."

I'll be the first one to say I'm no good at playing coy, but after his little show, it's a little easier than normal.

His hand still lingers on my arm, his thumb mindlessly stroking over the crook of my elbow. Goosebumps break out wherever he touches, and I lean into the touch, angling my body toward his as my breasts oh-so-casually graze against his arm. I let out a shaky breath at the jolt that shoots through my system at the small amount of pressure against my nipples, tight against the inside of my dress.

His eyes darken with something entirely different, and I lick my lower lip, noting the way his eyes track the movement.

"No problem." His eyes dart to the bar, like he's replanning his whole evening. "Can I get you a drink?"

"I'd like that."

It only takes one drink before he's opening the back door of his SUV, mouth pressed against mine in a scorching hot kiss. His tongue works against mine as I undo the buttons of his shirt one by one, while he pushes me back until I'm lying across the seat with a hand loosely holding the base of my throat.

My legs fall open on either side of his hips, my short dress riding up my thighs as Alexei settles his weight between them. He shrugs off his suit jacket while I pull his shirt out of his pants, almost desperate to have his skin against mine.

The door slamming shut behind him has me pulling back, meeting his smirk as his hands move along my calf, his touch briefly lingering over the small birthmark on my shin. He rubs the muscle until he reaches my ankle, thumb stroking along the skin above the strap of my heel.

"I like this dress," he says, his voice even deeper with want. "I'll like it even more on the ground." He looks ravenous as he takes me in, his eyes following every line of my body like I'm a work of art. "Ditch it."

I shiver under the weight of his gaze.

He releases me to shrug off his shirt, making quick work of his belt. When he pressed me against the vehicle, the strength of his muscles was obvious, but seeing them is an entirely different beast. I can't help but stare at the defined lines of his abs, his obliques painting a tantalizing arrow that disappears into his waistband.

Every inch of him is smooth and unmarred—no scars or tattoos to take away from the body he appears to have carved from marble.

Alexei nips at the sensitive skin on the inside of my knee, and it startles me enough to shock me back into motion. He lets out a throaty chuckle as I quickly undo the zipper at my side and lift my hips so I can slide free of the dress, leaving me in just my bra, thong, and heels.

"You're fucking gorgeous," he murmurs, slipping his pants down enough to expose the sizable bulge in his boxer briefs.

I undo my bra, dropping it into the footwell as he groans, a low rumble that I swear I can feel in my core. I shift my hips, feeling his gaze like a physical touch as he takes me in.

Fuck, when was the last time I was this wet? And he's hardly even touched me.

He pauses just long enough to pull a condom out of his pocket before he hooks his thumbs into his waistband, pulling his pants and boxers off to let his hard cock twitch free.

He takes his length into one hand, squeezing the base as he rips open the condom wrapper with his teeth, and I gape at his cock. He's absolutely stunning, every part of him. Thick and veiny, long enough that I know he'll hit all the right spots.

I bite my lip to hold back a whimper.

I kind of hope he's terrible in bed, because if he isn't, I'm handing him a prime opportunity to absolutely ruin me for anyone else.

No man has the right to be this good-looking.

Alexei sheaths his cock in the thin rubber before he drapes himself over me, his breaths scorching against the length of my neck as his fingers tease the edges of my thong. His teeth are sharp along my collarbone, and I gasp as he twists his hand sharply, tearing my thong from my body. He smirks while I stroke my fingers through his hair, pushing back the strands that have fallen to obscure his brow.

Fuck, his hair's soft.

He moves his lips to my tits, eagerly taking a peaked nipple into his mouth while he traces his hands over my ribs. I hiss when he brushes against the bruise there, cursing internally. I forgot about that. Fortunately, his car's parked in the back lot, and it's dark. The overhead light clicked off a while ago, so I doubt he'll be able to see it.

He pulls his mouth away, so I buck my hips against his stomach, forcing an airless giggle. "I'm ticklish," I tell him with a cheeky smile.

For a moment, the air in the SUV is frozen, and I hold my breath. He must believe me, because he returns his focus to my breasts, trapping a nipple between his teeth.

He alternates between sucking and biting, soothing away the sting with his tongue.

Normally, I'd tell a guy to be careful not to leave marks, but every time I collect myself enough to think about saying anything, Alexei does something new to make me gasp or moan, pushing my worries so far into the back of my mind I might never find them again.

His thick fingers swipe over my cunt, taunting my entrance and teasing my clit in slow circles.

I'm not sure if it's me or if he managed to turn on the car and crank up the heat while I wasn't looking, but my blood is on fire. My hips work against his hand, unable to resist him. My head falls back, eyes clenched shut against the onslaught.

His tongue traces over the small tattoo on my right hip bone as he hooks my calf over his shoulder, opening me further.

When his finger pushes inside me, I sigh in relief, only to cry out when his tongue takes over, working the sensitive nub. Instantly, my hands are back in his hair, and I can't tell if I'm trying to hold him in place or tear him away from me. He takes my clit into his mouth, sucking gently, and it's so perfect I could cry.

"Oh, shit!" I cry as my hips jerk. My muscles are like a spring coiled to its breaking point.

He crooks his fingers against a spot that has me seeing stars, and it's more than I can stand. The tension snaps, and my ears are filled with static as my vision flashes white.

"Fuck!"

Alexei laps at my release, drawing out each wave of pleasure with every torturous lap of his tongue. I pull his hair to move him away before the stimulation pushes over the line too much, dragging him up my body.

His lascivious smirk is enough to reignite the smoldering embers of my arousal. With his lips just a breath from mine, I lick over the seam of them, groaning when I taste my own arousal.

And as much as I enjoyed it, if I don't get to feel his thick cock inside me soon, I'm going to start getting desperate. And I refuse to beg.

"I need you to fuck me," I tell him, pulling him back by his hair until his eyes meet mine. His eyes are hooded, but it does nothing to hide his amusement.

"You know, I don't typically take orders." He hums, shifting so I can feel the crown of his covered cock nudging against my pulsing entrance. "But just this once, I'll oblige you." With that, he enters me in a single stroke, making my head fall against the door in pleasure.

I'm consumed by the delicious stretch, unable to think as he sets a steady rhythm. My nails sink into the smooth skin on the back of his neck in an attempt to ground myself. He lets out a low groan, and on his next thrust he finds my G-spot, forcing a cry from me.

"God, this fucking cunt," Alexei groans, holding my hips like it's the only thing keeping him grounded.

He nips my earlobe, forcing my attention back to him. "You're going to come on my cock," he coos. "Your tight little cunt is going to milk me until I drain my balls inside you, until you're begging for me to stop."

My breath stutters in my chest as he chuckles, a low rumble that rolls through me. "Do you understand, Emiliya?"

I only have enough wherewithal to nod, beyond caring that he knows my name, that he knows exactly who I am.

Not when my name sounds so damn good on his tongue.

He's relentless, driving into my pussy with single-minded determination, like it's the only thing he cares about. A familiar pressure builds, and when he moves just right, my clit dragging against him, it explodes.

He stills, and I can feel him pulsing inside me as he spills into the condom.

Slowly, I sink back down to earth. First, I feel the tingling in my limbs, aftershocks of my orgasm still sparking along my nerves. Then, I feel how raw my throat is, like I've been screaming. Only then do I realize Alexei's still on top of me, his breathing ragged even as he pulls out and takes care of the condom.

Without him there to keep me warm, the cold rushes back in to take his place.

Alexei's shoulders are relaxed, and I take his cue, cleaning myself up the best I can while refusing to acknowledge the awkward, self-conscious feelings trying to filter in past the pleasant buzzing under my skin.

What are you supposed to say to someone after the best sex of your life? *Thanks, let's do it again sometime?*

Ugh.

I can't find my bra, but I'm sure Alexei will get a chuckle out of it when he eventually stumbles across it. I slip on my dress as he buttons his slacks, and I'm once again struck by how unfair it is that he's so fucking hot.

His hair's even more ruffled than it was inside the club, his shirt's hanging loose around his shoulders, and he still manages to look like he just walked away from a photoshoot.

A filthy photoshoot, but still.

Biting the inside of my cheek, I run my fingers through my hair, doing my best to tame what I'm sure has become a rat's nest.

When he opens the door, I slip out with him. Even in my heels, I have to stand on my tiptoes to press a kiss to his cheek.

"I'll see you around?" he asks.

I nod, and the corner of his mouth quirks up in a sinful smirk.

"I'm sure you will."

# CHAPTER 2

# Emiliya

The clatter of cutlery against dinnerware pierces through the numbness I've tried to hide behind, making my skin crawl.

In another life, the house used to be full of laughter, music, and smiles. Mom and I would tell stories, play noisy games, and dance along to the music coming from her old record player. Father didn't love it, but he tolerated our noise because we were easier to put up with when we were happy.

But his tolerance has become paper thin since Mom started getting sick.

Now, we both flinch at anything louder than a whisper when he's around. We tiptoe on eggshells, doing everything we can to stay out of his way.

After a lifetime of laughter and song, the silence is deafening.

I want to lash out. Throw dishes around the room. Scream in his face. Throw a temper tantrum that forces him to feel even an ounce of the rage and fear he's inflicted on us without a second thought.

Mom's better at playing the game than I am. She knows how to be as quiet as a mouse, so still you wouldn't even know she was there if you weren't looking.

Father always looks at me like he's picking apart every detail and storing it away to analyze later.

"Have you made any progress with Trenin?"

The calculating look in Father's eye cuts me deeper than I will ever let him know. I want to sink into my chair and disappear, but that's not a luxury I can afford.

I nod silently, hoping it will be enough to satiate him.

If he prods—if he makes me think too hard about what he's asked me to do—I'll end up feeling like nothing but a pretty body, an empty shell for everyone else to just put away when it gets inconvenient.

It's easier to dole out breadcrumbs than it is to linger over the thought, wondering just how close to the truth that is.

"Use your words, Emiliya," he snarls. "You aren't a fucking bobblehead."

The food the cook prepared tastes like dirt under his withering glare.

"Yes, Father." I force my tone to morph into something pleasant and cheerful, a far cry from the disgust and simmering venom brewing in my chest. "I ran into him at his club the other night, and we spoke for a while."

Of all the roles and masks I've spent so long mastering, the happy one Father demands fits the worst. Even thinking about forcing a smile wears at my nerves and makes my stomach turn, threatening to purge itself of the food I managed to choke down.

Father hums dismissively, and I allow myself to go back to shuffling the food around my plate, wordlessly begging time to pass without his notice.

God, I wish he were distracted by Maksim. I had hoped that his death would at least distract Father and make him turn his attention elsewhere. Without a clear leader to take charge, the whole of the Bratva should be in a state of chaos, but Father looks as relaxed as a man like him can get.

The lines on his forehead are no more pronounced, and for once, his hands aren't balled into fists.

He takes a sip of whatever liquor is in his glass, his eyes drifting shut as he savors it.

I hope he fucking chokes on it.

The way he lords himself over Mom and me is exhausting. I can never tell what's going to set him off, and I don't know how much longer I can keep my guard up while I prepare for his next mood swing.

At least he's been focusing his rage on me and not Mom. I can try to avoid being home, just in case, but if Mom's having a bad day, she doesn't have the same luxury.

If I were braver, I'd ask her if he was like this when I was a child. I'd ask her if she took his abuse behind closed doors to protect me.

But I'm a fucking coward, and I'm terrified the truth will break me. It's bad enough that adulthood has shattered the illusion of my happy childhood.

I sip my water, watching as she delicately puts down her cutlery, her throat bobbing as she tries to swallow.

*Oh no.*

"I wanted to wait a few days to reach out to him again," I blurt out before Father can notice her struggling. She shoots me a grateful look, her whole head moving in my direction as she discreetly massages her throat, trying to force the food down.

Having difficulty chewing and swallowing isn't her most visible symptom, but it's the one that Father has the least patience for.

Last time I asked her about it, she said her doctor gave her a list of exercises that can help, but they're useless if she doesn't do them.

"I expect you to do more than talking."

A familiar flush of contrition blankets my cheeks, hollowing out my stomach. I meet his eyes, refusing to let him see the effect his words have on me.

"Of course, Father."

I smile.

He's like a shark in the water. If I spill a drop of blood, he'll go right for the kill.

"You've already fucked up once. Don't disappoint me again, *printsessa*."

I bite the inside of my cheek, forcing myself to go through the motions of eating.

This is far from the first time he's used my relationship with Daniil Krutikov against me, but it's no easier to stomach.

I was stupid enough to let Daniil use me in an attempt to get back into Maksim's favor, but that doesn't make it easier to swallow. If I could go back in time and scream at myself to stop being a moron, I'd do it in a heartbeat.

I'd shake myself until something finally rattled around in my empty head and clicked, and run far away from that *ublyudok*.

It's bad enough I let him fuck me when I knew he was a married man, but letting Father manipulate me into keeping the affair going so he could progress his own agenda only made everything even worse.

I can't undo the past, but I'm not going to let myself be that stupid again, either.

Mom makes a small sound in the back of her throat, and Father's cruel eyes flash in annoyance. Faster than I can say anything to distract him, he's already glaring, the knuckles of his clenched fists white where they rest on the table.

"Is there a problem, dear?" he sneers, voice sardonic as my mother shakes her head, face turning red as she struggles to hold back a cough.

She looks so miserable. Her cheeks are thinner, her normally tan skin is pale and sallow, and she looks so tired I'm worried she'll fall asleep at the table.

"Then get it together," Father snaps, the harsh sound of his voice a dull roar in the quiet room. It's enough to startle Mom into another coughing fit, eyes clenched shut as she tries to take a clear breath.

"Jesus fucking Christ," he mutters, taking another sip from his glass.

I shove my fear deep, rushing over to pat her on the back as firmly as I'm able to with shaking hands. When she's finally able to breathe again, her eyes lift to mine.

"*Spasibo, lastochka.*"

I nod, grabbing a napkin to wipe up the water that spilled down her chin with a small smile.

"Get her cleaned up," Father orders, pushing back from the table with a clatter, eyes spitting fire as he watches me. "And clean up the rest of this shit. When you're done, meet me in my office."

I look at the half-eaten plates on the table, and the glasses that have been knocked over, then glance at the doorway just in time to watch the maid scurry away, apparently taking his words as a dismissal for the night.

He doesn't wait for a reply, stalking away like everything in the room doesn't deserve his notice. To him, we're nothing but burdens, reminding him of everything he doesn't have.

"Are you alright?" I ask Mom.

She takes the napkin from me and nods. "Sorry for the mess," she mutters hoarsely.

"Don't worry about it." I smile. The embarrassment on her face hurts. I'd do anything to erase it. "Besides, I've probably still made more messes in my lifetime than you. You'll have to work on your numbers if you want to outdo me."

She laughs, but it's brittle.

"Give me time. I'll get there."

She hates it when she can't hide her symptoms. In Mom's ideal world, we'd all pretend everything's fine, and we'd go back to acting the way we did when I was little, but Father's temper has been getting worse for years, and even if she wasn't sick, he's never going to change.

\*\*\*

Father's office reeks of the sweet cigar smoke that follows him like a shadow. It's cloying, threatening to choke me before I even open the door. I smooth down my skirt, keeping my chin up as I knock, gritting my teeth until he calls for me.

There are papers scattered across his desk, a mess of scribbled notes, invoices, and printed documents for him to look over. I can count on one hand the number of times he's invited me into his office over the course of my life, and I'd still have fingers to spare.

That he's summoned me now sets my teeth on edge.

I look around the room, but the shelves and smoke offer me no answers to the questions I'm too cowardly to voice.

"Sit," he orders with a tilt of his chin, taking a long drag from his cigar.

The old leather chair groans under my weight, worn from years of use. I keep my chin up and shoulders back, my hands folded loosely in my lap while he considers me, looking for any weaknesses he can exploit.

"How's your mother doing?" he asks, tone deceptively casual.

"She's great." I do my best to look benign as I answer. Pleasant, mindless, and happy. Not anything he needs to focus on. "She's sorry for what happened at dinner. I'll make sure to talk to her doctor at her next appointment, so it doesn't happen again," I promise.

It doesn't matter that I can't keep that promise. It doesn't even matter if my failure is inevitable. If lying distracts him for now, I'll gladly deal with the consequences later.

I watch the cherry at the end of his cigar burning red. There's a steadily growing tail of ash at the end, primed to fall at the slightest shift of his hand.

He hums, smoke swirling around his head like a halo formed from brimstone. "Dr. Bonilla, right?" He waits for me to nod. "And she's comfortable with him?"

I force my heel flat on the ground, pushing my hand into my thigh like it'll keep my knee from bouncing.

"She is."

Mom is more than comfortable with Dr. Bonilla.

He's been a godsend. He listens to her. He stays on top of the latest treatments, and he actually seems to want to improve her quality of life. He can't cure her, but he can make sure she's able to love the life she still has.

Father leans forward, his cigar dangling loosely in his hand. The ash hangs over a stack of loose papers precariously, mindless to any embers it may be hiding.

"I've been lenient with you, haven't I, *printsessa*?"

I refuse to cringe, both from the nickname and the question.

The fresh bruises on my shoulder should be enough to answer, and if I have to entertain his delusion with a verbal response, I'm going to end up puking all over his fancy rug. Instead, I focus on a shiny gilded bust sitting on a shelf behind him.

"You need to come to terms with exactly what's at stake here, Emiliya." His elbow rests on his knee, and I itch to grab the ashtray from the corner of his desk and shove it in his face.

"You have a good life. Pretty clothes, a nice car, a credit card to buy whatever you want." With agonizing slowness, he taps his cigar, the ashes landing harmlessly on the papers. The soot stains every surface it touches, and when he blows out a long breath, the dust settling across the glass flies to land on my skirt.

I don't dare move, no matter how badly I want to brush it away.

"If Trenin isn't brought to heel, all those things will go away. He'll destroy everything I've built, and he won't feel an ounce of guilt over it. Unlike you." He shrugs. "And your *poor* mother. She isn't what she used to be, is she?"

Ice fills my blood as he shakes his head, a portrait of false sympathy.

"Perhaps it would be better if I sent her away. Relieve you of the burden and make her someone else's problem."

My mask slips away as panic grips my throat. "It's no burden," I rush to say. "I'll take care of her. I'll fix this, I promise."

"Will you? I know how soft-hearted you can be, dear girl." His grin promises violence, but I'll shoulder that, too. "I wouldn't want to set you up for failure."

My throat is thick, and I know if I blink, the tears I'm holding back will be set free. I will them—along with everything inside me—to hold still. To wait until I'm free from his prying eyes.

"I'll do whatever it takes."

"I know you will, *printsessa*. And once you do, we can put all this unpleasantness behind us."

# CHAPTER 3

# Alexei

I throw the paperweight so hard my shoulder burns. It hits the door just as it slams shut, clattering loudly when it hits against the floor.

Lev's mocking laughter echoes down the hallway as he retreats, blissfully ignorant of exactly how much I'd like to chase after him and wrap my hands around his throat.

Every time he darkens my doorway, he comes bearing more bad news.

It's always *Nikita needs something*, or *The Outfit fucked us again*, or *someone lost their cool and there's a corpse in the back room, should I call someone*?

When they say that you shouldn't shoot the messenger, did anyone consider that the messenger is really fucking annoying?

Lev seems to have a sixth sense for knowing the exact moment I try to close my eyes and relax, knocking on my door with a shit-eating grin plastered on his face, ready to ruin my fucking day.

I glare at the damage the paperweight did to my office door before I slump down in my chair, head pounding as I take in the growing pile of memos, license renewals, insurance forms, and invoices cluttering every available inch of space. I grab the invoices first, opening a drawer and dropping them inside without a second glance.

I have a plan for dealing with those.

A plan that involves seeing my sister, pawning them off on her, and asking her to deal with them. It's a flawless plan that has never failed me before, and I'm foolishly hoping it won't fail this time, either.

Nadya always said that I'm good at managing logistics and people, but the trade-off is that looking at numbers makes me dizzy.

When I was a kid, the schools forced me to see someone about it, and they said it's because I have dyscalculia.

But lucky for me, my big sister is both a genius and a saint, and she was so kind as to go to school and get all the certifications needed to let me hire her as my accountant.

The downside of our arrangement is that when I need something done, I have to deal with her. Which, when you don't want to deal with her needless worry and maternal hovering, is a problem.

Maybe I'll call Andrei over on some made-up business and make him take the invoices with him. Nadya's become attached to Blair, his wife, so she's probably going to run into him before I make time for her.

Looking up at the ceiling, I rack my brain for a plan around Nikita's latest insane demand.

Another two hundred grand and a contact for an arms dealer in Jersey.

I don't know who he thinks I am, but I'm not his fairy fucking godmother.

The money isn't an issue, and typically, I don't have a problem with making an introduction. I'm good at getting to know people and earning favors, but I can't pull them out of my ass.

Building relationships takes time.

Getting large amounts of cash that are clean enough to avoid detection takes time.

For all his many faults, Maksim at least understood that much. And at least under his rule, I had my independence. As long as the cash flowed freely, he didn't give a fuck what I did, and I was able to operate my clubs with little oversight.

As long as the cash flowed freely, he didn't give a fuck what I did.

But Nikita? He has to micromanage every little thing.

Even if I hadn't already hated that shit stain, it would be enough to make anyone check how much it costs to hire a hitman these days.

As it turns out, not as much as I was expecting. It's just the fallout I can't afford.

Every time he opens his mouth, Nikita demands more and more. More money, more time, more resources that I don't want to part with. He might have declared himself king, but I never pledged my loyalty to him.

Hell, none of us did.

The only reason he's even allowed to pretend he's owed it is because no one else has stood up to him. Until someone does, the men will fall in line, and he'll claim the title by default.

If he weren't such a pathetic excuse for a man, maybe it would have been a natural progression for him to take over the Bratva. He was Maksim's right-hand man, after all, and with no apparent heir, why shouldn't he take over?

Too bad Nikita's determined to run us into the fucking ground, trying to control every detail of everyone's lives as if it'll fix the rapidly spiraling war with The Outfit.

Explaining to him that he's asking for things that will never happen isn't worth the time or effort. It'd be like talking to a brick wall.

As much as he wants to pretend otherwise, he can't just unilaterally declare himself pakhan. No one can. He needs men to throw their weight behind him. He needs trust. He needs to prove he can hold his own.

Until he gets that approval, his crown might as well be made of paper.

Grabbing the license renewal forms, I grit my teeth and get to work.

I need my main clubs to hold up to any amount of scrutiny, or my whole kingdom will crumble to nothing but dust. My nightclubs, Enclave, Riot, and Savage, need to have every license, every inspection, and every permit. Morning Star, my legitimate strip club, needs to be operated in a way that's above repute, no matter who's looking into it. And I pay enough bribes to make sure no one looks at Virgo closely enough to worry about it.

My managers can handle the day-to-day, but I won't risk entrusting them with the little things that can either make or break everything I've worked for.

By the time I make it through a single stack of forms, my eyes are dry and there's a knot forming at the base of my neck. I roll it to alleviate the ache only to jump up, hand on my gun, when the door slams open. Just as quickly, I drop it when I see Nadya, fuming as she tries to take up as much space as she can.

Despite being tall and skinny as a rail, her presence is enough to suck all the air out of a room. Just by showing up, she's choking me with her anger, bringing back a childhood instinct to apologize even though I have no clue what I've done wrong.

She stalks into the room, throwing the door shut with all her might, and I cringe when one of the frames on the wall clatters to the ground, the glass shattering.

"Nadya," I mutter as she flops down onto the couch, her arms folded across her chest as she glares at me. "Please, come in. I'm so glad you could make it."

"Try a little more sarcasm. I'm not sure it's coming through."

Her voice is dripping with derision, and if I were a lesser man, I'd try to run out of the room and find a place to hide.

It doesn't matter that she's only a year older than me, her anger is more oppressive than our mother's ever was. Then again, I've had to deal with Nadya's anger for longer than I ever had to deal with Mom's.

"What do you want?"

"You've been avoiding me." She rolls her eyes, holding out her hand, palm up, as she makes a grabbing motion. "Give me all the scary numbers so I can do my job."

"You know," I say as I pull the infernal invoices out of my desk drawer, "if anyone else talked to me like that, they'd be having a bad day."

"Good thing I'm not anyone else, then." She smiles, but it doesn't meet her eyes. "I'm your sister, and you love me."

"It'd be easier if I didn't."

"Poor you." She shrugs as she puts the papers away neatly in her bag. "Guess you'll have to keep suffering until the end of time."

I hum, like I'm considering it. "I could always fake my death. But you're still the beneficiary of my will, and do I really want to give you everything that easily?"

"If you're open to suggestions, I have another one." She props her chin on her hand, her jaw held tight.

"Are you going to give me the option to decline?"

"We could stop talking about you dying. Even if it's just a threat."

"Why are you being like"—I wave a hand in her direction—"this?" She doesn't answer, and something about the worry lingering in her eyes puts me on edge. "Did something happen?"

In general, things are more dangerous than usual, but I've worked my ass off to shield her from it. Hell, it's why I haven't taken a more involved role in the grand shit show Nikita's been directing. If my work for the Bratva is blowing back onto Nadya, I'll have to find a way to shut it all down.

As soon as I figure out what *it* is.

My sister is off-limits. Always has been, and always will be.

By the time she sighs, shaking her head, I've boxed myself into a frenzy, halfway out of my chair and ready to storm out of the room to hunt down whoever's upset her.

"I'm just worried about you. That's all."

All of my fire fizzles out.

*Fuck, not this again.*

I blow out a long breath, looking anywhere that isn't her sad, worried eyes. "I'm fine, Nadya. I stay safe. So just... drop it, alright?"

"You know what?" She grins, eyes manic while she glares at me. "You're right. What's a few shootings and a couple of men disappearing from the streets? No big deal, right?"

It doesn't matter how hard I've worked to avoid making myself a target, she'll only ever see my lifestyle as a risk, and she's never going to let me forget it.

"I've been working at the older clubs." I gesture around us at my office.

Enclave has a lot of things going for it, but when I had it built, I didn't prioritize a workspace for myself nearly as much as I should have. The space I've claimed as my office is cramped. It's dark, gloomy, and half the time I have to step over a stack of papers before I can find what I really need. It's nothing compared to the luxurious space at Savage, but it'll do until the dust settles with The Outfit.

"If I have to go out, I've changed up my routines. My hours are inconsistent at best. I'm being fucking careful."

"Oh, is that why I was able to get to your office without running into a single soul? Is that why the front door was un-locked?" A muscle in her jaw ticks as she swallows, hands balled into fists on the arms of the couch. "Is that why you were at the *first* place I looked?"

"Lev should have locked the door when he left," I mumble lamely, unable to meet her eyes, because, yeah, that's a big fuck up on his part.

But I don't deserve her worry. She's wasted far too much of her life looking after me. When she should have been spending her teen years hanging out with friends and making dumb mistakes, she was helping me with homework and making sure I slept in my own bed every night, doing everything she could to keep me out of trouble.

"Well, he didn't. You need to get a guard."

"Even if I had one, they wouldn't stop you from coming in. You're my sister. You work here, for fuck's sake."

The look on her face tells me she isn't swayed at all.

"Fine. Let's pretend you're right. We'll play make believe and say you *are* being careful. Lev clearly isn't. Is Nikita? Do you trust him enough to look me in the eye and tell me that he's not going to do anything stupid that leads back to you? Do you really believe he won't set you up if it'll give him an advantage over someone else?"

I blink at my sister, who has, for as long as the Bratva has been a part of my life, happily stuck her head in the sand and pretended to be ignorant of everything about it.

"And why do you suddenly know so much about what's going on?" I ask slowly.

Nadya takes a deep breath, forcing herself to sit still when she looks like she wants nothing more than to storm out of the room.

"Like I said, you might be careful, but Lev isn't. He likes to run his mouth, and Aunt Vera likes to call me and complain."

*Fucking Lev.*

Either he's going to shut up, or I'll make him.

"Listen, I've handled everything that's come at me so far. I'll handle this nonsense with Nikita, too. It just might..." I trail off, shrugging. "It might take a while."

"I don't want you to end up like Dad," she whispers, sounding agonized. "I can't afford to lose you."

*Blyad.*

Dad took the fall for someone else on a murder charge, expecting to become a legend among his peers, but instead he was forgotten almost as soon as the cuffs were secured around his wrists.

Without him, Mom didn't stick around, and Nadya and I were left with only each other for comfort. Two scared teenagers who had to stumble through life without any guidance.

And Nadya did her best to raise me, but I'll never forgive Dad for doing that to her.

She should have been focused on boys and the latest trends, not worrying whether I was getting enough to eat and making sure I went to school often enough to keep child protective services from sniffing around.

"In that case, I have great news," I say somberly. "I make far too much money for anyone to use me as a fall guy."

Despite herself, the corner of her mouth lifts.

"Just... don't let your arrogance come back to bite you. That's all I'm asking."

I circle to the front of my desk, pulling her into a hug. She leans against me, and for once, it feels like it's my turn to take care of her.

I want her to be happy.

I bought her an apartment that she loves. I gave her a job in a field where she thrives. I make sure she always has money to enjoy whatever she wants, but none of it makes a dent in the debt I've racked up with her over a lifetime.

No matter what I do, it will never be enough.

But I can make sure I'm safe if that's what she needs. I can keep the worst of the coming violence away from her.

"I promise, alright?"

"And you'll get a guard."

"Don't push it."

"Fine." She sniffs, pulling back and blinking rapidly. "In that case, do you want to talk about my plans for my birthday?"

Ah, shit.

My expression must give me away, because she lights up with a devious grin.

# CHAPTER 4

# Alexei

Andrei's bright yellow front door mocks me, laughing in my exhausted face. I bet his wife, Blair, picked the hideous color, but I can't for the life of me figure out why he would've allowed it. Counting to ten, I glare at its derisive cheer before knocking again.

I tried his phone on my way over here, but apparently, he couldn't be bothered to answer it. I check my watch, aware that every second passing creeps closer to the hour Nikita's decided to summon everyone he considers important to the Bratva.

The brigadiers, the money men, the cleaners. Everyone except the lowest soldiers is expected to be at his house at the time he demands for no other reason than *because* he demands it.

I don't give a fuck, but I need to keep up appearances until I'm in a better position to show Nikita exactly what a moron he is.

But in the name of playing nice, I said I'd collect Andrei, who apparently doesn't give a fuck about pretending with the useless dickhead.

I ring the doorbell as my impatience builds. If he doesn't pull his head out of his ass in the next thirty seconds, I'm going to leave Andrei here and let him deal with the consequences of ignoring Nikita on his own.

As soon as I think it, the door is ripped open, revealing a surly Andrei, his pistol firm in his hand.

"What do you want?"

"Nikita wants a meeting," I tell him, not even bothering to acknowledge his weapon.

His brows draw together as he tucks his gun into his waistband, looking coldly over my shoulder before he gestures for me to come inside.

"I called, but you didn't answer your phone."

"It's dinnertime." He shrugs, like that explains everything, pulling out his phone and checking his missed notifications. "There are no phones at the table." I roll my eyes, but he ignores me as he stalks off, leaving me alone in the doorway.

Laughter echoes off the walls as soon as he's gone, shortly followed by muffled voices. I count to three before Niko sprints down the hall, the pitter-patter of tiny feet giving away any attempt at stealth.

"Alexei!" he calls as he rounds the corner. I crouch down just in time to catch him as he launches himself at me, nearly knocking me off my feet.

"Hi, Nikolai."

He grins at me in the way only a child can, open and absent of any self-consciousness, either ignorant or mindless of the remnants of his dinner smeared on his chin.

"You're here!"

"I am, but only for a little while." His smile drops like a sack of bricks, and if he didn't look so mad, I'd laugh. "I have some work to do with Andrei." As if summoned, Andrei rounds the corner with Blair at his side.

I pretend not to notice the way she glares at me, keeping my focus on Niko so I don't let her know exactly what I think of her.

I hate that woman. And despite what Nadya says, I don't need a reason for it, especially not when the feeling is clearly mutual.

"But if your parents agree, maybe you could come over next week. We could catch up and let your mom and dad spend some time together."

He looks at them with big eyes, silently begging them to agree.

I don't like it when Andrei drops him off uninvited, but I do like spending time with Nikolai. And truth be told, I've been busy. I've missed having him follow me around everywhere I go, curious and wanting to understand everything I do.

I've missed him. He's a good kid, and he's thrived under Andrei's watchful eye.

Andrei and Blair exchange a look, and when Andrei shrugs, she nods.

"Thank you, Mama!" Niko cheers, wiggling free so he can go to her, still beaming from ear to ear as she ruffles his hair.

In contrast, Andrei looks far less thrilled, but he won't make a fuss when Niko's around.

"What's up?"

I look at his loose jeans and gesture toward the front door. "Nikita's called a meeting."

"I heard you the first time. What *kind* of meeting?"

I shrug. "Get dressed, and we'll find out."

Begrudgingly, he nods, leaving to change into a suit and only stopping to hug Niko before he leaves, promising Blair that he'll be back before morning while he kisses her forehead.

***

The lights of Nikita's mansion are bright, and his driveway is full of all manner of cars. Some still running, others with drivers playing on their phones as they wait. A few are dented, scratched, and practically falling apart.

I double-check the clock on the dash, but we're still early. I shove my hands in my pockets, feigning an air of nonchalance as we pass through the gates and make our way inside.

Nikita's mansion is decorated exactly like I thought it would be. Expensive furniture that looks like it was carefully chosen by an interior designer who was salivating for a payday, boring but no doubt valuable pieces of artwork hanging on the walls, and men lingering in the entryway like they aren't sure what to do.

It's one of the many fucking problems with Nikita.

He puts so much effort into appearing civilized—going so far as to open his home like it'll garner the admiration he craves—that he doesn't stop to consider that no one here is civilized.

It doesn't matter how many hors d'oeuvres he sets out or how nice his home is. At the end of the day, every man here will still lie, cheat, and kill as long as they can get the job done.

The illusion of respectability will do jack shit to whet our appetites.

My eyes flit over each man, watching as they shift uncomfortably, before Andrei makes a scoffing sound behind me.

I follow his gaze, trying not to freeze when my eyes land on Emiliya, laughing as she chats with someone, smacking her hand flirtatiously against his arm. Even with a smile on her face, she doesn't look relaxed the way she did in the back of my car.

She looks on edge, like she's hyperaware of every predator in the room and fully prepared to either defend herself or flee at a moment's notice.

Beside me, Andrei rolls his shoulders, trying to shove aside his agitation.

"You know, she does live here. You can't be shocked to see her." I don't know whether I'm reminding him or myself.

Because, stupidly, I thought I'd be able to get away without having to deal with her again. We had our fun, but it's over. It won't happen again, and I need to knock it through my skull until it takes root.

But, fuck, if seeing her smile at another man doesn't make me want to pull her to my side so I can stake a claim on her.

I don't know what she was doing at Enclave, and I don't know why she was pretending I don't know who she is. Whatever she was doing, it doesn't change how her cunt gripped my cock like she was fucking made for me. It doesn't change the way I've been reliving the sound she made when she came every morning in the shower.

I've spent longer than is probably healthy thinking about the way her long hair looked haloed around her head, her tits flushed as they bounced every time I sunk my cock into that perfect pussy.

A quicky in the back of my SUV wasn't nearly enough.

Seeing her here, surrounded by everyone gathered to see her fucking father, should only reinforce how far I need to stay away from her, but I still want to drag her away from all the prying eyes and repeat that night all over again. But this time, I want her in my bed so I can take my time.

"All the more reason Nikita shouldn't be in charge," Andrei mutters under his breath.

"Because of his daughter?"

Andrei looks like a wet cat: pissy, and ready to lash out.

"You don't see the way Blair looks at me when I have to leave in the middle of the night."

"You can fault him for plenty of shit, but I don't think it's his fault Emiliya slept with your wife's dead husband."

The look he levels me with is scathing.

"Maybe not, but it doesn't change the fact that he can't control her. She's a liability."

Emiliya looks up, her cheeks turning a gorgeous shade of pink when she spots me. Her blush even prettier under bright lights than it was in the club. Her lips shift into an inviting smile as she pulls herself away from her conversation, walking toward us with a tantalizing sway to her hips.

Even with the conservative cut, so unlike the other night, the deep red of her dress makes her smooth skin look luminescent, highlighting every line and soft curve. She looks absolutely sinful.

Fuck, I want to feel those pretty red lips wrapped around me as she takes every inch.

Andrei takes a half step toward her, and it's enough to snap me out of my reverie. I cut him off, moving to intercept her. The closer I get, the more her satisfied grin grows.

"Hey, Alexei," she purrs. Her smile dies when I wrap a hand around her upper arm, dragging her away from all the curious eyes watching. "Hey!"

"We aren't doing this here."

"Doing what?"

I shove open a door at random, only taking a glance to confirm it's empty. A powder room isn't ideal, but it'll work. I push her inside and close the door, flipping the lock behind me.

The quiet *click* makes her smirk, and not a moment later, she's leaning into me.

"Oh. Doing *that*. Why didn't you just say so?" Her hands press against my chest, a simple touch that's full of intent.

"Nope. Not that." I pry her hands away, and the bones of her wrist feel as delicate as a bird's in my grasp. Something flashes in her eyes—something vulnerable and almost scared—but it's gone before I'm able to decipher it.

In a flash, her eyes are hooded as she blinks at me from under her lashes.

"Come on, Alexei. We had fun, didn't we?"

Even in the small room, her chestnut brown eyes are blown out under the single light. Her lips are parted, and I want to rub my thumb over them to see if they're as soft as I remember.

"We did, but it was a one-time thing."

I feel like a jackass, but I have to put a stop to whatever she's trying to build between us. For both our sakes.

"Oh, come on," she pouts. "You know I can make it worth your while."

"No. In fact, do us both a favor and forget it ever happened."

I don't tell her that it was a mistake, because it sure as fuck didn't feel like one, but I never should've let it happen.

Andrei's right. Emiliya's a liability, and one I can't afford. I couldn't the other night, and nothing's going to change that.

"Once was enough," I lie through my teeth. "Go find your fun with someone else."

She pulls her hands back as if she's been burned.

I leave her alone in the room, closing the door to give her space to compose herself before I head back to the masses, seeking out Andrei. He shoots me a dark look, but I shrug it off, trying to reclaim the cool professionalism I had before I spotted Emiliya.

Fortunately, Andrei doesn't have time to question me before Nikita ushers everyone into the dining room. Most of the room is consumed by a large table, but it's far from enough space for everyone in the room. In unspoken accord, the oldest brigadiers take the limited seats, forcing everyone else to stand awkwardly, much to Nikita's apparent delight.

He wears his pride like a new suit, flashing it around and desperate for someone to compliment it. It doesn't matter if it doesn't fit, or how hideous it is, he wants everyone to know that it's *his*.

I lean against the wall, pretending his lack of composure isn't enough to give me secondhand embarrassment.

"Gentlemen"—Nikita grins as I hold back an eye roll—"it's time that we take care of The Outfit. Their petty attacks have gone on long enough, and they need to end."

I blow out a slow breath. Despite what I told Nadya, their attacks have been far from *petty*. Nearly daily shootings have put everyone on edge, and the men who have gone missing are probably going to be found eventually, but when they do, we all know we're only going to find bits and pieces of them.

The chaos is starting to draw the attention of the feds. In the last week alone, three of their undercover agents have been spotted in my clubs. They left without incident, but I don't want them there at all.

"Attrition isn't working. We need to go after them hard and fast, put this whole *war* to bed and wrap things up." He looks around the table, but the few nods he's getting are far from the gushing praise he's looking for.

"I'm going to call their underboss and set up a meeting, get him into an environment that I control, and you're all going to surround the building. Go in guns blazing. We'll send them scrambling and cut down someone they rely on at the same time. Two birds, one stone."

That'll be nothing short of suicide.

Beyond the honeypot he'd be setting for the feds, this isn't the sort of plan that can be pulled off with more fingers in the pot than necessary.

A massive undertaking like this needs to be handled discreetly. Telling this many people that he wants to kill someone so high up in The Outfit's structure is just begging to have someone run their mouth.

Artyom, a brigadier who runs a tight crew just outside the city limits, clears his throat.

"And how're you planning on getting him to agree to a meeting?"

Good fucking question.

Carlo Di Veroli isn't an easy man to get a hold of under the best of circumstances, and with blood in the water, it'll be nearly impossible. It'd be easier for Nikita to get a meeting with Marcell Renzuto, The Outfit's front boss, but I doubt either of them would even take a phone call from this conceited prick.

He rarely even acknowledges me, and we share a fucking tailor.

"If I demand a meeting, I'll get one," he boasts. "We'll set an ambush. Invite Carlo into our territory for a peace negotiation, and after a little wining and dining, he'll be eating out of the palm of my hand."

Around me, men shift, murmuring their agreement.

They're hungry for blood, for revenge for the men we've lost. They don't care that only a man with no honor would attack someone approaching under the banner of peace. They don't care about all the ways Nikita's showing his cards.

How long will it take for his plan to dissolve?

What would it take to satiate the men enough to see past his bullshit?

I'd love to watch Nikita hang himself with his own arrogance, but manpower isn't something that can be replaced as quickly as he's trying to lose it.

And he's budgeting for a whole lot of it.

"Where're you gonna take him?"

Nikita's eyes flash to me, and only years of practice keep my lip from curling back in a snarl.

"Savage would work nicely, don't you think?"

All that practice flies out the window when I bark out a bitter laugh, no longer able to hold my tongue.

My newest club? Really? It's only been open for a few months, and he thinks I'll agree to having it closed for who knows how long for this stunt?

"And what makes you think that?"

To his credit, Nikita doesn't show any signs of offense at my blatant lack of respect, but this is the stupidest plan I've ever heard, and dragging my club into it burned away the little patience I had to pretend otherwise.

"Any damages would be an inconvenience at worst, but in the long run—"

"In the long run it would be equivalent to cutting off your own hand."

The room has grown uncomfortably tense, nearly silent except for the quiet sounds of men shifting from foot to foot as they try to figure out how to play this.

"What?" A vein throbs in Nikita's forehead, his knuckles white where he digs his nails into the edge of the table.

"Assuming Di Veroli *does* walk into your trap, which is a big fucking if, the firepower you'll need to pull it off will cost more than you can afford. Not just the initial attack, but you're going to need to defend against the inevitable retaliation. Guns are expensive. Bullets to feed them are expensive. Do you have the cash to back up what you're suggesting? Or is everyone else going to fund your plan?"

He glares as everyone turns to me. If looks could kill, Nikita's sting at best, but he's going to have to learn that he holds no power over me.

"If you have the money, it's only because *my* clubs keep your money clean. *My* work keeps you in this grand home, with your fancy cars and meaningless art. If you have a shoot-out at Savage, all those things are going to go away. The feds are already sniffing around, and if they realize we're at a full-blown war, they'll shut down all my clubs for their investigation. Do you know what that means?"

He opens his mouth to tell me off, but I cut him off before he gets a chance.

"It means no more money. We'll be dead in the water because you can't be bothered to take your time. War is slow. You can't win overnight."

Beside me, Andrei stands firm, arms at ease while he keeps an eye on everyone. The more upset Nikita becomes, the more Andrei relaxes, eyes calculating as he watches him.

"If you want to make the Italians hurt, don't go after their leadership. A power vacuum won't grant the advantage you seem to think it will." I give him a pointed look. "If you take out Di Veroli, what's to stop someone even more ruthless from filling the void?"

I can't deny the men their shot at blood. Any chance of that happening was gone the moment Nikita promised to satisfy their appetites, but we can't be reckless about it.

"If it's blood you want, don't settle for ours," I continue. "Several soldiers are harder to replace than a single king. If you lure their men to a neutral location, you can do far more damage. The feds have less reason to look into a single fight than they do if there's warfare on the streets."

I shrug. "If we can intercept one of their shipments from Boston, they'll have no choice but to meet us halfway. And if we get a valuable enough package? They'll bring plenty of bodies to ensure they get it back."

"Easier said than done." Nikita sighs as he leans back in his seat, shaking his head. "They aren't known to leave their contraband out in the open for anyone to stumble upon. Your plan's a nonstarter."

"Not necessarily," Artyom says slowly, looking contemplative. "They have a warehouse in my territory. We've never had issues before, so I haven't bothered to worry about it."

"And you think you can stroll right in and rob them blind?" Mikhail scoffs. He's seated the closest to Nikita. Like most of the older generation, he's content to throw his weight behind a familiar face, stubborn and resistant to any change.

Under Nikita's dubious watch, I doubt anything ever will.

Artyom shrugs, the glare Mikhail's leveling him with having as much of an impact as water on a duck's back. "I can't promise things won't get a little hairy, but if I'm given some time to do surveillance, I'll have a better idea of what I'm working with."

"No." Nikita shakes his head. "It's not a worthwhile use of time. And Trenin," he barks, "learn your place. The meeting will be at Savage within a week."

I roll my neck, listening as men shift in discomfort, tension thick in the air.

At Maksim's funeral, Andrei planted the idea that I take over the role of pakhan.

I hated it then, but the old regime had been running us into the ground for years. Now that we're preparing to fight a war on two fronts, the cracks in our foundation are getting bigger than we can ignore.

I don't want to be pakhan.

I don't want to risk exposing Nadya to more threats than she already faces, but as I watch Nikita settle into his chair, smug and self-satisfied, I realize I won't get a more opportune moment to let him know exactly how little he controls.

"No."

All movement in the room ceases, no one willing to risk doing anything that will turn any more attention to them than necessary. All the air is gone, and it's so quiet you could hear a pin drop. The wooden table creaks as Nikita leans against it, his jaw working.

"What do you mean, *no*?"

"I'm not going to let you use my properties to drive us into the grave. Artyom, do the surveillance. You have two weeks. After that, we're moving forward." I wait for him to nod his acknowledgment before I turn and leave the room, unable to stomach the disgust brewing in my gut.

Andrei follows me silently until we're outside, lingering by our cars at the end of the long driveway.

"You know this is going to be messy, right?" he asks, his relaxed shoulders belying the grim shadow over his face.

I nod.

"He didn't give me a choice."

# CHAPTER 5

# Alexei

Virgo is my only property that isn't squeaky clean. It's the one place I actively conceal my involvement with, and it's the only one I don't let my sister touch. Hell, as far as she's concerned, it doesn't even *exist*.

It's the last place anyone will look for me, which makes it the perfect place to hunker down and try to come to terms with what the fuck I just did.

Hours of childhood lectures, of lessons beaten over my head, and apparently, I still couldn't internalize the only thing Nadya and Dad would repeat over and over again.

*Your choices don't exist in a vacuum.*

It's one thing for me to make decisions that will make my life more complicated, but I just plastered a target on Nadya's back.

When she finds out I'm going to have a man watching her around the clock, she's going to kill me, but I can't risk her safety.

A smart man wouldn't be in this position to begin with, but no one's ever accused me of being smart.

I take another sip of my rapidly cooling coffee, scrolling through my text thread with Konstantin Lavrov. He's a pakhan out in California, but he's been making more and more visits to Chicago lately, and I can't tell if it's because he's working an angle, or because he's keeping an eye on the chaos.

He's well-connected, opportunistic, and if I'm fucking doing this, he could be a powerful man to have on my side.

For the hundredth time, I roll the idea around in my head. Konstantin can help me, but if he chooses to, he could just as easily crush me. But I can't control him, and putting myself in his debt is a fucking gamble.

As little as I want to, I need to talk to Nadya. She'll work herself into a frenzy, but there's no way around it.

Money is the only thing I can reliably offer Konstantin, and if I don't want him to laugh me out of the room, I need to make sure I have plenty to offer him out of my own pocket without touching any of the Bratva's money.

And if it all falls apart, and he decides to throw my request back in my face, I need to have a plan to make sure Nadya's protected. A place to lie low until everything blows over, maybe, or a way to get her away from here so she can start over.

Either way, it'll be expensive.

I sigh as I push away from my desk, my head throbbing.

By the time I get home, it's late, and I'm ready to collapse in my bed and pass out. I'm dead on my feet, but not so dead that I'm beyond noticing the signs that someone's in my condo.

The decorative bowl next to the door has been moved. The coat closet is partially open. The light to the back hall is on, when I'm certain it was off when I left. And most importantly, the toe of Nadya's favorite sneakers is poking out from around the corner, just waiting for an ambush.

"Hello, Nadya," I call out, flipping all the locks on the door.

She lets out a deep sigh, stepping out into the front hall with a put-upon expression. I step around her, ignoring the way she glares at me.

"I'll get you one of these days," she mutters under her breath.

"And eventually the sun will die and consume us all. You have a better chance of seeing that day."

Nadya flips me off. "I hate you."

She's been trying to sneak up on me since we were kids, and I can count on one hand the number of times she's been successful.

My sister is wonderful, but she's as stealthy as a drunk elephant wearing tap shoes.

Her steps echo no matter where she's walking, and if there's a single creaky floorboard or door, she'll find it every single time. The only way she's going to be able to sneak up on me or surprise me is if I'm either dead or in a coma.

"What're you doing here, anyway? I don't know if you've noticed, but it's the middle of the night."

"To be fair"—she smiles sweetly, putting me on edge—"I called you. And went to every single one of your clubs. And I even called Lev, who says he needs to talk to you, by the way. But I still couldn't find you, so I came here. Now imagine my surprise when I didn't find you dying in a puddle of your own blood, but just missing." She crosses her arms over her chest, but her building anger overtakes the looming disappointment on her face, so I'll take it.

"I do have a life, you know."

"No, you don't. You work, you come home, you brood, then you go back to work. On a good day, you go to your tailor and spend too much money on custom suits, but you typically reserve that for Saturdays."

And *I'm* the one without a life?

"Well, I'm fine. And actually, I'm glad you came over. I need to talk to you about something."

"Everything alright?"

"Yeah." *Probably.* "I just wanted to see if you could take a look at my personal accounts, Give me an estimate of how much cash I can stand to lose, that sort of thing."

She freezes as she looks me over, but I've spent a lifetime training myself to keep her from reading my body language. If she finds out I'm more concerned about things than I'm letting on, she won't figure it out because of me.

But she's clever enough, and if I'm sloppy, she'll figure it out. I won't delude myself into thinking I can hide everything from her, but I'll sure fucking try.

"And I'll ask again. Is everything alright, Alexei?"

I nod, deciding to throw her a bone. "I'm trying to set up a few things, and I thought it would be smart to ask my accountant if I can afford them first. I'm being responsible. You should try it sometime."

She rolls her eyes.

"Since when do you know anything about responsibility?"

"You're always prattling on and on about it, so I thought I'd give it a try."

Her worries over my safety and what I'm not telling her melt away with her excitement at the prospect of pouring over numbers and spreadsheets. She agrees to look over everything and get back to me in a few days. Or the next time she thinks I'm home and free to be ambushed by her particular brand of overbearing affection.

I love her, but the weight of Nadya's worry is crushing under the best circumstances. It's been better since she forged her friendship with Blair, but she still holds everything so close to her chest that I worry it'll end up suffocating her.

I sit for an hour after she leaves, waiting to make sure she isn't going to turn around and storm right back into my condo before I pick up my phone and call Konstantin.

On the third ring, he answers, voice authoritative over the whirring sounds in the background.

"Yeah?"

"It's Alexei. Any chance you're in Chicago?"

There's a pained grunt followed swiftly by the sound of flesh hitting against flesh.

"Shut up. I'm on the phone. Don't be rude."

His voice is more muted, and I roll my eyes.

Fuck knows I don't want to know what he's up to.

"Sorry about that, I couldn't hear you over my guest. Can you believe the gall of people these days?" I make a noncommittal sound, but Konstantin forges ahead as if nothing had happened. "What do you need, Alexei?"

"I take it you're back in California?"

"I am. Do you need me elsewhere?"

He sounds eager, and I hate it. I've never needed to know the details of his organization, and I still don't particularly want to, but rumors spread. Tales of his brutality, of his bloodlust, have made it all the way to the Midwest, and I wouldn't be surprised if they made it all the way back to Russia.

Men like Konstantin are built to make a name for themselves, and god help anyone who tries to stand in their way.

"I was wondering if you'd be open to a meeting later this week. I have a proposal for you."

"Business or personal?"

"A mix."

He hums. "Consider me intrigued. I might be there in a few days. I'll let you know."

"Wonderful. I'll send you an address."

He chuckles, dark and low. "Oh, you don't want to meet at one of your *wondrous* places of business? Are you trying to hide, Alexei?"

"I'm not going to spell everything out on the phone, Konstantin. Some of us are still fans of discretion."

The whirring of a drill kicks up, followed by a cry from whatever poor soul he's playing with. "I don't know what you mean. I'm always discrete." I pull the phone away from my ear as the line is filled with screams, the drill only getting louder. "I'm afraid I have to cut this short. It was a pleasure, Alexei. We'll talk soon."

\*\*\*

I'm willing to admit it when I make mistakes, and giving Konstantin my address was definitely a mistake.

Not that I had much choice.

Meeting him in public would have been idiotic. Nikita would have found out, and sure, there's a chance he will anyway, but hiding Konstantin away in my condo makes it less likely.

But now that he's in my space, poking around like I gave him permission, I understand why Andrei laughed in my face when I told him what I was planning on doing. He laughed, but he didn't tell me I was being an idiot.

*Ublyudok.*

I lead Konstantin to my office, grinding my teeth together as he treats himself to a tour of the room, looking over all the trinkets I've collected over the years, the dying plant in the corner, eventually stopping to linger on a photo of Nadya and me when we were kids.

I sit in my seat, letting him look to his fill while I silently seethe.

He trails a finger along the shelf like he's checking for dust, and I close my eyes, taking a deep breath until I'm able to feign a sense of calm that I don't feel. In the few interactions I've had with him, I've learned that Konstantin isn't the type of man to be rushed. He'll sit and listen to what I have to say when he's good and ready.

"So, what do you need?" he asks when he finally makes himself comfortable in a chair, spreading his hands in front of him. His black hair is pushed back, expression bored, but he can't hide the curiosity shining in his eyes.

I've mulled over what to tell him, how much of my hand I should show, but I figure my best bet is to put all my cards on the table.

Nothing's going to make me happy about inviting a rival boss into my home to ask for his favor, but the sooner I make my case, the sooner he'll leave.

"I was hoping you'd be open to working with me."

"As a business venture, or as an alliance?"

"Are the two mutually exclusive?"

Konstantin leans back, smirking as he shakes his head.

"Guess not. But last time I checked, it was still up in the air who was going to run your ragtag little group. Signs were pointing toward Dyomin."

I scoff. "Nikita couldn't control a flock of sheep. He's assumed temporary control, but it was always going to be just a matter of time before someone else took the reins."

"And that someone's going to be you? Or are you still acting as proxy?" He grins, sharp and deadly, as he meets my eyes. "I'm sure I've already told you I don't work with middle-men."

"You have, but your spies are apparently slow."

He raises a brow, not denying he's planted men among us. He's always known too much, been too aware for anything else to be the case, but it's nice to have confirmation.

"I've already made it clear I don't work for Nikita," I continue.

"And who do you work for, Alexei?"

"Myself."

"Interesting." He hums. "It's no secret how much they all rely on your money. And with your current power struggles with the Italians..." He shrugs. "Nikita would be dead in the water without you, wouldn't he?"

"That seems to be the general consensus."

Among the money who aren't too stubborn and stuck in their ways to see beyond the end of their own nose, anyway.

"If you're so sure of your position, what do you need me for?"

"Manpower. We have the firearms to hold the line, and I can provide the financial backing we need. But if you can spare men, we'll be able to force the Italians to fall in line." I shrug. "Whether that would be diplomatically or through more violent means remains to be seen."

"And what am I supposed to get out of it?"

"We'll cut you into our revenue streams for the next five years, and of course you'll have our support in the future." He squints at me, and I grind my teeth. "I know you already have the means to make your profits appear legitimate, but my accountant loves to remind me that diversity insulates against risk. Between that and cutting you in for twenty percent of the profit, you won't have to worry about money."

He laughs, shaking his head. Sweat beads against the back of my neck.

"Money is already the least of my worries. In fact—"

The front door slams, and Konstantin's easy demeanor drops as he rises to his feet, drawing his gun before he turns toward the door to my office.

*Fuck.*

There's only one person who would dare barge into my space uninvited, and I gave her the damn key.

"Put that away!" I snap, rushing to the doorway before he gets a chance to storm toward Nadya with guns blazing.

"If this is a setup, you're even stupider than I thought you were," Konstantin snarls, teeth bared. He raises his gun, gesturing for me to step into the hallway.

*Fine.*

If he points that thing anywhere near her, I'm going to kill him, and I'll be damned if I let Nadya see that.

"Nadya!" I yell, and the sound of her steps comes to an abrupt stop down the hall. "Go wait in the living room. I have a guest."

"Let me guess," Konstantin hisses sharply. "Your girlfriend?"

"My sister. Now put the gun away."

"Is everything okay?" she calls. My heart is in my fucking throat, my eyes glued to Konstantin's.

"Yeah. Just wait out there."

Konstantin raises a brow but makes a show of clicking the safety on his gun and slipping it back into his holster. "Sister?" he asks skeptically. I force myself to nod calmly.

"And accountant. I would *highly* appreciate it if you would restrain yourself from threatening her or aiming any weapons at her."

"No fucking promises," he mutters as I take a single step out of the doorway. He shoulders me out of his way, prowling toward the living room like he's still expecting an ambush before I'm able to stop him.

I want to shove him back into my office, to keep him as far away from her as I can, but if I want to salvage this meeting, I'm going to have to tiptoe on a goddamn high wire to avoid setting him off.

He comes to a dead stop at the end of the hall, looking in the direction of the couch. Dread builds in my gut as he stares at Nadya like she's the most interesting thing in the room. It takes more than I'll ever admit to bite my tongue.

A slow grin splits his face as he looks at her. She sits on the couch with her legs crossed, a folder dropped carelessly on the coffee table in front of her.

"Your sister, huh?"

Konstantin doesn't wait for an answer, walking over to her with his hand outstretched, palm up. "You must be Nadya. I've heard so much about you." Warily, she puts her hand in his, blushing when he lifts her hand to press a kiss against her fingers. "I'm Konstantin Lavrov."

"N-nice to meet you," she stutters.

*Okay, nope.*

"I'm afraid we'll have to finish this some other time, Lavrov. I forgot I was supposed to have dinner with Nadya tonight," I lie.

The sly smirk on his face has me ready to pull my gun.

"What a pity."

Nadya pulls her hand away, and his smirk only grows. "I'll be in touch, Alexei. I'm sure we can find a way to work together." With a wink, he turns on his heel.

I remain silent, pinning Nadya in place with a pointed look until the front door closes quietly behind him. She lets out a heavy sigh, leaning forward until her forehead is resting on her knees.

"I thought you didn't bring your work home," she grumbles under her breath, the sound muffled as I flop into an armchair, running a hand over my forehead.

"And *I* thought I told you to call before you waltz in here uninvited."

"Well, why would I?" she huffs, throwing her hands in the air in exasperation. Despite the lingering stress, it almost makes me laugh. "Your place is supposed to be safe! You don't work here, you don't bring women here, and when I *do* call, you find an excuse to be anywhere else."

She's not wrong, but it doesn't sit right with me, either.

"Yeah, well." I lean forward and rest my elbows on my knees as she rolls her eyes. "Next time I have a meeting here, I'll be sure to give you my itinerary ahead of time."

"Would you? That'd be so great," she drawls, voice dripping with sarcasm. "Thank you so much, Alexei. I really appreciate your concern for my well-being. Seriously, you're the *best*."

Her words grate against my ego like sandpaper, but I've long since numbed myself to the sting she is so quick to thoughtlessly dole out.

Instead of taking the bait, I point at the folder.

"What's that?"

Just like that, she stops being my annoying big sister and snaps into the role of seasoned accountant. "*That* is a full report of your personal finances. If you want me to go over the business accounts with a fine-tooth comb too, I can, but it'll take a while."

If Konstantin does decide to work with me, I have a sinking suspicion it won't be in exchange for money, but I don't want to disappoint her and cut her off. She pulls out color-coded spreadsheets, pointing figures out as she goes over everything.

I don't understand most of this crap, and based on the way her lips are pursed when she's done, she knows it, too.

"Anyway, all of that can be summed up by saying you're good. Unless you're planning on buying another four buildings and renovating them all at once, you don't have to worry about money."

I nod, trying to smile. "Thank you, Nadya. I don't know what I'd do without you."

"Watch your empire fall apart at the seams, probably."

Yeah, probably.

# CHAPTER 6

# Emiliya

I listen for the smallest sound, but I can't hear much of anything over my heart pounding against my ribs, doing its best to tear through muscle and bone and escape from my chest. Each minute creeps by with agonizing slowness until I'm so keyed up, I can't tell if I'm imagining the groan of the front gate opening and closing or not.

Having no choice but to hope I haven't completely lost my mind, I fly down the stairs and through the halls toward the east wing of the house.

Father's been on a warpath since his big meeting last week, and I've made a point of avoiding him like the plague. I don't know what the hell happened, but he was furious when everyone left.

Since that night, I've done a decent job of avoiding his attention and letting all the cuts and bruises he gave me heal. And for the most part, I've been getting away with it.

Sure, I've had to sneak around at three in the morning to make sure I can get something to eat without worrying about running into him, but it's better than the alternative.

The only downside is I haven't been able to check on Mom as much as I'd like to.

Father tends to keep her sequestered in the east wing, only allowing her to leave the house under very specific circumstances, and when there's company over, he makes it very clear that she is to remain out of sight and out of mind.

Avoiding Father means I can't sneak around to see her, and I miss her so much my heart hurts.

It isn't fair. Both his neglect and his avoidance of her, and a decent daughter would make sure he knew it. But I'm not sure I'll be able to cope with his wrath if I call him out.

The last time one of his associates saw her and asked what had happened, I ended up with a broken rib and a sprained wrist.

I'm not looking for a repeat, and Mom asked me not to stand up for her after that. And, frankly, I'm too much of a coward to let her know how much I appreciate the out.

I flit from room to room as I look for her, ignoring the maids and security that wander the halls, refusing to meet my eyes. I don't have to look hard. She's exactly where I should have expected her, in her favorite chair in her sitting room, face turned toward the window with her earbuds in as she listens to an audiobook.

Her shoulders are slumped and dark circles make her eyes look sunken, but whether it's from dealing with Father's shit or her illness, I don't know.

I don't know which one would hurt more, either.

Still, she's never looked so beautiful. I want to trace over her smile lines and crow's feet, proof that at one point, she was happy. She looks older than she is, but she carries a poise any woman half her age would kill to have.

Will I ever be able to age like that? Or, when Father gives up and sells my hand in marriage to the highest bidder, will my husband demand I pump my face so full of Botox and fillers I'm unable to express my emotions in any way that matters?

Even thinking about marriage makes me feel like I've swallowed a stone.

No matter how much I try to avoid it, that day's probably coming sooner than I'd like.

I shake my head, forcing my attention back to Mom.

With her eyes shut, she doesn't have to deal with the nausea and frustration of her eyes darting back and forth. Lately, it's her most visible symptom, but I'm more concerned about how much it frustrates her. She wants nothing more than to have control of her body again, but that's never going to happen.

Not if Dr. Bonilla was right in diagnosing her with Progressive Supranuclear Palsy, anyway. Since the last two doctors said it was Parkinson's, the jury's still out, but I like Dr. Bonilla.

I like to think he's right, and he knows what he's doing when he's taking care of her.

I knock on the door, and when she smiles back at me, I'm able to breathe for the first time in a week. She pauses her audiobook, gesturing me further into the room.

The sun streaming through the window makes it look like she's glowing, despite the bland, lifeless room she spends so much time in.

"I haven't seen you in ages. How are you?"

I swallow down the urge to apologize to her for how absent I've been, for the way I've let her be isolated, for the fact she has to deal with any of the shit life's thrown at her.

"Missing you, but I'm alright. How're you doing?"

"Missing you, *lastochka*." She smiles. "Always missing you."

I sit next to her, biting the inside of my cheek to avoid hissing in a breath when I sit too hard on a lingering bruise. The marks have faded, but the ache is still there, happily reminding me to get out of Father's way faster next time things don't go according to plan.

"How was your physical therapy appointment yesterday?" She shifts in her seat, looking back at the window with an irritated expression that puts me on edge. "Did... did it not go well?"

"It might have gone just fine, had I been allowed to go." Something flashes in her eyes, her hands shaking as she folds them over each other.

"What do you mean?" I ask, a pit opening in my gut.

She can't drive herself anymore, but she still has a driver. Father doesn't like her being where other people can see her, but he's never kept her from going to her appointments.

"Are you having problems with your driver?"

That's the only thing I can think of. The only explanation for why she wouldn't have been able to go. Because otherwise—

"Your father told him not to take me anywhere without his approval." She laughs bitterly as she shakes her head. "Apparently, doctor's appointments aren't on the approved list."

My father is the scum of the earth, but it's incomprehensible to me that he'd keep her from seeing her doctor. She needs physical therapy to stay mobile and active. She's already stuck at home, and if he takes that single reprieve from her, she's going to be even more depressed than she already is.

I'm going to kill him. I don't know how, and I don't know when, but I'm going to fucking kill him.

Mom stares out the window, lips pursed tight, and it cuts even deeper than Father's violent outbursts.

She'll never say it, but we both know he's doing this to punish me. I haven't even tried to talk to Alexei since that damn meeting, and Father's making sure she bears the weight of my inaction.

"I'll talk to him, okay?"

Resigned, I gently squeeze her forearm and press a kiss to her temple. Whenever she gets upset like this, she retreats into herself, locking her emotions away and acting like I'm not even here.

Sometimes, I wish she'd lash out instead.

I swallow my hurt and walk away, the sound of my heels clicking on the marble floors barely registering over the rush of blood in my ears.

If my father wants to make this house oppressive and unbearable for me? Fine. He wants to hurt me? I'll deal with it. He decides I can't make my own money, so I have no choice but to live in his house? That's alright; I like being close to Mom, anyway.

But she's off-limits, and I don't care what I have to do to get that through his skull.

I try to call him, utterly unsurprised when it goes straight to voicemail. I leave him a dozen angry messages and stand on the patio, wrapping my arms around myself to keep warm while I wait for him to come back and force him to listen to me. The guard by the door gives me a look but otherwise ignores me.

For hours, I stand in the cold, and by the time his cherry red Bentley pulls up, the wind has frozen my anger, leaving the familiar fear his presence always brings.

As he approaches, Father looks me up and down in a dismissive gesture that says I'm as worthy of his attention as the dirt under his shoes.

"What do you want?"

"I need to talk to you." My voice is quiet, and I clear my throat, bracing for a fight. If there's anyone I can force myself to defend, it's Mom. I can't be a timid thing that lets Father bully me into silence.

Clearing my throat, I continue, "You can't keep Mom from her appointments."

He raises a brow, striding past me without a word. But his silence screams for him.

Of course he can. He already has.

I follow him, feeling like a moron.

He loosens his tie as he stalks toward his office.

"When's the last time you made yourself useful?" he eventually asks, his glare pinning me.

"What?"

"I've asked you to do *one thing*, Emiliya. But have you done it?" He searches my face, and my eyes drop to my shoes, desperate to avoid Father's scrutiny.

Alexei's rejection still stings, and I've needed time to lick my wounds before I try to pursue him again, but will Father care about that?

No. Why would he?

"I tried, and I'm still working on it, but—"

"But you can't even find a way to make a single man pay attention to you. Then again, you weren't able to capture Daniil's attention the way I hoped, either." His eyes finally cut to mine, his disappointment falling over me like a bucket of ice water. "You're just as useless as your mother, aren't you?"

His face contorts into a mask of revulsion so deep, it freezes me in place.

"I just need more time. The plan was to go out tonight and try a new angle. I just..." I shrug, searching desperately for an escape. "I just wanted to talk to you about Mom first."

He raises one skeptical brow. "Make yourself useful to his family. Until then, there's no point in talking about your mother."

Desperation crushes my chest, so heavy it's painful to breathe.

I remain rooted to the spot, his silhouette growing blurry with tears as I bite my lip to keep them from falling.

He slams his office door in my face while my mind scrambles to find a way out of this.

Even if I wanted to find Alexei, I have no clue where to start looking. I glance around me, but the empty halls and unfeeling decor have no answers for the questions I can't bring myself to voice.

The only way I'll be able to convince Alexei to do what my father wants is if I'm able to trick him into my bed and convince him to give a shit about me. It was always a long shot, but, fuck, Father's right. The only person I've been able to dupe into caring about me is Mom.

I have no shot of convincing Alexei I'm worth caring about.

Mutely, I slink into my room, not wasting time on my doubt and insecurity.

I turn on the shower, staring into the mirror while I wait for the water to heat up, hating the view more than I ever have. My father stares back at me in the curve of my nose, the slope of my cheek, the set of my eyes.

An unforgettable reminder of exactly who I am.

Just as worthless, and just as easy to hate, but without the power to control anything.

I wait until the view is obscured by steam before I turn away, dropping my clothes into a pile to deal with later. The scorching water shocks me out of my numbness and forces me to focus on what matters.

Delaying Mom's treatments is pure fucking evil.

I take a deep breath as I wrap myself in a towel and dig through my closet for something suitable to wear. Everything feels like too much.

Too flashy.

Too short.

Too desperate.

Alexei made himself clear. We were a one-time thing, and he has no interest in a repeat. Whether that's because he was disappointed or because he doesn't want anything to do with me, I don't know, and I'll never ask.

I settle on a simple dress, pairing it with a flashy set of heels for a pop of color. Not so much that I look like I'm begging for someone to fuck me, but enough that people *will* look. By the time I'm done with my hair and makeup, I only want to crawl into bed and have a good, soul-cleansing cry.

But time isn't a luxury that I have, so I strut out the front door, wink at the guards at the front gate, and head toward one of Alexei's clubs.

My confidence is a brittle veneer, but I cling to it as I waltz into Enclave, smirking when the doorman gives me a slow once-over. Automatically, my eyes drift up to the mezzanine where the VIP lounge is, searching the faces one by one.

The crowd is bigger than I was expecting, a throng of people eager to let go and forget about their lives for a few hours, granting the small bit of hope in my chest a swift death.

I can't pretend I know him well, but I've never seen Alexei taking part in the thick of it. He's always been on the fringes, watching the chaos around him as much as he is directing it.

*Maybe he's in his office*, I tell myself. *Maybe he'll be out here any moment, and he'll fall for my charms without a second thought.*

Or maybe I'm delusional.

I twist my hair in my hands as I make my way to the bar. I could spend my whole night sprinting between his clubs, and the odds are I'd still miss him. Despite the urgency of the situation, I need to be patient if I want to have a real shot at getting his attention.

Even if that means I have to take my time.

My skin crawls with every new person who looks in my direction. I ignore them, settling in for a long night.

# CHAPTER 7

# Emiliya

F our agonizing, hair-pulling nights later I'm right back where I started, making small talk with a woman near the bar to keep myself occupied as my mind spirals out of control. I've spent every night cycling through each one of Alexei's clubs, and I have nothing to show for it.

If I don't find him, I'll go somewhere else tomorrow, then I'll do it again, and the next until I finally run into him.

I grin at the bartender as I take my drink, promptly spilling most of it when I turn away and run smack-dab into Alexei's chest. Humiliation and relief war in my chest. I try to take a half step back, stumbling when my heel rolls underneath me.

Before I'm able to make things even worse, Alexei's strong hands grab my arms, keeping me from falling flat on my ass and flashing my underwear to half the bar.

I take a moment to compose myself, and as soon as I see the gold flecks in his hazel eyes blazing with fire, I relax into him, resting my hands on his chest.

For balance, of course. Only for balance.

If I happen to like feeling the way his muscles flex under his suit, that's neither here nor there.

His face is stormy, but for the first time in days, I don't feel like I'm going to puke. Instead, a weight has been lifted from my shoulders. I smile, hoping the way I'm blushing comes off as sexy instead of childish.

"What're you doing here?" he grits out, his lips pressed into a firm line. Despite the crowd around us, and the fact that we're in his workplace, he looks far more hardened than I've ever seen. For the first time, he looks dangerous. I shove the inkling of unease to the side and grin, enjoying the way his eyes flare in response.

"I was thinking about dancing. Care to join me?" I flutter my lashes, not bothering to contain the way I laugh at his unamused expression. His grip loosens enough for me to take a step away, but I don't miss the way his hand pauses before he lets it fall away entirely.

"No. What are you doing in my club, Emiliya?"

I bite my lip at the way his white dress shirt pulls tight across his chest. He's wearing an emerald green suit, and his slacks hug his thighs like they were made just for his body. When I look up, I don't miss the way his eyes linger over my body even as he glares.

"You said you didn't want me." I shrug. "In fact, you told me to find someone else to have fun with."

I don't wait for a response before I strut away. The weight of his gaze is heavy as I make my way toward the mass of people dancing. It's only a matter of time before that tightly held control snaps.

Three steps later, a hand curls around my hip, right over a bruise. Alexei pulls me against his chest as I bite my lip and look up at him with hooded eyes.

"Are you *really* going to keep me from having a good time?" I ask with an eye roll.

For a long moment he doesn't answer, staring at my mouth like he can't figure out whether to chew me out or kiss me stupid. I relax against him, letting my head fall back against his chest.

"What're you so afraid of, Alexei?" The sound of his name on my tongue destroys something behind his eyes, his resolve snapping in an instant.

He drags me away from the crowd and through a door marked for employees only. He's still glowering as he pins me against a wall, far away from any prying eyes. In this private alcove, things are far quieter, and the change is almost dizzying.

I lift my chin to meet his glare. "Is there a problem?" The way his brows draw together reveals a small scar that cuts across his eyebrow, and I have the inexplicable urge to trace it with my thumb.

"I think you're a problem," he murmurs. His eyes search my face. God, I hope he finds what he's looking for. I need him to fall for the pretty mask that hides all the ugliness hiding underneath.

He's more than a head taller than me, even in my heels. With his face tilted toward mine, his breath is warm against my lips. I can feel the distance between us like a physical ache.

I hate that I know how good we can be together. If circumstances were different, we could've been electric.

"And what're you going to do about it?" My tongue traces my bottom lip, and his eyes track the movement. Before he pulled me into this hallway, he looked angry, but his anger has been consumed by hunger. Now, he looks like he wants to devour me.

He closes the gap until all I'm able to focus on is the weight of his body against mine, a steady thrum of heat passing between us.

"I'm not sure yet," he breathes. "I should scare you off and tell you to find a new hunting ground."

For a moment, he's as still as stone, a silent debate taking place behind his eyes. Then, faster than I would have expected, he opens a door, pushing me through it and twisting me around until my back is pressed against the cool wood while he flicks the lock, cutting us off from anyone that could try to interrupt.

Alexei's hand rests loosely at the base of my throat, making my breath hitch. The implied threat makes my heart beat an incessant tattoo against my ribs.

His thumb strokes over the hollow point between my collarbones, and I want to lean into the touch, to challenge him and ask him to press just a little bit harder, to show me how far he's willing to push me.

"But you aren't," I challenge.

"I guess I'm not."

"Why?"

I'm stupid to push him. I should be thanking my lucky stars that he's close to me at all, not doing something that risks pushing him away. Alexei doesn't answer, his eyes peering into mine before he shakes his head.

"I don't know."

His pupils are blown out and wild. I want to pull him flush against me. I want to push him back and shove him into a chair, get on my knees and take him in my mouth. I want to take the power out of his hands and make it my own.

Before I can work up the nerve, Alexei's lips crash against mine.

I gasp, and he takes full advantage, his tongue lashing against mine until I'm not able to think of anything at all. All I can do is feel, even when he hooks his hands under my thighs, lifting me like I'm weightless.

I wrap my arms around his neck, winding my fingers through his thick hair as he shifts until the bulge of his erection is lined up with my pussy.

I bite down on his lip, just hard enough to get his attention. He pulls back, his eyes flashing dark, glinting with a promise that makes me grateful he's holding me, because otherwise I'd probably dissolve into a boneless puddle before him.

"No claws this time," he growls, taking measured steps toward the leather sofa against the wall. He sits, leaving me no choice but to settle myself on his lap, and I take full advantage of the leverage he's given me, grinding against him, my own slickness easing the slide of fabric against flesh.

My clit throbs, my body buzzing from the inside out.

I trail my lips over the line of his jaw. "You didn't seem to mind them last time." To prove my point, I drag my nails down his chest. Even through his shirt, it's impossible for him to hide the shiver that racks down his spine.

He tilts his head to the side, granting me access to the long line of his neck. His hands are tight where he grips my waist, and I scrape my teeth over his jugular while I undo the buttons of his shirt, grinning at the way his breath hitches.

"Don't leave any marks," he orders again, voice firm. It's a stark contrast from the gentle way he runs his hands up my thighs.

"Don't be such a buzzkill, Alexei. It's killing the mood."

I undo the last button, wasting no time in pushing his shirt off his shoulders. I might not be able to control everything else, but I can at least take advantage of this to fulfill *one* of my fantasies. I slip off his lap, falling to my knees in front of the couch, making quick work of his belt.

Making him care about me as a person might be an impossible feat, but I can definitely get Alexei to care about me as a warm body. If nothing else, I can be a willing tool for his pleasure.

And maybe I can get something out of it, too. Some nice memories to make this easier to stomach when I'm alone again at the end of the night.

If this is all I'm going to get out of Alexei, then I want to feel the weight of him on my tongue.

As soon as I pull his cock free, Alexei groans a sound of pure pleasure, making me shiver as I stroke him slowly.

He's slick with precum, making my mouth water. Part of me wants to drag this out, to make him squirm, but that plan goes out the window as I run my tongue up his length, wanting to taste him far more than I want to tease him. He grunts, his hands toying with the straps of my dress.

"Why're you still wearing this?" he grunts, and it might be enough to startle a laugh out of me if I weren't so focused on taking him deep, swallowing so I don't choke. I roll my eyes, but oblige him, shifting the straps free and pushing the dress down my chest as my head bobs up and down, greedily running my tongue along the vein on the underside of his cock.

He leans forward the instant my breasts are exposed, lightly tracing a finger around my nipples. I pull back with a gasp that has him smirking when pinches them between two fingers.

If he thinks I'm going to let him run the show this time, he's fucking insane. I take his balls in my hand, rolling them as I position my lips right over his tip, teasing my tongue against the sensitive slit.

"You know, it won't kill you to give up control for a moment," I murmur, my lips brushing over his velvet-soft skin.

"We'll see about that."

His hips buck, and I smile as I take him back into my mouth.

Alexei really is a marvel to look at, especially from this angle. Lounging like a king, he still manages to look put together, even as his head falls against the couch.

I want to break that composure.

Sitting up on my knees so I can take him deeper, I swallow until he hits the back of my throat. Saliva drips down my chin, and I suck even harder as I pull back, using my hand on the part of his length I can't fit in my mouth.

His hand tightens in my hair, keeping me in place while his hips twitch like he's trying to hold back. The unyielding control he has over himself is infuriating, making me even more determined to see him let go.

My thighs squeeze together, and my whole body is pulsing with need. If I don't touch myself soon, I'm going to lose my mind. Giving in to temptation, I slip a hand between my thighs, but he shakes his head. I pull back, sucking his balls into my mouth until he forgets to care what I'm doing with my hands, moaning loudly in the small room.

*"Fuck."*

I work him with my spit-slicked hand, mindlessly chasing my own high until he pulls me up by my hair, digging a hand in his pocket before he kicks off his pants. I have enough time to slip my dress down my hips before he's pulling me into his lap and taking a nipple into his mouth, biting down until I'm a whimpering mess in his lap.

I shift until he's lined up with my slit, running my fingers through his hair as I grind my clit against him.

When he pulls back, I hold his hair tighter to keep him from giving my other nipple the same attention.

"If you don't fuck me in the next two minutes, I'm putting my dress back on and leaving to find someone who'll get the job done," I chastise. He chuckles darkly, the sound vibrating all the way down to my aching pussy. "I'm serious, Alexei."

He slips a finger along my soaking wet cunt, pressing a single one inside. It does nothing to alleviate the need.

If anything, it just makes it worse.

I want to feel him stretching me open again as much as I want my next breath.

"Relax, you'll get what you want."

His lips ghost over my pulse point. I bite my lip as I tilt my head to the side, giving him room to do whatever he wants.

"But it'll be on my time. Not yours."

He thrusts another finger inside me, making me cry out. My thighs shake when he brushes over my G-spot, his fingers massaging my walls like his goal is to drive me to the point of insanity.

If he keeps it up, every patron in the main room is going to hear me, the pulsing music be damned. I bite my lip to the point of pain.

Alexei uses his free hand to hold my chin, forcing me to meet his eyes.

"No," he snaps, grip just shy of bruising. I swallow hard as his thumb pulls against my lip. "Don't hide those reactions from me. I want to hear exactly what I do to you, sweetheart. I've earned every little gasp and cry out of those pretty lips."

His pace is unrelenting, fucking into me with single-minded focus. My core flutters around his fingers as he works ceaselessly, shoving me closer and closer to the point of ecstasy. I shiver, scraping the pad of his thumb before I lick the sting away.

"Please," I beg. "*Please*, Alexei, I need you." My voice is nothing but a breathy whine, and I have to make an effort to keep my eyes open. Just a bit more, and I'll be putty in his hands. Like he can read my mind, he flicks his thumb over my clit, and I shatter.

Collapsing against him, I cling to his shoulders to stay grounded while my body shakes with pleasure. Over the ringing in my ears, I can hear him tear open the condom, his hands grabbing my ass, urging me to stand on shaking knees.

The instant the head of his cock nudges against my entrance, I'm clamoring for another orgasm, desperate to feel him inside me. I gasp at the stretch as I sink down onto him. It's fucking exquisite, and even though it isn't the first time I've had him, it's still more than I was bracing for.

He grunts against my shoulder while I try to adjust.

Holy shit, one time with Alexei was not enough.

He keeps still, hands stroking over my back until I manage to catch my breath. I raise up until only the tip is inside me, then, with a wink, fall back heavily on him. And, *god*, it's so good. He feels so fucking good.

He meets me thrust for thrust. Feeling petty, I rake my nails down his chest, leaving long, red scratches behind. His head falls back on a groan, his breathing rough where I lay my hands over his pecs.

"Fuck, you feel good."

His hands flex against my hips, like he's trying to take charge of the pace.

Well, if he wanted to make sure he was in control, then he shouldn't have let me be on top. Rolling my hips, I shiver as I watch the way his abs tighten.

"Slow down," he rasps, his voice strained.

I bring my face down next to his, taking his earlobe between my teeth.

"Make me."

I feel his growl before I hear it, and next thing I know, he's throwing me to the side. My head spins as I catch myself on my hands and knees, and before I can protest, he's behind me, pounding into me with punishing slaps of his hips against my ass.

His teeth sink into my shoulder, and I throw my head back on a moan, bracing one hand on the arm of the couch, arching my back.

*Shit.*

My skin feels too tight, like I'm going to burst at the slightest touch. When he reaches under me, pinching my nipples tight, I do just that. My walls spasm around him as my orgasm detonates like a bomb, destroying any coherent thoughts I might have been clinging to.

"So." *Thrust.* "Fucking." *Thrust.* "Good," he grunts as his cock pulses inside me, filling the condom with his release. I'm panting as I look at him over my shoulder, and he looks agonized, but it hardly registers over the bliss rushing through my veins.

I want to float in this feeling. Like this, nothing hurts. None of the worry that plagues every moment of my life can touch me. It's just the two of us. The rest of the world doesn't matter.

I close my eyes as I collapse in a wrecked heap, my face pressed against the leather couch.

Fuck, I want to hold on to this for as long as he lets me, to pretend this was something other than a hate fuck.

As the high of his orgasm fades, his lax muscles tighten up all over again, until he's back to a stoic, angry wall of a man. I swallow the lump that forms in my throat as he pulls away, the cool air rushing into the void he leaves behind, leaving me cold and alone as sweat cools on my skin.

By the time I sit up, he's already disposed of the condom and is zipping up his pants. It makes me feel even more exposed, but

I'm not sure my legs will hold me up long enough to hunt down my dress and slip it back on yet.

Alexei's hair is a mess, and the lines on his chest send an unexpected wave of possessiveness through me.

*He's not yours, dumbass. Get it together.*

"This isn't happening again."

He doesn't look at me as he says it, and I'm almost grateful. His dismissal makes it so I don't have to hide the way his words hit me like a slap to the face.

Beyond sex, I have nothing else to offer him. I pulled out every tool at my arsenal, and he still wants nothing to do with me. He won't let me slip under his skin. He won't keep me close enough to let Father manipulate him.

I fucking blew it. Not just for me, but for Mom, too. All because I couldn't keep my fucking clothes on and pretend I was worth giving a shit about.

Did I really think sleeping with him was going to help? What a fucking moron.

Now what the hell am I going to do?

"That's what you said last time," I say.

Somehow, my voice doesn't sound nearly as fragile as I feel. I don't know if I could deal with being humiliated on top of everything else. Taking a breath, I school my face and force myself to stand, scooping my dress off the floor.

His eyes pin me in place just as I'm running my fingers through my hair, trying to tame the mess before I have to face anyone else.

"I mean it this time," Alexei says as he shrugs his shirt back on, taking care as he rebuttons it. "It isn't happening. I'm not going to see you again, and you need to stop hanging around my clubs. Find somewhere else to catch your hook ups."

My cheeks flush, and I bite my tongue to keep myself from begging him to reconsider. If nothing else, I need to be able to walk out of this room with my head held high. My pride is all I have left, and I won't let Alexei steal it from me.

Not tonight. Not over this.

"Sure thing, handsome," I smirk, turning to leave the room as soon as I'm dressed.

He doesn't call after me. He doesn't even acknowledge me as I leave, strutting out of the club and back to my car like there's nothing wrong. But as soon as I step outside, the open air and solitude is exactly what I desperately need.

I check the time on my phone before I toss it into the back seat.

Can I afford five minutes? Just a few moments to fall apart and cry. After that, I'll put myself back together, go home, and try to figure out another way to fix everything.

I bury my face in my hands just as the first tears hit my jaw.

# CHAPTER 8

# Alexei

Nadya chucks a stick of celery at my head, growling when it bounces harmlessly against the cabinet. Her frustration is so clear, I can't help but laugh.

When she shifts her glare to me, I only laugh harder.

"I'm only twenty-eight, you *mudak*. I'm not *pushing thirty*," she says as she rolls her eyes. "Besides, you're twenty-six! If I'm getting old, you're not far behind."

I had to work my ass off today in order to make time for dinner with her, and there's still a chance something will come up and cut this evening short. But knowing my sister, if it does, she'll throw a fit, and I'll have no choice but to stay until she's ready for me to leave. Then, I'll still be up until after sunrise dealing with whatever fire needs putting out.

"If I knew I was going to have to put up with this abuse, I would've told you to spend the evening with Blair instead of letting you insult me and throw food like a child."

She gives me a look so dry I have to focus my attention elsewhere to hold back another laugh.

"Unlike you, when I want to hang out with Blair, I can call her or show up at her place. Apparently, most people actually *want* to hang out with the people they care about."

"I think you're making that up. Like you did with the tooth fairy."

Any traces of amusement in her expression disappear.

"*I* didn't make up the tooth fairy! That was someone else."

"Alright then. Who? Give me names."

Her jaw works with her frustration.

"Either way, I can't hang out with Blair tonight because she isn't feeling well." I hum, turning to refocus on dinner prep, unable to dredge up the energy to care how Blair's feeling, but I'll pretend for Nadya's sake.

I just won't try very hard.

"You'll be glad to know that I'm hanging out with her next week, so you can't use her as an excuse to ignore me without feeling bad about it."

"You two going to another pottery thing?" I ask, ignoring her jab.

I adore my sister; I really do. She's my favorite person on the planet, but when she gets on a roll, she's the worst combination of a hovering, anxious mother and an obnoxious sibling.

She can't decide if she wants to yell at me or make fun of me when I do something stupid, and I don't have the heart to tell her that it isn't her responsibility to do either, but I'd rather have her worry than go without her, so I tolerate it.

"Nah, not this time. Turns out Blair kind of sucks at pottery, so we're going to try something different."

I grunt so she doesn't think I'm ignoring her, stirring the boiling soup on the stove.

"Do you have any plans this week? Other than working yourself into the ground."

"Not this again," I groan, steeling myself for a fight. "It's your birthday. Can we not fight?"

"You're right," she says as she shakes her head.

Instantly, my guard's up. I let out a slow breath, waiting a beat before I dare gloat.

"It's my birthday," Nadya continues, "which means what I say goes. And I say I don't want to watch you end up miserable because you're slaving away for men who don't give a shit about you."

The *like Dad* goes unsaid.

I can explain that I've done my best to make myself valuable to the Bratva until I'm blue in the face, I can tell her again and again that I'm not worried about glory the way Dad was, but she'll never believe me. It's a fear she clings to no matter what, and I doubt anything will ever be able to pry it from her hands.

Unlike Dad, I'm not the type of man to blindly follow arrogant men because I want to be respected. I'm not going to take the fall for someone else and end up locked up for the rest of my life in some misguided pursuit of honor or glory or whatever the fuck he thought he was going to accomplish.

I might be dumb, but I'm not that stupid.

I owe it to both of us to work my ass off to keep her safe no matter what.

"By the way…" I say, moving to put my body between her and the knife block before she gets any clever ideas when I say, "Lev's going to be hanging out with you for a while."

All traces of amusement are gone in an instant, replaced by a seething contempt.

"What?"

"When you go out, Lev's going to go with you." I shrug, like it's no big deal. Like I've always needed someone to watch her back when I'm not there.

Her hand flexes at her side, and I'm very conscious of the fact that she still has a clean line of access to her purse, and, subsequently, the knife I know for a fact she keeps in it. She's a terrible shot, but I've never seen a more terrifying figure than Nadya with a blade in her hand.

She takes a single step toward me, angling to the side like she's trying to figure out how to get past me. I plant my feet shoulder-width apart, prepared to grab her at the first sign of movement.

"Hey, you're the one that keeps saying we need to spend more time as a family."

"And you know damn well I wasn't talking about Lev. Why are you putting him on babysitting duty?"

I'd step forward to comfort her, but she's slippery when she wants to be. And the set of kitchen knives she got me last Christmas are real fucking sharp.

Despite what she seems to think, I'm not suicidal.

"I wouldn't call it babysitting, I'd call it…" I cast for a better word, but nothing comes to mind. "Guard duty."

"Why the hell do I need a guard, Alexei?"

"It's just a precaution. Things are fluctuating, and I'd feel better knowing someone has your back until they settle down."

"*Fluctuating*?" She shoves her hands in her pockets, but I don't miss the way they're shaking. "What did you do?"

"Nothing."

*Yet.*

She gives me the same look she used to give me when I'd hide my report cards or lie about sneaking out at night. Like she sees straight through me, and I was a fool to even try to lie to her.

"It's only temporary," I assure her, even though I don't know if that's the truth. "After things calm down, we can go back to business as usual, but I'd really appreciate it if you'd go along with this."

If I end up taking over the Bratva, there will be no going back to how things were. Nadya will need a guard around the clock.

But that's a problem for another day.

Even if it seems like it, I'm not going out of my way to ruin her birthday.

Nadya's quiet for a long, heart-pounding moment. "You could try saying please."

"Would it change anything if I did?"

Her whole body sags when she gives up, turning her face away. "Does it have to be Lev? Is there anyone else who can do it?"

Our cousin is loudmouthed, wouldn't know a social cue if it bit him in the ass, and always thinks his opinion is both welcome and wanted, but he's reliable. If I ask him to get something done, he does it. I don't need to hold his hand or follow up with him to make sure he's doing his job, and he'll understand the gravity of me asking him to protect Nadya.

"Unfortunately, you're stuck with him."

"And I'm sure the fact that you won't have to deal with him has nothing to do with it."

"Well…" I hedge, "it doesn't hurt."

She flips me off and pulls dishes from the cabinet before she storms out of the kitchen. "I'm going to set the table. Try not to drown in your own bullshit while I'm in the other room." I roll my eyes as I turn off the stove.

That wasn't her permission, but it was close enough. She didn't say no, and that's all I can ask for. We can go back to fighting about it tomorrow.

I follow her lead, moving the food to the dining room, sitting next to her while she chatters mindlessly about whatever's on her mind, letting her distract herself.

We eat. We laugh. We chat about anything except for what's important.

And it's easy.

She lets me pretend that everything's fine, and I let her pretend that I'm nothing but the little brother she wishes I was. Like this, things aren't messy. We're just celebrating her birthday, and we don't have to worry about anything beyond tonight.

I need this just as much as she does, if not more, but fuck if I'm going to admit it.

When the conversation dies down, I go to the kitchen and grab the cake I got from her favorite bakery and the gift in the fancy wrapping I paid far too much for.

Her face lights up with a quiet smile that makes all the bull-shit worth it. The ribbing, the hovering, the fact that she's going to be furious with me when she finds out I'm planning on deposing Nikita.

It's all worth it to see her happy.

She throws her arms around my neck, pulling me into a hug that's tighter than someone as small as her has any business giving.

"Happy birthday," I say, letting her hold me for as long as she wants.

Neither of us ever mentions it, but the absence of our parents hits harder on occasions like this.

Holidays are too quiet without them.

Special events too often go ignored.

Birthdays are a little too lonely.

Sure, we could have driven three hours to go see Dad, but what's the point? He doesn't want us there, and prison's fucking depressing, even if you're just visiting.

Fuck, I should probably go see him and let him know that Maksim's dead. But that can wait.

Nadya gasps as she tears into her gift, tossing the tissue paper over her shoulder without a care.

"How did you get your hands on these? They're impossible to find!"

Nadya clutches the set of cutting tools to her chest, like she's worried I'm going to snatch them away from her.

She's not wrong, though. It feels like everyone in the state got into pottery at the same time she did. Finding any of the tools she's been ranting about has been nearly impossible.

It took me six weeks, and I still had to pay way more than I should have, but I managed to find them.

"I know a guy." I shrug. She shoves my shoulder, but smiles, looking like a kid again.

"You're the best. You know that, right?"

"Any chance I can get you to put that in writing?"

"Never. In fact, I have no idea what you're talking about."

She laughs right until I'm getting ready to leave, shrugging on my coat.

"I guess I'll see Lev in the morning?" Her dejected acceptance loosens the rope around my neck enough for me to take a deep breath, letting me to think clearly for the first time in days.

"He'll be here before you leave in the morning."

The drive home is cold.

As soon as my office door shuts behind me, I call Artyom. The deadline I gave him is rapidly approaching, and now that someone's keeping an eye on Nadya, it will give me room to throw myself into preparing for the fool's errand I've set for myself.

"Alexei," he answers, a grin in his voice. "I was just about to call. I have wonderful news."

# CHAPTER 9

# Emiliya

The door clicks softly when it closes behind Dr. Bonilla. I dig around in my purse, like it'll somehow hide the way my hands are shaking.

After a long beat, Mom says, "Your father will be glad to hear I'm getting Botox." She smiles, but it doesn't quite meet her eyes. "We just won't tell him about the other part."

The *other part* being the antidepressants she was just prescribed.

Botox to help with the uncontrolled eye movements, and pills to make her life a little less miserable.

The bitter part of me wants to snap that Father doesn't know she's here, and it isn't his grace that allowed her to get the care she needs, but my stubbornness.

I'll gladly spend all my time driving her wherever she wants to go, making sure she gets what she needs, but she's not ready to let go of the fantasy that Father still cares about us.

For now, she can keep her pretty lies.

"Sure, Mom," I grin, face stiff while everything she said to Dr. Bonilla pounds around in my skull, an endless echo that threatens to send me to my knees.

*Not getting any better.*

*Feeling listless.*

*Maybe I've just been lonely.*

That last one is just as much my fault as it is Father's. If I spent more time with her, she wouldn't be as depressed. If I had fought harder, she wouldn't have had to wait to go to the doctor in the first place. She idly fiddles with her necklace while I stare at the clock on the wall, chewing on the inside of my lip.

"Once you're settled at home, I'll run to the pharmacy. He'll never have to know."

Dr. Bonilla saves me from my shame as he returns, a smile on his weathered face. "Alright, Irina, here you go." He hands her a slip of paper and a business card with the date of her next appointment scrawled across the back. "Come back next Monday at eight and call me if anything else comes up before then. Do you have any questions?"

I take Mom's polite smile as permission to leave, helping her stand and shuffling her toward the door so I can get home as fast as possible.

She can't keep missing appointments, and I refuse to let it happen again, but I don't know how long Father is going to be at his meeting, either. He probably won't notice if she isn't where he expects her to be, but if I'm gone too long, he'll start asking questions.

I take a deep breath as I pull out of the parking lot.

"Do you think your father will let me go to my appointments when he finds out about the Botox?" Mom asks, and my stomach turns at the optimistic note in her voice. Her hope is a killer, waiting to cut us both down the moment we fail to guard against it.

Ideally, she won't say anything to him, but I'll be the last person to tell her what she can or can't do. Besides, Father is already using her health as a pawn so he can control one single man. A man who wants nothing to do with me.

I turn up the music, pretending to enjoy whatever song's playing so I have an excuse to stay silent.

I need to find a way to get us both out of this hellhole.

Father was right when he said that everything I have is because of him. My car, my clothes, my money, he gave me all of it, and he can take it away whenever he wants. If I want to get Mom out from under his thumb, I'll have to find the means to support us both.

I run through the list of everyone I know, trying to think of someone who won't buckle when Father applies the right pressure, someone brave enough to help me, but come up blank. At the end of the day, everyone has a breaking point, and Father's an expert at hunting them down and commanding everyone to his will.

Every childhood friend, every tenuous connection I've formed as an adult, they all fall apart when he wants them to. Father has poisoned every relationship I've ever had, from quiet comradery with the housekeeper's daughter when I was twelve, to trying my best to find a sense of self-worth with Daniil Krutikov.

I shove the loneliness aside, focusing on getting us home before Father, sighing in relief when I see his car is absent from its usual spot in the garage. Without the need to rush, Mom and I take our time wandering to her wing of the house. She stops and straightens the frames on the walls, comments on the flowers in the decorative vases, and asks me to adjust the rugs to make sure they're lying flat.

It's a familiar routine, and normally, I love it. But right now, I feel like I've been struck by lightning, buzzing with a restless energy that I need to take advantage of.

If I'm going to get Mom and me away from this place, I'm going to need money. A lot of it. Enough for a place to live, a new car, new identities, and all her medical expenses.

My bank account might be in my name, but Father has just as much access to it as I do. If I take all my money out, he'll know exactly what I'm planning on doing.

I'll have to take out smaller amounts, space them out so he doesn't notice, until I have enough to get us both papers to set up new identities somewhere far away from Chicago and the Bratva's reach.

"Are you alright, *lastochka*? You seem distracted."

It's not going to be easy to talk Mom into leaving. I won't go without her, but Father has his claws so deep in her, I don't know if she'll ever feel safe enough to run.

"I'm fine," I say, smiling tightly.

Is she still in love with him? Am I already setting myself up for failure?

"I'm just tired, that's all."

Mom purses her lips, seeing straight through my lie, but I'm not ready to have this fight yet. I'll lay the groundwork before I even approach her, but unlike Father, Mom doesn't make a habit of forcing me to talk about things I want to ignore.

She trusts that I'll come to her in my own time.

As if to prove the point, she hums, strolling leisurely toward her rooms, already pulling her phone and earbuds out of her handbag. "If you say so, dear. I'm going to finish my book." Her hand trails along the wall, keeping her steady. "You know where to find me if you want to talk."

"Of course, Mom. Love you."

"Love you more." She sighs, a gentle smile playing on the corners of her lips as she disappears down the hall, leaving me to my own thoughts.

Without her, I can think clearly.

Right now, time is on my side, and no matter how brief this moment may be, I need to take advantage of it. I move from room to room like a ghost, mournfully tracing my fingers over the leaves of my dying plants.

Eventually, I stop to glare at the air vent above my scorched fiddle-leaf fig, practically choking on my frustration. It's taken years of pleading with the maids to leave watering the plants to me, but I haven't convinced them to leave my plants where I put them. They move them wherever they think they'll look nice, mindless to whether they can survive there or not.

And, once again, my poor baby has suffered the consequences.

Then again, if I hadn't been hiding away in my room for two weeks, I could've moved them back, and my plants would've been fine.

This is my own fault.

I make my rounds on the first floor, making sure the survivors have enough water, pruning off the dead leaves and tossing them in the trash as I go.

When we make our escape, I'll miss my plants. But I can get more when we find a soft place to land.

Shit, how am I supposed to get us out of here? Even if I drain every cent from my account, it won't be enough.

I have to find more somewhere else.

Fuck.

I can't get a job.

Even if someone would take a risk on a twenty-four-year-old with no work experience, the only places Father would ever *consider* allowing me to work would be affiliated with him, and he'd still control everything I earned.

I'll have to find a place where no one knows who I am, or who Father is, and hope they're willing to let me work whenever I can show up.

Either that, or I have to fall back on the only real asset I have.

No one in their right mind would trust me to work for them, but plenty of men will trust me in their bed.

Disgust creeps down my spine. I'm not quite desperate enough to wander along that thought, but if I play my cards right, I might be able to find someone with no children and one foot in the grave that I can con into marrying me.

It would take me away from Mom, but only until the unfortunate guy's dead and buried. Then I'd have my own resources.

It's so far from what I want, but I don't have years to scrounge and scrimp every penny I can find. Mom needs a better life than what Father lets her have. If I use my body to my advantage, I'll be able to get away from this fucking city that much faster.

If I don't think about it too hard, I can pretend it'll be fun. I'll go to my room and get all dressed up, then I'll go to a club that doesn't belong to Alexei Trenin and find someone with deep enough pockets to be my ticket out of here.

He'll either be ancient, or so cocky that he's begging for a bullet to the head, but Mom will be safe.

Once it's all over, I'll try to find a way to live with myself, but that's a long way out. I'll worry about that when terrified I'm going to end up with bruises and broken bones if I breathe too loudly.

# CHAPTER 10

# Alexei

I t's still early, and Underground is far from the most popular club in town. Hell, it's not even the most popular club on this street, but even still, the crowd is sparse.

Though for what I need, it's perfect.

The lack of people makes it easy to spot Carlo Di Veroli when he makes his way through the front doors, making no attempt to conceal the enforcers trailing after him.

With his dark suit and even darker eyes, it's impossible for him to blend in with the few people drinking and pretending to enjoy themselves.

I watch as he motions for the enforcers to stage themselves around the room while he eyes the VIP section. Half a dozen men make their way through the club, and he's bound to have more outside, ready to monitor everyone who so much as steps foot in the neighborhood.

The static in my head fades away when Lev slips past Carlo unnoticed, making his way outside.

Thank fuck Nadya already had plans to hang out with Blair tonight. Andrei can keep an eye on her, and I'll be able to focus knowing Lev has my back.

Ideally, Carlo won't need all his men. His only concern will be the shipments of firearms that Artyom managed to slip out of their warehouse. He managed to slip them out from right under Carlo's nose, undetected.

It's the best news I've gotten in weeks.

Even across the room, Carlo's frustration is tangible, swirling around him like a thick fog as he stalks toward me.

I make no attempt to draw his attention.

Underground isn't associated with either of our outfits, and the few people dancing and loitering at the bar appear oblivious to his presence. It's just as well. There's no reason for us to put on a show if we don't have to.

Besides, I'm sure Carlo's only had eyes for me since he first spotted me. I'd be flattered if he didn't look like he wants to deck me.

I rise from my seat as he approaches, his face blank and eyes blazing. I don't blame him for being pissed. Hell, I'd be concerned if he wasn't. It still might prove to be stupid, but provoking him has gotten an actual meeting better than any other negotiation tactic has so far.

"Carlo," I greet, shaking his hand. I practically roll my eyes at how hard he squeezes my hand. "I'm glad to see you again."

He nods, a swift acknowledgment and dismissal of my lie in a single gesture.

"I'm surprised you're leading this shitshow. Apparently, you're more of a snake than I'd given you credit for."

I bristle under the accusation, but cover it with a shrug as I return to my seat. "Restructuring can be messy. Things don't all end up where one would expect." I give him a considering look. "You know a little bit about that, though, don't you?"

He doesn't even blink. He gives away very little under the best circumstances, and now, when he's pissed off and I'm on edge, we're far from it. He turns his head, keeping one ear directed at me as he glowers at the bar below.

"I'd pass along my condolences for your fallen leader, but I doubt you want them."

I smile blandly.

As miserable as Nikita has been to put up with, at least he isn't forcing us into a war that neither side wants nor needs, like Maksim did. He also isn't lashing out at everyone who looks in his direction, killing the few men who manage to put up even a hint of resistance.

In time, he'll be the death of us all just the same, but it'll be a slightly cleaner ending than Maksim was preparing for us.

"We're getting off on the wrong foot," I say, raising my drink in a faux salute. "I'm supposed to be kissing your ass and thanking you for letting me meet with you instead of the front boss, right?"

His expression hardens as he leans back in his seat, taking a moment to survey his men along the outer walls, no doubt looking for the men I should've brought with me. There are a couple for him to find but not nearly as many as he was probably expecting.

The bulk of the men I've brought with me are outside the club, hunting down the rats that are so eager to report everything happening in the area to him as soon as he leaves. He might find them disposable, but if Carlo loses them, he'll be at a severe disadvantage.

"The boss only meets with bosses. Last I checked, you're not the boss."

"Not yet."

"Besides, after last time, Marcell doesn't want to make waves. And with our relationship already in the fucking shitter, you're stuck with me."

"Lucky me."

"Lucky you, indeed." His sneer implies he doesn't consider himself as fortunate, but I choose to let it slide.

A cocktail server stops beside us. Her hands are shaking, but her spine is straight in a forced display of bravery. While Carlo orders his drink, I take the opportunity to check where his men have ended up, eyes mapping a line to the closest exit, making sure there's still a clear path if I need one.

As soon as Carlo has his drink in hand, the server makes quick work of skittering away, apparently unwilling to linger in his violent aura.

Once she's out of earshot, he asks, "Do you plan on doing the right thing and returning what's ours, or are you going to bleed me dry for it?" Despite his casual tone, his knuckles are white around his glass.

"You make it sound like I'm extorting you. All I'm asking is for compensation for what my men found."

"Stole, you mean."

"Let's not argue semantics." I take a sip of my drink, taking a moment to savor the burn of the cheap vodka. "Regardless of how it happened, my men found your missing shipments. I'm simply trying to return them."

"For a ransom, of course."

"A finder's fee," I counter.

"Call a spade a spade," he practically spits. "What do you want?"

"Has anyone ever told you that you're not the most pleasant person to talk to?" I can't help but ask.

His expression is flat as he blinks at me, pulling his focus away from the crowd below. "Once or twice. Now get to the fucking point, Trenin."

"Cut me in on the deal. We get thirty-five percent, and your goods are right back where they belong, safe and sound."

Carlo scoffs.

"Give me a real offer, or I'm walking."

"Fine by me." I shrug. "If you insist, I'll take it all, and you get no part when I sell them. I thought you'd appreciate a show of good faith, but..." I shrug again and rise from my seat.

Hopefully it's been long enough for the men outside to satiate their need for revenge and do some productive damage, because when I leave here and Carlo finds out what happened, I'm not going to get another shot at negotiation.

Maybe I'll send his shipments back in a few weeks as a show of good faith.

A muscle in his eye ticks as I button my suit, nodding to Artyom at the bar, letting him know it's time to leave. Before I can step away, Carlo slams his glass onto the table, the sound ringing between us right before the muffled *pop* of gunfire sounds outside.

*Blyad.*

For a split second, the relatively relaxed room grows tense.

Frozen.

Like thin ice over a dark, raging current.

In a blink, everything shatters into chaos.

Carlo meets my gaze as we both go for our guns, an accusation glaring back at me. The rest of the room is a cacophony of noise and motion as people scramble, unsure if they should seek shelter further in the club, or rush for the exits.

As the first line of people reaches the doors, tearing at each other to get out, they're pushed back by even more gunfire.

This time, heading straight into the club.

"What did you do?" Carlo hisses.

"I promise you," I hiss between gritted teeth, "if this is one of mine, I'll have their fucking heads."

He watches me for a beat before I nod toward the exit at the back, one that leads out to the employee parking lot.

"Get the fuck out of here, Carlo."

My chest practically heaves with rage. Everything was going so fucking well, and if I find out that one of my guys is responsible for fucking this up, I'm going to turn him into a painful lesson for everyone else.

Between the gunfire that's continuing to tear from the doors, the screams of the terrified crowd, and the rush of blood in my ears, I'm surprised I can hear myself thinking at all.

Carlo's eyes cut to the door, watching as his men return fire at whoever's outside, and more particularly, at the man forcing his way through the crowd toward us, pushing a path against the panic like the bodies are nothing but water.

Artyom looks between him and me, a question in his eyes and his hand on his weapon.

I shake my head before he's able to get any bright ideas.

With the fragile trust I was trying to build with Di Veroli shattered, another fuck up is more than I can afford.

Carlo's gun is still at his side, and when he looks back at me, I can see how much he wants to tear me apart. Every ounce of him is dripping with barely contained fury, but we don't have time to duke it out right now.

With gunfire comes cops, and neither of us can afford to be here when they show up.

We're rapidly running out of time.

"You can bitch at me later, Carlo. Now leave."

His glare says more than he has time to right now.

That we'll be finishing the conversation one way or another.

That he doesn't trust that this isn't still a setup.

That he's glad I'm not using this opportunity to shoot him point blank.

Carlo nods as his enforcer reaches us, pointing his gun at my chest. He turns on his heel, shoving his goon along with him. More glass shatters behind the bar as the bullets continue to fly. I flinch as one embeds itself in the wall behind me.

Not sparing Carlo another glance as he makes his escape, I head straight into the chaos, rushing toward a half wall Artyom's ducking behind.

"What the *fuck* happened?" I bark as soon as I'm close.

"I don't fucking know," he snaps. "We're not going to know shit until we get the hell out of here."

Great. Fucking *wonderful*.

It was a stupid question, anyway. The shots started outside, and Artyom's one of the three men I brought with me. Lev slipped out when he was supposed to, and I don't see Philipp, but I can't worry about either of them right now.

I grind my teeth together while a woman screams somewhere out of sight.

"Get out and try to get as many of the men away from here as you can before the cops show up."

He nods. "You good to get yourself out? I don't want your sister coming after me."

*Fuck me.*

If Nadya finds out about this, he won't have to worry. She'll be too busy systematically carving the flesh from my bones to even think about anyone else.

Nodding, I stand, gun at the ready.

I've already been caught unaware once today. It's not going to happen again.

My resolve lasts exactly as long as it takes me to look up and spot a man in a suit that's far too nice for a place like this holding a woman by her hair, his grip tight as he moves her in front of him like a shield.

My gut drops, everything freezing for half a second, longer than it should to recognize her with her face twisted in pain as she claws behind her, doing everything she can to go for his eyes. But I know that vicious glare as intimately as I know the sharp tongue spitting obscenities at him.

*Emiliya.*

As soon as it clicks, I burst into motion. I point my gun at the man, shifting until I have a better angle. Fortunately, the chaos has provided me with an opening, because he doesn't notice me.

Unfortunately, Emiliya does.

She doesn't stop fighting, but she stiffens for a slit second, just long enough for the soon-to-be-dead man to notice. His head swings toward me, gun in hand.

"Drop!" I shout, only hoping she's able to hear me over the noise.

For the first time since I met her, Emiliya listens to me. Her knees buckle under her, giving me enough room to fire a single shot into her assailant's head. Before his knees give out, she's scrambling away from him, shoving him backward as he collapses to the ground, his unseeing eyes staring straight ahead.

"I could have handled that," she gasps, her chest heaving as she pants.

"I'm sure you could've," I bite, pulling her close to assure myself she's okay. "It's alright. You don't need to thank me."

Her breath is shaky as she wraps her arms protectively around her torso.

Before she gets a chance to run, I grab her tight enough that she lets out a squeak, keeping her close as I maneuver around the mess and the bodies toward the side exit.

She struggles every step of the way.

"Let go of me!" she hisses as I hold her tight against my chest. Her hands beat against my ribs, my pecs, my shoulders, against any part of me she's able to reach. "I swear to fuck, Alexei, fucking *let go*." She pulls her leg back to kick me, and I lift her enough to swing her to the side so she misses, her heel clipping my calf.

She clings to my jacket when my grip falters, like she's worried I'll drop her.

Not that I would. She weighs practically nothing, despite all her tight curves and outrage.

I'm torn between wanting to yell at her, demanding to know why she's here, and checking every inch of her to assure myself she's okay.

"Relax," I order as I step into the alley, taking a moment to check the opening for anyone waiting to ambush us.

Emiliya, predictably, does not relax.

If anything, she redoubles her efforts, coming at me with sharp elbows and even sharper heels. I drag her down the street toward my car, contemplating throwing her over my shoulder while she struggles.

Nikita shouldn't have known where this meeting was being held, but I don't know who's hiding their loyalties to play both sides until there's a clear victor.

Did he send Emiliya after me to keep an eye on things without having to put himself in danger?

I wouldn't put it past him.

I tighten my grip on her waist when I get to my SUV, struggling to keep her still with one hand while I pull out the fob with the other, throwing her into the back seat as soon as I get it unlocked.

She tries to scramble out, but I level her with a look.

"Stay. I'm not letting you out of my sight until I get answers."

Emiliya freezes, and I take the opportunity to engage the child locks, moving to the front and gunning it out of the area before the cops get a chance to set up roadblocks.

# CHAPTER 11

# Emiliya

I yank the door handle at every stop, ignoring the way Alexei glares at me through the rearview mirror.

No matter how I plead with him, scream, or threaten to claw his eyes out and shove them down his throat, he doesn't say a word.

He barely reacts at all.

Things at Underground had been going so well, too.

Sure, I wanted to crawl out of my own skin and I wanted to puke, but the guy I was talking to seemed interested. And even though the club wasn't up to my usual standards, the fine fabric of his suit and the way it was tailored to fit him let me know he had more money than he was letting on.

I didn't catch his name, but the man wanted me.

Well, he wanted my body, if not my personality, but I can hardly blame him for that.

With a little more time, I would have been able to go back to his place, and I could've laid the groundwork for a longer arrangement.

Then the bullets started flying, and he started pulling my hair in a way that was decidedly *not* fun, using me as a human shield.

Even if Alexei hadn't shot him in the face, I was going to kick his ass.

*Mudak.*

With each mile Alexei drives, taking us further from the guns and the blood and the smoke, my heart throws itself against my ribs, panic clawing at my throat until it's nearly impossible to breathe.

The adrenaline has nowhere to go, and Alexei's silence is too heavy for it to burn itself out.

My whole body is shaking as I throw my shoulder into the door at another stoplight. It doesn't budge, but, *fuck*, I need to get out of here.

My eyes burn, but I will not cry.

Alexei doesn't deserve to know how terrified I am.

What if he's like Father? What if the tears only make everything worse?

For all I know, he's going to use this as an opportunity to make sure he doesn't have to worry about me.

No one knows where I am.

Shit, *I* don't know where I am.

Alexei could do whatever the hell he wants, and no one would know.

Or he could dump me back on my front doorstep and tell Father where I was. Alexei could tell him exactly how useless I am to my family and let Father deal with me however he sees fit.

If Alexei wants me dead, he wouldn't even have to lift a finger. He could let Father do all the work.

"Alexei, if you don't let me out of this car, I fucking swear—"

"Do you ever shut up?" he snaps as he turns smoothly into an underground parking garage. Oh, fuck, this is where I'm going to die, isn't it? "I can't hear myself think over all your yelling."

"Let me out, and you'll never have to deal with how loud I am again."

"You know, for some reason I really doubt that."

He parks the car in a spot near the back under a burned-out overhead light. The whole place is empty, except for the two of us, doing nothing to alleviate my anxiety. Letting Alexei know how terrified I am is stupid, but when he gets out and walks to the back door, I still scurry as far away as possible, my back braced against the freezing-cold glass of the opposite window.

He throws open the door, and a blast of cold air makes me shiver even harder. I clench my hands to hide it. He's backlit by the fluorescent lights, but under the shadows, his broad shoulders and heaving chest make him even more intimidating.

His anger pours off him in waves, more animal than human. Like one small thing will send him into a frenzy, leaving nothing behind but blood and bone.

I wheeze for air, but there's none to be found.

The edges of my vision close in around me.

*Whatever Alexei tries to do, you've been through worse*, I tell myself. He can hurt me, crush my ego, humiliate me, and drag me through the mud, but I've faced tougher foes than him. Hell, if he'd left me alone at Underground, I would have.

It's going to take more than a prick in an expensive suit to finish me off.

I just need to breathe. Even if it feels like each puff of air is tainted with tear gas, burning my lungs just as much as the lack of oxygen.

"Why were you at Underground, Emiliya?"

"Finding a new hunting ground," I pant, pathetically wishing my voice would sound steadier than I feel. "Like you told me to." My eyes dart back and forth, desperate to find anything that will give me the room to get out of this car and run, something to give me a fighting chance.

"Stop looking at me like I'm going to hurt you," he snaps, the frustration in his voice bleeding through my panic long enough for me to focus on the way he rakes a hand through his hair in exasperation. "I won't, but I need to know what you were doing there, and I don't believe you were out looking for a quick fuck."

*Okay, fuck him.*

The derision in his tone drains the last of my fear, leaving me with a swift anger that makes me kick at him, the heel of my shoe barely missing his shoulder.

"It's none of your business." I take a steadying breath, the air even more cleansing than the outrage. "And what were *you* doing there? Checking out the competition?"

Alexei's eyes narrow even further, and I get the feeling that was the wrong thing to say, but I can't find it in me to care.

If he wanted me dead, he probably would've left me with the jackass in the nice suit. No one would've known that he could've saved me except Alexei himself, but he didn't. He put himself at risk and dragged me out and to wherever we are now.

"Cool. Neither of us want to talk about it. Glad we're on the same page. Now, move so I can get out of here." Reluctantly, I push myself away from the door, scooting closer to Alexei and gesturing for him to get out of my way. He doesn't, only glaring harder when I push him.

"Let me out, Alexei. I need to get home."

He scoffs. "You realize you could've died, right? If your *daddy* found out I let something happen to you, he'd kill me. And he'd have the right." I open my mouth to argue, but he doesn't give me a chance, his nostrils flaring as he continues, "Things are too hot for me to take you home right now, and I want to know how the fuck you were even able to find me."

I don't bother to hide the way I roll my eyes.

"Do you think I'm stalking you or something? I promise, you're not *that* good of a lay."

That's a lie; he is. But sleeping with Alexei leaves me with the shitty feeling I always get from doing what Father wants, even if it's far from a chore.

But Alexei doesn't need to know that.

"Not because you want me, sure, but if your father asked you to? I bet you'd do anything," he sneers. I flinch, and the curl of his lip lets me know he doesn't miss it. "Is that what this is? Daddy asked you to keep an eye on me, and you'll do anything to make him happy?"

My teeth grind together as a familiar shame burns under my skin. I feel flushed, the sensation growing, begging to crawl up my throat until I can't hide it anymore.

"Does he know that you were more than happy to get on your knees for me? Or did you leave that part out?"

Alexei leans forward, putting a knee on the seat in front of me as he crowds me further into the SUV, his lips inches from mine.

He looks down at my dress, and I have to bat away the urge to cover myself.

When I got dressed, I wanted to catch a man, but the way Alexei looks at me makes me realize how far out of my depth I am.

Because, even if he's being intentionally cruel, my body still sings for him. I still want him to touch me, and if he ordered me to, I'd fall to my knees for him, wretched, disgraced, and ready to take whatever scraps of affection he'll toss my way.

Alexei is bad for me. He makes me desperate. He makes me want him far more than someone in my position can afford to.

He moves until my back is flat against the seat, involuntarily letting my legs fall open to make room for him as he crawls over me.

"You'd do whatever I ask, wouldn't you?"

His hands tease the place where my dress is bunched against my thighs, his breath warm against my lips.

Like a fool caught in a trap, I nod.

His thumbs burn my skin, and the cold air fades to nothing, unable to penetrate the fog wrapped around us. Everything fades away until I'm unable to focus on anything except his hands on my legs and the electricity building between us.

I should push back against him.

I should never let him touch me again.

Not when I know he's going to go right back to pretending there's nothing between us as soon as he's done with me. Not when the *after* hurts so much.

Alexei brushes his lips against mine, smirking when he pulls away. My tongue chases that point of contact, desperate to calm the sparks under my skin in his absence. He makes a sound in the back of his throat, a groan of pure male approval, and it's enough to snap me back to reality.

Alexei wants to be an ass? Fine. But if he wants to play, I'll fucking play.

Wrapping a hand around the back of his neck, I wait until he's fully in the car before I flip my leg over his hip, throwing all my weight into twisting us around so I'm sitting in his lap, yanking the thread of control back in my favor.

"Are you going to admit you're interested this time? Or are you all talk?" I bite his bottom lip, not bothering to be gentle. His cock is hard beneath me. I roll my hips, wanting to see him as worked up as I feel. "I need more than words, Alexei, so don't waste my time."

He exhales roughly. It's the only warning I get before he threads his fingers into my hair and pulls it back, exposing my throat. He licks against my pulse point, chuckling sinfully when I can't bite back my groan. Another roll of my hips, and the soft lace of my thong slides easily against him.

"We both know I can handle you, *printsessa*," he purrs, pulling me against his hard chest. He's scorching against my body, but my blood turns to ice at the nickname, making me flinch.

"Don't call me that," I snap, harsher than I mean to. "I'm not a fucking princess."

"No. No, you're not," he concedes, fisting his hand to pull my hair even harder. My already tender scalp burns in the best way. "Now, I'm going to ask you a question, and you're going to answer honestly. Can you do that?"

"Was that the question?"

"Brat," Alexei chuckles darkly.

I shiver.

Arousal buzzes under my skin as he scrapes his teeth over sensitive flesh, his thumb brushing over my jaw. Every movement is measured and controlled. He watches me with a singular focus, moving my head until I meet his eyes, imprisoning me with a single look.

"Before you got there, did you know I was going to be at Underground tonight?" There's a heat in his tone I wasn't expecting, an undercurrent of anger that makes me swallow thickly.

"No."

For a long moment, Alexei looks at me, searching for something I can't even guess at before he nods to himself.

"Good girl," he says as his lips meet mine in a bruising kiss.

I flush with the praise, raking my nails through his hair. Fuck, it feels good when he groans against my mouth.

I whine with how much I want him. I want him to take out his cock and fuck me until my knees are weak and I have to stumble home. I want him to make me forget he has the power to crush me. I want him to erase the weight of all my worries, even if it's only for a night.

My hips grind against his, and when his hands drop to his belt to free himself, it's like he's granting me the illusion of control.

This is a terrible idea. One I'm definitely going to regret, but I couldn't stop myself if I tried. Especially not when every beautiful, throbbing inch of him is free, so heavy his cock smacks against his stomach.

"I have an IUD," I blurt as he fishes in his pocket for a condom. "I got tested after the last time, and I haven't been with anyone else in months."

"Yeah?"

I nod.

"I haven't been with anyone since you, and I get tested every six months." I bit my lip, want pounding through every nerve in my body. "Are you saying I can fuck you bare, Emiliya? That you want me to fill your pussy until you can't move without me dripping down your thighs?"

"*Please*," I whine.

"Thank fuck," Alexei groans, tearing my underwear to the side while I balance on my knees, giving myself just a moment to enjoy feeling him against my entrance, the slight pressure before I fall, the tease against my sensitive nerves.

Alexei growls with impatience, grabbing my hips and surging upward, filling me entirely and knocking the wind out of my lungs on a silent scream. The stretch burns, but I fucking love it.

I just need a second to adjust.

A second that Alexei doesn't give me.

My next breath is a keening cry when he withdraws, not pausing before he's rutting into me again, pulling me down onto his cock with each thrust. I squeeze around him, and, fuck, I feel so full.

With his hands on my hips and his mouth a breath from mine, I can feel him *everywhere*.

My tits are full in my dress, my skin practically aching for his touch, but I'm not going to ask him for it. He doesn't deserve to hear me beg, no matter how much I want to. He's already torn my pride to pieces, and I'll be damned if I offer him more ammunition.

I fist my hand through the hair at the base of his skull, pulling his head backward, away from where he's watching my cleavage, my breasts threatening to slip free from the slip of fabric blocking his view.

I shift, trying to use the position so I can control the pace.

I need this.

*Goddamn*, I need this.

Moving hard and fast, I see stars with every thrust, until I'm digging my hands into his shoulders as I find the rhythm I want. Alexei's hips snap against mine. With one thrust, he hits just the right spot.

"Right there," I pant. "Don't you dare stop, Alexei."

My clit drags against his slacks with every movement, until nothing matters except the tension making every muscle bunch so tight I feel like I'm going to snap.

All the other bullshit fades away, and it's just the two of us. I don't care that I don't know where he brought us. I don't care that tonight was technically a bust for me. And I don't care that we're in a parking garage where anyone could see us.

If they want to watch us, let them.

My thighs burn, but I refuse to slow down. I can't let Alexei think he has the upper hand, or he'll run with it.

My skin prickles while he hisses a breath through his teeth, fingers so tight on my thighs, I'm sure he's leaving marks I'll be able to admire tomorrow morning.

"Did you know *I* was going to be there?" I ask lazily. He jolts when I run my nails along his throat. "If you wanted more of me, you only had to ask."

His chest rumbles with a growl as he reaches around, splaying a hand across the small of my back, holding me in place.

I struggle against him, but he doesn't even seem to notice. With his other hand, he grabs my chin, pulling my face right in front of his.

"You don't get to ask why I was there," he grunts before taking my mouth in a dominating kiss, his tongue lashing against mine until I have no choice but to focus on him while he moves, taking over before I can even protest.

He fucks me hard and fast, driving all thoughts away.

I should hate him, but it's so hard to cling to the emotion when he drives into me with single-minded focus, like the only thing that matters to him is making me come.

I cry out his name when his thumb flicks against my clit, sending me into a screaming orgasm.

It's like a bomb going off, ecstasy burning through me until there's nothing left. I curl forward until I'm moaning into his shoulder, the sound echoing against the concrete of the garage.

I can hardly catch my breath, only distantly registering Alexei's satisfied growl as he stills, his cock pulsing as he fills me with his release.

Too quickly the heat disappears, and I'm left shivering against the cold air, wishing I'd managed to grab my coat before Alexei dragged me out of the club. It's going to be a long, miserable walk home.

Whatever. At least it'll give me something to focus on other than the feeling of his cum on my thighs.

I'm such an idiot.

As his breaths even out, Alexei pulls his hands away, and I take that as my cue to slip off him, sliding my underwear back into place before I get out of the car.

I have no plans of waiting for him to dismiss me again.

Rubbing my hands against my arms, I look around, trying to find a way out of here, but I only see a gate that must have closed behind us and what looks like a set of elevator doors.

Alexei locks the SUV as he gets out, the sound of the door slamming shut bouncing back at us like a bark of laughter, mocking me. I risk a glance at him. He adjusts his belt, already put back together.

Seeing him so unaffected by what just happened hurts more than I'd like to admit.

"Is there a door I can go out of? Or a button to raise the gate?"

Alexei looks at me, squinting like he's not quite sure why I'm still here.

If I could find the fucking exit, I wouldn't be.

"You're not leaving," he says bluntly, turning on his heel toward the elevator doors.

"Excuse me?" Despite myself, I follow him. Wherever he's going, there's bound to be an exit.

"You heard me. I'm sick of fucking you in my car. If we're doing this, you're coming with me, and we're using an actual bed."

I stop in my tracks.

Out of everything he could have said, that's the last thing I would've expected.

But I'm adaptable. I can work with this.

"Oh, *now* you're admitting there's going to be a next time?" I call after him.

Alexei levels me with a look so serious, I have to bite my tongue to keep from laughing in his face. He looks as pissed off as he does resigned, and it's unfair how good it looks on him.

"In that case, lead the way."

# CHAPTER 12
# Emiliya

An ice-cold gust of wind makes me want to kick myself for leaving the warm comfort of Alexei's bed. My newly stolen sweatshirt is doing nothing to help ward off the chill, and I'm pretty sure my legs are going to freeze long before I'm able to make it home.

At least Alexei lives in a decent neighborhood.

But I don't trust my father not to track my phone if I order a rideshare. For as generous as Alexei was, I'm willing to bet he wouldn't appreciate me leading him back to where he lives.

And the last thing I wanted was to stick around to see if he'd order me one himself.

So, I waited for him to fall asleep after he practically collapsed underneath me, and snuck out. Now I'm three blocks away, freezing my ass off while I wait under a streetlight for the ride I finally requested with numb fingers, breathing out a sigh of relief when I see I only have to wait five minutes.

It's not that I'm worried about anyone trying to rob or hurt me—all it would take is name-dropping Father, and everyone except the most unconnected idiot would back off—but I don't want to hang out in the cold.

The mocking voice in the back of my head—the one that sounds suspiciously like Father—reminds me that my family name didn't protect me back at the club. That guy didn't give a fuck who I was, only that I was a warm body he could use to protect himself.

I push the thought aside and blow on my hands, trying to regain any feeling in my fingers.

I'll pick apart everything later. Until I'm home, I have to focus on the issue at hand.

Mainly, staying warm.

I'll have to ditch this sweatshirt before I get home, even if it's the last thing I want. It's just as cozy as Alexei's bed was, and it'd be nice to pull it out on occasion.

Not all the time. Just when I'm lonely and need to feel like someone's wrapping their arms around me. Someone other than Mom.

*God, I'm pathetic.*

Alexei and I had our fun, and maybe we'll have some more in the future, but I'm not going to trick myself into pretending we're going anywhere. Even if I were willing to throw myself down on the ground and beg for something as complicated as a relationship, if Alexei ever found out about everything Father told me to do for him, he wouldn't touch me with a ten-foot pole.

Honestly? He shouldn't. He should stay as far away from me as possible.

If Father wants more control over Alexei, it isn't for anything good. It definitely isn't because he wants to take him under his wing and see him flourish.

He's going to ruin Alexei, and I want nothing to do with it.

When my ride arrives, I greet the driver with a bright smile and make mind-numbing conversation about nothing, giving him a wink when he drops me off around the corner from Father's front gate. I wait until the taillights disappear before I pull Alexei's sweatshirt off, folding it carefully and tucking it behind one of the decorative hedges.

Maybe I'll be able to sneak out again later and get it back after Father's gone for the day.

Or maybe it'll become a warm bed for a raccoon. At least then it won't go to waste.

The image comforts me as I greet the guard at the gatehouse and head up the drive, clenching my jaw when I see that all the lights on the main floor are turned on. With each step, my hands get sweatier, despite my entire body feeling like it's chiseled from solid ice.

There's a sour taste in the back of my mouth, and if I thought I could get away with it, I'd turn around and find somewhere else to spend the night.

No one would wait up for me.

No one except Father.

My muscles wind tighter and tighter the closer I get to the house, and I need to find a way to calm the fuck down before I get inside. Showing weakness only pisses him off more. I have to look as calm and collected as possible and hope I can talk my way out of tonight's confrontation, whatever it may be.

Is he still up because I snuck out? Is it the shooting? Did he somehow figure out that I want to run?

My forced smile comes a little easier when I see Yan leaning under the light, already smirking at me. He's been a guard for my father since I was a kid, always there to offer me a friendly smile or a distraction when I needed one.

Out of everyone on Father's payroll, Yan is the only one I would consider a friend.

"Hey, Yan."

"Hey, hot stuff. You're out late tonight." His eyes sweep me up and down, a smirk on his face. He's always treated flirting like a game, and typically, I'm always down to play, but tonight it makes me want to crawl into a hole where no one can see me.

The weight of his gaze is too much, and his playful smirk is too intimate. I feel exposed in front of him, Alexei's taunts still hammering through me like a wave of bullets.

"Wherever you were, it agreed with you. You're stunning. Just as pretty as your Mama."

"You're not so bad yourself," I grin, infusing my voice with a false cheer. Hopefully, it's too late and cold for him to notice. "And as much as I'd like to spend the rest of the night with you, I'm freezing."

To prove my point, I rub my hands on my arms as I shiver.

Our breaths are visible, swirling in front of us. I'm just grateful it isn't snowing.

"I can see that," he chuckles, raising a dark brow while he looks at me, rubbing his bottom lip with his thumb.

I shudder, hoping he thinks it's because I'm cold while I give him my best puppy-dog eyes. Yan isn't cruel, just a flirt.

His eyes soften as he opens the door, gesturing for me to go inside.

"Fine, go thaw out while I stand out here, all alone and freezing my balls off."

"Thank you," I say, standing on my toes to press a kiss against his cheek as I pass him. "You're the best." He rolls his eyes, but remains silent as the door shuts behind me, motioning through the frosted glass for me to flick the deadbolt.

I do so, then slip off my heels so I can make my way through the house as quietly as possible.

If Father's waiting for me, I won't be able to avoid him for long, but I can sure as hell try. Heat seeps painfully into my bones as I take the most direct route to my room, tiptoeing past Father's office as silently as possible.

Maybe I finally got lucky. Maybe he didn't notice me. Maybe Father wasn't waiting for me at all. Maybe he—

My optimism scurries back to its hiding spot just as quickly as it emerged when I open my bedroom door.

Father dispassionately plucks a leaf from the plant sitting on my dressing table. He's dangerously calm, moving slowly like I'm not even here.

When he turns his head toward me, his face is blank. So emotionless, I can only guess there's a storm brewing under the surface.

It's too late to turn and run, so I beam at him, maintaining an air of nonchalance. "Hello, Father. You're up late."

"As are you."

His voice is even, betraying nothing of how he really feels. I remain frozen, bracing for whatever he's going to do to me.

Scream.

Throw the plant at me.

Demand answers to questions only he knows.

He's doing an excellent job of looking uninterested, but I'm not fooled.

His calm is only a facade, one that's casting a thin veil over a roaring fury he'll gladly turn on me with the smallest provocation. If time has taught me anything, it's that the calmer he is, the more dangerous the situation.

He thinks he's a king, but really, he's nothing but a pathetic waste of space. So dismissive of everyone around him that he's convinced we're all below his notice.

If he weren't such a threat, I'd let him know exactly what I think about his manipulative games, but I need to get out of this with enough strength to fight him again tomorrow. Provoking him isn't going to help me at all.

My hands curl into fists where I hold them behind my back.

Fighting will get me nowhere.

"Where were you, *printsessa*?" he asks, sounding bored.

I swallow my anxiety, trying to use it to prop up my anger. I can't answer him. Not if I want to keep my plans to get away from him a secret. I need an excuse.

Fuck, why didn't I spend the ride home crafting the perfect lie?

Father's gaze sharpens the longer my silence stretches. I try desperately to think of something, of *anything*, to tell him before he crosses the room, pulling me through the doorway with a bruising grip. He slams my bedroom door shut while I struggle to free myself without pissing him off even more.

"I said, where were you, Emiliya?" Any mask of calm is gone as he spits the words; his face contorted in a frown that coats my insides with thick, sticky fear.

He shoves me toward my dressing table. My hip knocks against the edge, sending makeup and my plant clattering to the ground while I try to catch my balance. My eyes are glued to the shattered remains of the ceramic bird Mom got me back when things were easier and we were both happy.

"You were out all fucking night, and when you finally come back, you look like you've been working every man on the street. I've been so fucking lenient with you, *printsessa*, but you're pushing my last nerve." I fix my hands on the table, turning before he can come at me again.

"I'll ask one more time. Where were you?"

"I was at a club," I blurt as he looms closer while I try to calm my panting breaths. It's close enough to the truth without betraying the kindness Alexei showed me.

He didn't have to rescue me. He didn't have to let me into his home.

He could just as easily have left me to fend for myself, but he didn't.

I refuse to betray Alexei's trust by telling Father who I spent my night with, and he can't know why I was out without his permission.

Not if I ever want to get Mom and me out of this house, this city, this fucking *country*.

As long as I'm within Father's reach, I'm always going to look over my shoulder, waiting for the next blow. I'll always be bracing for the day he tracks us down and drags us back. I need to do it right the first time, because I won't get a second chance.

"I'm sorry I didn't tell you. I didn't want to waste your time with something so trivial."

He looks at me like he knows every thought in my head, every transgression I've ever committed, and he's judged me and found me wanting.

"Right. You'd rather waste my time by being a leech on this family. Is that it?" The insult lances through me, but I push the pain aside, burying it as deep as I can.

"I—"

Father lurches toward me, cutting off my desperate excuses as he grabs my shoulder, dragging me to the ground while he crouches in front of me, a violent promise in his eyes.

"Shut up. Until you find a way to be more than a waste of my time, I don't want to hear a word out of you. I don't even want to fucking see you," he snarls, hand snapping to my jaw, pushing my head back until I cry out in pain.

There's alcohol on his breath, but his eyes are too sharp for him to be drunk.

He knows exactly what he's doing. He just doesn't care.

"You *and* your mother are both fucking useless." His chest heaves. "I should've been able to sell you off, at least. Made connections or forged an alliance, but you just *had* to spread your legs and ruin yourself, didn't you?"

"I didn't—"

He releases my jaw and wraps his hands around my throat, squeezing until my defense is forcibly cut off, trapped in my burning lungs.

My rage wins out as I kick at him, trying to shove him. I claw at his hands, but he doesn't let up. No matter how deep my nails dig, how hard I fight, it's like taking on a brick wall.

He doesn't budge.

None of this is my fucking fault. No one can live up to Father's expectations. Not a single soul can do everything he wants without compromising anything else.

My pride, my soul, my fucking heart.

I've lost so much trying to prove my worth, but none of it's ever been enough.

To Father, I'm nothing but a tool.

Black spots dot the edges of my vision, each beat of my heart more of a struggle than the last.

"I told you to shut up," he hisses. "I asked you to do a *single fucking thing* for this family. You couldn't even accomplish that much, could you?"

My lungs burn for oxygen while Father's wild eyes glare at me, devoid of any emotion at all.

I've only seen Father look like this a handful of times before, but I've never been on the receiving end of it before.

Tears flow freely down my cheeks.

*I'm going to die.*

My father's going to kill me, and I'm powerless to stop him.

There won't be anyone to look after Mom.

I don't give a shit about disappointing Father, but failing to protect her is the regret I'm going to take to the grave.

My fight fades along with my consciousness.

There was never going to be another end to my story, was there? I was never going to escape. I was never going to find my own pocket of joy in this world.

Father always controlled my life. It's only fitting that he controls my death, too.

I hope Mom isn't upset with me when she finds out. I hope she never has to learn exactly what happened. I hope she's able to cling to the way she loves me the same way she still loves Father. I hope Yan's the one to tell her I'm gone instead of Father.

At least he's always kind to her.

One moment, I'm giving up, ready to greet the infinite darkness waiting for me, and the next I'm on the ground, choking on bloodied, beautiful air. My throat feels like crushed paper, even as Father stalks away from me.

I'm not sure if I'm crying in pain, joy, or devastation. Why couldn't he just let me go? Why do I have to suffer through everything he demands of me?

Why can't I be free?

It was easier to fight when someone had a gun to my head. Now, I'm just tired. I can't take any more.

"I was with Alexei," I choke out while Father paces the room. I try to sit up, to scramble away from him, but my limbs aren't working. He sweeps his arm over my dresser, knocking the small tchotchkes I've collected to the ground, shattering the little figurines and destroying the small cactus I've grown from a seed.

"I was with Alexei," I sob again and again, begging him to believe me even while guilt burns away the last of my dignity.

Alexei might not give a shit, but he saved my life tonight. Letting all that effort go to waste seems like almost as much of a betrayal as giving Father an inch.

"And what did he say? Was he hurt?"

He yells questions faster than my foggy mind can follow. There's a lump in my throat blocking another sob.

"Where did you take you?" All his focus is on me, eyes alight with manic energy. If I weren't so exhausted, I'd run from him. "Did he tell you about the meeting?"

Father steps closer to me, and it's enough to send adrenaline shooting through me, kick-starting my legs enough to scramble backward until my back meets the wall, arms held out in front of me like I could ever have a chance of stopping him.

"He didn't tell me anything important," I cough, looking around for some sort of weapon. I spot a broken perfume bottle, but before I can even reach for it, it's crushed to dust under Father's shoe.

Even though my throat burns with every breath, each word tearing at the already ruined flesh until I can taste blood, I want to scream in his face. I want him to suffer for everything he's ever done to me. I want him to feel every ounce of the pain he's inflicted on me. I want to make him wish he were dead.

"That's not your decision, *printsessa*. What. Did. He. *Say*?"

That it wasn't my business why he was in some shitty club.

That I'd happily get on my knees for him.

That he can handle me.

He called me a good girl.

None of that is what Father wants to hear. But Alexei doesn't tell me anything he *would* want me to hear. He's more of a man of action than he is a man of words, and I doubt he trusts me enough to talk about anything other than what's in front of him.

Oddly, that thought settles me.

Though he isn't trying to, his silence is a form of protection. For both of us.

"Don't tell me you just showed up and took off your clothes?"

My silence is apparently all the answer Father needs, and he takes small, measured steps forward until he's hovering over me, a massive shadow prepared to erase my existence at a moment's notice.

I'm shaking, trying to prepare for another round when I know I can't.

I've survived everything he's thrown at me so far, but I can't take much more.

Still, I won't go down quietly. Father doesn't deserve that sort of grace. If he's going to kill me, I'm going to drag him right down with me.

Every breath is agony, but I'm going to make sure my wheezing is the last thing he ever hears before I tear out his throat with my teeth.

"If he isn't trying to keep you around yet, then newsflash, Emiliya, your cunt isn't working for him. You need to find a different way to make him give a shit."

I nod dumbly, though moving my neck makes everything hurt even worse.

Getting Alexei to want me is fucking impossible, but I'll agree to anything Father wants as long as he gives me time to lick my wounds and recover before his next attack.

"Soon, Emiliya. He's getting on my last nerve."

He's regained his control, calmly adjusting his sleeves. Except for the scratches I left on his hands, you wouldn't even know anything happened.

I continue to nod, silently begging Father to leave. If he demands a verbal response, I'll break.

I'll dissolve into tears so thick I won't be able to defend myself. Even now, my vision is blurry as he turns on his heel, grinding broken glass into the floor as he leaves.

The door slams shut behind him, leaving me more alone and terrified than I was at Underground.

I collapse onto my side, curling up as small as I can, ignoring the way the broken bottles and shattered glass cut into my arms and ruin my dress.

How the fuck does he expect me to get Alexei to care about me? Tonight was only the result of built-up adrenaline, and I couldn't manufacture a repeat even if I wanted to.

I cough, trying to clear the blood clogging my throat while I sob.

Tonight, I'll let myself have my pity party.

I'll clean up this mess and find another solution after the sun comes up.

Then, when I'm able to hide in the shadows again, I'll find a way to hold off Father until I can get the hell out of here.

# CHAPTER 13

# Alexei

Lev kicks his feet up on the corner of my coffee table, his legs crossed at the ankle while he plays on his phone. He hasn't said a word since he showed up twenty minutes ago, seeming to sense my need for quiet.

He should be with Nadya, but he showed up at the crack of dawn like the fucking ambush at Underground changed anything when it comes to her safety.

It didn't, and he fucking knows it. Now he's sporting a black eye, and I have to worry about her on top of everything else.

*Again.*

Nadya's promise to stay put until he gets back to her place is bullshit, and we all know it.

I'd kill him, but my aunt would have my head. The longer he sits there, the less I'm convinced I care.

"How many of my men are at the hospital?" I eventually ask.

"Five. Andrei already did his thing, so as far as the cops are concerned, they were all innocent bystanders that got caught up in the violence," he answers without looking up from his phone.

I roll my neck to relieve the tension that's been building since I woke up to an empty bed.

It's ridiculous. If anything, I should be grateful that Emiliya left on her own accord, but, fuck, I hated it. I was looking forward to seeing what she's like when she isn't working an angle. I wanted to know whether or not she's a morning person.

I shouldn't have even brought her here. If I were thinking, I'd have dumped her at Nikita's and left before he had a chance to ask questions. At least then I'd know she had made it home alright. I wouldn't be worrying about whether or not she's safe in her own bed.

"And they'll all make it?"

If they don't, I might as well go pick out a pretty plot in the cemetery before lunch.

I'll lose any respect the men have for me, and all the power I've managed to carve out for myself will burn away faster than I can defend myself.

My first time trying to control the situation and it ends in a fucking shooting.

The past twenty-four hours have been nothing short of a goddamn disaster.

Now, not only does Nikita have something to hold over my head, but everyone has ample reason to question my judgment.

Fuck, *I'm* questioning my judgment.

Everything was going so fucking well. It wasn't going to be the massacre Nikita wanted, but it would have been enough. From what I've heard, we managed to take out a number of The Outfit's spies, and Carlo seemed like he was going to actually work with me. We could've found a way to slow down this fucking war.

Until one *ublyudok* with a gun got cocky and fucked us over.

And I still don't know who it was.

"They'll be fine. Philipp got out of surgery a few hours ago, and the rest should be discharged tomorrow."

Even though no one died, I fully expect everyone who backed me on this to be fucking furious that I put them in this position. This whole mess was *my* call, and if I'd made different choices, they wouldn't have been there to begin with.

For all I know, they could be gunning for my head before they even make it home, and I can't blame them for it.

I steel myself and stand, straightening the cuffs of my shirt. No point in delaying it.

"Want to come to the hospital with me?"

"Uh…" Lev scratches the back of his head, avoiding looking in my direction. "Not really. If we're being honest, that's probably the last place you should hang out right now."

"I know," I concede, "but I'm the one who fucked up. Might as well stand by it." If I want to salvage this, it's not like I have a choice. Waffling now would make me seem spineless. "So, you want to come along and make sure no one strangles me with an oxygen tube when I'm not looking, or do you want to go back to Nadya's?"

"You know I'm more than a guard dog, right? I can do more than watch your sister."

"Just because you're scared of her—"

"I'm not scared." He stands, glaring. "But now that you mention it, I'd love to watch someone on morphine try to kill you. Sounds fun."

"You have to get over this ridiculous fear of her at some point, man." He gives me a dead stare. "You could take her in a fight."

"We both have the scars to prove otherwise. I don't need more."

"Right. We've been trained how to fight since we were kids, and she weighs a hundred and ten pounds soaking wet. Why would I ever doubt her?"

He huffs, but it helps lighten the mood.

He's right, Nadya's fucking terrifying, and when she wants to be, she's downright vicious. It's part of the reason I've put so much effort into avoiding her. Hopefully she's too caught up in being mad at me to connect the shooting with Lev not showing up this morning, because if she finds out I was there, she's going to be pissed.

He flips me off on his way to the door, a smile cracking through the grim expression he's had all morning.

***

"You know," Lev starts as he puts the car in park, the hospital looming over us like a specter, "this could have been worse." His smile is strained, but I appreciate that he's trying to keep things light.

Everyone who was at Underground agreed with the plan. I didn't twist their arms or force them into going along with it.

They trusted me enough to volunteer. And what did I do with that trust?

"If they're angry, they're entitled to it. If they want to scream and take it out on me, then we'll let them. I appreciate that you're trying to cheer me up, but if I wasn't willing to deal with the fallout, I shouldn't have stepped up in the first place."

He frowns, tension lining his shoulders.

"Let's hope the rest of them are as pragmatic about it as you."

Bracing for the worst, we march inside silently. Despite what I said, I'm not particularly worried about my safety today. My men aren't stupid enough to make a scene in public. If they're going to come after me, they'll do it later, when they're away from prying eyes and security cameras.

They'll either bide their time or return their loyalties to Nikita and let him kill me in his own time. Either way, it isn't worth worrying about right now. Intellectually, I know that, but I'm struggling to internalize it, and as I step into Philipp's room, my shoulders are so tight my muscles feel like they're going to tear off my bones.

Lev posts himself outside the door, giving the illusion of privacy while keeping an eye out for any possible eavesdroppers.

When I walk in, Philipp's propped up against the pillows, smiling at his wife as she fusses over him, tucking the blankets around his legs. He spots me over her shoulder, lifting his chin in acknowledgment. As he does, his wife whips around, glowering at me in the doorway.

It stings, but the way Philipp takes her hand and quietly hushes her before she's able to spew whatever vitriol she's thinking softens the blow.

"Heya, boss. You'll have to excuse Stella. She doesn't like hospitals."

"It's understandable. Can't say I'm a fan, either," I say, brushing her hostility aside. "How're you holding up?" He looks better than I'd expected for a man who had surgery this morning. Probably due to the steady drip of morphine in his IV, but I'm not going to look a gift horse in the mouth.

"My guts are being held together with staples, and the fancy doctor says I need to take it easy for a couple weeks, but I've got a steady supply of good drugs, and my girl's got an excuse to dote on me. So, overall, I'm great." He smiles at Stella, urging her to sit on the edge of the bed.

"Though, I gotta admit, being used for target practice isn't my favorite thing in the world."

"Let's make sure it doesn't happen again."

When I move to leave the room and let him rest, he stops me.

"Your idea was still better than the alternative, you know? It just didn't work out the way you planned."

It's a sentiment that's echoed by the others I visit in one way or another. They aren't pleased with how things played out, but they'd rather have tried than condemn us all to the bloodshed Nikita wants. Lev stands guard outside each room, and by the time we're leaving, he looks more relaxed than he has all day.

Even still, I'm on guard while we head outside, scanning the faces around us just in case there's another threat lurking in plain sight.

That vigilance is the only reason I spot Emiliya. Her face is tucked into her scarf as she marches toward the hospital, shoulders hunched in her wool coat. I motion for Lev to go ahead and lean against the wall near the entrance, watching her.

She's oblivious to everything around her, only focusing on readjusting her scarf.

The wind batters her, swirling her long hair around her shoulders.

Even wind-rumpled and distracted, she's gorgeous. Aloof and effortless, she winds her way through the parked cars and the few people coming and going as she moves with determination toward the entrance.

Like a fool, I can't look away. I won't approach her, and once she's inside, I'll go on with the rest of my day, but for now? I'm content to just lay eyes on her again.

My resolve crumbles the instant she swipes a hand under her eyes.

I don't like seeing her cry, and I've never been good at doing what's good for me.

"Emiliya," I call, pushing away from the building.

She startles, and when she looks up, all I can focus on is how bloodshot her eyes are. It's like every blood vessel has burst, far more damage than comes from just crying.

*What the fuck?*

Just as quickly as she meets my eyes, she looks away, trying to hurry past me. Fuck that.

I take her arm as she passes by, directing us toward a more private alcove. She twists around and tries to tear free, completely silent as we approach a couple of people in blue scrubs smoking. They eye us skeptically but hastily vacate the area when they see my thunderous expression.

As soon as they're gone, I turn around, lifting Emiliya's chin with a single finger so I can study her.

She flinches away, bringing her hands up like she's worried I'm going to hit her.

The whites of her eyes are beyond bloodshot, and even with her makeup, I can see how puffy they are, the dark circles under them prominent.

I tilt my head, trying to get her to look at me, but she refuses, looking anywhere else.

"What happened?" The question comes out harsher than I intend it to, and she clenches her jaw and pulls out of my grip, pushing herself further into the brick wall behind her. She tries again to wiggle away, but I pin my hands on either side of her ribs, forcing her to stay right where she is.

She was at my place less than twelve hours ago. She was fine.

I try again, my voice softer. "Emiliya, what happened?"

"Let me go, Alexei."

Her eyes blaze with anger, but her voice comes out as a broken rasp that's so unlike the snarky woman from last night.

The only time I've seen someone's eyes this bloodshot was when they'd had someone's hand around their throat. My hands flex against the rough brick, torn between hunting someone down and reaching out to comfort her.

"Tell me what happened," I plead.

Emiliya's unapologetic glare is the only answer she graces me with.

The wind tears into our little alcove like a wind tunnel, but she doesn't so much as shiver, even as dust and dirt swirl at our feet.

Using my weight to pin her against the wall, I trace a finger over the smooth skin of her jaw. If she doesn't tell me, I'll find out what happened on my own. I'll look in every shadow until all her secrets are revealed and I know who did this to her.

Then I'll make them pay for it. But I'd really prefer that she tell me herself.

I touch the edge of her scarf, and it's like someone lights her ass on fire with the way she tries to shove me away from her. I refuse to budge.

I've ignored the bruises on her ribs whenever we're together, the way she flinches when I move too fast. I've pretended not to see the way she tenses when I grab her hips too tightly, or the way she freezes when I grab her arms. I figured if she wants me to know what's going on, she'd tell me, because I sure as hell wasn't going to pry.

But if someone tried to fucking choke her, I'm not going to ignore it anymore.

"It's your father, isn't it?"

She stills, the way she pales answering the question more than her words ever could.

I'm going to fucking kill him.

"Is he the reason you're here?" I ask, nodding toward the hospital entrance.

She shakes her head before turning to the side to clear her throat.

"I'm picking my mom up from an appointment." She winces, like it hurts to speak. Killing Nikita right now would be stupid, but I'll gladly deal with the consequences, especially if seeing her like this is the price of inaction.

Her shoulders are hunched forward. She looks so fucking small, and the sad look in her eyes makes me want to do something reckless. Right now, I don't care if she's bad for me. I don't care if she's dangerous. Fuck, I don't even care if she's plotting to ruin everything I've ever worked for.

I don't want to see her look like anything other than the strong, unbearably annoying woman I know she can be. Emiliya should always be free to show off the confidence that possessed her last night.

"I don't remember the last time I saw your mom," I muse before I tell her something stupid.

Emiliya snorts a humorless laugh. "That's the way Father wants it."

"What do you mean?"

I shouldn't make her speak, not when it's clearly so painful. But when she's talking, I don't want to storm away from here and do something I'll come to regret. Emiliya's too stubborn to let me help her, but if she's here, maybe I can coax her into forgetting how to fight me for a while.

"She's sick, and Father doesn't want people to see her. It ruins the powerful image he's spent so long cultivating."

"Sick how?"

"Progressive Supranuclear Palsy. She's not going to get better, and he wants everyone to forget she existed altogether. So he hides her," she hisses bitterly. The disgust on her tells me how long she's fought him.

"But you look after her."

"I do." She looks again at some middle point over my shoulder. "And if I don't want her to ask questions, I have to go inside and meet her. So kindly get out of my way." She throws her full weight into shoving me aside.

I let her.

"Here," I call before she's able to storm away, pulling out my wallet and holding out one of the business cards Nadya made for me. Emiliya eyes it warily.

"What's that?"

"My number. The one your father has, but my personal number, too." Tentatively, like it might bite her, she takes the card from my hand. "If you need anything, you only have to call."

Her brows are drawn together as she flips the card in her hands, looking at both sides. When she tucks it into her purse, her hands are shaking. It's a crack in her facade that kills me to look at, so much so that I have to look away.

"Whatever you need, Emiliya. Day or night."

She nods, fixing her scarf and lifting her chin until she looks more reminiscent of her usual self, then turns on her designer heels and walks away like I'm not even here. I watch, pelted by wind until she disappears around the corner, heading into the hospital like nothing even happened.

I'm halfway to my car, Lev impatiently playing air drums against the dashboard, when my phone rings.

*"Da?"*

"Trenin." I stiffen at Konstantin's casual drawl instead of Emiliya's broken rasp. Not that I really expected her to call me right away. "Are you free for a meeting? I think I've found a way for us to work together."

All thoughts fade into the background, my focus sharpening to a fine point.

# CHAPTER 14

# Alexei

When Konstantin insisted Nadya join us for this meeting, alarm bells didn't just ring, they blared in my head, refusing to be ignored. Every instinct I have screams at me to keep him as far away from my sister as physically possible.

But my options are far more limited than I'd like them to be.

Nadya tried to assure me it was because he knows she controls my money, but my gut says otherwise.

I don't like the way he looked at her, and I don't trust him to keep this strictly about business.

Nadya talks me through the file she's brought with her, but nothing she says is sticking. I'm too busy trying to think my way out of having her here at all.

But no matter how I spin it, Konstantin has the resources to bring everyone who has thrown their weight behind Nikita to heel without slaughtering them, and he could hold the key to ending the mess with The Outfit.

If I had time, I could come up with something on my own, but it'd be expensive, and far more dangerous than I'm willing to risk when there are so many cards at play.

The longer this chaos goes on, the more likely someone will use Nadya to get to me. I need a swift solution, and Konstantin can provide one.

As long as I don't kill him first.

Nadya points to another column on yet another spreadsheet she's printed out, going over the color-coded numbers, and my jaw aches from how hard I'm grinding my teeth.

"So, tell me a single thing I just said."

I blink at her annoyed expression. "You said everything's great and you have it all handled, so I don't have to worry about it."

She groans in frustration, closing the file like she's finally given up on me. I grin.

"Alexei, you need to know this stuff. What happens if I'm not here?"

"But you are. And if I thought anyone was going to ask me about numbers, I'd learn." Well, I'd try, anyway. "And unless you have something to announce, you're not going anywhere, so I don't have to."

"What are you planning on doing if I want to leave? Or if I can't show up to one of these meetings you pretend I don't know about?"

"Then I have your perfectly good spreadsheets that speak for themselves." I motion to the folder in front of her, one she'd printed out before I even asked for it. "Because you're smart. And the best sister ever."

Twenty minutes after I called her, she showed up, sat me down, and proceeded to talk at length about the details of every account and investment I have. She was so well prepared I'm tempted to ask her if she's been practicing, but I don't want to push my luck.

"*And* you're a fucking nerd."

She rolls her eyes. "Did this guy at least tell you what time he was going to be here?"

"I wish," I grumble, shaking my head.

Lavrov holds all the power, and he knows it. All he told me was that he was willing to work with me, demanded Nadya also attend, and he'd be here later. When I tried to make him narrow down a time frame, he hung up on me, and he hasn't returned any of my calls or texts since I got home.

"So, for all you know, we're going to be waiting here for hours?"

I lean back, settling against the couch. "Sounds like plenty of time for you to go over your papers again. Who knows? Maybe I'll learn something this time."

She glares at me for a beat, but goes over everything she's said again, this time with exaggerated slowness.

I understand why she wants me to know what the hell she's talking about. I really do, but no matter how hard I try, it doesn't click. The numbers get flipped around in my head, and I end up so twisted around trying to make sense of them that it's easier to tune it out.

Nadya's never been deterred, though.

Not when she tried to help me with my algebra homework in high school, and not now. Rather than pointing out how futile the effort is, I choose to be grateful she cares enough to try, even if she is trying to teach a brick wall.

Fuck, is working with Konstantin even worth it? If it comes down to it, I have the resources to send Nadya away and make a new life for her. At least, I think that's what she's telling me. But if I don't want to lose her, I'd have to walk away from everything I've fought for, from everything I've built.

Besides Nadya, the Bratva has been the only constant in my life since Dad got locked up. For better or worse, this life has raised me to become the man I am.

And that man isn't good at quitting.

If Konstantin and I can't come to agreeable terms, I'll figure something out. Something that doesn't mean losing my sister and lets me get Emiliya out from under Nikita's thumb.

Nikita doesn't get to ruin this Bratva with his own incompetence. The men who have thrown their lives behind the brotherhood are worth more than that.

Nadya huffs beside me. "You know, you can at least pretend to listen."

"Why would I do that? I've gotta keep you humble somehow."

Her indignant reply is cut off by two firm raps against the door, dissipating the easy atmosphere and sending my walls shooting up in an instant.

"Would you look at that? It wasn't even an hour," I say with projected ease. Nadya rolls her eyes, trying to cover her nerves as she gathers her papers in an orderly stack, holding her folder in front of her like a shield. "Go hang out in my office," I tell her, pushing to stand. "If we need you, I'll come get you."

She nods, apparently content to listen to me for once. As she scurries away, I realize she doesn't want to be here as much as I don't want her here, but she still showed up without hesitation or complaint.

I've worked tirelessly to keep her away from the unsavory parts of my life. She doesn't pretend I'm not involved in organized crime, but she doesn't need to know all the ins and outs of the business. She can run her numbers and make sure everything looks good come tax season, and that's as much as she needs to know.

Nadya doesn't know details, she doesn't attend meetings, and she definitely doesn't need to be present when I'm trying to forge alliances with unhinged men like Konstantin Lavrov.

I wait until my office door closes softly before I open the door to my condo, tension a low boil in my blood.

Konstantin leans against the doorjamb, checking his watch with an infuriating smirk. His jacket is unbuttoned, showing off the gun tucked into his shoulder holster, visible to anyone who bothers to pass by.

I motion for him to come inside before he gives Mrs. Sullivan from down the hall a heart attack.

"Hello to you too, Alexei." He grins, taking his sweet time strolling inside.

"Konstantin." I shut the door securely behind him, trying to find a sense of calm. My anger and doubt have no place here. Not now.

He looks around, raising a brow, before he turns back to me.

"Don't tell me your sister isn't here yet?" His grin is still there, but there's a threat behind his eyes that makes my hackles rise, renewing my decision to keep him away from her.

"If she really needs to be here, then I'll call her."

He strides into the living room with a smirk on his face, his eyes lingering as he passes the hallway, every door open except one.

"Rest assured, she needs to be here."

"With all due respect, I'm going to wait until you convince me. So far, I'm not."

"Fine." He pulls out a stool and folds his arms on top of the island, looking unbothered. "Is it still fair to assume you're looking for my assistance? Or have you found another fairy godmother powerful enough to fix your problems?"

"Unfortunately, you're still my best option," I tell him. He leans back, the corner of his mouth lifted in amusement as he watches me, clinical and detached. I have to force myself not to react, to not broadcast exactly how much I'd love to punch him in the face. "Have you settled on terms?"

He tilts his head from side to side as if he's still considering it, barely holding back his grin. "I have, though I'm not sure you'll be willing to pay the price."

"Try me."

"I have three conditions, and either you agree, or I walk."

I grind my teeth, motioning for him to continue. Even if his demands are outlandish and over the top, I'm not in a position to push back, and we both know it.

He could ask for the moon, and if I want any chance of his cooperation, I'll have to find a way to get it for him.

"We'll start with the obvious. If I offer aid, I expect full reciprocation if the need arises."

"Financial or otherwise?"

"Otherwise." His chin tilts in challenge, but I nod my acceptance.

"That won't be an issue. What else?"

"I want assurances that you intend to take the crown. I worked with your last pakhan more than once, and I have to say, the fact that he lived as long as he did doesn't inspire much confidence in the rest of you."

I hope Maksim's enjoying his little pocket of hell, because if he ruins this before it even begins, I'm going to piss on his grave.

"I know the official story is he and some little rat from The Outfit took each other out, but I'm not buying it."

Face intentionally blank, I lean against the opposite side of the island. I won't insult his intelligence by telling him he's wrong, but I won't confirm the truth, either.

"Tell me, Alexei, are there more players in this fight than I'm aware of? Does the man who *actually* killed Maksim have his own designs for power?"

Under different circumstances, I'd laugh.

Does Andrei want to become pakhan?

Fuck no.

He's the one that's pushed for me to take the title for my own, and the only thing he seems interested in is being with his new family.

"No," I tell Lavrov. "He doesn't."

Konstantin hums. "Wonderful. Because, should we go through with this, I'll only work with you. Not your second-in-command, not that annoying cousin of yours. Just you."

"If that's the case, can I expect the same courtesy in return?"

"You can *expect* whatever you want," Konstantin laughs. "But this isn't a negotiation, remember? If you need me, you'll go through whoever you need to. I'm a busy man."

Fucking asshole.

"*Fine*. I'll pretend to have a modicum of respect for you and choose not to be a petty bastard. That work?"

"Perfect." He shoots me a cheeky grin. "In that case, why don't you be a proper host and pour us a couple of drinks." There's a tightness to the corners of his eyes, and he's watching me far too closely for the careless attitude he's projecting.

I tap my thumb against the counter.

"What's the third condition, Konstantin?"

"Pour yourself a drink, and I'll tell you." His infuriating smile doesn't falter, but there's a command in his tone that feels like sand over an exposed nerve.

"Lavrov."

"Yes, Trenin?"

"What's the third condition?"

He sighs, long and disappointed. "For the record, this isn't how I wanted this to go. I tried to pull the stick out of your ass."

My jaw aches, and I wouldn't be shocked if I cracked a tooth. "I don't need a drink," I say, a warning in every word. "I need to know what you're dancing around."

Konstantin rubs his thumb against his index finger, all traces of amusement dropping away as he shakes his head.

"I don't know about you, but I know one surefire way to secure an alliance." The air around me freezes, and I'm suddenly very aware of how close I am to all the weapons in the room. The gun at the small of my back, the knife block, the gun he made sure to show off when he came in.

In retrospect, it was a smart move on his part.

Because if he's implying what I think he is, that show of force will be the only thing that keeps me from trying to kill him.

"A marriage," he says. The words land like bullets.

"I'm flattered, but you're not my type. I prefer them a little bustier."

"But, Alexei," he bemoans, "I've added another set of bench presses to my routine just for you." He shrugs off his suit jacket, showing off more of his physique, and allowing him even easier access to his gun.

Tattoos decorate his skin from his neck to his fingers, and while I'm by no means a small man, Konstantin looks like he spends every spare moment in the gym. If it comes down to it, I won't be able to take him in a fair fight. And with Nadya in the other room, I'm not willing to make that gamble.

"Unfortunately, I prefer them with more curves."

"Damn," Konstantin drawls, keeping a hand close to his weapon as he hooks his elbows over the back of the stool. "And I prefer your sister, so where does that leave us?"

"Good joke. Find a new one."

I will not serve up my sister on a silver platter for a violent *mudak* like Konstantin Lavrov.

"I told you Nadya needed to be here tonight, Alexei."

I'm consumed by a flood of rage so all-encompassing, I'm almost numb with it. If he wants to fuck with me, that's fine; I'd practically expect it. But dragging Nadya into the fray isn't just crossing a line, it's jumping over it and setting it on fire so he can dance on the ashes.

"Get out," I grit out through my teeth.

"I can do more than end your little spat with Nikita. I can put an end to your fight with The Outfit with a single phone call. That's an offer worth considering, and you know it."

"Oh, I've considered it plenty. And now you need to get the fuck out of my condo."

If he doesn't, I'm going to end up doing something I can't walk back from.

"Alexei?"

We both whip our gazes toward Nadya's tentative voice at the end of the hallway. She looks a mixture of terrified and confused, her eyes darting back and forth between us.

*Blyad.*

Before Konstantin can run his mouth and try to say something else to set me off, I dart around the island, positioning myself between the two of them. If he so much as takes a step toward her, I'll rip his fucking head off with my bare hands.

"Go back to my office," I order, voice firm.

I can't tell which one of them I should keep my eye on. Konstantin hasn't moved, but I wouldn't put it past him to lie in wait until he smells even a hint of an opening. Nadya can fight, but she doesn't stand a chance against a man like him.

"You could try giving her a chance to speak for herself. She may be more receptive to the idea than you think."

"Get the fuck out, Lavrov."

I'm half ready to launch myself at him, but Nadya's hand on my shoulder stills me, forcing me to settle on snarling at him and hoping he can be convinced to listen. Though from the way he's still lounging in his stool, turning only enough to watch us, I'm not going to hold my fucking breath.

"If you'd relax for a minute, you'd see I'm offering you a good deal."

He stands, still making no move to conceal his gun, and the small inhale from Nadya when she spots it nearly undoes all of her work to still my hand. She pulls on my shirt, a small reminder of what's at stake.

"Do all of us a favor and *leave*," she pleads. Konstantin looks at her, something I can't name brewing behind his eyes. He grins in a way only a man with no sense of self-preservation can, looking her up and down.

I angle myself so I'm concealing her from his sight.

"For you, *solnyshka*, I will. But only for you." He winks. When her cheeks flush, my vision blanks with red.

"Don't worry, Alexei. Once you come to your senses, feel free to call me."

By the time the front door slams shut behind him, my chest burns with fury. I focus on the ringing in my ears, trying to calm myself down, because no matter how much I want to, I *can't* kill him. Not today, anyway.

I needed this fucking alliance far more than I was willing to admit.

But now that I know there's no chance of it happening, I'm fucked. Those hopes are dead and buried, and I have to pivot and come up with a new plan entirely.

I'll make it work. Somehow.

"Alexei?"

I take a deep breath, letting it out slowly, before I look away from the spot where Konstantin stood and face my sister. "We're not talking about this again after tonight, so if you want to say something, say it now."

She crosses her arms with a sigh, and I hate the vulnerability she's working so hard to hide. I've never been in control of her life, and I'll never pretend to be. I fucking hate that Konstantin might have made her doubt that for even a second.

"If I talk, are you going to listen, or are you going to shut me out and get all huffy?"

"I'll listen."

Of course I'll listen. I always listen to her. Unless she gets worked up about numbers. Or is intentionally trying to piss me off. Or nagging me about working too much. Or accusing me of avoiding her. Or I'm busy avoiding her.

But after tonight, the last thing I want is to avoid her.

I need to keep Nadya close until I know Konstantin's long gone and has set his eyes elsewhere.

She rolls her eyes. "Yeah, right," she mutters under her breath. "What are you trying to get out of that guy, anyway?"

I close my eyes, hating the way the walls are closing in on me from all sides, including from her, before I march toward the living room. Not a moment later, she follows, not giving me even a moment of reprieve. I sit heavily, pinching the bridge of my nose.

"I take it back. We're never talking about what just happened."

Whether it's because we actually like each other or because of the way we grew up, Nadya and I get along most of the time. There are only a few lines that we have to enforce to keep the peace.

One being that we don't talk about my job. We can talk about finances all day long, but as soon as things stray from the illusion of being on the straight and narrow, it's off-limits.

She doesn't want to know, and I don't want to expose her to it. Bratva shit is something I can talk to Lev, or, in a pinch, Andrei about. But not my sister.

Never her.

And Konstantin didn't just break that seal, he beckoned her behind the curtain, inviting her to take a peek at all the dark, dangerous things I've worked so hard to hide.

She tosses a pillow at me, watching with dismay when it bounces off my shoulder and lands harmlessly on the floor. "You said you'd listen."

"You asked a question. There was nothing for me to listen to."

"Then treat me like you care about what I think and answer it." I swallow when her voice waivers. She looks away. "This isn't just about you anymore. He dragged me into it, and as much as you don't want to hear it, that means I get to have an opinion. So at least tell me what you need from him."

This would be easier if she were mad. I can deal with anger, but the worry she's pretending I can't see cuts me to the bone. She blinks back tears, and I can't fucking breathe.

I'll kill Lavrov for this.

"I was hoping for an alliance."

The words are pried from the depths of my chest, her tears ripping an agonizing wound through me. I've never seen her cry before, and this shouldn't be how I see them for the first time.

It should have been when she got married to some guy she's crazy about, or when she had her first kid. Not because Konstantin Lavrov decided to nuke my life.

"But it doesn't matter, because I'm not going to use you as a bargaining chip."

"Why do you need an alliance?" she asks. I rub my jaw, looking around for something that can rescue me from this conversation. "Does it have anything to do with the shooting last night?"

I'm not surprised she knows about it.

I'm just surprised she waited this long to ask.

I shake my head.

"Does Nikita know you're trying to work with whatever that dude's name is?"

An unexpected chuckle breaks free.

"Konstantin. His name is Konstantin Lavrov." If he made her cry, she deserves to know his name. "And though Nikita probably suspects it, I didn't exactly ask for his permission."

"I was worried you'd say that." She sighs, her head hitting the back of the couch. "So, what's the plan? You want to dive headfirst into the corruption and bullshit and take control of it?"

"Don't." I give her a stern look. "I don't need this lecture again. You've made your feelings regarding my life more than clear."

We sit in tense silence, and when she finally speaks up again, her voice is tentative. "Is this why you have Lev watching me? Because you're worried about Nikita retaliating?"

"It's just a precaution. I have everything under control."

"And if Lev's watching my back, then who's watching yours?"

Nadya looks at me with worried eyes, not blinking until I force myself to look away from her.

"Will working with Konstantin make you safer?"

"Not really," I lie. He's the safest route toward ending this fight with Nikita. With his help, I'll only have to worry about fighting The Outfit, but I can't tell her that.

When I get the nerve to look at her again, she's picking at her nails, shoulders curled and looking smaller than she ever has.

"If it would help, maybe we should talk about what he said. About me marrying him."

"No."

I stretch my hands, forcing them to uncurl from the tightly held fists they've been contorted into. I'll never allow her to marry for my benefit, and even if she convinced me she loved him, I'd never let her marry a man like Lavrov.

His reputation is bloody and violent. He does whatever he needs to in order to secure his own wants, and that's the last person Nadya should be with.

"Put your ego aside and try to see things from my perspective. You're putting your neck on the line for an outfit that doesn't give a shit about either of us, and when I have an opportunity to help you, you won't even consider it. If I can do something to keep you safe, then I'll do it."

Guilt is a heavy burden around my neck.

I've done my best to ease the scales, to repay her for everything she's done for me, and the thought of letting her step back into that role burns like acid.

"I don't need your help!" I snap. She rears back like I've slapped her, and I regret my words immediately. "I'll be fine without Lavrov. I'll figure something out. So just... forget about it, okay?"

Her neck is red, an angry flush creeping to her cheeks like she's physically ill with how upset she is. Her resounding silence is kinder than I deserve.

When she stands, she smooths her skirt, making me feel even worse.

She dressed up for this. She put on a fucking blazer, and it was all for nothing.

"Fine," she breathes. "I hope you can. Since you don't need me, I'm going home, and you can go back to pretending I don't matter until it's convenient for you."

I don't stop her when she leaves.

Konstantin doesn't deserve her, but neither do I.

Everything from the past day echoes through my head, bouncing around in an endless cacophony that has me seeing double.

And there's still so much left to do.

I stare at the skyline out the window, and, like I have done a hundred times before, I wish I could tell Nadya everything and ask her to help me figure it all out.

# CHAPTER 15

# Alexei

I ronically, my clubs are the perfect place to escape from everything and focus on work.

In each one, my office is built far enough from the main room that I don't have to worry about running into anyone, but close enough that when I close my eyes, I can still hear the music. I can feel the energy of the crowd all through the night.

No matter how late it is or how long I'm holed up trying to find another angle to approach my problems from, I can tap into that well, and I can push through for another hour.

From the way Andrei's frowning as he shuts my door behind him, I doubt he feels the same way, even though it's early, and everything is relatively quiet.

The only sounds from the main room are the techs testing the new sound equipment, making sure everything's in working order before opening tonight.

Ideally, I would've called Lev or tried to find someone else to talk to, but my hands are tied.

Nadya's no longer content to play along and ignores her guard, fighting him at every turn and refusing to give him a heads-up when she leaves for the day. If I pull him away for a single hour, he's not getting back into her apartment.

Until I manage to fix that mess, I'm stuck with Andrei.

He sits silently; an ankle crossed over his knee, while he waits for me to say something.

As much as I hate to admit it, I need to talk to someone. Without Konstantin, I'm out of ideas.

I don't have the resources to end the fight with Nikita on my own, and as much as I'd like to pretend otherwise, we can only dance around each other for so long before it all comes to a head. If I want to protect what's important, I need to be in control when it all blows up.

And right now? Andrei and Lev are the only people I trust to have my back.

That doesn't make it any easier to figure out what to tell Andrei.

After several agonizing minutes, he clears his throat.

"Everything alright?"

I haven't so much as acknowledged him since he walked in, but if it bothers him, he hides it well.

Andrei's the one who introduced me to Konstantin. He's the one who planted the idea that he might be able to help me. And as mad as I am at Lavrov, I have to remember that it isn't Andrei's fault. I take a fortifying breath, forcing a sense of calm I don't feel to take over.

"Do you know of anyone other than Lavrov who would be able to assist us?"

"Did something happen?" he asks, arching a brow.

"Doesn't matter. He's off the table."

He blows out a heavy sigh, his head falling back. Tension lines his shoulders, his thumb tapping rapidly against his knee.

"Did Lavrov back out? Or was his price too high?"

"Since his price is letting him marry my sister, let's consider that lead dead and buried."

Andrei blanches. "He wants to marry Nadya?"

I nod, twisting a pen around my fingers. "He didn't have many demands, but that was one of them."

"I take it you threw him out on his ass?" I nod. "Anyone in your place would have done the same," he says with a sigh.

"But you aren't," I reply. He tilts his head to the side as he watches me. "And I'm curious how you really would've handled it."

I need someone to tell me I'm not insane. That I wasn't blatantly in the wrong. That I haven't ruined my relationship with Nadya and thrown away my best chance of ending this fucking fight over nothing.

"If I were you, I would've told him to go to hell."

"What else would you have done, if you were in my place?"

For the first time in all the years I've known him, Andrei looks uncomfortable. He shifts in his seat, not meeting my eye, and every breath fuels the disappointment and helplessness that blaze under my skin, refusing to burn out.

After a long pause, Andrei says, "I would have given him anything he asked for." He shrugs. "But Blair's pregnant. And the Italians won't touch her, but I don't have that promise from Nikita. And, honestly? I want to live long enough to meet my kid. If we're fighting Nikita *and* The Outfit, the odds of that happening are low."

He clears his throat. "If Konstantin offered me a bone, I'd take it."

Well, fuck.

When he puts it like that, I'm an asshole. I argued against letting more men die when I was talking to Nikita, but now I'm throwing away my best chance to prevent it.

Who can blame Andrei for wanting to live? For as long as I've known him, he's lived like a shadow, only noticed by the people who had use for him.

He's finally found a place for himself.

By refusing Konstantin, I'm putting that at risk. Not just for him, but for everyone. If I fail, Nikita's going to make sure everyone who backed me suffers for it. Even if they manage to escape unharmed, they'll have to watch as he ruins this brotherhood and morphs it into something beyond recognition.

If I concede now, there's a better chance everyone else will be spared. No one will go after Nadya, and even when Nikita does retaliate, he'll focus on me.

If the worst were to happen, Lev would watch over Nadya in my place.

They might not like it, but everyone would be safer.

Everyone except Emiliya.

But she's smart. She doesn't need me to save her if she doesn't want me to.

"Should I let Nikita take over?" I wonder when the weight threatens to choke me.

The silence drags between us, thick and heavy.

"No," Andrei says firmly. I blink in surprise, but he doesn't give me a chance to interrupt him.

"Nikita doesn't care about brotherhood, or a mutual cause, or anything besides himself. He'll gleefully turn every man against each other if it makes him a little bit richer." He runs a hand down his face, looking almost as exhausted as I feel.

"For most of my life, the only leadership we've had has willfully fostered greed and set pitfalls that will eventually topple our whole operation without intervention. And maybe I'm getting soft, but Niko deserves a decent pakhan when he grows up. Nikita won't be able to provide that for him. You can."

I'm not sure I've ever heard Andrei say so much in one go before.

"Niko's three," I point out rather than addressing his blind faith in me. "Isn't he a little young to be thinking about that?"

"If you bothered to visit, he'd gladly remind you that he's turning four in a couple weeks." Andrei shrugs. "I want him to have something better than the rest of us did."

The weight on my shoulders increases tenfold.

"Then I hope you can find someone else to help me. Otherwise, we're fucked."

My phone rings on my desk, the unknown number glaring back at me. Andrei's eyes flit to mine as I pick it up. The fact that it's my personal phone does nothing to alleviate my dread.

"*Da?*"

"Alexei?"

Even though Emiliya's voice is tentative and hushed, a single word is all it takes for my focus to zero in on her. She sounds like she's trying to make sure no one else hears her, her voice muffled like she's cupping a hand over her mouth.

"Can you talk?"

At least she sounds better than the other day, but that isn't saying much.

"I've got time. What's up?"

If she's calling for help, I'll gladly offer it, and if she's fishing for information, I'll have to figure out how to tell her to fuck off without making her think I won't help her get away from Nikita if she changes her mind.

Nothing comes to mind right away, but part of me never thought I'd have to come up with anything at all.

Mostly, I figured she'd be too proud to ever call.

I glance at Andrei. Thank fuck I didn't have Emiliya's number saved. Something tells me he wouldn't appreciate knowing I gave her a direct line to me.

"I just... Father said something the other day, and it didn't click until just now, but I thought you should know." Her words tumble over each other in one hurried breath. "He knew about the shooting before I got home. He kept asking if you'd said anything about it."

I close my eyes, feeling like a fool.

Of course, Nikita was behind that farce.

But how did he know which club I was in? Only a few men knew where that meeting was, and that means I have a fucking rat.

And while there's a limited pool to choose from, every man volunteered to be there, making it that much harder to figure out who's playing both sides.

"And what did you tell him?"

"The truth. That you didn't say anything."

*But she told him we were together.*

Resentment is a bitter pill to swallow, even if I know I shouldn't feel that way at all.

Whatever Emiliya's doing for her father, he isn't giving her a choice. She's only doing what she can to get from one day to the next without ending up half-dead.

Apparently, she takes my brooding as a dismissal, because I can hear her moving around before she clears her throat.

"Anyway, I just thought you should know. Keep an eye out for him, okay? I have to take Mom to the doctor, so."

She hangs up unceremoniously, leaving me to sort through the ticking bomb she dropped in my lap without so much as a proper goodbye.

*Blyad.*

"Who was that?" Andrei asks.

Lying to him would be so easy, but I don't trust myself to make the right call when it comes to Emiliya.

For all I know, she could be planting whatever seeds of doubt Nikita's told her to, and even if it's reckless, part of me would still believe her.

"Emiliya," I say.

"Emiliya?" he asks with a frown. I nod.

In an instant, Andrei's calm demeanor shifts to a mask of barely contained frustration. He threads his hands together as he leans forward, his face wiped free of all emotion as he eyes me.

"I'm sorry, I thought you said that was Emiliya Dyomina, but I must have misheard."

"You didn't." I sigh. So much for a productive conversation. "But on the bright side, it sounds like you can stop trying to find out who pulled the gun at Underground. She says Nikita knew about it before she said anything."

Maybe if I redirect his attention, he'll drop it.

"Oh, good. If Nikita's daughter says something, you don't immediately doubt it. That's great," he scoffs dismissively. "If you listen to a single word out of her mouth, you're shooting yourself in the foot, you get that, right?"

It's not my job to defend her, especially not against someone who has a decent reason to dislike her, but that doesn't stop something protective from rearing its head, ready to go to bat for her.

"You ever consider there's a chance you're wrong about her?"

"Sure. But with someone as conniving as her, I don't think I am."

"Like you're some saint. Does Blair know half the shit you've done?" I scoff. "Get off your fucking high horse."

"You're actually going to defend her?"

I don't justify him with a response, letting him see exactly how serious I am. Has Emiliya done some awful shit? Sure. But so have I. So has he. Hell, so has every man we know.

There are no hands free of blood in this life. It's only a matter of whose blood it is, and what you did to earn it.

Emiliya has her reasons for what she's done, and neither of us have the right to know what they are.

"Fucking Christ. Fine. Don't listen to me." He stands, not bothering to wait for a dismissal. "Ask any other man if she's trustworthy. If you find the one who agrees with you, you've found your fucking rat." He stalks to the door, apparently as done with this conversation as I am.

"And when she comes back around to bite you in the ass, maybe you'll figure it out. Until then, you know how to find me."

# CHAPTER 16

# Alexei

I don't waste time waiting for Andrei to leave before I take off for the hospital. If he's pissy enough to follow me, so be it. I need to find out what Emiliya knows, and if the other day was any indication, I don't think Nikita's going to bother joining his wife at her appointment.

It's an opportunity, and I'm not going to let it slip through my fingers.

I lean against the reception desk, flashing the nurse my friendliest smile, and forcing it not to fall into a scowl when she looks me over, seeming bored. When I wink, she squints at me like I'm a threat.

One she isn't at all cowed by.

"Can I help you?"

"I certainly hope so," I drawl, laying the charm on thick. "You see, my girlfriend's mom has an appointment today, and I was hoping to surprise them. Make a good impression, you know?"

"Very sweet," she replies without even a hint of a smile. "What does that have to do with you hovering in my space?"

"Well, that's the thing. Since it's a surprise, she didn't tell me which room they're in, and I forgot the doctor's name. Can you help a man out?"

"I'm only able to give patient information to people the patient has previously given authorization to," she answers without looking up from her computer, typing away like I'm not even here. "Sounds like you don't have authorization."

My smile turns wooden.

This wasn't a fucking issue when I was here with Lev. The nurse then was more than happy to tell me where my men were. She practically jumped over the counter to escort us to their rooms.

"Listen, I'm only trying to warm up my future mother-in-law, you know?"

Her eyes flick to me, apparently deciding in a single glance that I'm not worth dealing with.

"In that case, I suggest you call your *girlfriend*"—disbelief drips from the word—"and ask her to meet you down here. Otherwise, I'll have to call security and have you removed from the premises."

I eye the ID clipped to her pocket, squinting to read her name.

"C'mon, Sadie. I screwed up the other night, and this would go a long way toward fixing things."

"It's Nurse Hill to you. And if you fucked up, that's on you. Now, do you want me to call security, or are you going to march your happy ass out of here on your own?"

No wonder this woman's stuck at a computer instead of with a patient. She has the warm and comforting personality of a cactus.

"I appreciate that you're just trying to do your job here," I say, slipping out my wallet and slipping a few bills across the counter. "But maybe I can convince you to work with me."

Disdain drips from every fiber of her being. Her hand slips toward the phone, no longer willing to play with her threat to have me kicked out.

Apparently, healthcare workers have more integrity than hardened men.

Goddamn it.

"Fine," I grit out, snagging back the bills before she gets any bright ideas about keeping them.

Hopefully, Nikita doesn't keep track of Emiliya's phone calls.

She's quick-witted enough to talk her way out of explaining one call to a random number, but that number calling her back less than an hour later? She'll have a harder time waving it away without telling him exactly who she was talking to.

Nurse Hill's hand is still hovering over the phone while I storm away.

I could try waiting in the parking lot and catching Emiliya when they leave, but I was hoping to catch Emiliya alone, and if I wait here or try to track her down outside, I run the risk of running into the guards Nikita's bound to have watching her.

The nurse's spiteful glare follows me to the entrance while I rack my brain to figure out another approach. I'm just passing the elevator when the doors slide open and I nearly collide with Emiliya as she steps out.

"Excellent timing," I huff, catching her when she stumbles. She blinks up at me, her pretty eyes shining with equal parts confusion and alarm. It stirs something tender in my chest, aching to comfort her.

"What're you doing here?"

Behind me, I can hear the nurse calling for security, so I plaster on a smile, hoping that the witch can't read lips. "Pretend you're excited to see me, and I'll gladly tell you."

"Is this man bothering you, Miss Dyomina?" The nurse calls out. My blood pressure spikes at her harsh tone. "Security is already on the way."

I don't like that woman at all.

I have half a mind to tell her exactly what would happen if security tried to lay a hand on me, but instead, I take the mature route, and inhale a deep breath through my nose. I force every muscle in my face to smile in a way that looks pleasant.

"We're fine, Sadie," Emiliya says with an easy smile that makes me feel envious. She glances between the two of us and wraps an arm around my torso, patting my stomach.

My muscles flex under her touch.

"You're going to have to excuse him. He has the manners of a caveman, but he's *my* caveman." Sadie—because if Emiliya gets to call her by her name, then I'm going to call her by her fucking name—glares at me suspiciously even as Emiliya drags me further into the hospital, her arm looped through mine.

I let it go, if only because being this close to Emiliya feels good. I catch a hint of her perfume, a delicate scent that brings back flashes of her lying against my chest before I fell asleep that night, warm and content.

"What're you doing here?" she hisses as soon as we're around a corner, snapping me out of my reprieve. "Are you trying to get me killed? What if someone saw you?" Outwardly, her body language is still flirty and calm, but her eyes dart around.

Whether she's searching for threats or an escape, I don't know.

"How did Nikita know about the shooting?" I ask gently. Emiliya herds me past a doctor inspecting a clipboard, and I let her. As long as she keeps touching me like this, she can lead me wherever the fuck she wants, and I'll follow her.

Few things have ever felt as right as her arm in mine, and the way she leans her head toward me gives a sense of intimacy I didn't even know I'd been missing.

Emiliya is far more dangerous to me than she knows.

"I don't know," she says. When I pin her with a look, her eyes flare with anger. "All I know is that he was in a frenzy I got home. I was too busy trying not to die to ask him for specifics."

Guilt stabs me.

As we approach another nurse, Emiliya's calm and collected facade slips back into place.

I hate that practiced look. I don't want Emiliya to be polite and put on a show. Not with me.

I want to see her pissed off and lashing out, telling me everything that's bothering her without restraint or hesitation. I want to see her the way I have only when we're alone.

Wild.

Fearless.

*Free*.

Not this amenable, uncomplicated show she puts on for the world.

Not when her normally perfect hair looks dull, and her makeup is still doing very little to hide the dark circles under her eyes. Not when I can see a busted lip through her shiny lip gloss.

She should be screaming at everyone here, demanding justice for everything she's been through. I crave to feel her teeth as she tears me to pieces for my part in it.

"But he knew you were at Underground."

She shakes her head, a flicker of uncertainty dancing across her face before she smothers it.

"No. He just knows I was with you afterward." She smiles vaguely as she leads me out a set of doors and into a sunny courtyard, an area shielded from everyone else by tall trees bereft of leaves. "And even that's more than I wanted to tell him."

"So why did you?" I ask, bracing myself.

Emiliya stares straight ahead. "Why do you think, Alexei? I didn't want one of the maids to find my corpse in the morning."

A magpie takes off as we approach, and she watches the movement with an indifferent expression.

"I didn't want him to know I went out, and tossing him a stick got him to back off. I told him I was with you, and he let me be for the night."

I don't know what to say to that. I want to pull her into my arms, to take away all the pain she's suffered, but I don't know where to start.

"He wanted to know if you were hurt," she eventually says. "He wanted to know if you had said anything about what happened. He wanted to know if anyone had died."

I don't realize how tightly I'm holding myself until Emiliya flinches, trying to pull her arm free of mine.

If he wanted to know if I was hurt, that means he didn't have any eyes inside the club. That narrows down my pool of potential rats by exactly three: Lev, Artyom, and Philipp.

I'm no closer to figuring this out than I was an hour ago.

With a strength I don't expect, Emiliya rips her arm free. All her fire is back when she glares at me.

I breathe a little easier at the sight.

"Since he's the one who hurt you the other day, is it fair to guess that he's the one who gave you that split lip?" I move into her space until we're standing toe to toe. "And that he's the one who gave you the bruise I saw on your ribs the first time I fucked you? And your hip?"

My stomach turns as I force myself to contend with exactly how many times I've seen her hurt. And not once did I say a fucking word.

She blinks over my shoulder, refusing to meet my eyes.

She looks a hundred times better than she did last time I saw her, but what'll happen until I see her again? Is she going to be safe when she goes home tonight? Will Nikita hurt her so badly that I won't get a chance to see her again?

If he was trying to get me killed the other night, he's going to be pissed that he failed.

My heart stutters in its cage, rattling to life so hard it's impossible to ignore.

*Fuck*.

"Alright. Do you know if your dad is at home now?"

Emiliya sighs. Some of her tension lining her shoulders melts away, making her look more like the Emiliya I've seen flashes of.

"If you're asking because you're planning on attacking him, you're only setting yourself up for failure. And even though you're an asshole, I'm very fond of your dick. It'd be a shame if you were killed before I got a chance to enjoy it again."

The corners of her lips curl into a real smile. My feelings become impossible to ignore.

Teasing suits Emiliya.

"I was thinking more along the lines of taking you home to pack a bag so you can stay with me for a bit, but if you want my dick again, far be it from me to discourage you."

For a beautiful moment, she flounders for words, and it's such a lovely sight I can't help but smirk. I tap a finger against the bottom of her chin until she snaps her mouth shut so hard her teeth click together.

"Would you like your mother to come along, too?" I pause, looking back at the hospital. "Or does she need a special setup? I don't have any medical equipment or anything, but if you give me a couple days, I'll set something up."

"She doesn't need anything special," Emiliya says slowly, like she's unsure if we're speaking the same language. "But Father won't let her go anywhere he doesn't want her to. I already have to sneak her out of the house to get to her appointments. And he definitely won't let her stay with you."

"Is she safe in his house?"

The love she has for her mother is crystal clear to anyone who cares to see it.

If protecting Emiliya means I have to blow everything to hell and steal Nikita's wife and daughter from him in one afternoon, then so be it.

We're already barreling toward mutual destruction. Might as well get a few blows in while I can.

"Yeah. He doesn't hurt her, or anything like that. He just ignores her. Controls where she goes and who she gets to see."

Because Emiliya will do anything for her mom, and even if he pushes Emiliya hard enough that she stops caring about herself, Nikita knows that he still has an ace up his sleeve.

"Then do you want to stay with me for a while? Or would you be more comfortable there so you can keep an eye on her?"

Her eyes fall to the side, calculations I can't even begin to guess dancing across her expression.

If she says she wants to stay at home, I don't know what I'm going to do. Storm the building and drag her out? Drink myself into a stupor so I can forget for a moment?

Emiliya spends so much time hiding who she really is that the few glimpses I've got under her sarcastic, blasé armor have been few and far between. But they've been enough for me to know she'll do anything for the people she loves.

They've been enough to whet my appetite and leave me craving more.

I won't blame her if she doesn't want to come home with me, but no matter what she decides, I'm getting her out of that house.

Even if I have to force her hand.

The woman she hides from the world is far too precious to let waste away under Nikita's eye.

"Why are you even asking? Two weeks ago you would've told me to go fuck myself."

"Because I want to," I say firmly. "Maybe because I don't like seeing you wearing marks that I didn't put there. Maybe because I want another chance to play with your gorgeous tits while you squirm in my lap."

It's a fucking cop-out, and we both know it, but the truth feels like too much. Even to myself.

A half-truth will have to do for now.

"I do have pretty nice tits," she eventually hums, twisting her hands together in an uncharacteristic display of self-consciousness.

"I'd argue they're better than pretty nice, but maybe I should spend some more time with them before I make that call."

There's a conflict in her eyes that I want to pick apart and analyze.

Does she want to come with me? Even a little? Does she want to use me as a way to escape Nikita? Or is she trying to come up with a polite way to tell me to fuck off and leave her alone?

Emiliya looks almost dejected as she bites her bottom lip, but I don't take back my words.

If she wants to deal with Nikita on her own, she's going to have to tell me that. If she wants me to leave, she needs to say it.

Otherwise, I'm not going anywhere.

"Fuck it," she eventually says, resolved. "Mom's probably done with her appointment. You can follow us home and wait down the street. You can take me back to your place once she's settled."

Emiliya turns and winks at me over her shoulder, compelling me to follow her without any conscious input.

"How long are you planning on keeping me, anyway?"

"Let's play it by ear." I shrug. "Who knows? Maybe I'll enjoy having you around."

# CHAPTER 17

# Emiliya

"I'm going to stay with a friend for a few days," I say brightly as Mom settles into her favorite chair. She winces as she turns her head away from the window, studiously ignoring the headache that's been plaguing her since we left the hospital.

Between worrying about her, checking the rearview mirror to see if Alexei was still following us, and the annoying voice in the back of my head berating me for being an idiot, I'm exhausted. I want nothing more than to hide away somewhere and zone out for a while.

Something tells me things won't get easier when I'm alone with Alexei.

"If you're planning on running away, you should just say so," she replies, a teasing smile on her lips.

"Wouldn't that defeat the point?" Mom pats my arm, the corners of her eyes still stiff and swollen from the Botox injections. "I'm not running. I'll be back here to bother you again before you know it."

"Don't rush on my behalf. You deserve to have some fun, *lastochka*."

*Fun* isn't the point. I'm pretty sure this is more about feeding Alexei's ego and letting him think he's saving me.

"I have fun with you."

Mom chuckles, shaking her head. As long as it makes her happy, I'll let her think whatever the hell she wants.

"You're always worrying."

"No, I'm not."

She gives me a knowing look that makes my cheeks burn.

"Now, tell me about this *friend* you're staying with. Is he cute? Does he treat you well?"

"What makes you think they're a man? For all you know, I could have a gaggle of women who I hang out with."

Mom pats my cheek with a soft hand. "Yes, Emiliya. You're very mysterious. So, is he good in bed?"

"Mom!" I nearly choke on my tongue while she laughs, loud and amused.

"Don't be coy, Emiliya. I love you, but I also caught you in the pantry making out with one of your father's guards when you were a teenager."

Is it too much to hope the ground will open up and swallow me whole?

"You said you weren't going to bring that up again," I hiss, looking around for any witnesses to my humiliation. Fortunately, there's no one but the two of us in this wing.

"And until now, I haven't. But I'm old and lonely." She smiles sweetly. "Now give me something to keep my imagination busy while you're gone. Does he look good without a shirt? How tight is his ass?" Her eyes light up as she gets an idea. "You should bring him around some time."

Oh, god.

"We're not doing this," I mumble under my breath, moving around the room and checking drawers and shelves until I find Mom's headphones. I drop them onto the table next to her. Mom grins, bemused by my discomfort.

As little as I want to see her when she's upset, I want to talk to her about my sex life even less.

"Here. Listen to one of your books. They'll give you plenty of things to imagine."

Mom grins as I press a kiss against the top of her head.

For once, she takes mercy on me. "Fine, leave me to suffer my boredom alone. Just tell me one thing first."

"What?"

"Is he cute?"

I bite my lip, stifling a grin. Even if she is in a good mood, the last thing I need to do is encourage her.

But when I think about it, I can't find the words to describe Alexei's magnetism. Definitely not cute. He watches everything around him with an intensity that's searing, and when you're the focus of his attention, everything else fades to black.

There's only him and the pull in my chest that makes it impossible to look away.

"I wouldn't call him cute," I settle on. "He's too hardened for that, but he's stunning. Eye-catching and put together, maybe. He's handsome, but not cute."

"Hardened?" she asks with narrowed eyes. In an instant, her face twitches into a grin that makes me groan.

"I bet he's hard."

"*Jesus*, Mom." I roll my eyes, smiling as she laughs at her own joke. "I'm going to pack. I'll be back on Friday for your next appointment."

Her soft voice stops me when I'm at the door, her smile apparent even as she twists back toward the window. "You're a good girl, *lastochka*."

"I love you too, Mom."

***

I slink toward the front door more out of instinct than necessity. Father won't be home for hours, and even if he were here, he'd let me go the instant I told him where I'm going.

Anticipation and self-loathing combine in a toxic mixture that makes my head spin.

I want to get away from this house, and spending more time with Alexei is no hardship, but Father would only encourage me if he knew about this.

As much as it disgusts me to do anything that pleases him, I can't keep being terrified in my own home, even if that means accepting Alexei's savior complex.

When I step outside, Yan's concerned gaze bounces between me and the small suitcase in my hand. He lifts a brow.

The wind turns biting under his scrutiny.

"You going somewhere?"

Unlike the rest of Father's men, I like to think Yan gives a shit about me. He's discreet in how he looks out for me, but he's the first one to redirect Father's attention when he's on the rampage, drawing his attention elsewhere while I slip away.

He watches Mom and me so carefully that it almost looks like affection in the right light.

But at the end of the day, Yan's still on Father's payroll.

Even if he's only asking because he's curious, there's a real chance anything I say will end up being parroted to Father as soon as I'm out of earshot.

"I was planning on staying at a hotel for a few days." I shrug. "Need a break from everything, you know?"

He raises a skeptical brow, assessing me like I'm a threat.

Silently, I beg him to let it go. When allies are far and few between, losing Yan to Father's thrall would be devastating. He could gain a lot from prying, and we both know it.

But no one's looking at us. He'll lose nothing from showing me a small act of compassion.

"Fine," he eventually sighs. "But keep your phone on you in case your mom needs you, alright?"

Air rushes out of my lungs.

"You're the best, Yan."

"Get your sweet ass out of here before your dad gets home."

I practically skip down the drive, waving at him before I turn the corner and hurry back to Alexei's SUV, only detouring to duck into the bushes and look for his sweatshirt.

Even though it's been days since I left it there, disappointment weighs heavy on my shoulder when I come up empty-handed.

Despite feeling like I could cry, I grin as I settle into the passenger seat, tossing my bag into the back. Alexei doesn't smile back.

His eyes are too aware, constantly forcing me to up my game so he can't dig beneath the surface and find out exactly how shallow and empty I really am. Hiding from him is harder than it is with most people, and I have no clue how I'm going to keep up the act over a period of days, but I'll figure something out.

I always do.

"Why were you digging through that shrub?"

*He saw that?*

My smile falters slightly.

"I thought I saw a mouse," I lie, coughing to cover the way my voice cracks.

Alexei squints. "You know, you don't have to come with me if you don't want to. I'm not trying to make you my prisoner."

"I figured. Since you gave me a choice, and all."

I gesture to the open road in front of us, but Alexei remains unmoved, watching me like I'm the most interesting thing he's ever seen. His gaze strips me bare, pulling away layer after layer of my defenses until I'm more exposed than I've ever been.

I'm not sure if I'd rather give in to it, or crawl across the center console and into his lap so he looks at me like I'm not worth digging deeper.

Changing tactics, I lean toward him and reach across the center console to lay a hand on his muscular thigh, squeezing gently. "You know, the sooner you get me home, the sooner I can help you relax."

His shoulders drop a fraction of an inch as he shakes his head. As Alexei looks away, the tender feeling in my chest dims.

When he finally starts the car, the entire drive is silent.

***

Alexei leads me inside his apartment building, ignoring me as I follow him. I lean against the wall while I wait for him to unlock his door. It takes him a moment to dig his keys out of his pocket with my bag clutched in his hand.

He's just fitting it into the lock when a door down the hall opens and a head of white hair pops out.

"Hello, Mrs. Sullivan," he calls, not even sparing her a glance as he opens his door.

The woman frowns as she looks between the two of us.

"Who's your friend, Alexei?"

He closes his eyes, nostrils flaring as he takes a deep breath. I bite my lip so I don't laugh.

"Mrs. Sullivan, this is Emiliya. Emiliya, Mrs. Sullivan." Mrs. Sullivan opens her mouth to say something, but Alexei nudges me into the condo with a hand on the small of my back before she can. "I'm sorry, but it's been a long day, and I'd like to get Emiliya settled."

He slams the door behind us, rolling his eyes.

"I'm glad you have such a good relationship with your neighbors," I chirp, smiling obnoxiously when he glowers.

"*Good* and *Mrs. Sullivan* are two things that don't belong in the same paragraph, let alone the same sentence."

Without another word, Alexei prowls further into the condo. Everything looks so different than it did the other night. Light pours through the floor-to-ceiling windows, revealing modern furniture, clean lines, and a neutral color palette that begs to be complemented by a forest of plants.

There's so much more personality than I saw when I was here last. Not that I spent much time looking around. No, that night, Alexei dragged me straight to his bedroom. But I saw enough to know that's not where he's leading me now.

"Here you go," he says as he opens the door at the end of the hall, revealing a guestroom entirely devoid of personality. It's so lifeless compared to the living room. Everything is white, minimalist, and boring as hell.

If I didn't know any better, I would double-check it's even in the same condo.

Alexei sets my bag at the foot of the bed while I try to figure out what to make of my vague sense of disappointment.

Alexei putting me in a different room is a *good* thing. It saves me from having to put on a show every minute of the day, and it'll be that much easier to keep my heart out of the game.

One day, Alexei's fight with Father is going to come to an end, and I can't afford to get caught up in the shrapnel.

Falling for him, like trusting Father, would be equivalent to shooting myself in the foot, because neither of them is going to protect me.

I have to do it myself.

Swallowing my unreasonable hurt, I smirk, blinking at Alexei through my lashes.

"What, worried you won't be able to keep your hands off me?"

"Maybe." He shrugs as he checks his watch. "But I thought you'd appreciate having some privacy. And even though I'm not home much, you deserve some space to yourself."

Alexei takes a step back, leaving me with little to do except poke through the empty dresser and stare at the blank walls.

"Which reminds me, I have to get to a meeting with my suppliers. I trust you can find everything you need?"

"Sure," I respond breezily, turning my back to him so I can look out the window.

If it weren't for my father, if it weren't for the bruises, would Alexei want me here at all? If I were just a woman he was hooking up with, would he still be running out the door to get away from me?

"If you need anything, text me. I'll answer as soon as I can."

I nod, but he's already walking away, moving onto something more important.

"Oh, and Emiliya?" he calls. I poke my head into the hallway, watching as he adjusts his cufflinks. "Please don't run off. I'm looking forward to seeing you when I get home."

Somehow, I doubt that.

# CHAPTER 18

# Emiliya

As interesting as Alexei's condo seemed at a glance, the more time I spend alone, the more I realize it's all a paper-thin front.

His shelves are full of books about business that bore me to tears just looking at them, the view out the window is nothing but the unchanging skyline, and I can only poke at his decor for so long before I feel like I'm prying.

The only interesting thing I find is a pink apron in the kitchen.

Part of me wants to pull it out and tease him about it, but the other part knows how precarious my place here is. A stupid joke isn't worth risking getting sent home.

I'm so busy trying to distract myself, I hardly notice when the sun sets behind the clouds.

It takes longer than I'll ever admit to poke at the high-tech panel on the wall until I can figure out how to turn on the lights, and it takes me longer still to figure out how to dim them enough so they aren't blinding.

Hours tick away, and when my boredom gives way to hunger, I end up raiding Alexei's fridge, sifting through the unexpected amount of vegetables he has stashed away.

For a second, I wonder if Alexei will mind me making use of his kitchen, but he *did* say I should be able to find what I need. And right now, I need food.

I haven't eaten since last night, and before Mom's appointment I was too worried about sneaking her out, and then I called Alexei, and...

And now I'm alone.

At least I don't have to worry that Father's going to walk in and start screaming at me for making noise.

Wait.

*Holy shit.*

I don't have to worry about figuring out what today's threshold for *too loud* is, because Father isn't here.

I put a pan on the stove, not acting like it's made of fine china. The sound clatters through the room so loudly I flinch. On instinct, I freeze, but no one comes stomping around the corner. No one shouts, and nothing crashes against a wall.

For once, I'm alone. I don't have to cater to anyone else.

I giggle like a little girl, sprinting to my room to grab my phone. The little speaker blares to life, screaming out loud, angry music I typically only listen to when I'm in my car.

Alexei's going to hate me when Mrs. Sullivan inevitably starts to complain, but I can't find it in me to give a shit. He's given me a little pocket of freedom, and I'm going to take full advantage of it.

As I cook, I dance and sing along, loud and off-key for no reason other than I can.

I'm in an unfamiliar space, waiting for someone who doesn't even want me here, but I can eat dinner without having to worry about my father's temper. I can walk around, and I don't have to worry about looking less than a hundred percent put together.

I haven't been this lucky since the last time Father went out of town for a meeting.

I wash the dishes, pack away the leftovers, and happily strip out of the nice clothes I put on this morning, putting on the sweatpants I threw in my bag on a whim. They're warm and soft, and after making sure I look nice for everyone else for so long, the thick fabric is a comforting hug, loose enough to allow me to breathe for the first time in weeks.

Twisting back and forth in front of the mirror, I almost want to laugh at myself. The steam from cooking turned my hair into a frizzy mess, and the only generous way to describe my outfit is *cozy*. With my makeup wiped away, I can make out the faint marks left from Father's last temper tantrum.

It's not much different from every other night, but for once, there's no one to witness it. No Mom, no Father, no gossiping household staff. I can just *be*.

Switching over to a more upbeat playlist, I throw my hair into a messy bun and dig into my luggage until I pull out a little jar.

After the last week, a little self-care sounds like exactly what I need.

Being able to relax is a luxury in my home, and if only for tonight, I'm going to let go. For a few hours, Father's expectations don't matter. I don't have to fret over Mom with every breath, and I don't have to care about keeping everyone else happy. I can forget myself for a single night.

There's a bitter irony in the fact that the only time I've been able to feel like myself lately is when I'm with Alexei.

When I'm with him, it's harder to overthink and second-guess everything until I can't tell which way is up. He gives me glimpses of what life might have been like if I weren't stuck under Father's thumb.

As long as Alexei keeps me around, I have a chance to hold on to this feeling.

I just have to remember that he doesn't really *care*. It doesn't matter if I thought he looked at me like he cared at the hospital. I'm nothing more than a means to an end. A little vanity project so Alexei can feel good about himself, but not an actual *person* worth caring about.

At the end of the day, I'm still just a manipulative bitch who lashes out and smiles pretty until she gets what she wants. The asshole who slept with a married man. A little spy.

My father's daughter through and through.

Turning up the music until I can't hear myself think, I dance around my new room, not caring that I'm sweating through my mud mask. There's no one here to see it, anyway. No audience, no crowd I'm expected to impress.

There's just me.

I throw my hands in the air, my hips moving to a rhythm only they know until I lose track of time. I turn and twist in a circle, practically screaming along to the song until I see a shadow out of the corner of my eye.

I whirl around, my mouth dry and heat flooding my face.

Alexei smirks, leaning against the doorjamb with his arms folded across his chest. He must have ditched his suit jacket at some point, because the sleeves of his shirt are rolled up to his elbows, exposing the flexing muscles of his forearms.

If I didn't want to disintegrate with embarrassment, I'd probably stare at them. Instead, I'm trapped by his bemused expression like a bug under a microscope.

Scrambling, I turn off the music, plunging the room into silence so rapidly, my ears ring with it.

"If you're hoping I'll kick you out over noise complaints, you should know that the soundproofing here is better than you'd expect."

"Damn. I worked so hard on that plan, too," I mutter, wishing I were invisible, that the ground would open up and swallow me whole. "Guess I'll have to walk out the front door on my own two feet instead."

"You could. But you might want to clean off all of"— his hand twists in the general direction of my face—"that. Whatever that is."

"Don't pretend you don't know what a mud mask is." He frowns in genuine confusion. I blink, taken aback. "You have a sister, Alexei. Don't play dumb."

"Why would you put mud on your face?"

"It makes my skin look nice. Do you think I look this pretty without a little work?"

"I mean, yeah? How does mud even—" He cuts himself off with a shake of his head. "I just wanted to check in on you before I go to bed."

Alexei runs a hand through his hair, making his blond waves stick up in wild angles that make him look... not softer, but less intense. It's a good look on him, and it makes his concern a little easier to stomach.

"Well, I'm fine." My voice is softer than I want it to be. I shrug, brushing aside the gratitude stirring in my chest. "Do you want me to turn down the music?"

"No," Alexei practically whispers before he clears his throat. "Be as loud as you want."

"Not that I was asking for permission, but good to know."

Alexei's eyes soften, like he hears the lie as if I'd shouted it, but he doesn't strip me of it, even though it'd be so fucking easy.

"If you didn't want me to make noise, you should have said something before you asked me to stay here, anyway."

The corners of his lips tick up into something that resembles a smile. My heart thumps heavily at the sight.

I meant it when I told Mom that Alexei isn't cute. He's impossible to ignore no matter what he does, but when he smiles at me like that, I wonder if he could be cute if he ever lowered his guard.

Maybe even a man like Alexei could be tender if he wanted to.

"You're right. I'll keep that in mind next time." He turns away. The desire that compels me to follow him, to stay in his company, is a dangerous thing.

"If you're still hungry, I cooked dinner. There are leftovers in the fridge," I call out before he can retreat to his room. "If you want some."

One corner of his lip twitches upward, his expression tender when he looks at me over his shoulder. "I think I'll take you up on that."

I smile to myself as I close the door behind him, pressing my back against it while I work to calm the fluttering of my heart.

# CHAPTER 19
# Emiliya

My sleep is plagued by nightmares where I'm standing on a cliff with a strong wind pushing me forward. No matter how I twist or turn, the land beneath my feet falls away whenever I move.

When my alarm goes off, I'm panting and sticky with sweat. I count backward from five, willing my pounding heart to calm with every breath.

When time's up, I throw myself into looking presentable to start the day and shrug off the lingering unease.

If I'm only here out of pity, then I'll have to work twice as hard to convince Alexei to care about me enough to do Father's bidding. So, for every morning for the past week, I've made sure to go all out before Alexei even wakes up.

Perfect outfit, perfect hair, perfect makeup.

Each morning, I tidy up the already immaculate condo, prepare breakfast, and brew coffee before he's even out of bed.

Not that it seems to matter.

We've spent every day silently moving around each other until one of us leaves. Me, to go see Mom, and him to do whatever it is he does throughout the day. The few times our paths do cross, he has nothing to say, and I can't find my voice to say anything to him.

Since anything I find out would only be another weapon Father can extract from me, I'm not sure I ever will.

Swiping on a final coat of mascara, I run through a checklist. My hair is perfect. My outfit is suitably sexy without looking like I'm trying to seduce anyone. There are no signs of the sleepless nights and even longer days where I'm constantly trying to find the balance between keeping my head down and wanting Alexei to notice me again.

If it were anyone but him, they'd at least spare me a second glance before they headed out the door. But he doesn't even look up from his phone as he passes the kitchen on his way to the door. He can't even be bothered to say a word.

I take a sip of coffee and glare at the second fruit bowl I prepared as if my apparent invisibility is its fault.

It definitely isn't mine. Because if were mine, then I was delusional in thinking that if I put forth some effort into including Alexei in what I'm doing, he'd act like I'm something other than a coat rack that mysteriously changes places every time he leaves.

Nope. It's the fruit's fault that the only person I've spoken to in the past week is my mom.

*Whatever*.

Lingering in an empty space that almost feels as hostile as my childhood home isn't going to help, either.

I pack up the untouched breakfast and stroll out the front door.

If Mom's up to getting out of the house today, maybe she would enjoy a picnic in the park. We can get some fresh air and take our minds off everything that's been going on.

Anything but wallow over Alexei, or Father, or her doctor's appointments.

I'm sure she needs the distraction just as much as I do.

At least Alexei took me back home the other day so I could get my car and some more clothes. He said I wasn't a prisoner, but it wasn't until I had the ability to leave freely that I really started to feel like it was true.

Now all I have to worry about is whether Father is home or not.

So far, I've been lucky. But how long will that last? When I pull into the driveway, I blow out a slow breath when his car isn't around. Still, my steps are light as I make my way toward Mom's wing.

She watches the few leaves left on the dead grass through the window, a lone magpie picking at whatever's hiding underneath them.

Before I'm even able to step into the room, my shoulders tense. There's a solemn air around her that makes my limbs heavy, makes me want to turn tail and pretend I never came over at all.

She wears her heart on her sleeve, broadcasting her feelings for everyone to see. And lately, the lows are coming so frequently, so harshly, that it's hard to choke past the fog.

"Hey, Mom," I greet cheerily, hoping to snap her out of her funk. She doesn't respond, just keeps watching the bird like I'm not even here. I move around the room, tidying up her trinkets, and pretend not to be hurt by her silent dismissal.

It'd be so easy to lash out or give up on her when she's despondent like this, but she deserves better.

Mom spends her days alone, and when she's alone, she retreats back into her head. And even if her new drugs should help with the depression, she knows how to hold a grudge just as well as anyone else. If Father weren't such a dickhead, he'd spend time with her, and she wouldn't be left thinking none of us cared about her.

"I was thinking we could go to the park for breakfast. It's nice enough out."

The sun—a miserable, spiteful thing—disappears behind a cloud, making the room that much darker. I swear under my breath.

"Language, Emiliya," Mom mumbles. I could do a little dance for how happy those two words make me feel. Even a reprimand, even if it's only out of instinct, is infinitely better than being ignored.

"If you want to talk about my swearing, you'll have to do it outside. I'm tired of being cooped up. And I made fruit bowls. With all your favorites." With more grumbling and halfhearted argument, she eventually relents and lets me help her to the car.

None of the guards or staff gives us so much as a second look, but when this gets back to Father, there'll be hell to pay.

Oddly, I find it hard to care.

***

Mom leans against the side of the car while I pull a blanket out of the trunk, glaring at everyone and everything that crosses her path. Closing my eyes, I grant myself two seconds to be upset before I plaster my smile back in place and loop my arm through hers, helping her keep her balance as we cross over frozen, uneven ground.

"Do you want to sit under the tree or on the hill?" I ask. "The sunshine might feel nice."

The air bites my cheeks. Sitting in the sunshine is probably the only way this field trip won't have to end in both of us freezing to death, not that I'll admit it out loud.

If we pull the plug on this outing, I'll have to go back to Alexei's and fill his condo with noise until he comes home. After so long being ignored by him, and terrified when I'm home, I'm ready to crawl out of my skin.

Cautiously, I dig through my purse, making sure the key Alexei gave me is still there.

It is, but it's a cold comfort as Mom points to the hill. Silently, we shuffle toward the sunny spot. The longer we walk, she slower she moves. I pretend not to notice.

She's still scowling when I lay out the blanket, putting out our breakfasts while she makes herself comfortable.

The wind cuts between us, sending a shiver down my spine.

"How's Father been?" I ask, desperate to distract us both from the silence swirling around us.

I've spent so much time in my own head that I'm starting to spiral. Without anything to distract me, I'm left with the vicious thoughts and bitter feelings that have me wanting to bury myself so I can sleep uninterrupted.

No expectations.

No demands.

Just merciful peace.

"He hasn't beaten me, if that's what you're asking," Mom mutters bitterly, not looking at me.

A bone-deep weariness presses between my shoulders, making every movement feel next to impossible.

"I didn't think he would."

"He'd have to care about me to do that."

I sigh, not sure if I want to shake her until she sees reason, or cry at how futile it would be. Father's nothing but a monster, and no matter how she sees it, his neglect is the greatest sign of affection he could ever give her.

I only wish she weren't haunted by the way things used to be.

"I haven't seen him since you left," she spits, turning away from me. "He sticks to his wing, and only the maids bother me in mine."

There's a quiet longing in her words that cuts me to the bone, exposing every doubt, callously digging them out for all to see.

Staying with Alexei is my best chance to distract Father. Once he's happy, I'll be free enough to work on my plans. Then, we'll both be free to live the rest of our lives.

But until then, is leaving her in isolation doing even more harm? What's the point of escape if she's going to be even more miserable?

"I can come home, if you want."

My throat squeezes tight as I consider it, but I will. Besides, all I'm really accomplishing is pissing off Alexei's neighbors and letting him feel like he's doing something for me. I'm no closer to him giving a shit about me than I was before the shooting. If anything, I'm only drifting further away.

"No," she declares, spearing a strawberry like it's the one who wronged her. "Your father's going to be angry when you come back. It's better for you to stay away until things blow over. You know how he gets. Even from across the house, I can hear him yelling about one thing or the other."

Unfortunately, I do know.

But why is he being testy this time?

If I want to avoid stepping on a land mine next time I see him, I need to find out.

I need to know if it's because of Alexei, or because I've been gone, or if it's the shooting. Or if it's simply because he woke up on the wrong side of the bed.

I'm quiet while Mom pokes at her food, studiously avoiding looking at me as she continues to glare at anyone who gets within a dozen feet of us.

I can only hope my luck holds out.

***

When I get back to Alexei's, it feels like gravity is going to drag me down through the floor. Pretending everything's okay when I'm with Mom takes everything I have, throws it in a blender, and sets what's left on fire, leaving me drained and unable to carry on with the pretense anymore.

But now that I don't see her every day, this mockery of positivity is even more necessary. If I'm not there to help her manage her own loneliness, then she can't know about mine.

Mom has to see that I'm happy and enjoying myself away from home, or we're both going to buckle under the weight of our disappointments.

Here, in Alexei's condo, there's no performance to put on. I have no audience, and I can let my mind linger on things that matter to no one but me. I can forget all about the doctors, Father's threats, and the stupid feelings for Alexei that refuse to be snuffed out.

I can turn on some music, make as much noise as I want, and cook.

When Alexei gets home, I'll retreat to my room and endure my disappointment and despair without having to appear unbothered.

Then I'll go to bed and prepare to do it all again in the morning.

Picking a playlist that's loud and angry enough to drown out my spiraling thoughts, I pull ingredients out of the cupboards at random until inspiration strikes. With my hands busy and my mind beaten into submission, I let go.

The morning routine of being ignored and avoided is nothing short of agonizing, but in the evenings? I love it.

I'm free to look things up online when I have questions, make a mess, and experiment. Because there isn't anyone to smack my hand with a wooden spoon or glare at me when I don't do exactly what they want me to.

And if Alexei cares, he hasn't said anything.

Every night since I got here, he's been out until long after I'm done cleaning up after myself. And aside from the brief good morning or goodbye when he leaves, we haven't exchanged more than ten words.

But he knows I'm stealing his food.

When I get up every day, the leftovers I set aside for him are gone, and the Tupperware has been washed and put away.

I'll take it as permission to keep going until he says otherwise.

For all I know, he's throwing them out because he thinks I'm trying to poison him.

I snort at myself. I wouldn't put it past him.

"What's so funny?"

I shriek, twisting around with a knife in my hand. Alexei's hands are folded in front of him as he leans against the island.

His eyes glint with amusement, and his self-satisfied smirk pisses me off. If I weren't relying on him to stay out of my way, I'd chuck a knife at his head.

There are other men in the world. Alexei's handsome face and delightful cock can be replaced.

"Where the hell did you come from?"

"The front door." He shrugs. "Mrs. Sullivan doesn't approve of your music choices, by the way."

"Good thing I don't care what she thinks. How long have you been standing there?"

"Long enough to know you're thinking too much."

My cheeks feel hot under his scrutiny.

"Careful," I tell him. "Keep watching me like that, and it'll become a habit."

"There are worse ones to have."

Instead of dissecting his comment too hard, I turn back to the task at hand, expecting to hear his footsteps retreating to either his office or bedroom so he can go back to his usual habit of avoiding me like the plague.

Instead, he pulls out a stool and folds himself in to it, continuing to watch me as I work.

I try to ignore him as I try to finish cooking dinner, but my hands shake more than they should. The whole time his eyes burn a hole in the back of my neck while I curse myself for making enough for two people.

"What did you do today?" he asks.

I sigh, straightening my spine so I don't cave against another wave of nerves.

"Why do you care?"

"I'm curious."

"You know what they say about curiosity, right?"

"I do. But fortunately, I'm not a cat."

No, he's not. A cat wouldn't torture me by asking about my day. A cat would simply accept the free food and leave me alone.

"If you really want to know, I took my mom to the park for a picnic." His brows draw together, and I realize my mistake. Of all the lies I could have told, all the tales I could have spun, I went with the truth.

*Fucking idiot.*

"It's January," he points out.

My hand flexes on the handle of the pan, measuring its weight. "I'm aware."

"Then you know it's fucking freezing, right? Why the fuck would you go on a picnic?"

Because I'm just as selfish as my father and didn't care if we froze our asses off. Because I wanted to enjoy the sunshine with my mom. Because I got Mom's looks, and no one's brains.

I didn't think it through. I just wanted an easy morning.

I don't need to spell out all my flaws for Alexei.

They're already lit up like neon signs over my head. He can find them for himself.

"How's your mom doing?" he asks when the silence drags on to the point of discomfort.

"She's fine," I bite out through gritted teeth.

After the disaster my day was, I don't want to pretend to care about his day, and I don't want to subject myself to Alexei pretending to care about me, either.

"That's good."

"Yep."

The only sound is the food sizzling in the pan. If I thought it would ease the tension, I'd turn back on my music, but every time I glance at my phone, my hands clam up, and I'm paralyzed all over again.

"Aren't you going to ask me about my day?" Alexei prompts. There's no judgment in his voice, only expectation. My jaw clenches.

"I wasn't planning to."

I turn off the stove and stand in front of the cabinet while I try to figure out how many plates I should grab.

There's obviously enough food for both of us, and Alexei's been letting me stay here. He might be an asshole, and I might be being a total bitch, but plating up food for him is the least I can do to say thanks.

"Alright," he sighs, "who pissed you off?"

The tension I cling to bursts, giving way to a surge of frustration that I wield as a shield.

Grabbing a single plate, I put it down harder than necessary. If Alexei wants to eat, he can serve himself.

"Why are you pretending to care? Did you get tired of pretending I don't exist, or do you want something?" My anger reaches a boiling point in my chest. "Or are you planning on giving up this charade and telling me to go home? If you're trying to soften the blow, rest assured, I'll be just fine without you."

Alexei raises his brows as I plate up my dinner, stabbing at it from my spot on the other side of the counter. He keeps staring at me, still and serious, but I refuse to wither under the weight of his stare.

My resentment poisons every cell in my body as the silence stretches between us until I'm exhausted and miserable all over again.

At some point I'll have to get used to feeling unwanted, and for the most part, I am. But with Alexei, it hurts in a way I can't shrug off. I've buried it under layers of nonchalance and hours of practiced ease, but I'm so tired of being hurt by the way he's able to cut me out while I'm still so desperate to impress him.

He stands, and I brace myself for whatever he decides to do, still not looking at him.

He hasn't hurt me yet, not physically anyway, and I don't think he's going to start now, so what's the worst he can do? Throw me out on my ass and make me crawl home with my tail tucked between my legs?

I've faced more humiliation than that and survived.

His arm brushes against mine as he opens the cabinet, and I flinch away from him. He doesn't say a word but gives me space as he loads up a plate with the rest of the food.

I watch out of the corner of my eyes, and the only word I can think of to describe his expression is stoic.

"I'm sure you would be," he finally replies as he sets his plate on the counter next to mine.

"What?"

"I invited you here, but I've been a shitty host. If my sister finds out, she'll tear me a new asshole."

He digs into his food like that's all there is to be said. No apology. No excuse. Just an acknowledgment, and then he treats himself to eating dinner with me for the first time since I came here.

My instincts scream at me to snap at him and tell him to go to hell, maybe to have dinner in my room so he has to eat alone like I've been doing.

But isn't that what he's been doing every night, anyway? And maybe I'm just feeling vulnerable after Mom's terrible mood, but I'm willing to admit that I'm lonely.

Maybe Alexei feels the same way. Maybe he doesn't know how to navigate having another person in his space, but wants some companionship, too.

He's standing close enough that his elbow knocks against mine, causing sparks of something I don't want to acknowledge to dance under my skin, soothing away the lingering irritation.

He won't say he's sorry, but he'll stand next to me and share a meal.

My throat's tight as I swallow my pride.

"How was your day?"

"It was alright." One corner of his mouth lifts, softening his expression. "Better now that I'm home."

# CHAPTER 20

# Alexei

I 'm off-kilter, and I can't figure out how to find my balance again. I can say I was trying to give Emiliya space to settle in, but that's a fucking lie.

The tender feelings she inspires have me in a death grip, and I was clinging to the hope that ignoring them would make them go away, that knowing she was safe would be enough.

So, I ignored her.

I wonder which part has been pissing her off the most. Not having anyone to talk to, or having to make peace with the thoughts in her own head. Based on the way she's been playing music as loud as she can at every possible opportunity, I'm guessing it's the latter.

But I'm not going to complain. Having my condo filled with noise is a relief.

While she's clattering around, I can actually think.

If I could, I'd spend all my days working from home, taking advantage of it, but I need to get out of here and head to another round of meetings. There are no hard feelings from the shooting, at least not from my men, but I've been working around the clock to smooth things over with the Italians.

Giving them back their shipments didn't have the impact I'd been hoping for, and I can't say I blame them for it. Urging Carlo to get out of the fray might have calmed him down, but his boss still assumes it was a planned assassination attempt.

If it were, it would've been a piss-poor one.

I was in just as much danger as Carlo.

Antonio Volotto rules The Outfit with an iron fist, but he seems to assume we're a bunch of bumbling morons. Either that, or he's taking advantage of the chaos to shore up morale on his side.

From what I can tell, he's been successful, too.

At least Emiliya's safe. Everything else is a fucking nightmare, but Nikita can't get his hands on her.

I'm working around the clock, getting out of bed every morning before dawn, but I don't have a nagging voice in the back of my head worrying about her with every breath.

Having her in my condo is far more comforting than it should be. But the fact is I don't know her, not fully, and I don't know what ulterior motives she might have. For all I know, she agreed to stay here because she's hoping I'll fuck her again.

Which I would. Gladly. But she also could be here to gather intel for her father, something that will get him to back off her for a bit.

I wouldn't blame her if she were, but I can't make myself believe that's what she's doing.

As far as I can tell, the only places she's been in my condo have been her room, the living room, and the kitchen.

When I get home each day, my office and bedroom are undisturbed, and she hasn't exactly been asking me for anything Nikita would be interested in, either.

She's just been around, haunting my space like a ghost. A noisy one who leaves leftovers that make it worth coming home at four in the morning, stealing a couple hours of sleep, and leaving again while I'm still half asleep. Her presence is there, but she's a ghost, nonetheless.

After the other night, I've been making a point of coming home so I can hang out with Emiliya for an hour or two before she goes to bed. Sometimes I make it back in time to have dinner with her, but most of the time I've only been lucky enough to sit and have a conversation with her.

It's helped melt the ice wall between us, but the jury's still out on whether that's a good thing or not. At best, having her here is a risk.

I know that, but the alternative makes my skin crawl.

My eyes water as I check my email. Emiliya's been awake before me every morning since she's been here, but she's still asleep. The sun isn't going to rise for hours, but I have to be across town in forty minutes to meet with Artyom.

I should leave her a note so she doesn't think I'm trying to avoid her.

As I search for a pen, there's a pounding knock on the door.

My hand flies to the grip of my gun, ready to pull it out if someone tries to force their way in.

Only Nadya would try to get a hold of me this early in the morning, and if she were on her way, Lev would've given me a heads-up.

And, despite how many times I've told her to, my sister doesn't knock.

My hands are steady as I look through the peephole, swearing under my breath when I see Andrei's surly face.

Fantastic.

"What do you want?"

"Open the door, Alexei."

"Son of a bitch," I mutter under my breath as I swing the door open. Andrei's blank stare greets me as gently as a freight train when he shoves past me. I poke my head into the hall to ensure Mrs. Sullivan isn't hanging around, sticking her nose in my business, but she's nowhere to be seen.

All the noise Emiliya makes has only made her worse. Maybe lying about the soundproofing was a poor choice on my part, but I can't find it in me to regret it when I am greeted by evidence of Emiliya's presence as soon as I step out of the elevator after a long day.

"You know, you could've called."

"So you could brush me off?"

"You sound like my sister."

"Funny you should say that," he scoffs, shooting me a glare, "since, unlike you, I can actually get a hold of her."

"Keep your fucking voice down. I've been busy, alright?"

For a man that everyone complains is too quiet, he sure isn't afraid of being loud as fuck now. I keep my eyes trained on him.

It's only a matter of time before he wakes up Emiliya.

And everyone else on this floor, for that matter.

"Busy," he says with an eye roll. "Then do you want to explain to me why Nikita's been telling everyone who'll listen that you're going to work with him?"

*"What?"*

"He seems to think you're going to do what he wants. And I need you to tell me *why*."

"How the hell should I know?"

He doesn't answer.

Mentally, I flit through everything that's happened since the shooting, searching for answers, but come up empty. Nikita hasn't so much as tried to reach out.

"If he's worked himself into a state of delusion, that's on him, because I have no clue what he's talking about."

Andrei's eyes flash as he spots something over my shoulder, his face thunderous. I take a deep breath, closing my eyes when there's a squeak of surprise, followed by the hurried footsteps of Emiliya darting back to her room.

"Are you fucking kidding me?" Andrei hisses, his nostrils flaring.

"I told you to keep your voice down," I mutter under my breath.

"You're a fucking moron, Alexei."

My skull throbs with tension, and I still haven't had any coffee.

Every line of Andrei's body is vibrating with rage, but I'd expect nothing less. He's made no secret of how he feels about Emiliya, and given she is probably still in her pajamas, I can't brush off her presence as a one-night stand.

I can't pretend she's here for any other reason than because I want her to be. Of course, Andrei's going to view this through the worst lens possible.

"No fucking wonder Nikita's so confident. He has his daughter playing like a violin."

"That's not what this is."

"Yeah?" he seethes. "So, you're not fucking her? She's not running around behind your back until she finds something new to help her climb the social ladder?"

I rub my temples, ignoring the impulse to punch him.

*It's too fucking early for this.*

"No. She isn't."

And I really don't think she is.

As soon as I stood up to Nikita, I needed to be sure of everything I'm doing. The price of uncertainty is higher than I can pay, and if I want to keep Andrei's loyalty, I need him to believe me, too.

He's an infuriating asshole, but he's worth his weight in gold when it comes to getting information or finding a way to make a mess disappear. I need him to back me, because if he's on the other side, he could ruin everything.

"She's doing whatever Nikita tells her to do, *mudak*. If he told her to get whatever she can out of you, do you really think she'd say no? For fuck's sake, she probably fucked Daniil on his orders."

That's a gross thought, but my gut tells me she isn't here because he told her to be. I don't owe Andrei an explanation, but if Emiliya was doing her father's bidding, she would've jumped all over the offer to stay here for a while. She wouldn't have hesitated.

But she did.

Her reasons are her own, and I'm not going to insult her by questioning them. Especially not in front of Andrei. I'm balancing on a high wire where a single wrong move could cost me my life, but I trust her.

"The only person that woman is loyal to is herself," Andrei spits, still glaring at the spot where she was. "She doesn't care who she hurts or what she has to do, only about serving her own interests."

"That's bold coming from you. Last I checked, you pledged your loyalty to your pakhan," I snarl. "How'd that work out for Maksim?"

He doesn't flinch. He doesn't so much as blink. Instead, he rolls his neck, taking a step back so we both have room to breathe.

If it came to light who killed Maksim, Andrei would be dead and buried before he had a chance to do anything about it, but he doesn't look the least bit concerned.

"Fine." He hooks his hands into his pockets, as causal as anything. "If you want to question me and what I've done, you're going to have to pull your head out of your own ass." He sighs.

"You're still our best shot at a decent leader. I've given you my loyalty, and that isn't changing, but don't ask for my help when your relationship with her blows up in your face."

"Get the fuck out, Andrei," I bite out.

He doesn't so much look resigned as he does disappointed as he nods, turning on his heel and striding away.

I'm still grinding my teeth together when the door closes softly behind him.

Several minutes pass before Emiliya pokes her head around the corner, showing off her barely tamed hair, and I'm pissed that Andrei got me mad enough that I can't even enjoy seeing her looking messy and disheveled.

"What was all that about?" she asks.

Checking my watch, I run a hand through my hair. I still have to get to my meeting, and now I have no choice but to be late.

*Motherfucker.*

"Nothing. Try not to worry about it."

"It didn't sound like nothing."

She's uncharacteristically timid, twisting her hands together in the hem of her sleep shirt. If I had time, I'd reassure her that it was all unimportant. I'd tell her that Andrei was talking out of his ass, and I don't care what he says.

But I don't have the fucking time right now.

"Listen, I'm late for a meeting. You going to be okay here?"

"Yeah," she answers a beat later than she should. "I'm good."

I clear my throat and nod, following Andrei's footsteps to the door.

# CHAPTER 21

# Alexei

"All of my contacts are saying it's a no-go. They want nothing to do with you."

"Let me guess. They don't want to work with someone unknown and run the risk of me not being able to finish the job?" I ask, rubbing my temples.

It's the same song and dance no matter where I turn. The Outfit has gladly been sweeping our clients out from under our feet, sending me scrambling to make up for the lost profits.

On top of that, too many men who push product for us have either ended up with bullet holes or in jail, and moving contraband through the state is suddenly nearly impossible, making me wonder exactly how the Italians have managed to get as many cops in their pockets as quickly as they have.

But with my attention split, I can't give the issue the attention it needs.

"That's a polite way of phrasing it, but yeah, pretty much."

Artyom shifts in his seat, antsy, not that I'm surprised. He's not the type of man to be content to sit around and talk. He'd rather be out on the streets, using a combination of wit and force to get what he needs, and under normal circumstances, I'd leave him to it.

But right now, we need to be tactful. We can't afford more violence, no matter how hard holding back has been riding him.

The hope was that Artyom was far enough removed from both me and Nikita that his contacts would still be willing to set something up, but apparently not. Every door and window that's ever been open is summarily being slammed in my face, leaving a path that leads right back to Nikita fucking Dyomin.

"Fan-fucking-tastic," I sigh. "At least tell me everything else is going according to plan."

Artyom glances over his shoulder, his knee bouncing. "Well..."

*Fuck me.*

If he tells me he's having issues with our narcotics suppliers, I'm going to start day drinking.

"Just fix it, alright?"

"Sure thing, boss." He nods easily, standing to leave without any further prompting.

I don't like questioning myself. I've always known exactly what I'm doing, and I've always been able to make a fair guess of how things are going to play out, but now?

I have no fucking clue what I'm going to do. No matter what I try, it's like Nikita's one step ahead, sabotaging me at every turn.

I'm constantly reacting, and if this keeps up, I'm going to crash and burn. I need to be proactive, but there aren't enough hours in the day.

Tension builds behind my eyes, a pounding reminder of how little sleep I'm getting. When the door opens and Andrei walks in, I do my best to trap the snarl in my throat, but I don't know how effective it is.

He folds himself into a chair, observing me as much as I am him. If he feels any remorse for what he said this morning, he shows no sign of it. He's buried his anger away, like it never happened at all.

"You're one of the last people I want to see right now," I tell him honestly.

"I figured."

"Then why are you here?"

I'm too fucking tired to put out any more fires right now, and I don't have the wherewithal to fight with him again. All I want to do is go home, join Emiliya for dinner, and have a single uninterrupted night in my own bed.

"Have you been able to get another meeting with Di Veroli?"

"If I had, do you think I'd be sitting on my ass? His boss thinks I tried to have him killed. They're not exactly champing at the bit to have another chat."

Andrei leans back in his seat, face pensive. "I wonder what Nikita's telling them."

I pause, squinting at him. "What makes you think he's said anything?"

"If The Outfit thinks you tried to have Di Veroli killed, they'd want revenge. So why haven't they done anything?"

Great fucking question.

They've started giving a shit about our dealers when they never have before, and they've been making their presence known along the edges of their territory, but they haven't been outwardly aggressive.

If they had wanted revenge, they would've lashed out by now. If not at me, then at whoever they think is in charge of the Bratva. They'd respond in a hail of bullets and bloodshed. Not gifting us with steely silence and distance.

"Are you suggesting someone's been smoothing things over?"

"I am. And it doesn't sound like it's coming from you."

*Motherfucker.*

From what I've gathered, Nikita's men have been untouched. Hell, they're practically ignoring him. If I could sit down and figure out exactly how many of my problems are caused by that *mudak*, I'd be willing to bet almost all of them would trace back to him in some way.

"I don't suppose you know of anyone in Nikita's camp that may be sympathetic to our cause, do you?"

"Beside your girlfriend?" He raises a brow, his eyes asking a question I don't have the answer to. "No. But I can keep an ear out, and when I find someone, I'll let you know."

That's more than I had an hour ago.

"If this is your version of an apology, it's not the worst one I've ever had." Honestly, it's far more than I would have expected. He could've cut me off entirely, and I wouldn't have had any cause to blame him for it.

That he's here now is an olive branch. One I'm grateful for.

"Don't say that until I find someone. I might still come up empty-handed."

"You never have before."

"No," he agrees. "But I can't make something out of nothing. If there are holes in his ship, I'll find them, but they need to exist first."

"Speaking of," I say slowly, "do you have any leads on my own rat problem?"

Andrei gives me a look, but I cut him off before he can say a word. He can think it's Emiliya all he wants, but if it was her, how did she know I was going to be at Underground when I met with Carlo? Why hasn't she given Nikita the key to my condo and told him exactly where to find me?

If we want to find out who the rat is, we need to look among our own ranks, not at her.

"Fine. We'll say it isn't her." He rubs his jaw. "No one's being forthcoming, and there's only so much I can do without raising the alarm. It's going to be a slow process if you want me to keep digging."

"Then, by all means, take your time."

As sick as I am of sitting around and talking about things I can't fix, I don't have a whole lot of choice. I can't prevent more fires until I put out the ones around me, and I have no choice but to put off any action until either Nikita or Andrei gives me something to work with.

Once he's gone, I dive into some paperwork, only taking a break to check in with the managers at my clubs. When I finally leave, it's dark, and I'm exhausted.

I haven't seen the sun in weeks, and I doubt that's going to change anytime soon. I've been working over every angle for so long that I'm missing the obvious shit. And if Andrei's visits are any indication, others are starting to notice.

I'm burning the candle at both ends, and I need a break before I have nothing left to give.

Tonight, I'm going to try to forget everything else so I can come back fresh in the morning.

As I step off the elevator, I'm immediately assaulted by the dulcet sounds of Emiliya screeching along to her music, a melody best compared to a pack of rabid dogs howling. A glance down the hall confirms that Mrs. Sullivan's door is still shut, and I idly wonder if it's because she's gone for the day, or if she's finally given up.

Either way, it works for me. Emiliya's noise has distracted her from her habit of keeping track of when I leave and when I get home, and if I were more generous, I'd have to find a way to thank her for it.

I follow the racket into the kitchen, where I'm graced by the sight of Emiliya shaking her ass in a pair of loose-fitting sweatpants, dancing with her hair piled on top of her head in a messy bun. As quietly as I can, I sit at the island, all my stress fading away at the sight of her.

With bare feet and wearing a loose crop top, this is easily the least put-together version of her I've seen since her first night here, and it's gorgeous. She dances around the kitchen, happy and carefree, effortlessly making the space her own.

She looks so happy. So free. So mine.

I have to use a hand to adjust my dick in my slacks, almost consumed by just how much her ease affects me.

Emiliya is undeniably sexy when she's all dolled up and putting on a show for the rest of the world, but like this? When she doesn't know she has an audience? She's the kind of beautiful men would go to war for.

And for some reason, she's in my kitchen, making dinner. At ease, even though she doesn't trust me, and all I've managed to do is push her away.

Though I'm loathed to disturb her, I clear my throat, aching to see the way her cheeks flush when she realizes I'm watching.

"What're you making?"

She freezes for a single, nearly imperceptible moment before she whips around with a shriek, throwing the towel that was in her hand at my face. I catch it, chuckling as I drop it on the counter while she glares, pressing a hand to her chest.

Her outrage is cute. I like it far more than I should.

"Stop doing that," she snaps, her face flushed.

"Doing what?"

"Sneaking up on me."

I smirk at the way she rolls her eyes, crossing her arms with a pout as she shifts from foot to foot, like she's self-conscious.

"How do you know I didn't say something when I got home? It's not like you would have heard me." I nod at her phone, and she rushes to grab it.

The silence when she pauses her music is deafening.

"Sorry," she mumbles, throwing her phone into her pocket and ducking her head. Her shoulders slump forward, brows twitching in a frown that she works hard to bury as she turns away.

I fucking hate it.

"Just so we're clear, I wasn't complaining. Be as loud as you want. I don't give a shit, but don't blame me when you can't hear anything happening around you."

I round the island and wrap a hand around her hip, pulling her back against me until her ass is flush with my groin. A flash of heat tears through me, but I hold myself still, content to enjoy the weight of her body against mine for the moment.

It's been far too long since I've had her, and I'm not going to be able to restrain myself for much longer, but for now, I'm content to hold her. I'll gladly keep her with me until I forget what it was like to ever be without her.

"Don't hide from me, Emiliya. Be loud. Be messy, nosy, be whatever the fuck you want, I don't care." I roll my hips just enough to let her feel exactly what seeing her like this does to me. "Whatever you are, I can handle it."

I loosen my hold enough for her to turn in my arms, watching as she eyes me curiously. This close, I can inspect every inch of her face, bare of any makeup. Her split lip has healed, and she looks more tender and vulnerable than ever before.

I lean forward until my forehead rests against hers, our noses bumping together.

She's stiff as a board, and every part of me wants to chase away that tension, eliminate every worry she has.

I want to hold her when she's calm, like she was before she knew I was here. More than once, I've lain awake at night, craving to know who she is when there's no one watching her.

"What if you can't?"

I hate the uncertainty in her voice.

I hate that I can't answer her even more.

"But what if I *can*?"

Her lashes flutter as her eyes drop to my lips, trapping her lush bottom lip between her teeth. I want to pull it free and soothe away the sting with my thumb, but instead I brush my fingers along the exposed skin above her waistband, skimming over the goosebumps that break out on the sensitive flesh of her midriff.

*Give me a chance*, I want to beg. *Give us a chance.*

Even if we're a disaster waiting to happen, I want to hold my breath and jump into the deep end with her. I just need her permission, some indication that I'm not the only one who feels out of control when we're together. Something to tell me she's feeling even a *portion* of the unstoppable pull that I'm feeling.

In answer, she tilts her head to the side, breathlessly granting me access to her lips.

The band that's been stuck around my ribs loosens, letting me fill my lungs for the first time since the night of the shooting when she licks along the seam of my lips, falling against me like she needs this as much as I do.

Fuck, her kiss is the sweetest thing I've ever tasted. She's so fucking hot against me that I wonder if her touch will burn, if she's going to set me on fire and leave behind nothing but ashes.

As I pull her tighter against me, every line and curve of her body fits against mine like she was made for me, and I decide that I don't care.

Let her burn me. Let her ruin me and leave my life shattered. When Emiliya's in my arms, everything feels right. All the struggles are worth it and coming home to her erases all the bullshit and stress that I put up with.

She's worth it.

Reaching around her to turn off the stove, a possessive thrill goes through me as her arms hook around my neck. It's dangerous, but I can't force myself to push it aside right now.

A woman like Emiliya will never belong to anyone but herself. She's a bird that's too majestic to be caged, and even if it means I'll never be able to keep her, I want to see her fly again.

She's giving me the illusion of possession, but I'm setting myself up for failure if I pretend that it's anything other than that.

"Take me to your bed," she breathes against my lips, an unspoken question in her eyes.

It's all the permission I need.

Her weight in my arms is a welcome distraction from the buzzing in my head and the throbbing of my cock as I carry her to my bedroom, my only focus on spreading her across my bed.

Even though the last time we were together, I got her back to my bed, it wasn't for long enough. Not at all.

I want access to all of her beautiful body. I want to see her silky hair spread across my pillow. I want the luxury of time to explore her the way she deserves to be.

With deliberate motions, I slide her sweats and panties down her long legs, running my tongue over every inch of newly exposed skin while I tease my fingers under the hem of her shirt, urging her to pull it over her head. I trace my lips over the birthmark on her shin, a sight that's haunted my dreams since our first time together.

That tiny mark, that little imperfection, only makes her even more stunning, more impossible to ignore.

Regardless of why she's here, no matter what her reasons are, I'm lucky to have her. When this all inevitably goes to shit, I'll find a way to make peace with it. I'll use moments like this to comfort myself when Andrei gloats, and I'll swallow down my bitterness and regrets until I find a way to cope with losing her.

Even when she's inevitably going to ruin me.

When she's bare before me, I take my time pressing kisses against her thighs as I use my shoulders to spread them wide, exposing her wet slit to me. My mouth waters, dying for a taste. I part her lips with my tongue, moaning as I savor the taste of her.

Emiliya gasps, hips bucking against my mouth while I suck on her clit, flicking it with the tip of my tongue.

When she collapses against the pillows, I grind my hips into the mattress, making a mess of the inside of my boxers. Her hands creep toward her tits, and I can't restrain myself from pushing them away so I can take over, rolling her nipples with my thumbs.

She gasps. "*Fuck*, Alexei, your mouth."

I redouble my efforts around a grin.

"You're so fucking gorgeous," I tell her, my voice husky. "And you're even sexier when you come. You're going to scream for me. You're going to give me every drop of your cum until you can't say anything except my name. Can you do that for me, Emiliya?"

Emiliya nods, her cheeks flushed bright red and her lips parted.

"Good."

I'm going to make her understand everything I feel for her in the only way I know how.

Working slowly, I drive her right to the precipice before I pull her back, chuckling against her thigh while she groans in frustration. A light smack against the side of my head only makes me harder.

"Be patient," I tease while she glares at me. "I'll let you come. Eventually."

Her breathy sighs and throaty moans fuel me as I drive her relentlessly to the point of madness, relentlessly working my fingers against her G-spot until she's pulling on my hair. When her pussy begins to flutter around me, I once again pull back before she can topple over the cliff's edge of bliss.

There's a red flush on her chest when she rakes her fingers through my hair, eyes spitting fire while her nails send shivers down my spine.

"If you think you're going to stop me, you're sorely mistaken," I say, my voice husky with desire. "Let me enjoy this, sweetheart."

She's panting when I pull her back for a third time, her pleasure and anger combining in a beautiful storm as I press a kiss against her clit, still refusing to give her the last push she needs. My scalp burns when she tightens her grip in my hair, pulling my head back so I have no choice but to look her in the eye.

"If you don't make me come, I'm going to kill you," she hisses breathlessly.

Her hair has fallen out of her bun, and her lip is pulled back in a snarl, teeth exposed.

Every time I've seen her outside of this condo, she's always neat and put together, but like this, in my bed, in my arms, she's absolutely feral. All her inhibitions are gone.

I'm desperate to see more.

"If I don't, then I'll deserve it."

She releases her grip, urging me back to the task at hand, and I don't waste my time. I fuck her with my tongue, working my thumb in tight circles over her clit that has her throwing her head back.

God, she's fucking soaked, and I've never been so proud to have made a mess.

Her thighs shake around my head, squeezing tight enough to hold me in place, threatening to drown me in her ecstasy. Her climax overwhelms me. The taste of her, the smell of her arousal, the way her muscles seize before her muscles turn to liquid.

I need her. In my home, my bed, my life. I need her in more ways than she's willing to hear, but this will have to be enough. For now, it's enough.

She's still panting as I tear out of my clothes and thrust myself into her, groaning at the sweet relief of her tight cunt, still clenching around me from her orgasm. She's limbless as I pull her hips down, digging my fingers into her sweet flesh.

Emiliya mewls into a kiss, lips bitten-red and slick while I set a slow, hard pace that has me seeing stars.

Thank fuck she's still out of it, because it's an embarrassingly short amount of time before I'm grinding as deep as I can, unloading all my tension as I fill her with my release. I'm only coordinated enough to brush my lips against her, sharing her air while I wait for the ringing in my ears to stop.

# CHAPTER 22

# Emiliya

"Stay put," Alexei says, voice still husky as he presses a kiss to my shoulder before he gets up and heads toward his bathroom. While I'm still blinking back stars in my eyes, he comes back with a warm washcloth, taking his time to carefully clean away the mess before he flops down next to me, twining his arms around me and pulling me close.

My legs feel like they're jelly, and I'm not sure when I'm going to feel up to walking away from him again. And if he decides to give me another demonstration with his tongue, I might never want to.

His arm acts as a weighted blanket, giving me a sense of security and comfort I shouldn't learn to rely on.

But as I take in the relaxed lines of his face, it's a hard thought to cling to.

This is the first time I've ever seen Alexei look so at ease. Without conscious effort, I reach up and trace over the scar on his eyebrow.

From what I've seen, it's the only scar on his body. Alexei's all lean, chiseled muscle and hidden strength, waiting to strike when you least expect it.

A muscle in his cheek ticks, and I pull my hand back as if burned.

"My sister gave me that one," he says, his deep voice rumbling in his chest. His eyes are still closed, seemingly unbothered. Still, it feels safer to rest my hand on his chest, idly stroking the unblemished skin.

"How'd she manage that?" I ask, hoping my voice isn't as shaky as I feel.

My interactions with Nadya have been limited, but she's never struck me as violent.

Uptight and a little bitchy, sure, but what can I really expect? She's protective of Blair, which makes me the villain in her eyes. Whenever I see her, Nadya's bristly and standoffish before I even open my mouth.

I understand it, even if I don't like it.

"When Dad decided I was old enough to learn how to fight, Nadya tagged along to most of our training sessions."

"And he let her?"

"He didn't have a say in it." Alexei shrugs. "When he told her to leave, she refused, and when he tried to force her to, she'd fight back." He huffs out a tired laugh. "She couldn't do much, but she knew how to bite hard enough to make him bleed. Eventually, he gave up."

I try to picture what Nadya must have looked like back then. She's tall and built like a model, but as a kid? She was probably a willowy little thing that could have snapped in half if she were stuck in a strong wind.

And Alexei wants me to believe she fought a grown man and won?

"There weren't any issues until he started teaching us how to use weapons. Turns out my sister is a fucking menace when she has a knife in her hand. It took her less than an hour to teach Dad that you're not supposed to start with real blades, and for me to learn the importance of dodging."

His hazel eyes are warm in the dark room, his expression somehow fond.

"Dad figured I was only bleeding so much because she got my face, and facial wounds always bleed like a fucking fountain, but Nadya cut me to the bone. I'm lucky she didn't get my eye."

I burrow even further into his embrace, shoving my guilt far away from here. I shouldn't be here listening to stories about his childhood while I'm safe in his arms. Not when I'm still holding back so much, still pretending Father has no role in our relationship.

"It'd be a shame if she got your pretty face again."

"You think I'm pretty?"

I hum noncommittally, and his chest shakes with poorly concealed laughter. "Did Nadya learn anything from her first attempt at murder?"

"She learned what it looked like when our dad freaked out," Alexei chuckles. "He was so rattled he botched the stitches, leaving me with this." He taps the line on his brow, his eyes glimmering with amusement. "He didn't let her spar with me after that. He dragged Lev along and worked with Nadya himself."

I smile into his chest as he twists a lock of my messy hair around his finger. My instincts scream at me to go back to my room and make myself presentable, but Alexei doesn't seem to mind what I look like.

If I have to, I'll run damage control in the morning.

For now, I'm going to enjoy being wrapped up in the smell of his cologne and ignore the way my stomach flips as he plays with my hair. I sink into the comfort until I start to drift off, feeling weightless in Alexei's arms.

"I think you two would get along."

Like he's dumped a bucket of water over my head, reality shatters my daydreams and chases off the warmth that's suffused my limbs. I jerk back, putting a gap between the two of us.

"Me and Nadya?"

"Yeah." Alexei's brows furrow. "Why wouldn't you?"

How can he be so smart about some things, and completely oblivious of others? Nadya's best friend is Daniil's widow. No woman would want to buddy up with their bestie's dead husband's mistress.

Just because Alexei gives me room to pretend I'm something else, doesn't mean the rest of the world will indulge me. Especially not his sister.

"Your sister is close to Andrei's new wife, right?" I sit up, clenching my hands in the bedsheets. Without Alexei pressed up against me, the air is cold and sharp, piercing against every exposed inch of skin.

The affection in his expression is gone, giving way to confusion that only makes the creeping sensation under my skin that much more potent.

"Yeah," he sighs. "They've gotten pretty close."

I'm more relieved to hear that than I'm willing to admit. If anyone deserves to have friends, it's Blair. It isn't her fault Daniil was a self-serving jackass, but it is *my* fault for letting myself get caught up in his shit.

Despite what Andrei said this morning, I wasn't doing my father's bidding when I started sleeping with Daniil. I dove headfirst into that shitshow because I was dumb and he was nice to me.

A few kind words and a charming smile. It didn't matter to me that I was hurting someone. I just wanted something for myself. Even if I had to ignore his wedding band to get it.

"I'm not proud of what I did to Blair," I admit, unable to look at him.

Andrei's bitten-back words from this morning echo in my head, burrowing under my skin like splinters I'll never be able to dig out. Father's untampered pride in me for my role in the affair made me feel dirty in a way I know I'll never be able to scrub clean, and I'd take it back if I could, but this isn't a fairy tale.

Wishes don't come true just because you want them to, and the past won't change to heal your regrets.

I have to own my actions, even if they're impossible to make peace with.

Alexei frowns, clearing his throat. "You're not the one who did anything to her."

"I knew he was married."

"So did he. Like you said, *he* was married. Not you." My arms slip around my knees. "Listen, I wouldn't say I'm close to Blair, but I never got the impression she was mad at you. Just the situation."

"Yeah? Is that what Andrei told you?"

His jaw flexes in answer.

Because the truth is, Alexei doesn't know shit. Not about Blair, not about how she feels, and not about me. Before I came along, Alexei didn't give a flying fuck, and the only reason he cares now is because I'm here.

In his bed. His life. His head.

Once I'm gone, he'll go right back to his indifference.

"I'm not looking for redemption, Alexei. I fucked myself out of that ages ago. I'll get over it."

My hair is tangled when I run my fingers through it, trying to control the mess and squeeze back into a familiar role.

My clothing is in a crumpled pile on the floor, right next to his. It's so domestic, and I hate that I have to ruin it, that we can't just pretend we're in some sort of relationship which is based on anything other than ego and lust. But as much as I want to keep up the illusion that we're together because we want to be, it'll only make the inevitable crash hit that much harder.

With layer after layer of denial and false bravado, I bury my feelings with a smirk.

"Anyway, this was fun. Thanks." I wink as I stand, only stopping when Alexei grabs my hip with a firm hand.

He looks both ravenous and furious, like he wants to consume me, bones and all. My heart feels like it's going to explode.

"What, are you looking for a second round already?" I ask, lifting my chin.

I need to get out of here. Away from Alexei. Away from this condo. Away from the riot of emotions threatening to drag me under.

Alexei scowls. "Don't do that." He pulls against me until I'm lying down next to him, then covers me like a blanket. He holds himself up just enough to give me room to breathe, but he's too solid for me to squirm free.

"I thought I told you to stop hiding under that seductive act. I like you better when you're being yourself."

I suck in a harsh breath as he presses his forehead to mine, removing my ability to look at anything but him and the fierce intensity burning behind his eyes.

Alexei's tenderness is bruising, tearing through my walls and threatening to show him all the hollow voids I'm desperate to hide.

"I don't know what you're talking about."

The tenderness in his eyes flickers, like he's holding it on a tight leash. One moment, he looks at me like he needs me more than his next breath, and the next, there's only disappointment.

That single look hits me harder than Father ever has.

Rather than dealing with it, I arch my back as much as I can, making sure Alexei can feel the way the cool air around us has my nipples pebbling against his chest.

I've never been shy about exploiting someone's weaknesses before, and I'll be damned if I give up the only advantage I have now.

"Are you saying you don't like it when I'm trying to get in your pants?"

Alexei sighs, rolling over, and pulling me with him until his arms trap me against his chest. Even though there's a bone-deep ache weighing me down, his arms are so comfortable I could happily lie like this forever.

Eventually, Alexei will move on to something new, and I'll be right back where I started. Even worse, I'll have to deal with knowing what his tenderness feels like, how whole I feel when I'm with him.

With his arm draped over my waist and his breath tickling the back of my neck, it's agonizingly clear that I'm already in too deep.

It doesn't matter if I'm with Alexei because I want to be. Our relationship will always boil down to the original reason I sought him out. And when Alexei finds out the truth, he'll hate me.

He's going to find out. I'm not that lucky, and the world can't be that cruel to him.

Even if I'm terrified of it, he deserves the truth. His disappointment and anger will fucking ruin me.

I have to go home before he finds out.

I'll face Father and whatever punishment he wants to deal out. Then, when he realizes I can't get what he wants from Alexei, I'll face it again. I'll just focus on protecting Mom from the flames when he explodes.

All night, I lie awake, silently begging for sleep, for a break from this torment.

Despite the crushing agony in my chest, I can't bring myself to leave Alexei's arms. With each passing hour, my mind spirals, spinning plan after plan to distract myself.

When his arms tighten around me, I do my best to pretend I'm fast asleep. My mask is brittle as he presses his lips against my forehead before he carefully rises, making sure the blankets are wrapped around me, so I don't get cold in his absence.

Tears burn like red-hot coals held against my flesh while I listen to him get ready.

Once the front door closes, I gather everything I brought with me. It takes twice as long to collect the broken pieces in my chest, clutching them together so I don't fall apart before I get home.

It doesn't matter that I never really unpacked; my limbs are heavy, dragging along as I gather the few things I've left out. A pair of boots here, a hairbrush there. Another sweatshirt I stole from Alexei's closet. All of it gets shoved back into my bag.

I don't know what I'm dreading more: facing Father or Mom and her lingering disappointment. She wants so much more for me, and it kills me that I'm going to remind her of all the reasons I can't have it.

My focus has to be on survival, not reaching above my means. Maybe there's a distant future where I can want things like forever, but that day is a long way off.

"What are you doing?"

I blink, Alexei's voice startling me out of my fugue as I finish putting on my boots.

The pathetic part of me that can't help itself compels me to look up, choked by an unnamable emotion when I see Alexei holding two takeout coffee cups. The same displeased look from last night is still there, cracking my chest in two.

"Figured it was time to head home. We've had a good time, but I'm ready to move on, you know?" I grin, feeling like I'm spitting in the face of something wonderful. "No hard feelings, but I want to see what the other fish in the sea have to offer."

He looks far more composed than I feel. His face is set in stone, but it's impossible to miss the way the paper cups crinkle in his hands.

"That's not happening."

"It is, actually." I wink. My insides feel like they're being carved away one by one. "Thanks for the orgasms. I'll see you around, alright?"

Silently, I beg him to let this go. I don't have the strength to argue with him. Pulling myself out of the wish I didn't know I was still holding on to is the last thing I want, but leaving now is my only chance of surviving the fallout of this.

"You're not nearly as opaque as you think you are, Emiliya," Alexei says, thrusting one of the cups in my direction. He scowls until I tentatively take it from his hand. "But I'm glad to see that you're ready to go, because you're coming with me."

There's no room for argument in his voice, but will that stop me from trying?

No, of course not.

"No, I'm not."

"You are."

With his free hand, Alexei scoops up my bag, snags my keys off the dresser, and walks away, not giving me a second glance. Frustration wars with relief when I storm after him.

"Alexei, give me back my things!"

I chase him all the way to the elevator.

I watch as he uses one hand to hold the doors open and the other to pocket my keys. When he raises a brow, I glance between him and his closed condo door.

Without my keys, I can't get back inside. And it's supposed to be cold as hell today. I stand there, torn, but when Mrs. Sullivan's door cracks open, I make my decision.

I join him on the elevator.

"Would you look at that? Looks like you're coming with me after all."

I turn away before he can see the way my lip trembles.

# CHAPTER 23

# Alexei

E miliya spends the entire drive to Savage pouting. Her arms are folded firmly over her chest; her face is turned toward the window as she does her best to give me the cold shoulder.

It's cute as fuck, but I get the feeling that telling her that would only piss her off more, so I keep my mouth shut.

She can pretend she wants to leave all she wants, but I'd have to be the biggest moron on the planet to miss the truth: last night was more than she bargained for. Whatever this thing is between us, it feels huge, and she doesn't know how to deal with it.

Neither do I, but I'm not going to let her run just because she's scared.

She wants to hide from this mess between us, but I want to cultivate it and see what grows.

Will we crash and burn in the end? Leave each other broken and bitter? Probably, but apparently all those talks Nadya gives me about looking on the bright side have managed to take root, because last night I was taunted by the thought that we might be okay.

In fact, we might end up being something pretty fucking great. But first, Emiliya has to let her guard down and learn to trust me.

And if that means I have to chain her to my side until she's calm enough to handle this shit like an adult, then that's what I'll do.

When I left to get coffee, I wasn't expecting my morning to pan out this way, but since when has Emiliya ever done what I've expected? Being with her keeps me on my toes, but adapting to her is far more fun than it should be.

I just wish she would time it better when she decides to throw a wrench in my plans, but there's plenty of things she can do at Savage to keep her entertained. There are books in my office. We can chat when I'm between calls, she has her phone, and if she really wants to ignore me, there's booze.

When I list it like that, I sound like a real asshole for dragging her here with me.

When I pull into the back lot, Emiliya doesn't move. She continues to stare impassively out the window, not actually seeing anything around her.

"C'mon, Emiliya," I grunt as I get out. In a silent standoff, she finally looks up, meeting me eyes with a challenge I'm not afraid to face head-on. I pat my pocket to double-check that both her keys and mine are still there and lean against the hood, fully prepared to wait her out.

It's freezing cold out here, and even though she was shielded from the wind when she was inside the car, my wool suit is going to keep me warmer than her little dress and boots will her.

Only a few minutes pass before she throws her hands in the air and gives up, slamming her door shut and stomping after me through the back rooms to my office, isolated from the cleaning staff working to prepare for another wave of people tonight.

She's silent even when she sets herself up in the chair across from my desk, covertly taking quick peeks around the room while I dig through the stack of papers in my desk, trying to get everything in order before I call my suppliers.

Still, her silence is far better than the alternative. If I got home tonight and she was gone, I don't know what I would've done, but something tells me it wouldn't be pretty.

Even thinking about her back in Nikita's house is enough to have a murderous rage filling my chest.

Virgo's manager quit on me last week. I need to find a replacement, but between my regular work, taking care of his damn job, and all the other shit, I haven't had the time.

If I weren't drowning in work, I'd at least think about tracking him down and letting him know what I really think about him running out on his responsibilities with no notice or care.

Maybe I'll do it when things settle down. After I've cleaned up the mess he's made of my fucking club and undone all the damage he left behind.

Idly keeping notes, I keep half an eye on Emiliya while the man on the other end of the phone drones on and on about numbers that mean nothing to me.

More than once, Nadya's lamented about how I won't let her handle these calls, but I can't reasonably expect her to negotiate deals for me. I might not be willing to split hairs, but I know enough to understand profit margins and what isn't selling. If I have a constant overstock of certain drinks, I have more wiggle room to negotiate for a lower price point.

But even if I cared about listening to his sales pitch, every time Emiliya so much as sighs, she effortlessly seizes all my attention. With her legs curled up next to her, her boots lying where she discarded them almost immediately, she somehow manages to look perfectly put together and domestic.

Like hanging out with me while I'm working is so common it's unremarkable.

How am I supposed to get anything done when she looks like that? But what other choice did I have?

She was going to run, and I can't let her go. Not now that she's managed to fly free of her gilded cage. When she inevitably flits back home, Nikita's going to lock her up so tight I'll never get another chance to be alone with her.

Who knows what's going to happen to her when she's behind those doors again?

The way she smiles when I see her at the end of the day is the only thing that gets me through the day right now, and when she was in my arms last night, even though she was as stiff as a board, it was the closest I've felt to being happy in ages.

I don't know if I've ever slept as well as I did last night.

If I had the words, I'd tell her I can keep her safe. I'd tell her that if she's with me, she doesn't have to worry about Nikita, but Emiliya's not that gullible.

Every moment of softness she's shown me has an edge to it. She's always holding something back, hiding behind a prickly attitude and an even sharper tongue.

Somehow, I feel like that's Nikita's doing, too.

Emiliya's only ever given me glimpses of who she is when she lets go of everything. A stolen moment over dinner, a flash of something carefree when she thinks she's alone. She's bristly, sassy, and sensitive. And despite everything, she still looks after me, even if she doesn't realize it.

Does she even know what it's like to have someone take care of her?

I want to strip back the layers of hurt and seduction she hides behind until there's nothing left except the woman she spends so much time guarding from the rest of the world.

When she sits up straighter, eyeing me with a mischievous look that promises nothing but trouble, I have to hold back a sigh.

*Goddamn it.*

Nothing good has ever come from that look.

With exaggerated slowness, Emiliya stretches her arms above her head, showing off the long lines of her body, her dress stretching over every curve like it was made for her.

"I assure you, Mr. Trenin, it would be well worth the added expense," the voice on the phone says, loud and excited when I grunt noncommittally. I'm far too focused on the woman in front of me to know a damn thing he just said.

Emiliya tilts her head to the side, evaluating before she stands, moving around my desk with a wicked grace until she's able to urge me to sit back, and slowly sink into my lap, her knees on either side of my hips.

"I'll call you back," I bite out, hanging up even though the supplier's still arguing with me. My phone lands face down on the top of the glass desktop while I eye her, curious how she's going to play this.

Of everything I adore about Emiliya, one of my favorite things is that she's as transparent as glass once you know what to look for.

From the conflict behind her eyes, the insecurity, she wants to distract me. She wants me to think about anything else so I'll let down my guard and she can slip away while my back is turned.

For once, I'm not going to give her what she wants.

Seduction is a careful dance with her, and this time I'm not going to get caught up in it. Not until we sort this out.

Her eyes are calculating, and she slips her hands around my neck, capturing her plush bottom lip between her teeth.

Fuck, why does she have to look so pretty like this?

"What're you doing, Emiliya?" I ask, running my thumb over her cheek bone.

"I'm bored," she says, voice lilting before she leans forward, brushing her lips against mine, practically begging me to let her pull my attention away.

She turns me on as easily as she breathes, and there's no point in pretending she can't feel the way my cock tests the limits of my zipper underneath her.

I ignore it.

She grinds down, her heat scorching through the layers of fabric between us. There's a small smirk gracing her lips when my hands drop to her hips, but it fades when I hold her just tight enough to still them.

"You can't fuck me until I forget about this morning, Emiliya."

She freezes. Only for a moment, but long enough.

"What makes you think that's what I'm doing? What if I just want to feel your cock stretching me open?" She bats her lashes. "What if all I want is to make you feel good?"

"I'm not going to let you run. That's not what's going to happen between the two of us."

Her eyes dart away, and I move one hand to the small of her back, holding her against me when she tries to stand.

If she didn't want to have this conversation, she could've stayed on the other side of the desk and ignored me. Instead, she pushed the issue.

Now she's going to listen to me.

No woman has ever made me feel even a fraction of what I feel for her, and part of me wants to tell her the truth: I'm falling for her.

I'd rather she threatened me—rather she told Nikita everything about me—than suffer through her leaving, even if she's not ready to hear it.

"You can be scared, but you don't get to act like there's nothing here. Don't insult me like that." Her only movements are the rapid rise and fall of her chest. She looks like a panicked bird, desperate for escape.

"I don't know what you're talking about."

"You do." She turns her head away. "You *do*, Emiliya."

She shifts, unsuccessfully grasping for the bravado she clings to whenever she doesn't know how to deflect attention. When she presses her hands against my chest, her pulse flutters in her throat, rapid and terrified.

"Are you saying you don't want me, Alexei? Because if you don't, I'm sure I can find someone else who does."

My hand lands on the back of her neck, pulling her even closer. I press my forehead against hers, waiting until she meets my eyes.

Outside this room, everything presses down on us in every moment. But not now. For a moment, a single, peaceful moment, it's just the two of us.

"Forget everything else and focus on me. For once, just trust me."

Her breath is hot against my lips, conflict apparent in her darting eyes. Will there ever be a day when she trusts me enough to tell me what she's thinking? Or will she always pull back and push me away?

When I kiss her, it's slow. Almost luxurious, even. It feels like a promise; one I hope she understands.

*I won't hurt you.*

*I can take care of you.*

*You're safe with me.*

She doesn't flinch, content to let me control the pace. When I pull away, she looks as vulnerable as I've ever seen her. Content and scared, with something tender mixed underneath it all, something that she works so hard to hide.

It echoes everything burning in my chest.

Being with Emiliya feels like coming home. She makes all the chaos and uncertainty bearable. I can't let her go because I won't be able to hold it together if something happens to her, and I'll destroy anyone who tries.

Even her father.

*Especially* her father.

Sooner or later, everything with him is going to come to a head. If I'm being honest with myself, it's no longer about the Bratva. If he hadn't appointed himself pakhan, I'd still be working toward his death.

No matter what, I'm going to protect Emiliya. It doesn't matter if she wants me to or not, she doesn't deserve to go through everything alone. She never has, and she never will again.

"I don't know how," she whispers, her eyes half closed as she leans into me.

I don't either, but, fuck, I want to try.

I brush my fingers against her hip, over the spot where her tattoo is hidden. I picture it in my mind, the cluster of flowers, each one remarkably detailed for how small they are.

"Tell me about your tattoo," I say, the request coming out like a prayer.

She blinks, slow and dazed, like she's confused. "What about it?"

What can I say to make her understand?

I want to know everything about her. Her favorite color. Her dreams. Her favorite song. Why she only dances when she's alone.

There's no detail about her that's too small, too minute, to be unremarkable.

"Anything. When did you get it? What kind of flower is it? Did it hurt?"

With time, I'll learn more, but we can start with something small.

We can start with this.

Her face is wary as looks at me, chewing the inside of her cheek. "It's alyssum. I got it when I was seventeen and going through a phase." She huffs a breath, not quite a laugh, but close enough. "Mom lost her mind when she found out. She threatened to never let me leave the house again."

"Is that why you only have one?"

A corner of her lips lift, and she looks more like herself.

"No. Turns out I hate getting tattooed." She raises a single shoulder.

"Really?"

"I don't like the pain," she chuckles. My heart thuds painfully at the broken sound.

"Does it mean anything?"

There's a long pause before she answers, "Alyssum means worth beyond beauty."

My chest cracks open at the soft way she says it, like she's bracing for me to laugh. I rub my thumb in slow circles over the back of her neck, refusing to let her hide.

"You have that in spades, sweetheart."

Slowly, she relaxes until her muscles are no longer coiled tight, prepared to flee at the first opportunity. It's everything I want and more.

My office door slams open, making my blood run cold in an instant.

Using one hand to press Emiliya's head against my chest, I use the other to rip my gun out of my waistband, ready to lay waste to whoever is disturbing us, whether they're a threat or not.

And when I look up, for the first time in my life, I see my sister look afraid.

Nadya is pale, frozen mid-step. Her mouth gapes. She's terrified.

Because of *me*.

Betrayal flashes in her eyes even as I do my best to minimize the damage, dropping my gun on my desk as quickly as I can. She watches every move like she's worried I'll strike at her.

"What have I said about knocking?" I all but snarl, wishing I could take it back when I notice the way Nadya's shaking, her eyes still glued to my gun. She takes a half step back.

I can't undo this.

All the groveling in the world won't change the way Nadya's looking at me, like she thinks I would actually hurt her. It won't calm my racing heart.

"You've never— I didn't think you'd pull a gun on me for it." Her eyes flick to Emiliya as she tries to turn her face further away from the doorway, doing her best to hide when she's right in the open. I wrap my other arm around her shoulders, doing what little I can to comfort her.

Nadya's cheeks are pink, her eyes fixated on Emiliya's discarded boots.

"I wanted to talk to you about the Konstantin thing, and you've been screening my calls." She refuses to look at me, ignorant of the way I freeze, desperately willing her to shut the fuck up.

Emiliya's stiff as stone, tilting her head as she listens. All of Andrei's warnings come rushing back, filling the space left behind as she pulls away.

"I want to help, Alexei. I'm sorry for interrupting, but your problems aren't going to go away just because you're ignoring me."

Any knowledge of my association with Lavrov would be priceless to Nikita. If he ever gets his hands on Emiliya again, it would be a get-out-of-jail-free-card next time he goes after her.

It might even be enough to buy her freedom.

"It isn't a good time, Nadya."

She snorts weakly, her eyes flicking back to Emiliya and me.

"Clearly."

Emiliya takes a peek over her shoulder, and it's just my luck that it's at the same time Nadya is looking.

Her lingering fear disappears into the ether, replaced by the disappointment that always pops up when she spends too much time with me, no matter what I do to keep it at bay.

"Really, Alexei? Out of everyone, you picked her?"

Like every time since I was a kid, I don't know how to react to the fact that I'll never be the brother she deserves. I go numb, hardly fighting when Emiliya turns around, eyes blazing with an anger I'd probably find attractive if the situation were different.

"What the fuck do you mean, *her*?"

Nadya sighs, taking in the room with new eyes. I expect to see judgement, but if it's there, it's buried under her dismay.

"I mean that I thought my brother had better judgment. I thought he'd avoid someone who's gone out of their way to hurt other people."

"At least I know how to be something other than a frigid bitch who not even her own brother wants to deal with."

Nadya sucks in a shocked breath like she's been slapped.

"Emiliya, that's enough!" I snap, but her lips are still curled in a snarl, her muscles tense enough that I'm worried she's going to go after my sister.

"And at least I'm able to get people to like me without having to jump into bed with them," my sister snipes back.

"Nadya, *enough*," I command.

Her jaw snaps shut as she glares at me. It's enough to tear down the remains of the numb walls I'd erected, and the force of her anger hits me full force, gutting me as she lifts her chin dismissively.

I'll always defend my sister until the day I die, but I'm not going to let her tear down the woman I love.

As much as I don't want to admit it to myself, that's exactly what this is. I'm not just falling for her, I'm already flat on my ass in love with Emiliya.

I'm fucked. Totally, completely fucked.

Taking a deep breath, I will the smell of Emiliya's shampoo filling my lungs to calm me as she pulls away.

"Nadya, go home. I'll call you later. We can talk about the issue after you've cooled off, but until then, get the fuck out of my office so I can get some work done."

Her back is stiff as she nods, swallowing thickly.

"Fine." Her face is carefully blank, but she can't hide the way her eyes shine with hurt. "I sincerely hope you can be bothered." Turning on her heel, she walks out, leaving us alone.

Emiliya's chest is still heaving, ready to defend herself. I slump backward when I let her go.

She stands like she's been burned, her hands shaking.

When the door at the end of the hall slams shut, it feels like a death knell.

I don't even know what I'm more upset about: Emiliya's distress, or Nadya thinking I won't call.

"I'm sorry."

Emiliya's quiet voice draws my attention back to where she's standing. Her shoulders are curled forward, and her gaze is fixed on the ground at her feet.

"I shouldn't have let her get to me."

This is all my fault. If I hadn't put off dealing with my sister, none of this would have happened.

"I'm not the one you need to apologize to. Besides, she owes you one, too." There's no conviction in my words, only an empty sense of failure. I've managed to fuck up everything in less than a day, and I don't know how to fix any of it.

"C'mon. Let's just..." I clear my throat against an awful wave of emotion. "Let's go home."

The paperwork will still be here in the morning, and the negotiations can wait. I need to spend some time nursing my wounds before I'm ready to face anything else.

# CHAPTER 24

# Alexei

The few birds brave enough to face winter head-on jump from branch to branch, not even pretending to have the energy to sing in this biting cold. My fingers flex in my gloves as I try to restore some semblance of feeling while I check my watch.

Again.

Another five minutes had passed, but Nadya isn't here. I'd worry if Lev hadn't already sent me a text letting me know she still hasn't left her place.

I just wish I knew whether she was avoiding me because she's still shaken up, or because she's pissed and punishing me for what happened.

Nadya's the one who said we should meet in this fucking park in the freezing cold, so here I am. If making me wait is her path toward justice, then fine. I'll sit here until she either deigns to show up or until Lev tells me to give up and go home.

If he can be bothered. It's not like he gave me a heads up when Nadya apparently decided to systematically check each of my clubs in order to hunt me down.

Probably because he thought it was funny.

Fucking asshole.

It's fine. As long as she doesn't shut me out entirely, I'll find a way to deal with it. Even if it means I have to sit in this park and freeze my dick off.

A squirrel tries to snatch a small hoard of breadcrumbs from a couple of geese, only to be chased off in a flurry of hissing and flapping wings. Undeterred, he plasters himself to the side of a tree, shuffling around while he watches the geese, waiting for an opening.

He skitters behind a tree, snapping my attention to the figure making their way down the path toward me. One that is definitely not my sister.

Nikita adjusts the sleeves of his coat, his eyes burning with malice and his posture oozing with his trademark sleazy charm. I don't know how the fuck he found me, but I have to give him some credit for it.

I'm alone here. I didn't bring anyone else.

Why would I? This wasn't supposed to be a whole showdown, just a chance for Nadya and me to hash things out.

And, because I trusted things to be straightforward for once, I've left myself wide open, sitting on a bench in the back of a nearly empty park, hidden from view by barren trees and frozen foliage.

It's the perfect spot for an ambush.

Sitting stock-still, I sort through my limited options.

If I go for my gun, I'll have an unknown number of them pointed right back at me. If I try to fight him, someone will make sure I don't get to finish the job. And there's no chance in hell I'm running from this.

With next to no effort, Nikita's pinned me into a corner of my own making.

At least Nadya isn't here, too. I've never been more grateful for her vindictive streak than I am now.

"You're a difficult man to track down, Trenin."

"Did you consider calling? I have business cards if you need my number."

"Not necessary." His glare does its best to burn, but the cold wind has long since left me numb.

How the fuck did he know I was going to be here? And how am I supposed to make sure Nadya doesn't come now? The fact that my phone remains silent in my pocket is a pitiful comfort against the panic clawing up my throat.

"How has the dust settled since your little attempt to work things out with The Outfit?" At a glance, Nikita seems calm, despite the annoyance glinting in his eyes.

"Better than you likely suspected."

Is it smart to taunt him? No.

Have I ever been someone who is praised for my intelligence? Also no.

But if I'm going to walk away from what I hope is just a conversation, I need time to figure out a plan. I need time to work through how severely fucked I am, and stalling is the only tool at my disposal.

"You think you're clever, don't you?"

"Not particularly."

"Just as well." Nikita smiles like a shark, practically salivating for blood. "You're not smart enough to lead an army of ants out of a paper bag. But I will give you some credit, Alexei. You managed to inspire loyalty in more men than I thought you could."

"How generous," I deadpan.

How anyone manages to put up with his condescending attitude, I have no clue. And with his all-consuming delusion that power is something owed to him, he's a walking recipe for disaster every time he opens his mouth.

"Watch the attitude, Alexei."

The amount of fear he's managed to invoke in Emiliya is mind-boggling. She doesn't suffer fools, but she's so terrified of Nikita that she doesn't say a word against him, even when she's safe in my condo.

Without a care in the world, Nikita sits on the bench next to me. Every violent thought, every silent promise I've made to Emiliya, demands I lash out and exact revenge, but this isn't the place.

Anything I do to him would be returned to me tenfold, likely before I'm even able to blink. I glance around, searching for the audience he's no doubt planted.

Since we were teens, this is where Nadya and I would come to escape from everything else. When we've wanted to forget, or talk without worrying about anyone else listening, we've sat on this bench. Whether we loved or hated each other on any given day, we had this.

Nikita being here has ruined it. I'll never be able to come back without looking over my shoulder, even if I do manage to walk away from this.

"I'm willing to work with you," he continues, "so long as you're willing to give up the silly notion that you're fit to run anything. Other than your little nightclubs, of course."

I clench my jaw so hard it aches.

"You mean the little clubs that clean more than eighty percent of our cash? The ones that keep the IRS from breathing down our necks?"

He rolls his eyes. "Your pet projects do just fine for what they are, but let's not pretend someone else couldn't do better. Really, Alexei, your father would be disappointed in you. At least he knew his place."

I scan the tree line to cover the instinctive response trapped in my chest. My dad was an idiot who believed in a cause that never really existed, but he always made it clear that he wanted more for Nadya and me.

If anything, he'd be proud of what I've accomplished without him.

Now that I'm taking the time to look for them, Nikita's men don't blend in with nature as well as they think they do. To my left, the tip of a worn boot pokes out by the roots of a tree. In front of us, the hem of a wool coat rustles with the breeze, flashing one moment and settling back behind the trunk the next. Like he can read my mind, someone behind us clears their throat.

He isn't close, but when I can't see him, he's far too close for comfort.

How the fuck did I miss them moving in? I was distracted, sure, but that's no excuse to waltz right into a waiting attack and be caught unaware.

My hand itches, but I'm not sure if I want to reach for my gun or my phone more.

Fighting would be suicide, and calling for backup would be pointless. But if someone comes, they can warn Nadya off from coming here.

If someone gets here before things go too far, there's a better chance she'll have something to bury other than an empty coffin.

Nikita runs a hand over his mouth. "I would have thought you would be more eager to claw your way out of obscurity, you know. At one point, I thought that might have been why you're fucking my daughter, but perhaps I was giving you too much credit."

*What?*

My face has been fixed in an emotionless mask since I first spotted him, but I'm not sure if I'm able to cover the way my blood boils and static screeches in my ears.

How the fuck does he know about my relationship with Emiliya? The number of people who know anything about us is so small it's negligible, and every time Emiliya has left my place, she's either been with me, or she's been with her mother.

*Or so she says,* a scornful voice in the back of my head taunts, digging its claws into every doubt and every shadow I try to ignore, dragging them to the light. *You don't really know where she's been.*

I only know what she's told me, and I can tell myself that she has no reason to lie to me, but that doesn't make it true. It's entirely within the realm of possibility that she's been taking every morsel of information I've given her and feeding it right to Nikita.

For all I know, she's telling him everything the moment she's alone.

The only people who knew where I was going to be today were Nadya and Lev, but Nikita still managed to figure it out. How much of a stretch is it to think Emiliya might have found out?

She was right down the hall when I talked to Lev last night. It wouldn't have been hard for her to stand outside my office and eavesdrop. For all I know, she might have even planted bugs when I was out, and I'd have no fucking clue.

I've all but given her free rein of my condo with the intention of giving her space and making herself comfortable, but I have no assurances that she hasn't abused it.

Maybe this is the wake-up call I've needed.

Emiliya has hesitated and fought against me every single step of the way. I thought it was because she was scared, but maybe she's just a nervous rat.

*No.*

She couldn't fake the bruises. She can't fake the way she flinches every time I've ever moved too fast or when I reach toward her to tuck her hair behind her ear.

Maybe she's just looking out for herself and her mom. What if she's only ever told me the truth, and our relationship is just a byproduct?

*Blyad.*

The air in my lungs is heavy, threatening to drown me.

Somehow, Emiliya knew I was at Underground. She could have found out where I was today. Every time something's gone wrong, she's been right there.

As much as I hate myself for it, at some point, I have to admit that my feelings are enough to give me a mile-wide blind spot when it comes to her.

All she had to do was smile, and I looked the other way while she set me up.

"Oh, don't tell me," Nikita sighs, his sympathetic grin belied by the sharpness of his teeth. "Did you manage to fall in love with her?" When I don't answer immediately, he laughs, the sound loud and echoing among the frozen trees. "Oh, Alexei. I thought you were smarter than that, but the truth is written all over your face."

He leans back, his legs crossed at the ankles. Triumph pours off him as stretches, savoring this victory.

"What a shame to see a man collapse under the weight of his own arrogance."

If I walk away from this, Andrei's never going to let me live this down. Honestly? I hope he doesn't. I hope he reminds me that he told me exactly what was going to happen, but I was too blind to see it.

This isn't the kind of lesson I want to learn more than once.

"Did you think Emiliya actually *cared* for you? Let me give you a tip: women like her are good at lying to get what they want. They make you think they give a shit, but they're only interested in themselves and what you're able to do for them.

My *printsessa* got what she wanted, and, really, what can you do other than keep her entertained?"

I don't even bother arguing with him. The only thing I'm able to offer Emiliya is safety, but even that's temporary. Beyond that? I'm useless.

Nikita already funds her whole life, and if she wants a quick fuck, she's made it clear she can get it from someone else.

While I've been falling right under spell, Emiliya's never seen me as anything but another tool in her arsenal.

The worst part is she never pretended it was anything else. She's always been clear about what she wants from me. I'm just the idiot who thought I was different.

"You seem to be under the impression that what I have with her is anything more than physical." I shrug, the lie bitter on my tongue. That might be all it is to her, but it was so much more to me. It was something that felt a lot like forever.

But it was all smoke and mirrors. A mirage in a barren, lonely desert.

"Has it ever occurred to you that if she's running her mouth to you, she might be doing the same with me? Your daughter doesn't exactly have a glowing reputation. Only an idiot would trust her with anything sensitive."

Nikita smirks, seeing right through my bluff.

"And yet you welcomed her into your home." He shakes his head, every inch the patronizing dick I thought he was. "But don't be hard on yourself. We've all been distracted by a pretty face, haven't we?"

This morning, I would have said that I never had, but that's because I'm an idiot.

I invited a mole into my home, into my bed, and then I had the gall to fall in love with her. The word *moron* might as well be tattooed across my forehead in big, red letters.

"I have other appointments to get to, but I'll see you around, Alexei. Let me know when you pull your head out of your ass and fall in line like a good soldier. After all, you know how to find me, don't you?"

As he walks away, I wait, watching every man emerge from their hiding places, weapons in hand as they eye me. Five men glare at me as if I've personally wronged them while they stand guard for a coward. Each one heard everything Nikita said and will waste no time gossiping like children about how their chosen leader has thoroughly duped me.

I'll have to add the fight to recover my reputation to my to-do list.

But first, I need to deal with everything I learned today.

In approaching me, Nikita showed more of his hand than he likely thought he would. He hasn't gone near Nadya the whole time this feud has been building, but he approached me himself. Because Emiliya doesn't know what Nadya's doing or where she is.

Emiliya only has access to me.

Thank fuck, because I need Lev at my place as soon as he can get there.

I don't move, checking and rechecking my surroundings to make sure there isn't anyone else lying in wait before I pull out my phone.

"I'll be there in ten minutes, just hold your fucking horses," Nadya snaps as soon as she answers. I close my eyes, my heart rate returning to something closer to normal.

My life is falling apart, and I can barely tell which way's up, but at least Nadya's safe.

"Actually, I have to reschedule."

"Fucking of *course* you do."

I smile at the exasperation in her voice, able to picture her eye roll and the way she throws her hands up in frustration no matter the distance between us. I can't trust my own judgment, or my heart, or anything else, but I can trust Nadya.

She's exactly who she says she is. She has my back, even when all I do is piss her off.

"I'll make it up to you. How about I come over sometime this week? I'll bring takeout and we can catch up."

A beat of silence, then she hums with a smile I can hear. "Fine. But if you cancel again, I'm going to quit my job and go work for a bank."

"Why would you want to work with those criminals?"

Despite how strained things have been lately, she laughs, and it settles the ground beneath my feet. It does nothing to ease the ache in my chest, but it makes me feel like I can breathe around the heartbreak.

# Chapter 25

# Emiliya

I'm not sure what I was expecting to happen as a result of my standoff with Nadya, but I wouldn't have put my bet on things remaining largely unchanged. If anything, things between Alexei and me have been even easier.

The compulsion to run still screams in the back of my mind, and the way Alexei clings to me when we're together gives me the sense he knows it too, but it's getting easier to ignore it every day.

As soon as he gets home, he seeks me out, either joining me for dinner, or sharing a drink while we talk about our days. Even if all I do is rearrange his kitchen out of sheer boredom, he wants to know every detail.

Then, when there's a comfortable silence between us, he beckons me into his room, either fucking me until I pass out or holding me against him until I give in and fall asleep, safe and secure in his arms.

I must be the numbskull my father accuses me of being, because I like it.

No matter what I do, the soft, delicate feelings in my chest that I've worked so hard to ignore have taken root, and if I don't treat them like the invasive species they are, I run the risk of losing myself to them completely. They'll choke out all other signs of life and leave me with nothing but a broken, cracked foundation.

Instead of doing everything in my power to eliminate it, I've been leaning into it. Fanning that little ember when it grows dim, letting myself kiss Alexei tenderly when I should be worrying and finding an emergency exit.

I fiddle with a leaf on Alexei's sad excuse of a pothos as I try to figure out how much liberty I should try to take here. I've taken free rein of the plants in his kitchen, living room, and bedroom, but this is my first time poking around in his office.

Am I overstepping if I try to save this plant?

Then again, Alexei pays so little attention to them, I doubt he'd even notice if I threw it out and replaced it with a new one.

From how limp the few leaves are on this guy, I might have to do that anyway, no matter how much I want to save it. I pluck off another dead leaf with a sigh, dropping it into the trash with all the others.

"What'd you do to be treated like this?" I ask idly. "Did you look at him the wrong way? Tell him you didn't like one of his suits?"

I exhale as I find an entire strand of leaves that are dead, tracing the rot and decay all the way back to the roots.

This thing doesn't need TLC; it needs a fucking necromancer.

Regardless, I have to try.

I've already worked my magic on the plant in his bedroom, and it looks a hundred times better than it did the first time I saw it. The snake plant in the living room was a goner, but hopefully I can get a chance to run to a plant nursery next week and pick up something to replace it.

When I'm done, I'm going to make careful, foolproof notes for Alexei so he knows how to do something other than make his plants suffer.

Seriously, how the hell did he manage to kill a snake plant? Even the maids at home haven't managed to kill one, and I'm pretty sure they put rat poison in my plants when I'm not paying attention.

I'm so focused on pruning that I don't notice Alexei coming home and standing in the doorway until he clears his throat, making me jump so high the dead vine in my hand snaps in half.

"I thought I told you to stop sneaking up on me," I grumble, even though it's impossible not to smile at him.

He doesn't return the gesture, but he rarely does.

He shows more emotion in his actions than he does with his face, but right now the typical ease I usually find in the set of his shoulders is missing. His mouth is twisted into an uncharacteristic frown as his sharp eyes carefully take in every move I make.

Dropping another leaf into the trash, I turn to give him my full attention.

"Is everything alright?"

"What're you doing in here?" he asks sharply.

"Trying to keep your plant out of the grave." I shrug, pretending his cold tone doesn't hurt. Even though I know he won't hurt me, my muscles are coiled tight, prepared to flee if his dour mood takes a turn for the worst.

I'm no stranger to someone taking their frustration on me.

I'd rather be wrong and prepared for him to lash out than add him to the list of people I picture bleeding out when I can't sleep at night.

"Right," he scoffs under his breath, making me sit up even straighter.

"Are... Are you okay? Did something happen?"

He's a blank slate, just like he was when Nadya and I argued the other day. He gives me no indication of what he's feeling.

My stomach drops.

"There's been a change of plans."

Dread settles in around my shoulders, a familiar, awful weight.

"Which plans?"

He looks over his shoulder, and for a moment, he almost looks conflicted, but in a blink, it's gone. He's back to looking at me with a stone-cold stare that makes the breezy winter roaring outside the window look warm and cozy.

"Come with me. We need to talk."

I dust my hands off over the trash can before I reluctantly follow him, the dread growing until it's sitting like a stone on my chest.

Is this about my argument with Nadya? Did it just take a few days for my fuckup to sink in? Because if he wants to chew me out, that's fine. I can cope with words, but the waiting, anticipating his every move and focusing on every micro-expression on his face, is going to wear my nerves down to threads.

I take my usual seat on the couch, but rather than joining me, he remains standing, hands deep in his pockets.

When there's a knock at the door, a corner of his lip curls up in a smirk that doesn't meet his eyes.

"Perfect timing." He strolls out of my sight to answer the door, while I try to push off the unease that's threatening to choke me. "You know my cousin Lev, right?" Alexei motions to the man following him, then leans against the wall, his eyes looking through me, oblivious of my distress.

I nod slowly, recognizing him from the first night at the club. I raise my hand to wave, but my anxiety only gets worse when he greets me with a dead stare in return.

With his dark, buzzed-short hair and hooded eyes, Lev is dark and malevolent, where Alexei is charming and cunning. I never would have guessed they were related.

"Great, then we can skip the introductions. He's going to be keeping an eye on you from here on out. He's going to drive you to your mother's appointments, and he's going to ensure you stay exactly where you're supposed to."

"Like a guard?" I ask hopefully.

"No. Not a guard." Gone is the gentle way he looked at me when he kissed me this morning. Instead, he's looking at me like I'm nothing but a stranger. "When I invited you here, I told you that you weren't a prisoner." I swallow the lump in my throat. "That is no longer the case."

The blood drains from my face so fast I'm dizzy, falling back and dragging my knees to my chest, clinging to all my pieces before I shatter.

"Did something happen?" My voice is barely a whisper.

*Why are you looking at me like I'm less than gum on the bottom of your shoe?*

Out of the corner of my eye, Lev makes a show of coughing into his fist to cover a laugh. I toss a glare in his direction, but Alexei doesn't even react.

For some reason, that hurts more than anything he's said so far.

"I was supposed to meet my sister today. But you already knew that, didn't you?"

When he pauses, I nod hesitantly. "You mentioned it."

"And can you imagine my surprise when instead of seeing Nadya, I was greeted by your father?"

Oh, *fuck*.

Father's been suspiciously quiet since I left, and the relative tranquility with Alexei has made it all too easy to forget.

For once in my life, I haven't spent every moment straining my ears for his footsteps, and that oversight was a mistake I'm not sure I'll ever make up for. If he's tracking down Alexei, he hasn't just noticed my absence, he's decided to take advantage of it.

He's pissed. And he's going to make sure I know it.

"Are you alright?" I look him up and down, checking for signs of injury I might have missed, any sign that Father's gone after him.

"Oh, I'm just fine. Nikita was feeling generous today. But you knew that too, didn't you, *printsessa*?"

"Don't call me that," I protest on instinct before the accusation in his eyes hits me. For a moment, I'm stunned into silence. "D-do you think I told him where to find you?"

"No, of course not," he drawls, his voice dripping sarcasm. "I know you did. He told me as much. Your father was so kind as to let me know all about your arrangement with him."

My stomach drops like a stone, making me dizzy. "What arrangement?"

"The one where you're doing whatever he tells you to. You know, the one where you play me for a fucking fool and you both get everything you want from me."

I swallow, but my mouth is bone dry. "I'm not—"

Fuck, aren't I, though? I'm doing exactly what Father would have told me to, and I haven't tried to push back against it. No matter how much I protest, I'm still here, doing exactly what he wants. I'm still keeping an ear out for anything that I might be able to use for leverage when I need it.

"I didn't tell him where you were. I didn't even know!" My protest sounds weak even to my own ears.

"Then who told him, Emiliya?"

"I don't know." He raises a skeptical brow. "I don't, but it wasn't me."

"Right." He rolls his eyes. "Given your history, what else should I have expected? The apple never does fall far from the tree, does it?"

Casually, without a care in the world, Alexei checks his watch while I blink back tears.

"I don't have any more time to waste on you today. Lev, I take it you can handle this?"

*This.* Like I'm a burden. Not a person, but an inconvenience that he has to work around.

"Sure thing."

"Great. I'll see you later."

He doesn't acknowledge me before he leaves, and my breaths are shaking while I look around. The space is unchanged from this morning, but now everything looks unfamiliar.

I can deal with this.

I *have* to deal with this.

Alexei might hate me, but he isn't going to hurt me.

I feel like my heart's being put through a food processor, but I'll be fine. I can go to bed and mourn my only shot at an actual relationship, and then I'll wake up in the morning and wait for Mom's appointment.

Nothing's changed. I only have to wait two days, and then I'll get to see Mom. She'll make it better.

My breathing is choppy. I bite down on my lip before a cry slips free.

Even when everyone else has given up on me, Mom's always there. I still matter to her.

Lev whistles long and low, tearing me out of my thoughts.

"You must have really fucked up. I don't remember the last time I saw him that pissed off."

His smirk feels like salt over an open wound, but I set my mouth into a firm line before I stand. Giving him the haughtiest look I can while I'm barefoot and in my pajamas, I march to my room, steadfastly ignoring the way he laughs at my back.

If Alexei doesn't want to deal with me anymore, fine. But I'm not going to play nice with his little sidekick.

# CHAPTER 26

# Emiliya

Lev smacks my hand with more force than he needs to when I reach for the radio.

"What's wrong with you?" I demand, cradling my hand against my chest.

Over the past couple of days, I've spent more time than I'd like with him. Definitely long enough to know I can't expect anything close to sympathy, but it almost feels like he is *trying* to hurt me.

He shakes his wrist to readjust his solid metal watch before returning his focus to the road. I glare at it, the stupid crystal gleaming in the sunlight. I can't make out the brand while he's driving, but at a glance, I can tell it's more expensive than anything else he's wearing.

It's completely out of place with his off-the-rack suit.

"You're fine. Stop being dramatic."

Even if I want to be as far away from him as possible, Lev's the only person I've spoken to since Alexei decided to cut all ties.

Not that I've worked very hard for his attention. In fact, I've done as much as I can to stay as far outside his notice as possible. It's like I'm back at home, walking on eggshells and pretending I'm not holding all the broken pieces of my heart together with chewing gum and paper clips.

I've even been too scared to go back into his office to get my phone. Every time I've so much as looked at the closed door, Lev's been right there, glaring at me with so much malice that I have no choice but to retreat to my room.

I'm bored, sad, lonely, and Lev is doing nothing to alleviate any of it with his stony silence as he drives toward the hospital.

I tried to tell him that we needed to pick up Mom first, that Father's drivers won't take her to her appointments, but he rolled his eyes and told me to get in the car.

*Fucker.*

Hopefully, when we get there, we'll have enough time to turn around and pick her up before Dr. Bonilla has to reschedule. If she misses out on treatments because Lev's a dickhead, I'll be livid.

"You could've just told me not to touch the radio. You didn't need to hit me with that heavy-ass watch."

"I could've. Or I could save my breath."

"It was uncalled for," I mutter under my breath.

"Was it?"

I cross my arms as he pulls into the hospital parking lot, getting out so I can be as far away from him as possible. From what I can tell, Lev's nothing but a conceited asshole with an inflated ego.

I'm already striding toward the entrance when Lev snaps his fingers behind me. Literally snaps his fingers, like I'm a dog and he's commanding me to heel.

Fuck. Him.

"Uh-uh," he bites as he rushes after me, grabbing my upper arm hard enough that I have no hope of wrenching free. "I'm not letting you out of my sight. Now, come on. We don't want to keep anyone waiting, do we?"

Muttering under my breath about how little I care, I'm helplessly dragged through the hallways. All the nurses and staff who are typically ready to greet me with a smile do a wonderful job of keeping their eyes averted and pretending nothing out of the ordinary is happening.

Even Sadie, who's always happy to see me and chat about the latest hospital gossip, doesn't so much as glance in our direction, her gaze glued to the linoleum at her feet.

My glare drills daggers into the side of Lev's head.

This hospital is one of the few places I can feel like myself, and if that changes because he insists on manhandling me, then I don't care who he is or how close he is to Alexei. I'll hunt him down and make him regret even thinking about laying a hand on me.

I bat my lashes sweetly. "Would you mind letting go of me so I can go where I need to? Because you're dragging me in the opposite direction."

"I know where I'm going."

My nails dig into my palm when he doesn't stop, moving further and further away from the physical therapy rooms and toward parts of the building I've never had any reason to explore.

When he comes to a stop outside a private exam room, I'm doing everything I can to pry my arm free. His grip is bruising, pulling the skin so tight there's no way he isn't leaving marks, but I don't care.

If Mom's here, then I need to get to her.

"This isn't even the right department, asshole."

Ignoring me, Lev tosses me toward a closed door so hard I crash into it.

My glare bounces right off him as he leans against the opposite wall, lifting his chin in a silent command.

"Fine, but when this isn't the right place and we're late, it'll be your fault."

"Sure thing, sweetie," he says with a condescending smirk. "Now shut up and do what you're told."

If I'm quick, I can dart around him. If I kick off my heels, I can probably make it down the hall and to the elevator before he can catch me.

But then he'll complain to Alexei, who will just have even more reason to hate me.

Damn it.

I grit my teeth and open the door. Almost immediately, I stumble backward into Lev's hard chest. Father's dispassionate stare watches from where he leans against the exam table.

"Hello, *printsessa*. It's been a while."

My heart is a dead weight in my throat, freezing me on the spot, but Lev shoves me into the room before I can find my feet, slamming the door shut as soon as I'm inside. Over the ringing in my ears, I can hear someone flick the lock behind me.

My eyes dart around the room, and I'm not sure if I'm relieved or terrified that Mom isn't here.

*Maybe she's with Dr. Bonilla.*

Or maybe Father's going to demand something else before he lets her see him again.

"How are you?" I ask around my panic.

I risk a glance over my shoulder, freezing for half a second when I see Yan standing next to the door, his hands folded in front of him. His friendly grin is nowhere to be found, and an unjustified wave of betrayal washes over me.

Since when does he tag along with Father? He's supposed to be low-ranking, the kind of man that only watches the house. I haven't been gone long enough for that to change, have I?

Yan was supposed to be something like a friend.

How little did it take for him to become another one of Father's puppets?

"It's been brought to my attention that you're finally doing the one thing I've asked of you. Such a pity that you couldn't be bothered to let me know yourself."

A familiar heat slashes my cheeks, begging me to take the bait. I bite my cheek until the impulse fades.

"I didn't want to say anything until I was able to give you good news," I lie.

If I had my way, I wouldn't have told him anything at all. I would've happily stayed with Alexei until either he got bored of me, or someone did me a favor and ended Father's miserable existence.

I should've known Father wouldn't let me have even a small modicum of happiness. Of course, he tracked down Alexei and ended any of the illusions I held about what was happening between us. Of course, he needed to make sure I'm as miserable as he is.

"You mean you wanted to keep fucking the little bastard, and you didn't want to do what needed to be done, right?" When I don't bother responding, he sighs. "See, this is your problem, Emiliya. You have no *vision*. You never do anything unless you're provided with the right motivation."

With a disappointed head shake, he contemplates me while my skin crawls.

He's never been more wrong. I do have vision.

It's just that Father's vision ends in him ruling over everything like a king and seizing more power than a man like him can ever control, and mine ends with Mom and I dancing over his grave while any traces of his legacy burn to dust.

"I have a deal for you. I need Alexei to be at Savage on Saturday. Say, around ten. And you, *moya printessa*, are going to make sure he's there."

Like hell I will.

"Alexei isn't exactly happy to be around me right now," I confess. "I'm not sure I'll be able to convince him to have dinner with me, much less go to his club."

"What a shame. Because if you don't manage to get this done, I'm afraid your mother isn't going to be able to go to her appointments anymore. In fact, all those medications, all that physical therapy, it'll all stop."

He doesn't so much as blink as my heart stops entirely.

"She'll get to sit in my home, and we'll both watch as she gets worse and worse. And when she's suffering and miserable, it'll be all your fault."

All my blood drains from my face so quickly I sway where I stand.

"You can't do that."

"I can do whatever I want, Emiliya. It's time you figured that out."

*But I need her.*

I need Mom, or none of this is worth it. She deserves the world, but if all she gets is me, then I can't let her suffer for it.

She's the only thing that matters.

"You can take it out on me, but not her," I tell him, desperately trying to hold back the panic in my voice.

"See, we tried that. But you're too dense to have any sense of self-preservation. If something happens to you, you don't care. Your mother, on the other hand..." Father rocks his head back and forth. "You care about what happens to her. Far more than I do. Which means you're going to listen to me, aren't you?"

My chest burns with hatred. If Yan weren't standing behind me, no doubt ready to take me down without hesitation, I'd attack Father. I'd go after him with everything I have and then I'd find a little more until he's unrecognizable.

But Yan's here. And even if I can't trust him anymore, I don't want to have to look him in the eye when he does my father's bidding.

With hate and resentment seeping through my veins, I brokenly answer, "Yes, Father."

I'll do whatever he tells me to do, because he's right. I have no choice.

I'll prostrate myself in front of Alexei. I'll degrade myself and strip away any pride I have left, but I'll make sure he's at the fucking club on Saturday.

"Good."

Father heads toward the door, and when he opens it, Lev is still standing outside, watching the door like he's expecting me to run.

"Oh, and be a dear and make sure no one finds out about this conversation, *printsessa*. I'd hate to see what happens to your mother when she's deprived of her medication."

***

Lev doesn't have to worry about me touching the radio on the drive home. In fact, I don't want to do anything that will move me even a fraction of an inch closer to him. I'm tucked against the door, facing the window like it'll somehow protect me.

Part of me wants to ask Lev if he knows what he's helping set Alexei up for, but to what end? He set me up, he's setting Alexei up, and I'm willing to bet he's the one that set him up when he was supposed to meet Nadya.

Does Alexei know what his cousin is planning behind his back?

What a dumb question.

Of course he doesn't. After his little run-in with Father, Alexei assumed he was telling the truth, and I was the one running my mouth about his business.

Has he even thought to look at anyone else?

Does it even matter that this was the first time I've spoken to Father since I moved into Alexei's?

Lev is hiding right under his nose, but Alexei's been handed a perfect excuse to blame me for everything.

And I can't do a thing about it.

He's already decided I'm to blame, and I have no chance of convincing him that he needs to be looking at the man he trusts with his sister's life.

At least if Lev's stuck babysitting me, he isn't with Alexei. He won't be able to give Father any firsthand information.

On the one hand, I'm relieved. On the other, I know it only makes me look even guiltier.

When Father doesn't have any new information, Alexei will assume it's because he has me under constant guard. And when Father doesn't have anything, he'll find a new way to apply pressure until I get him something to work with.

Either way, I lose.

"Do you know where my mother is?" I eventually choke out. My throat aches from holding back all the vitriol I want to unleash on everyone.

Alexei, Lev, Yan, Father.

They all deserve far worse than they're going to end up getting, and I'm going to have to bear the weight of the consequences regardless of who ends up on top.

If I have to convince Alexei to go to Savage on Saturday, I only have two days to get it together and make him view me as something other than the parasite that's taking up space in his guest room. And if I'm going to do that, I need to put everything else aside and focus.

But I still don't know if Mom's safe. And no matter how hard I try to ignore it, she takes priority over everything else.

I can't rage against the injustice, I can't lash out and expect things to be different, and I sure as hell can't coddle my broken heart.

I need to dust myself off and focus on what actually matters.

What was I thinking, leaving her behind?

Father's still the one pulling all the strings. I'm still nothing but a tool, and he's still going to get whatever the hell he wants.

I might have gotten a break, but is Mom's safety worth it?

"Why would I know?" Lev scoffs.

"Because if Father wants me to do his bidding, then I need some sort of reassurance that he's going to hold up his end of the deal."

Without proof that she's safe, there's no point.

"If you're really worried about it, you should take it up with Nikita, because I don't know jack shit about your mom, and I'm sure as fuck not going to ask."

"Well," I start, ticking reasons off on my fingers, "I don't have my phone, you practically rip my head off any time I step near Alexei's office, and if I go home to check on her, I'm going to come back with a black eye. How do you think your cousin's going to react to that?"

Lev hardly reacts, and I wish I knew if it's because Alexei already told him the whole sordid tale of my family drama, or if it's because he's so dead inside he's beyond giving a shit.

"Since you're so cozy with my father, ask him for a picture of her. Something so I know she's alive, at least. Tell him that you're using it for motivation if he pushes back, but I need this."

A little crumb to let me focus on the task at hand without losing my mind. Something to keep me from losing my mind entirely, because I already feel like I'm drowning, and I need to know there's a light at the end of this.

The drive passes in silence, each minute dragging out until I'm blinking back tears, my throat bobbing uselessly. I'll beg if I have to. Cry, shout, plead.

"And what am I supposed to get out of it?" Lev eventually sneers.

"Other than what you're getting from Father?"

"Yeah." He shrugs, smirking at me like he's more amused than anything else. "I know why I'm helping him, but why should I help you?"

Dread is heavy on my chest, the voice of reason in the back of my head telling me to bite my tongue and shut the fuck up before I spit out, "I'll do whatever you want."

Slowly, he turns to look at me. He appraises me like a piece of meat.

His eyes make me feel dirty, and my skin crawls, but what else do I have to offer a man like him?

"Anything?"

I nod, no matter how badly I want to take back every word.

"Fine. For the small price of *anything*, I'll talk to him." Lev pulls into the underground garage, eyes straight ahead while I nearly weep with relief, even when I'm consumed by the weight of him accepting my deal.

I can only offer him the only thing I'm any good for. The thought of anyone but Alexei touching me makes my stomach turn, but I don't have any other leverage.

He can have my body if he demands it. Anything I own. Shit, if he says he wants my hand in marriage so he can get closer to Father, then it's his.

"But Alexei's not going to hear a whisper of any of this. If things go sideways, you don't mention me and Nikita in the same fucking breath."

His hard eyes cut to me, pinning me in place.

"If Alexei says anything—hell, if he asks one odd question—I'll tell Nikita you're refusing to work with him. Whatever threats he's holding over your head, I'll make damn sure he follows through faster than you can cry for help. Got it?"

I snort, a hysterical sound that's just shy of a sob.

There's no time for tears. Not anymore.

"Even if I told Alexei, it's not like he'd believe me, right?"

Lev hums an agreement as he gets out of the car, waiting while I try to steady my nerves enough to follow him.

One day, Mom and I will still get away from this. We'll be able to laugh and sing along to old records again. We won't hold our breath and count the moments of freedom when we're alone.

It just might take more than I thought I could stand to lose.

I'll sacrifice any lingering fantasies as long as I'm still whole at the end of this. I'll pretend I never pictured a world where Alexei and I were happy.

That was always a stupid pipe dream, and I should probably thank Father for reminding me before I got too caught up in my feelings to get out cleanly.

Lev knocking on the window impatiently makes me jump, and I fix him with a glare. Neither of us says anything as I follow him toward the elevator, only briefly glancing at the dark corner in the back of the garage where Alexei usually parks.

His car isn't there, just shadows.

"Thank you for driving me," I say, like it'll change any of the cruelty that consumed him when he looked at me. When he comes to collect, it's going to hurt. My body, my mind, my soul. No amount of ingratiating myself or being polite will change that.

"Not like I had a choice," he mumbles as the elevator dings, coming to a stop.

"You're a prisoner, remember? You don't get any time outside your cell without supervision. And Alexei might be the warden, but I'm still the man making sure you don't run away. By force, if necessary."

*Right.*

He shoves against my shoulder until I stumble past the front door.

"Stop pushing me everywhere, *mudak*."

"Go run along and do what you've been told, alright?"

"Heaven forbid I forget to think about what Father wants from me for more than a single minute at a time."

The click of my heels and the blood swooshing through my ears chase me back to my room while Lev makes himself comfortable in the living room, content to put on a grand show of how bored he is before Alexei gets home.

I don't want to sulk, but it's hard to figure out what else I can do.

How am I supposed to convince Alexei to go anywhere with me? Especially into a trap so obvious it might as well be lit up with neon signs.

Father wants Alexei to be at Savage at a time he's chosen because he wants to end their fight on his terms. He doesn't want to deal with uncertainty or doubt. He wants things to be *done*, and the easiest way to do that is to make sure the competition is no longer around to fight.

Shutting the door behind me, I focus on the flimsy click of the lock before I kick off my shoes. The thin wood and weak lock won't do anything to keep me safe, but it'll buy me a little warning. It'll give me time to collect myself before I have to face anyone else.

As soon as my bare feet hit the floor, my legs fail. I slump against the door, the sting of my tailbone hitting hardwood reverberating up my spine.

Father wants to kill Alexei, and he wants me to make it happen.

He isn't giving me the illusion of choice; he's teaching me another one of his lessons.

He has the power to kill everyone I've ever loved, and in his eyes, it has nothing to do with him, and everything to do with my failure.

If I didn't love Mom, he wouldn't be able to use her as leverage. If it didn't hurt me to kill Alexei, Father wouldn't have any power.

But I love both of them, so he's making me choose. The only person who has ever shown me unconditional love, or the man I've fallen for, the one that gave me hope for the first time since I was a child.

Either way, I'm giving up half of my heart.

I wipe a hand over my cheek, ignoring my tears.

If I linger in my misery, the hole in my chest will consume me, and I can't afford that. I need to push my emotions aside and make a plan.

I need to accept the situation for what it is.

Alexei's going to die.

He's going to die hating me and thinking I'm nothing but a traitor.

And when he's gone, and Father's done using me to manipulate the men around him, when he's sold me to either Lev or the highest bidder for my hand in marriage and I'm left with nothing but memories, I'll have a few happy moments to keep me warm.

They'll give me something to cling to until I can escape. Because no matter what, this is far from the end of this war. It's just another battle, and I won't be a casualty. I'll come out the other side bruised and bloodied, but I'll be alive.

# CHAPTER 27

# Emiliya

A s soon as I'm able to get myself together, I wash my face and redo my makeup.

No matter how miserable I am, it's nothing a fresh coat of mascara won't be able to hide. I move from product to product, until the foundation and eye shadow bury my despair and piece my mask back together, patching the cracks until all anyone can see is the image I want the world to.

If Alexei wanted me to leave, he would've kicked me out, not locked me up with a jailor whenever he isn't here.

Pretending I'm invisible only benefits him, but it's a luxury he's going to have to learn to live without if I want any chance of getting him to Savage.

Besides, I'm sick of hiding away in my room. If I'm going to be his prisoner, I don't see any reason I should be a well-behaved one. I'm not going anywhere just because he hates me, and if he has a problem with it, then even better.

Lev watches me like a hawk as I move around the kitchen, glaring at me like he's offended by my mere presence while I make dinner.

Every *snick* of the knife against the cutting board sounds like a roar. Each time the pot clatters against the stove as I adjust it grates like nails on a chalkboard.

The absence of music is harder to cope with than I thought it would be, the din and hum of the relative quiet banging around my head like a jet engine without anything else to drown it out.

I feel like I'm trespassing in a space where I was previously welcome, and the air itself knows I'm no longer wanted. Or maybe it's just the way Lev stares at me, his shoulders tensing every time I so much as look in the direction of the knife block.

Only now that it's gone do I realize how much I loved being able to exist without being stuck under a microscope. Every flick of Lev's eyes drives a splinter of annoyance under my skin, so deep I'm not sure I'll ever be able to get them out.

Why does he care what I'm doing, anyway?

It's not like he's on Alexei's side. He checks his watch again, and my eyes linger on it before scanning over his cheap suit.

For whatever reason, Lev made his choices, and he chose Father.

Ignoring the way he looks at me, I focus on the vegetables I'm supposed to be chopping.

"Are you trying to treat us like fucking rabbits? Why isn't there any meat?" Lev grunts at me.

"I wasn't planning on sharing, but if you want some, I'll gladly garnish everything with some cyanide. Do you know where Alexei keeps his?"

Lev rears back, shooting me a look that makes me want to tear the words out of thin air. The promise of *anything* I owe him claws at the back of my skull, threatening to consume me.

"There's no need to be a bitch. I was just making conversation."

I swallow thickly, my chest tight. "Then find your own dinner."

He rolls his eyes, muttering something under his breath that sounds suspiciously like *fucking cunt* as he turns his attention back to his phone.

Pissing Lev off will do me no good in the long-term, but it's hard not to when he looks at me like a prize to be won.

Alexei, on the other hand? I don't just want to piss him off. I *need* to.

Being sad and pathetic was fine and good when I was just waiting for this train to hit the end of the line, but I need to step up my game if I'm going to redirect it.

Alexei's dismissal does nothing for me, but if I'm able to piss him off, I'll be able to gently guide him until he remembers that he used to give a shit about me.

Anger is useful. I can work with anger.

I can use it to manipulate him into doing whatever I need him to. Alexei's pride will let me drag him wherever I need because if he thinks I have a leg to stand on, he'll do anything to prove me wrong.

By the time dinner is ready, I finally have a plan.

I'll push all of Alexei's buttons, do whatever it takes to piss him off, and draw him into a fight.

And honestly? I can't wait.

I need a chance to take out my hurt and fear, and Alexei will make an excellent target. I can't wait for him to yell and tell me every cruel thought he's ever had about me. I'm on the edge of my seat anticipating him throwing all my insecurities in my face and letting me know exactly how worthless I am to him.

I hope he makes me hate him. I hope that he takes every hope I've ever harbored and crushes them under his heel until they're nothing but a smear on concrete.

Anything to break my heart before I have a chance to.

I barely touch my dinner before I pack away the leftovers and shove them into the back of the fridge.

Time clicks away, and ten minutes before Alexei typically gets home, I clean up, take the leftovers out of the freezer, and put them in his normal spot before I retreat to my room, working myself up for the next part of the plan.

I didn't bring my flashiest clothes when I came here, but I have more than enough that are high on sex appeal and low on modesty.

Besides, a little creativity never hurt anyone.

I take my time dolling myself up, making sure my makeup is giving off the perfect *fuck me* vibe, styling my hair until it's practically begging to be wrapped around someone's fist. With a final coat of lipstick, I'm dancing on the edge between looking hot and not looking totally desperate.

It's fine.

I look *fine*.

It's far from the best I've ever looked, but how much can I really expect when I feel like nothing but a husk?

Looking good isn't just about the physicality, it's about the confidence. And at the moment? I have none.

My outfit shows off every curve, the lingerie I picked up on impulse the other day is working for me exactly the way I hoped it would, and if that's all I'm capable of, it'll have to be enough.

It's just a shame Alexei won't be able to enjoy it the way I wanted him to.

My hands shake, but I look like I have my shit together. It doesn't matter if I don't feel it. All that matters is that everyone around me believes that it's true. I haven't had to pull out all the stops in a while, but it's like riding a bike, right? It feels foreign, but you don't forget even if it's been ages since you last did it.

Still, it feels weird to be all glammed up and getting used to not caring about my appearance.

Before, a tight dress would fit me like a second skin, but now it makes my skin crawl. I want nothing more than to pull on a pair of sweats and hide somewhere no one can see me.

I take a fortifying breath when the front door slams, listening to the murmur of low, masculine voices as Lev catches Alexei up on his version of today's events.

If he wanted to help me out, he would have prepared me for whatever his story is so I don't walk straight into a pit I can't talk my way out of, but Lev doesn't strike me as a man I can count on to so much as spit on me if I was on fire.

When the door opens and closes again, I take it as my cue.

I'll play my role, because at the end of the day, that's all this is.

A show. A production.

I've played my part for years, and I can keep it up for a few more days. With a deep breath, my shoulders fall, and I smirk at my reflection as I cap my lipstick.

If there's anything I know, it's how to use my body to get what I want.

"Alexei," I sing-song as I sashay toward the kitchen. To my surprise, he's sitting at the island, glaring at the dinner I left for him like it's a personal insult.

I hope it's stone cold and disgusting.

"Can you call your vicious guard dog and tell him to come back? I want to go out."

"No," he says without so much as pretending to consider it.

Slowly, he takes me in, squinting like he's mad at himself when his gaze lingers on my chest. "Why the fuck are you dressed like that?"

"Like I said, I want to go out. Have a little fun." I shrug. "You know how it is."

Alexei rolls his eyes. "We aren't playing this game, Emiliya. Go back to your room."

"Why? If you don't want to play with me, shouldn't I be able to find someone else?"

"I wasn't aware prisoners expected hook-up privileges."

"We could ask your dad. He'd probably know." His jaw flexes as my arrow finds its mark. *There we go.* "If you don't want to fulfil my needs, I might as well let someone fill them."

"That's not going to happen."

I make a show of folding my arms over my chest, each motion calculated.

Alexei might think he knows me well enough to see through my charms, but at the end of the day, he's still nothing but a man.

He's still beholden to all his wants, and he still forgets to protect all his soft spots when he's comfortable.

If he feels like I'm backing him into a corner, he'll get defensive, and I'll get my argument, and then some. As soon as he lashes out, I just have to pull the right strings.

"Listen, I'm not asking you to *watch*. That's why I told you to call Lev. He seems like the kind of guy who'd be into that sort of thing." With a thoughtful tilt of my head, I tap a nail against my chin, even as my stomach twists at the thought. "Actually, that's a great idea. Call Lev. I bet he's a freak in bed."

"No," he snarls, his dinner forgotten as he turns his glare to me. "The only person you're going to have any fun with is yourself, so get that through your pretty little head."

I'll give him some credit; that's not a terrible suggestion, either.

Besides, I might as well drag out this little game, right?

"So, what? You're going to trap me here until you get sick of me? And I'm supposed to just take it? Entertain myself and stay out of your way until you get bored?"

The look on his face makes it clear he's already sick of me, but to my dismay, he doesn't lash out.

He clings to his impenetrable calm, not giving me an ounce of the frustration and anger I need from him.

Why does he have to leave me wanting the one time I'm really counting on him?

I need him to hate me as much as I hate myself, or I'll never be able to move on.

He raises a single brow, dismissing me as he turns back to his cold dinner.

I huff, hating how much it hurts that a cold, limp stir-fry has captured his attention when he can barely stand to spare me a glance.

Whatever.

He already told me how to get his attention. Might as well call his bluff.

I stroll into the living room as if he's still watching me, even if it's only in the reflections of imaginary mirrors, and pretend I'm the center of his world as I drape myself over the sofa, propping one heel on the coffee table, uncaring whether I scratch the glass surface or not.

Even when Alexei doesn't want me around, I've always had his attention while he fucked me. If he wants to tell me I'm the only one that gets to satisfy my needs, then so be it.

He never said I had to do it in private.

Though, fuck, this would be easier if I had my phone.

I'm too wound up to get in the right headspace to put on a show on my own. A video would make it so much easier. The television remote catches my eye.

That'll work, too.

I mute the TV as soon as I turn it on. In no time at all, I'm scrolling through videos until I find one of a blond man having his way with the faceless woman beneath him.

I pause. If I squint, that might work.

I force myself to focus on the video until I'm not worrying about the fact that Alexei's only a short distance away, ignoring me.

I click play and watch as the man on the screen urges the woman onto her hands and knees, running a reverent hand over her back while he kneels behind her, still fully dressed in a T-shirt and jeans.

It's so far from the man I really want to watch, the one who's across the room in a three-piece suit, but beggars can't be choosers.

With the television muted, I can't hear what he whispers to his partner causes her to gasp, but in my mind, he's telling her everything he plans to do to her. Every wicked thought that's plagued him until he's consumed by nothing other than her. Her body, her presence, her every move.

His fingers run along the band of her panties; the only scrap of fabric she's still wearing.

Still hyper-aware of Alexei's presence, I shift as wetness pools between my thighs.

I pull my dress up over my hips. Suddenly, the fear of Alexei's judgment is far away. The only thing I'm worried about is the heat curling low in my belly as I trace my slit with my fingers, slicking them with every slow, teasing pass.

That heat blazes into an inferno as I work my clit, spreading my legs even further so I can work two fingers inside.

My eyes flutter shut while my nerves sing with pleasure.

The man on the screen has one of his partner's breasts in his mouth, torturing her nipple while he thrusts his fingers in her pussy. Still dressed, he grinds his hips in the mattress below him, desire written plainly on his face.

I move to match his pace, and it's good, but the angle is all wrong.

I can't get as deep as I want, and I whimper softly in frustration.

I'm so close, but I need just a little more. If only I'd thought to grab a toy, something to help push me over the edge. I need—

"Is this the show you wanted to give my cousin?" Alexei growls, snapping me back to reality. While I was wrapped up in my pleasure and frustration, he must have moved across the room.

The fire blazing in his eyes should strike me with enough fear to drown my arousal, but seeing him at the end of the couch only stokes the fire.

It's unfair that even his anger is attractive.

It doesn't matter that he's furious. Having his eyes on me is exactly what I want. Not the couple going at it on the television, not any image I can conjure for myself.

Just Alexei.

I moan as I nod, holding his eyes while I come all over my hand.

His hair is a mess, he's pissed as hell, and still, Alexei can't hide how hard his cock is, straining the fabric of his pants.

*He still wants me.*

The realization hits me so hard I almost weep with relief.

In a flash, he's in front of me, bracing his hands on either side of my head. His huffed breaths scorch against my skin, even as I tilt my chin toward him, our lips barely an inch apart. I pant, tentatively brushing my hands, still wet with my release, against his covered chest.

His eyes track the movement, dark and hungry.

I want to feel his skin against mine, let him make everything from the past two days fade into the background.

But there's no warmth in Alexei's expression. He wants me, but the affectionate way he looked at me a week ago is nothing but a distant memory. No matter how close he is physically, he still wants to push me as far away as possible.

"I didn't realize you were an exhibitionist."

"I'm not," I admit against my better judgment. If it were anyone else, I would've hated being watched. I would have run away from this, praying I never had to see them again. "Only with you."

"Understand this, Emiliya."

His teeth grind together, conflict painted in every line on his face while the vein in his forehead throbs. He looks terrifying, but I want to rub my face against him like a cat. No matter how mad I make him, he won't hurt me. For as long as he lives, no matter how long that may be, he'll never raise a hand against me.

"Whatever happens, no one else gets to see you like this. You're. Still. *Mine.*"

A small thrill shoots through me faster than I can squash it.

"Prove it," I challenge with a tilt of my chin.

He flashes a smirk so sharp, I start to understand why Father sees Alexei as a threat. I can picture the way he'd command a room, not just demanding, but *earning* it.

"It's not a good idea to provoke an angry man. You never know when they'll snap."

I bite my bottom lip.

"What if I want you to?"

With a snarl, Alexei slams his mouth against mine, dominating my body as easily as he does my mind. When his tongue forces its way into my mouth, I melt against the couch, clutching onto his shirt like a lifeline.

This is so far from the fight I was looking for, but I can't find it in me to complain.

As much as I want to hate Alexei, I want to be close to him even more. I want him to be my soft place to land, the person I'm safe with no matter what.

I just can't forget that he doesn't care about me. My feelings need to stay locked in a box in the back of my head if I'm going to have any chance of protecting my heart.

Alexei pulls me against him, flipping our positions so I'm straddling his lap, and I have to brace my hands on his shoulders to keep my balance.

He doesn't give me any time to orient myself before he's pulling down the front of my dress, apathetic to the way the fabric tears under his strong hands. With even less care, he slips his fingers into the cups of my bra and pulls until the pretty lace is ruined in his hands.

I don't have a chance to complain before he's freeing his cock and thrusting into me hard enough to make me see stars.

He fucks me like he hates me, like this is a punishment.

Every time his hips meet mine, I'm not sure if I want to cry out in rapture or loss.

It was a mistake to even think I could have more than a purely physical connection. With anyone, but especially with Alexei.

Fantasies are one thing, but losing him is going to destroy me.

Another orgasm overcomes me as I bury my face in his neck, desperately panting his name.

He doesn't stop.

Even when the burning in my eyes and the pounding in my heart nearly overwhelms me, Alexei fucks me until he stills, groaning his pleasure while he pulses inside me.

This is so much worse than if he'd just let me pick a fight. Instead, he took a jackhammer to the already unstable ground beneath my feet.

Taking a deep breath, I mourn the loss when I slip off his lap. His cum drips down my thighs, and it's pointless to try to adjust the ruined remains of my outfit, but that doesn't stop me from trying.

Anything to keep from looking up and letting him see how wet my lashes are.

"You know what?" I ask, hoping he ignores how hoarse I am. "That was even better than going out."

Alexei doesn't answer, his face devoid of any emotion. No lingering bliss, no anger, no happiness.

Just a blank mask that hurts as much as anything else that's happened tonight.

He doesn't give a single fuck whether I'm here or not.

I toss him a wink over my shoulder as I stride away. I can't be around him anymore. Not tonight.

My knees feel like they're going to buckle underneath me, but I keep my spine straight and my shoulders back, doing everything I can to make it look like I have everything under control.

The time for tears has come and gone. I need to get it togeth-er, and I need to do it now.

I take the world's coldest shower, scrubbing at my skin like there's a chance I'll ever be clean before I slip into bed, hating the way the cold sheets embrace me, I berate myself over and over until my door cracks open.

My eyes snap shut, feigning sleep. That plan falls apart like everything else has when Alexei pulls back the blankets, scoop-ing me into his arms.

"If you think I'm going to let you out of my sight after that bullshit, you've lost your mind," he mutters, carrying me to his room. He ignores my questioning looks and instinctive protests, not even looking at me.

Alexei's touch rubs against all my raw emotions when he tucks me into his bed, lying down beside me. He cradles me and my tender heart for hours, holding me close as much as he is holding me together.

Regret and hope battle in my chest for hours until I finally fall asleep.

# CHAPTER 28

# Emiliya

Over the span of the past few days, the ficus in the corner of Alexei's room has taken a sharp turn for the worst.

The early morning sun is obscured by the swirling snow outside, but there's just enough light to show every dead leaf and emaciated branch. Even if I were granted access to it long enough to try to save it, there's no point. I'd be better off hunting down a nice, sunny spot to bury the remains.

Who's going to take care of Alexei's plants when Father kills him? He neglects the hell out of them, but they don't deserve to be thrown in the trash and left to rot.

Alexei's heat burns against my back. With his arm banded across my chest, it'd be so easy to let myself fall back into the comfort and go back to pretending. Instead, I stare at his stupid, dying plant with sore, swollen eyes and tell myself to focus on what I *know* instead of what I feel.

I know Alexei turned his back on me at the first sign of trouble. I know Mom would never abandon me that way. I know Alexei has to die if I want to keep Mom safe.

As Alexei wakes up, his breathing changes, and for a single, wonderful moment, he seems to forget.

He smiles against the back of my neck before pressing a soft kiss there, content and sleep-soaked. It's everything I don't deserve. I bite my lip to keep it from trembling.

This warm bed is perfect, and in another life, this is all I could've asked for. Knowing I'm going to lose it before I even had it is one of the hardest parts to stomach.

Then the delicate moment shatters into a million pieces.

Alexei stiffens, sending reality crashing back down, but instead of pulling away, he only holds me tighter.

His voice is gruff with sleep when he says, "You and Nikita had a good game going."

When Alexei first wakes up, he has nothing to hide. Every word out of his mouth rings with overwhelming sincerity.

Even now, his resentment is laid bare.

Will I ever hear him speak kindly again? Or will everything he tells me from here on out be coated with bitterness and anger?

"Your father took one look at me and knew I was in love with you." My eyes snap shut while Alexei chokes out a humorless laugh. "You two managed to play me so fucking well, sweetheart."

He rolls out of bed, taking all the warmth with him. I shiver, wrapping my arms around the pillow.

He's lying.

He *has* to be lying.

He's never loved me. Because I'm nothing but an empty shell of a person, another weapon for my father to wield.

I don't deserve his love, and if Alexei ever thought I did, he's just as much of an idiot as I am.

The bathroom door closes behind him while I choke on a meaningless sob.

He didn't just *say* love; he spit it out like he's already cut the fragile emotion out of his system and forgotten about it.

The past tense hurts more than any punishment Father's ever doled out.

Pressing my face into the pillow, I take a fortifying breath.

I just need to find a way to spin this.

Alexei's acting like he doesn't care anymore, but not that long ago, he did. And even if he's acting blasé, I know better than anyone how hard it is to kill affection, even when the embers are so small you could ignore that they're there at all.

Affection consumes everything in its path, and as long as a single spark remains intact, it's liable to come back and rear its ugly head when you least expect it.

Just like when I find myself missing Daniil when all he did was use me. Like it does when I find myself wanting to make Father proud, even when the only thought that lets me sleep is knowing that one day, he'll be dead.

It's what makes leading Alexei into Father's clutches so unbearable.

At least I can comfort myself knowing that all three of them were only looking out for themselves. I was only ever a messy byproduct of their own wants and ambitions.

But with Mom, I'm more than that.

She spent so many years of her life taking care of me, it's only fair that I return the favor, even if I have to break my own heart to do it.

"Get dressed," Alexei snaps. He ducks into his walk-in closet with a towel wrapped around his waist. "I have places to be, and you're coming with me."

I make no move to get up as I make a show of rolling my eyes. "Isn't this what the babysitter's for? So I don't have to be chained to your side?"

Not that I mind taking a break from Lev, but I need time to get my shit together, and I was looking forward to reminding myself of what's at stake while Alexei was gone for the day.

Lev owes me a photo.

When he emerges from his closet, Alexei's wearing navy suit pants, an unbuttoned shirt hanging loose around his shoulders as he runs his fingers through his hair, doing his best to style it while it's still wet.

"I hope you got what you wanted out of him, because after that little stunt last night, you're not going anywhere near Lev. You're stuck with me, and I'm not going to let you manipulate me into doing whatever you want. Those days are over."

My stomach drops.

As little as I want to be around that fucking creep, I need him. He's the only connection I have to Mom.

"Are you sure about that? Because I got what I wanted just fine last night."

"Because I wanted to fuck you?" Alexei scoffs as he buttons his shirt, fingers working in quick, practiced movements. "That doesn't mean you can get jack shit from me, sweetheart."

He grabs the blankets and pulls them away before I can stop him, yanking them out my grasp. I shiver, screeching indignantly when he drops them in a pile at his feet.

"Unless you want to go out like that"—he looks at my pajamas with a disdainful quirk of his brow before he glances at the snow beating against the window—"I suggest you get dressed. It wouldn't be my choice, but it's not like you care what I think."

"Fucking asshole," I mutter under my breath as I throw one of the pillows in the direction of his face. Alexei doesn't so much as flinch, snagging it midair and adding it to the pile of bedding at his feet.

"Fine. Give me twenty minutes."

"You have ten."

I stop, half standing with one leg still folded on the mattress. "I won't even be able to get my hair done in ten minutes."

"Tough. You're not in control anymore, *printsessa*."

"Stop fucking calling me that!" I shout. "I get it, alright? I'm so far from a princess it isn't even funny, so give it a rest already."

Even if I had the energy to explain that I've never been in control of anything, Alexei won't fucking *listen*. I'd just be wasting my breath. To him, I'm nothing but a selfish bitch, which apparently makes it fair for him to taunt me with a nickname he knows I can't stand.

"I'll call you whatever I like. Now, hurry up. I have work to do."

Mentally, I scream every curse and obscenity I know at his retreating form before I dart to my room so I can slap on enough makeup to cover my puffy eyes and throw on the first warm outfit I can find.

I'm only half dressed when Alexei yells my name from the front hall. Deciding against pushing my luck, I hurry to grab my boots and a warm coat before he loses patience and drags me out into the snowstorm.

Alexei grants me a reprieve from being manhandled on the way to his car, but he sticks close like he's worried I'm going to run if he gives me more than a few inches of space. As soon as he's convinced I won't jump out of the car, he's tearing out of the garage and driving headfirst into the storm.

I watch the snow flying past the window faster than my eyes can track it until he pulls to a stop in front of an apartment building. Not wasting any time before he gets out, I follow, the knot of dread in my gut pulling tighter with each step.

The elevator stops on the fifth floor, and confusion filters in around the edges. Don't most Bratva men take pride in living in the flashiest, most expensive places they can afford? Who would he possibly be meeting with that's content to live on the fifth floor of a nondescript building so far away from all the action further downtown?

Is he planning on dumping me with a new guard?

The hand he has clamped on my shoulder is so tight there's no way he doesn't feel my pulse rocketing out of control.

Within moments of Alexei knocking, the door is ripped open to reveal Nadya glaring at us as she looms in the doorway.

"I thought you were too busy to see me," she says, her voice dripping with sarcasm. "Or did you decide to get off your high horse and deem me worthy of your time again?"

Alexei responds by dragging me closer to him. Surprise flashes in her eyes for a moment before she turns it into a glare.

"I get it, alright? I'm a shit brother, and we need to spend more time together. But right now, I need you to keep an eye on her." He tilts his head toward me, a dismissive gesture that takes a hammer to the already shattered remains of my heart.

"No," she says, unmoved by his no-nonsense tone. "Find someone else."

Ignoring her protests, he shoulders past her, dragging me with him. Her apartment is full of warm wood and candles, plush pillows decorating a comfortable-looking couch.

Her contempt for Alexei and me keeps the entire room warm despite the storm raging outside.

"It's either you, or I'm taking her to Andrei's." He stays close as he faces Nadya, whose expression can only be described as thunderous. "I'm sure Blair would love that. Stress is good for pregnant women, right?"

"Or I could stay at your place with Lev," I protest weakly.

The weight of their combined glares makes be stumble backward.

"I don't trust you around Lev, and I don't have time to deal with you myself. So, who's watching her, Nadya? You or Andrei?"

They're locked in a silent standoff that makes me feel like little more than an unwanted pet, and I don't want to stick around and listen to them argue over me like a burden.

No matter what they think of me, I'm still a fucking person.

Testing the water, I shuffle toward the door, but Alexei notices immediately, pinning me with a hard stare.

"Fine," Nadya grumbles. "But I'm working, and if she gets in my way, I'm tossing her out on her ass, whether you're here to pick her up or not."

"Thank you. I owe you one." He turns to me with a bland expression and says, "Don't be a pain in the ass."

"I'm the obnoxious one here?" I ask incredulously. "That's news to me." I give him a look, but with his back turned, he misses the corner of Nadya's mouth twitching up.

Alexei turns, knocking his shoulder gently against Nadya's as he passes. "I'll be back in a few hours. Try to call me before you dump her in the cold."

Nadya mutters under her breath as she follows him, slamming the door shut as soon as he steps through it.

If I had to rank my options today, I would've picked being thrown out in the storm in my PJs first, then being sent home to Father, and then ending up alone with Nadya. Actually, throw fighting the raccoon that stole Alexei's sweatshirt with my bare hands in the mix, and it'd still rank above where I am right now.

But no one bothered to ask me, did they?

I eye Nadya warily, Alexei's story about her talent with a knife playing like an omen in the back of my head.

She won't hurt me, will she? Nadya doesn't like me, and she clearly isn't happy that I'm here, but that's too far for a girl like her, right?

"So, what'd you do to get on his shit list?" I flinch as Nadya brushes past me, curling up in an armchair and pulling a laptop off the coffee table. "For how fiercely he protected you the other day, he barely looked at you now."

I could try to make a run for it, but even if I get away, where will I go? It's freezing out there, and I'm not familiar with this part of town. I have no phone, no friends, and no plan.

"Oh, you know," I say, waving a hand in the air. "I have that effect on people."

Nadya snorts, turning her attention back to her computer. "Most people have that effect on my brother." I pull off my boots and set them on the tray next to the door before I shove my hands into the pockets of my coat. "Alexei doesn't typically change his mind, though. Once he's settled on something, it's set in stone. So, I'm curious as to what made him flip."

"Would you believe me if I said he decided you were right about me?"

"I'd sooner believe he sold everything he owns and has decided to live as a monk."

I blink. Whatever I expected her to say, that definitely wasn't it.

"That'd be a travesty. His hair is far too nice for him to shave it."

Nadya laughs, tossing me a smile over her shoulder. "Well, if you're stuck here, you might as well take off your coat and have a seat. I wasn't kidding about having work to do, but feel free to poke around. Watch TV, read a book, whatever you want."

That grabs my attention, sinking its teeth so far into me I'm going to bear marks for the rest of my life.

"You have a job?"

I don't remember the last time I heard of a Bratva woman working. It's a point of pride for all the ego-driven men in our lives. They provide everything we need, even if they have to buy, cheat, or kill for it.

But Alexei lets her work?

I want to badger her with questions, but if I want answers, I'm going to have to slow-roll them. I need to figure out where she works, what she does, and how I can make this work so I can get a foot in the door.

A job is a gateway to escaping.

Does Nadya even realize what a privilege that is?

"Yeah," she answers. "I wouldn't want my degree to go to waste."

I freeze, my coat still half on as I gape at her. "Your brother let you go to school?" My parents were so sure an education would be a waste for me that they encouraged me to drop out of high school. Refusing caused the biggest fight Mom and I have ever had.

And Nadya when to *college*?

Unaware that she just blew my mind, Nadya says, "First of all, Alexei doesn't *let* me do anything. I wanted to go to school, so I went. Even went to community college for a year so he wouldn't have to be on his own before he graduated."

"I thought you two stayed with your aunt and uncle after your dad got locked up?"

At least, that's the impression I got when I poked around after Father told me to start working Alexei.

"Kind of." Nadya shrugs, fingers flying over her keyboard. "We stayed with Aunt Vera when Child Protective Services would come sniffing around, but for the most part, we looked after ourselves. The house was paid for, and people made sure we had food most of the time. It worked."

*What about heating?* I think as I sit on the couch. Who made sure they were warm? Who made sure they were happy and looked after? Who made sure they had everything they needed?

Her stalwart focus on the screen gives me the impression she doesn't want to tell me anything else.

As much as I want to learn more, there's something else I need to know.

"What do you for work?" I ask, trying not to sound overeager.

"I'm Alexei's accountant."

Disappointment hits me like a sack of bricks. Thank god she's not looking, because there's no way it isn't written plainly over my face.

I'm so crestfallen, I barely notice when my coat falls to the floor, soaking in the melting snow Alexei and I dragged in.

"So, you know how much he spends on hookers and blow?"

She shakes her head and chuckles.

"I have no record of what he does with his cash, and I don't want to."

Gathering myself, I stare mindlessly at the television as she works, trying to dig deep enough to find the confidence that's typically so readily available, but just like with everything else in my life, Alexei wandered in and took it with him.

When I shift with discomfort, Nadya looks at me, and her narrowed eyes look so much like Alexei's it hurts.

I scramble for something, anything, to make her stop looking at me like that.

"Why doesn't your brother know what a mud mask is?" Out of everything, that's what I ask?

"What?"

"I wore a mud mask a few weeks ago, and he acted like he had no idea what it was. How the hell does your brother not know about basic skincare products?"

She blinks for a moment before she closes her laptop, leaning forward and looking at me gravely. "Listen, my brother already has thicker hair, longer eyelashes, and all the power over my career. If he starts getting ideas about having better skin too, I'll have nothing left."

Like a dam breaking, I begin to laugh, settling in while she talks.

For a few hours, Nadya puts aside her work and treats me like a friend. She doesn't act like she hates me, and I pretend I'm not about to ruin her life. We watch ridiculous soap operas and ignore everything else, telling pointless stories and laughing.

She tells me about the trouble Alexei got into when they were younger, and I lament the sad state of his plants and how I plan to replace them when I get a chance.

It's easy. Fun.

More fun than it has any right to be, really. I keep waiting for her to say something snarky or tell me that she doesn't want me around her brother, or even point out how much I fucked up by letting Alexei hate me, but it never happens.

Instead, Nadya treats me like a friend.

It's an experience I'm not sure I've ever had before.

# CHAPTER 29

# Emiliya

Knocking on the front door resounds like a death knell, sucking all the air out of my lungs. Unaffected, Nadya happily gets up to let Alexei in. His eyes dart back and forth between us, making sure we're exactly as he left us.

"You want to tell me why your girlfriend's been acting like I'm going to hurt her all day?" Nadya asks as he inspects us. I shift uncomfortably under his gaze, but it goes unnoticed.

"I told her about your knife skills."

"It was *one time*," she huffs. "When are you going to let it go?"

"I don't see any reason I should."

"Maybe because it hurts my feelings?"

"Well, in that case..." Alexei shoves his hands into the pockets of his coat, one corner of his lips lifting in a smirk. "Never going to happen."

Nadya makes a show of acting annoyed, but it's impossible to miss her gentle smile and the way her entire body relaxed when she saw her brother standing on the other side of the door.

For all their ribbing and teasing, their love for each other is clear for anyone with eyes to see.

"Fine, then get your girlfriend and get out of here. I have places to be and people to do."

Alexei's lip curls in disgust, and I have to turn my head to hide my smile. There's no doubt in my mind that she's trying to get him out of her apartment as quickly as possible, and from the way he swallows a curse and urges me to put on my boots, she knows exactly what to say to get what she wants.

I only wish I could do the same.

With every step away from Nadya's apartment, the emotions from this morning rush back in, torturing me.

I want to go back to pretending. I want to stay in her cozy apartment where Father can't find me and Alexei's words can't hurt.

*I was in love with you.*

*Was.*

Every time I fail to distract myself, that *was* is an endless echo beating against my skull like gunfire, pounding and pounding away until I want to scream. And every time I close my eyes, I see Father's face as he threatened Mom.

He was so casual, so nonchalant with his treat that I have no choice but to believe he'll follow through on every word.

Alexei's eyes are hard as he focuses on the road, gripping the steering wheel so tight his knuckles bleed white. And though the distance between us is the same as it was on the ride to Nadya's, now it feels like a cavernous gap.

I'm running out of both time and ideas.

What if I tell him the truth? Will he believe me?

Fuck it. What do I have left to lose?

"Father is obsessed with you," I say, unable to look in Alexei's direction. Throughout the day the fluffy snow has been turned into brown slush splattered all over the sidewalks, making everything an unsightly, sloppy mess. "He wanted me to get close to you before Maksim died, but now, it's all he talks about."

I clear my throat, self-loathing threatening to choke me. "You make so much money he considers you a problem, and I think he wanted me to bridge the gap between you two." I huff out a bitter laugh. "Clearly, that hasn't worked."

For several quiet minutes, the only response he graces me with is the roar of the engine and the windshield wipers doing their best to keep the falling snow from blinding.

"Nikita has enough money. He doesn't need me for that," he eventually mutters.

I shrug. "Father doesn't like how independent you are, so he told me to do whatever it takes to get you to fall in line."

When I glance at him, Alexei's nostrils flare as he frowns.

"And you went along with it." It's a statement, not a question.

"You saw what happens when I don't listen to him." I turn back to the window, twisting my hands together in my lap.

"Are you saying he made more of a habit of hurting you than you've let on?"

I roll my eyes.

"Do you really want me to answer that?"

It's not like he doesn't know, but if he's looking for confirmation, he won't get any from me. Spilling the details of Father's abuse serves no one at this point. I won't get any more sympathy, and Alexei's pity won't help anything.

"If it makes you feel better, he only tried to kill me that one time."

The wave of menace that rolls off Alexei and burns through the car is so sharp and sudden that my shoulders curl forward, bracing for whatever comes next.

"No, Emiliya," he says through gritted teeth. "That does not make me feel better."

I laugh, but it's devoid of any amusement. "Well, since you moved me in, I've only seen him once, and he didn't even threaten me."

Alexei's eyes cut to me as he sits up straighter.

"When did you see him?"

*Blyad.*

In any version of the truth, I run the risk of exposing Lev. He was right there with me, and as far as Alexei's concerned, he was supposed to be glued to my side anytime I left his condo.

And if I so much as mention Lev's involvement, Alexei will dismiss anything I say as a lie, and Mom and I will be well and truly fucked.

But if I try to take it back, if I keep feeding him nothing but half-truths and lies, how can I expect him to trust me again?

"He was at the hospital yesterday, and he wasn't happy I haven't been home."

Alexei frowns. "Why didn't Lev say anything?"

"Father was in the exam room." I shrug, picking at my nails. "Lev waited in the hallway so Mom could have some privacy."

"Let me guess, Nikita didn't tell you anything that would be helpful to me?"

For reasons I refuse to examine, that pisses me off more than anything else he's said to me since he gave up on me.

I am more than a pawn for the two of them to trade back and forth. I'm an actual person with thoughts, feelings, and ambitions that neither of them gives a single fuck about.

My heart squeezes tight. If anyone could see me as something other than a tool, I would have thought it would be Alexei, but I was wrong.

And you know what?

Fuck. Him.

Fuck both of them.

They can have their pissing match, and whatever comes from it is *their* fault, not mine. I don't care anymore, no matter how hard my traitorous heart screams otherwise.

I'm so sick of taking orders from everyone else. As soon as Alexei's dead, I'm going to throw myself back into my escape plans. I don't need him, I don't need Lev, and I sure as hell don't need my father.

"Nope. Just threatened to kill my mom. But if he lets anything slip next time I see him, you'll be the first to know."

The fact that Nadya is able to have a job gives me hope. I can't work in a field that requires brains like hers, but I'll find something. When we get back to Alexei's condo, I'll demand my phone back, and I'll start putting in applications everywhere I can.

It doesn't matter where. As long as it's beneath Father's notice, it's worth a shot.

Maybe I can look into the sketchier strip clubs downtown.

At least I have something to offer at a strip club.

"He threatened your mom?"

With a mixture of determination and despair, I nod.

"Why not, right? No one's noticed that she's been out of the public eye for the past two years. Besides me, no one cares about her." My throat burns, but I ignore it as Alexei pulls into the underground garage. "It's all a game of leverage, and he has nothing to lose. I have everything."

I run my fingers through the ends of my hair, anxious to get out of this car and as far away from Alexei and this oppressive silence as I can.

"By the way," I say as I get out of the car, not quite able to meet his eyes, "can I have my phone back?"

He gives me a curious look. "I'm not keeping it from you."

"Right," I sigh. "I can just wander into your office and get it, and you won't say a word? What if I go poking through all your drawers and files? I might find something to tell Father."

Alexei's hand hovers over the call button for the elevator, his eyes boring into the side of my head. "How long have you gone without your phone? How're you checking on your mom?"

I give him a flat look, hoping he understands without my having to say it.

Even if I get my phone back, she probably won't answer. Normally, if she needs me, Yan will shoot me a text and tell me to come back. She gets too frustrated trying to get her eyes to cooperate to bother with her phone anymore.

Hell, I wouldn't be surprised if she keeps her phone on *Do Not Disturb* at all times. She only uses it to listen to books anymore.

But if I have my phone, maybe Lev can get in touch with her for me. If I weren't so mad at Yan, I'd call him and ask him to check on her, but he made his loyalties clear, and I'm never going to encourage him to look after her again.

From now on, I'm going to be very selective of who I let have power over us.

Yan doesn't deserve it anymore.

"You can have your phone," Alexei says gently.

I want to hate that I even had to ask for this small act of kindness, but Alexei looks at me with so much concern that my bitterness gives way to the desire to sink into his arms.

Even after everything, he makes me feel safe. He hates my guts, but he makes me feel like I have somewhere I can safely fall apart, some place where I can let the panic attack that's threatening the edges of my vision consume me. And I trust him to help me put the pieces back together afterward.

It's a pretty lie, but it's still a lie, regardless.

Still, I cling to the tattered edges of it until my phone is in my hand and I'm free to hide in my room, chewing on my nail while I wait for it to charge.

Every second that passes before it has enough juice to turn on takes years off my life.

I crowd against the wall, refusing to risk pulling the cord out as I text Mom a heart emoji. I wait, but as expected, she doesn't answer.

With shaking hands, I pretend everything's fine and dive straight into my job search, looking up strip clubs that are well off the beaten path. Hopefully, they're all so far removed from everything that they're below the Bratva's notice.

None of them look like the kind of places with an actual hiring process besides talking to a skeevy manager, but worst-case scenario, I can find a couple of phone numbers to call later tonight.

I scroll through page after page, cross-checking between Google Maps and dodgy websites.

The longer I sit here, the dirtier I feel. I'm almost ready to call it quits when I find a website that actually has a link to submit applications.

Feeling beyond pathetic, I fill one out, pausing long enough to strip down to my underwear and take a few full-body photos to attach when they request them. What's it matter if some creep sees them? If I want to work there, I'll have bigger things to worry about than some faceless nobody seeing me in my underwear. I might as well get used to it.

Even if every other door and window slams in my face, I know I can count on my body to work in my favor. A nice set of tits and a tight ass will always afford an opportunity, even if it isn't one I actually want.

*There are plenty of women who find sex work empowering,* I tell myself. *Maybe I'll be one of them.*

With my heart in my throat, I submit the application and flip my phone over, burying it under my pillow like I can shove away the gnawing resentment tearing at my insides.

Hopefully, Alexei's content to feed himself, because I'm in no state to make dinner.

All this worry and anxiety, and it's probably fruitless. For all I know, someone set up that website to get gullible, desperate women to send them nudes, and they're using them to keep the relationship with their hand interesting.

At least I have enough functioning brain cells to crop my face out of them before I hit submit.

Half an hour later, my heart is just starting to slow enough to allow me to get a deep breath when my door slams open. Instinct has me scrambling away until the bed is between me and the door.

"Do you mind telling me why I have an application with your name on it sitting in my inbox?" Alexei snarls, his chest heaving.

The blood drains from my face in an instant, pooling at my feet until they're practically glued to the floor.

"What?" I ask breathlessly.

"Why are you applying to be a dancer at my club, and why did you attach pictures?"

I'm frozen, unable to focus or run away. "What do you mean? That... Virgo isn't yours."

I know all of Alexei's clubs. I made a point of it. He has his three nightclubs and one strip club, but it's a nicer one uptown, and that's not where I applied. But he knows about the photos and—

"I don't exactly advertise it, but rest assured, Virgo belongs to me. Now, you're going to be honest with me and tell me why your nearly naked pictures are sitting in my inbox."

Oh, fuck. I'm going to be sick.

"Quickly, Emiliya."

"I wanted some extra spending money," I blurt in a rush. "I found a Blancpain watch that I'd kill to get my hands on."

His eyes narrow at me in that all-too-knowing way of his, and even though I pulled on my comfiest pajamas after I took those photos, I feel naked under his gaze. Even more than I did when I thought I was sending those pictures to a total stranger.

Oh, fuck me.

Alexei has those photos.

And he can do whatever he wants with them.

Send them to everyone in the Bratva. Show them to father. Use them to humiliate and debase me.

"Don't lie to me, Emiliya."

I'm sweaty, guilt coloring my cheeks.

"Why do you have a secret strip club?"

"It's not a secret. It's unlicensed. There's a difference."

"Why do you have an *unlicensed* strip club?" I ask instead, desperate to divert his attention.

"Why would anyone involved in organized crime have a business like that?" he replies. "Discretion is an asset, as is having a building that no one gives a shit about. Now, I'm going to ask you one. Last. Time." Alexei's eyes blaze, the gold flecks burning so hot they appear molten. "Why are you trying to get a job at an illegal club?"

He prowls across the room, and I stumble away from him.

"I already told you."

Step by step, he pursues me, eating up the distance until my back meets the wall. I couldn't run from him even if I wanted to, not with how his furious glare keeps me pinned. Trying to keep some sense of dignity, I bury my shaking hands in the hem of my shirt so I don't do anything stupid.

Like push him away. Or pull him into a kiss.

He's so close my chest brushes against his with every rapid breath.

"If you want pretty things, you know how to get them. And taking off your clothes for strangers at a fucking dump like Virgo won't get you enough for a five-figure watch, no matter how sexy your body is. Neither of us is stupid. So, for once, stop *lying* and tell me what you're hiding."

"I'd rather suck your dick."

My palms are damp when I rub them against my thighs. In a flash, he pulls me against him, his fingertips biting into my hips tight enough to make me squirm.

"Despite what you think, I *know* you, Emiliya. Stop trying to use sex as a shield and answer the fucking question."

I can't decide if I want to reach out and claw his eyes out or twist around until I'm free to run away. Run out of this room, this building.

I want to run straight out of Alexei's life.

Between flight and fight, my body chooses the worst possible option.

I freeze.

I can't move, and I don't realize I'm crying until he cups my chin, brushing away a tear before it hits my trembling chin.

"What's going on, Emiliya?"

If I didn't know any better, I'd say he looks concerned.

Alexei should be screaming at me until he's blue in the face, not touching me like he's scared I'm going to shatter in his arms.

"Is it your mom? Did she say something when you called her?"

"I didn't," I find myself admitting. "Even if she answered, I don't want to worry her. She's got enough going on. Too much for me to add anything else to her plate."

"Isn't that her call to make?"

"I can't." I shake my head, and something behind his eyes shutters closed, a desperate lifeline I didn't even know I was still looking for. "I just have to get her out."

# CHAPTER 30

# Alexei

Emiliya's fucking playing me.

But because I'm a fool, and seeing her cry is carving massive crevasse through my chest, I want to believe her anyway. I want to tear everything to shreds until every tear has been avenged and she's smiling again.

Watching every emotion that plays across her face is one of the best parts of my day.

She wears them all so well, so fully, that I want to savor each subtlety and nuance. When she's angry, it's hot as fuck. When she's feeling sassy, happy, sexy as sin, or relaxed and at peace? I've never seen such a beautiful sight, and I want to spend the rest of my life inspiring every smile, every flicker of joy that crosses her face.

But like this? With her shoulders hunched and blinking back tears like she's terrified I'll dismiss her? I want to tear apart everything and everyone in my path until I find what upset her and destroy it with my bare hands.

Even though I know these tears are probably fake.

She's trained me like Pavlov's dog, and when she rings the bell, I come running.

Telling her I loved her was one of the stupidest things I've ever done, but in that moment, it didn't feel like I had a choice. With her soft and warm in my arms, it felt like the words were going to strangle me if I didn't let them free.

The untrustworthy organ in my chest doesn't care that she's doing her best to ruin me. It wants me to pull her into my arms, to keep her so close I never have to live another day without her.

It'll be the death of me if I let it.

Besides, Nikita won't kill his wife. If he wins this fight, whoever's left standing will disapprove. Any one of us would lie, cheat, steal, and kill anyone that stands in the way of whatever we want, but our families are supposed to be off-limits.

*He still hurt Emiliya.*

Tossing the thought aside, I focus on what's in front of me.

When I stormed in here, I was certain Emiliya had somehow found out I own Virgo and was trying to fuck with me. But the panic when I confronted her about the pictures was impossible to ignore.

Fuck, now I really want to hunt down the old manager so I can kill him.

Using my business to get women to send him photos of themselves like his own personal porno? Then quitting and leaving me to clean up his bullshit? He's given me even more reason than I already had, and he'll come to regret it.

At least Emiliya was smart enough not to include her face, but even if her name hadn't been plastered all over the phishing scam dressed up as an application, I would have known it was her.

Her body. The birthmark on her shin. The fact that those photos were taken in my fucking *guest room*. Any idiot who knows her at all would've been able to identify her.

I'm furious that she would ever put herself in that position.

Aching to punish her.

Livid that she was going to let another man look at her. Not just a single man, but any asshole with a handful of cash to throw her way.

She wanted to dance and show off her body for a few dollars.

Emiliya doesn't care that I still think of her as mine. She isn't. No matter what the primal part of my brain says. She never was, and she never will be.

"Why do you need to get her out?" I ask her.

"I can't let him kill her." Her lower lip wobbles, fear making her eyes wide as saucers. My jaw aches from how tightly I'm clenching it.

"Then let me help," I offer, the tone almost pleading as I watch her.

If she cares about me at all, she'll jump at an opportunity to get away from Nikita, right?

Impossibly, she grows even paler, and it's an answer to a question I can't dare voice.

She doesn't want an escape.

She really does just want to toy with me until I fall so far under her spell that I have no chance of getting out. My chest squeezes so hard I have to fight for another breath, working hard to cover up how much it hurts.

"I can't. I have to do this without you." Her voice waivers, more broken than I've ever heard it. Desperation and determination are evident in every word, but I refuse to listen.

I can't do this again. I can't let her tear my heart out with crushing honesty and tears running down her face.

But I can't give up without trying again, either.

"Right." As I take a step back, a chill fills the space she's thawed out in my chest. "I know I'm a fool for falling for you, and you and your father have probably been laughing about it behind my back, but I'm a fucking idiot. So, I'm still offering my help. If you want to get away, I can do it. Money, a car, new identities. Whatever you want."

With every word, Emiliya grows increasingly more still, until I'm not even sure she's breathing.

"And if you want to stay with your father, if all you want is for me to fuck off, then I'll drop it. We'll never talk about this again."

She considers it, debating with herself, but as soon as she pulls her shoulders back, I know I've lost. Choking down bitter regret, I nod and leave the room, in desperate need of a drink.

I close her door to block out the sound of her cries and pull a bottle of vodka out of the freezer, pouring a healthy amount into a glass.

I should call Nadya. At least she'd get a kick out of this. Or maybe Andrei. I still can't leave Emiliya unattended, but I might be able to convince him to come over for a drink if it's under the guise of planning our next move now that we've found our rat.

I hiss as the alcohol burns the whole way down as I swallow.

What am I going to do when Emiliya leaves?

I can pretend she's my prisoner all I want, but if she demands I let her go, I will. I don't want to give her back to Nikita, but if she's determined to end up there anyway, who am I to stop her?

I'm pouring another glass when a sound down the hall catches my attention. I pause, straining to listen with the glass halfway to my mouth, and it doesn't take long before I hear it again.

Reluctantly, I creep toward Emiliya's room, feeling like a jackass as I stand outside her door.

If I know what's good for me, I'll turn around and walk away, maybe even swallow my pride and call Lev so I can use him as a buffer.

Anything other than lingering outside her room and listening to Emiliya crying.

That's just pathetic. Even for me.

Steeling myself, I take a single step away before I hear another cry, a choked-off sob that shatters my resolve.

I open her door, feeling like a monster when I see her curled around a pillow, doing her best to stifle the sound of her sobs. Self-loathing is like acid in my chest, destroying everything in its wake. Before I decide to, I'm across the room, propping one knee on the bed.

I pry the pillow out of her arms, encouraging her to roll over until her tears are soaking into my chest, her shoulders shaking with every breath.

I press a kiss against the top of her head, murmuring softly while Emiliya shoves her face against my shirt, muffling her cries.

"I'm sorry," she sobs as I rock her back and forth.

Emiliya's far stronger than she gives herself credit for. She manages to put up with my bullshit with her head held high, and she hides her father's abuse so well that no one would know it was there at all if they weren't already looking for it.

Seeing her break down like this is fucking crushing.

I don't know how to comfort her, and I don't even know if she *wants* my comfort, but I hate this. I hate that she's upset in the first place. I hate that I played a role in it. A helpless feeling fills my chest, leaving no room for anything else.

Before I can second-guess myself, I carry her. With her solid and secure in my arms, it's easier to breathe. Still, it feels like it takes ages to maneuver her down the hall so I can lay her in my bed and wrap her in the soft bedding.

Only then am I able to tell myself she's safe.

Miserable and hurting, but safe.

"I'll fix it," I whisper as I curl around her, shifting until her legs are tangled in mine, not a single inch of her not pressed against me in some way. "Whatever it is, I'll fix it." I run my fingers through her tangled hair until her sobs dissolve into distressed hiccups, her face still buried in my chest.

As she settles, I'm filled with a sense of peace that's evaded me since I was sitting in that fucking park.

My heart doesn't care what Emiliya's motives are, or what danger she's putting me in. It only cares about comforting her and making her happy.

If I didn't have to look out for Nadya, I'd give Emiliya whatever she wants. I'd let her serve me up to Nikita on a silver platter if she'd only smile at me again.

But I do have to protect Nadya, and I can't do that if I'm six feet deep.

Nikita isn't the only threat. Konstantin is still circling the edges of my periphery like a shark, waiting to strike at the first sign of blood.

I'll handle him, but I have to deal with the more pressing threats first. Like Emiliya, and the fact that she could crush me with one flick of her little finger, and I have no power to stop her.

"This isn't what I want," Emiliya whimpers, the sound muffled against my dress shirt. "None of this is what I want."

It would have hurt less if she'd stabbed me with a knife.

I trail a hand up the smooth skin of her arm, lingering over the curve of her shoulder.

"No?"

"I just want Mom to be safe. I don't want anyone else to get hurt. I want to be safe."

Something in me cracks open, chills spreading through my whole body, and suddenly, Emiliya's scorching against me. I'm practically sweating, torn between pulling her closer and getting as far away as I can.

"I'm so sorry," she whispers tearfully.

I could ask her what it takes to make her feel safe, but I don't.

"I know," I sigh, wondering if I'll ever get another chance to hold her like this.

I have to let her go.

And I will.

Tomorrow.

For a few more hours, I'll pretend and cherish the time I have left with her.

"I'll fix it, sweetheart. I'll fix it."

# CHAPTER 31

# Alexei

All night long, I'm plagued by an unceasing ache in my chest. It keeps me awake, staring at the snow until it eventually stops and the sun breaks through the thick layer of clouds.

Emiliya is warm as she rests. For as long as she sleeps, I'm going to cling to every moment, treasure every breath I can share with her.

No matter how many moments I steal, it will never be enough. It won't be enough time to memorize every inch of her, to stare at her sleep-slackened face, wondering what she'll look like ten, fifteen, twenty years from now. Even with all the money in the world, I can't afford the time I need.

And even if I could, I can't force Emiliya to give it to me.

*This isn't what I want.*

I need to take her home, and she needs to assure herself that her mother's safe.

Emiliya's lashes flicker against her cheeks as she stirs, making me smile even when I feel like a wrung-out husk of the man I thought I was. She managed to strut into my life and steal my heart, but now I have to let her walk away, taking part of me I'll never be able to get back.

When she blinks awake, she sleepily looks around the room before her gaze settles on me, her face full of so much affection that it crushes me.

The more she wakes up, the faster it fades away until it's gone completely, replaced with the same despondent anxiety from last night. She doesn't try to escape my arms, but she's stiff as a board.

The bright sunlight, so soft only a few minutes ago, is now blinding, harshly exposing everything I desperately want to hide. Slamming my eyes shut, I drop my head against the pillows as Emiliya shifts, her long hair brushing against my chest.

"Are you feeling better?" I ask.

"Yeah." Her voice is still hoarse with sleep, and I want to revel in it. I want to capture the sound so I can play it back whenever I want.

"Do you want to talk about it?"

"No. Actually, I'd rather you pretend it never happened."

That's not going to happen, as much as I wish I could.

She must read it in my body language because she sighs, laying her head down over my heart as she looks toward the window.

"I wasn't lying last night," I tell her. "If you want me to help you get out, I will. No strings attached."

"I know," she replies, her voice just above a whisper. The blanket of snow muffles the sound of traffic that typically floats up here, and even the wind seems to have taken a break from its howling rage. In its place is an awful, excruciating silence. "But I really need to do this on my own."

Guilt threatens to squeeze all the air from my lungs. When I try to speak, it feels like my voice is caught in a vice.

I have to clear my throat when I say, "If you change your mind, you know how to find me." She turns to me, her pretty eyes filled with confusion. "C'mon. Let's get up so you can pack. I'll take you home as soon as you're ready."

All color drains from her face.

"What?"

"I can keep you here, but it isn't going to make you feel any better, is it?" I look away, blinking up at the ceiling. Emiliya's pretty eyes are going to ruin the last vestiges of my resolve, and I can't let that happen. I need to find a sense of strength to rely on until I'm able to learn to live with the ghost of her haunting my condo.

Or, if I live through all this, maybe I'll move somewhere she's never been so I don't have to live with the memories hiding around every corner and behind every door.

"I was talking out of my ass yesterday. I still love you. I want you to be happy, and I'm man enough to admit that it's not going to happen with me."

"What do you mean when you say *home?*"

"Your father's house." Then, because I'm weak, I wonder if that's what she wants. Is that the place she calls home? Or is she still looking for one? "Or I can set you up in a hotel. Wherever you want to go, I can make it happen."

*Stay*, I want to beg. *Tell me you want to stay with me.*

"You can't do that." There's a bite to her voice, a resilient rod of steel under her skin that gives me a moment's pause.

"Why not?" I ask.

"I..." I play with her messy hair, her skin so soft under my fingers. "Did you mean that? When you said you love me, did you mean it?"

With my pride stripped bare, I have nothing to hide behind. No lies, distractions, or hindrances. I can't deny my feelings for her anymore. Not to myself, and certainly not to her.

"Yeah," I sigh. "I meant it. I'm so fucking in love with you I'm not sure how there was ever a time where every thought wasn't consumed by you." I shrug helplessly. "But I'm stuck like this, because there will be a day where my heart doesn't ache. I know you'll never be mine, but no matter what happens, I'll always be yours."

Her breath hitches in her chest before she pulls away, dragging the comforter with her, cold air rushing in to take her place.

"Then do me a favor. Please." Emiliya's voice breaks on that single word, and I'm helpless to deny her anything.

I nod as her eyes water. She hesitates, twisting her fingers in her lap while she swallows, gathering her thoughts. When she finally does speak, she turns around, looking at the plant I keep next to the window.

"Can you take me to Savage tonight? Before you take me home, Father needs..." She closes her eyes, her hands shaking delicately before she bunches them into fists. "It'll be easier for me if Father still thinks I have a chance with you."

She's lying again. Whatever she needs, it isn't because she wants it, and it isn't because Nikita wants me to pretend with her.

He wants me dead.

I look around the room.

When Emiliya leaves, when her things are gone, there will be no sign she was ever here. Even if circumstances were different and she had wanted to be with me, I tossed the possibility of it ever happening the instant I treated her like she meant nothing.

She deserves so much more than what I can give her. But she deserves more than she has with her family, too. If I'm lucky, I'll get a chance to eliminate Nikita from the picture and make things better for her so she can find her happily ever after.

She just won't be standing at my side when I do it.

"If I do, will give me a favor in return?"

"Anything." Her voice is as soft as I've ever heard it.

I wish she would look at me again. I wish she would grant me the opportunity to decipher the array of emotions playing across her eyes, just a hint so I can see if she's struggling with this as much as I am.

"Whatever your father has planned for me tonight, stay out of the way. Don't get caught up in it."

If I know something's coming, I can prepare.

I can have extra security and pay attention. I can put in extra precautions to make sure there aren't any weapons. I can have Lev sweep the place before opening to make sure everything's exactly as it should be.

I can call Nadya and tell her I love her before I go. Just in case.

Because even if it kills me to admit it, she'll be fine without me. I've always needed her far more than she needs me.

But if something happens to Emiliya, I lose any advantage. I won't be able to focus on keeping myself alive if I'm putting everything I have into making sure she's safe.

With a sniff, Emiliya nods down at her lap, picking at a stray thread on the comforter. Her obvious reluctance to hurt me cuts deeper than her lack of a denial.

"I need your words, sweetheart. I need you to promise me you'll stay out of the way."

"I won't get involved," she offers. "I'll stay out of his way."

***

Savage has only been open for a few months, but I'm still proud of everything I've put into it. Out of all my businesses, this is the first one that feels like it's more mine than it is the Bratva's. Though Maksim pushed me to, I was able to refuse any of his money for the purchase of the building, and I was able to fund the renovations on my own.

I allow the Bratva to clean their cash here, but at the end of the day, this place is mine.

No one gets to have a say on any part of it.

It's my name on the line whether it fails or succeeds.

So far, it's been nothing but a rousing success.

There's a crowd of people lined up every night, eager to get in and partake in all my hard work, and tonight is no exception.

I keep an eye out for Lev as Emiliya and I walk through the entrance, waiting for his signal. According to the reports I got from my security team before we left, everything is going exactly as it should, but I'm still on edge.

No matter what Nikita has planned, and I have to assume things are far more dangerous than they seem, and every person in this building is a threat.

Emiliya's a statue on my arm, and when I loosen my grip, she doesn't step away. If anything, she presses herself even closer against my side, lit up and glamorous under the strobe lights flashing overhead.

Under different circumstances, I'd spend all my time admiring her. But, for once, I want her as far away from me as she can get. No matter how much I insisted, she refused to stay home.

As soon as I track down Lev, I'll have someone take her back to my place.

I keep one eye on her as I scan the room, hoping she'll give me some hint of what Nikita has planned, but from the way her eyes are darting back and forth, she doesn't know any more than I do. I'm hesitant to move any further into the crowd before I can find Lev, but Emiliya's so tense I'm not sure I'd be able to pry her off me with a crowbar.

Security is packed along the bar, and one of them can get her to safety without causing a scene.

Once she's safely away from here, I can rely on everyone else to hold down the fort long enough to pull out my phone. Maybe Lev found something and is handling it somewhere out of sight, but if he is, he should've sent me a message.

It isn't like him to fall off the face of the earth.

The longer we linger, the longer Nikita has to do whatever he needs, and the more danger Emiliya's in.

I lean close to her ear, lips brushing against her hair.

"Let's get a drink."

We're in the middle of the crowd. Anyone could slip in behind us, and I'd never know. I need to get her to the edge of the room, somewhere where I can signal for someone to come get her.

There's a crawling sensation on the back of my neck when I urge her forward, but Emiliya's frozen on the spot, her feet glued to the floor as her eyes linger on something I can't make out over the crush of the Saturday night crowd around us.

"Is everything okay?" I ask, my face close to hers.

With a practiced smile that doesn't meet her eyes, Emiliya nods, shaking off whatever freaked her out before she squeezes my arm, her nails digging into my sleeve with every step.

With every step, my heart pounds in my chest. Where the fuck is Lev?

Every muscle in my body is tight when I make eye contact with one of my men, nodding for him to join us as we approach the bar.

The bartenders are all busy, but I'm not looking for service. If Emiliya wants something, she's more than free to imbibe from what's available in my office, because that's exactly where I'm going to tell the security guard approaching to take her.

Until I know there isn't an ambush waiting for me outside, she isn't going anywhere.

I turn to tell her as much when she throws herself in front of me, pushing be backward with all her might.

"Emiliya, what the fuck—"

My words are cut off by a blast of white-hot heat, a huge *boom* deafening me as I'm thrown backward, and everything goes dark.

***

From my head, to my back, to my arms, all that registers is *pain*.

The overhead strobe lights have gone dark, replaced by the flashing of the fire alarms that are making everything bright one second and pitch-black the next. There's screaming, but it feels like my head is wrapped in cotton, making everything sound distant.

I blink dumbly, trying to get my bearings in the utter chaos.

My chest heaves as I cough so hard I gag. My mouth tastes like ash and plaster, and when I turn my head to spit, I can feel something running down my face.

My eyes focus between one flash and the next, until I can make out the debris and dust still falling, coating everything. All around me, there are bodies. Some moving, others writhing in agony, even more not moving at all.

I swipe my hand over my forehead, and it comes back red.

Blood.

On the floor, on the bodies. The pools of blood bubble around me where they meet fire that's destroying everything in its path. Flames creep up the walls and through the shreds of drywall and torn clothing like it's being fueled by the stench of fear and panic.

There's pressure against my shoulder. I swipe for whatever it is, but when I make contact with a hand, they only tighten their grip.

Like someone punched me in the gut, I suck in a sharp breath.

*Emiliya.*

Where the fuck is Emiliya?

My eyes flit from person to person, body to body. Someone is dragging me over shattered glass and broken drywall, away from the flames, but I don't see her.

Using all the strength I have left, I struggle to get away from whoever's touching me.

"Boss, you've got to get out of here!"

His voice is muffled, like I'm underwater. I shove him away, heaving onto my knees.

We were close to the bar, weren't we?

That's the last place I saw Emiliya.

I need to find her.

I shuffle toward the fire, my heart dropping when I see an unmoving body. They're coated in ash, but they're so close to the flames.

I can't make out any details, but they have long hair. They're wearing a short dress.

What if it's Emiliya?

"Boss!"

Glass cuts into my knees, tearing my hands open as I crawl. With every movement, my head spins. The heat makes it impossible to breathe, but I don't stop, not until I'm shoving away a broken stool and brushing dust. Not until I can finally breathe again when I see Emiliya's slack face.

My heart is bruising against my ribs, threatening to give out entirely.

She's so fucking still. Unnaturally still. And when I drag her closer, she's limp. Her body flops uselessly as I pull her against my chest, like she's boneless.

I hold her to my chest, my hands shaking so badly I'm barely able to hold still enough to find her pulse, but it's there.

*It's there*, and that's the only reason I don't collapse on the spot.

There's blood pouring from a vicious gash on the back of her shoulder, soaking into her dress and mixing with the dust around us to create a toxic mixture that makes my stomach turn. I'm afraid to jostle her, to cause her any more pain, but she's not waking up. I pat her cheek, silently begging for a flutter of her lashes, a single glimpse of her fire, but she doesn't stir.

"Boss, c'mon!"

I glare at the guard when he reaches for me again, focusing on the way her breaths puff sluggishly against my chest.

I'm not sure if it's blood, sweat, or tears that's pouring over my cheeks, and I don't fucking care, either.

"Call a fucking ambulance!" The guard hesitates for a half a second, and if I could, I'd throttle him.

But nothing will make me leave Emiliya behind. Not the pain, not the threat of violence. She's going to get out of this, and she's going to be *fine*.

I'll make sure of it.

I move to one knee, doing everything I can to pick her up, to carry her far away from here. My leg buckles as soon as I put weight on it. I pull her close, twisting so my back is facing the flames, making sure she's protected.

Slowly, I shrug off my jacket, draping it over her. If nothing else, it'll protect her from the chunks of ceiling still falling down around us. I hunch over her, protecting her face.

"Come on, sweetheart, open your eyes for me," I beg, pushing her hair back so I can see her. "I need you to wake up. I need you, Emiliya."

She was supposed to stay out of the way.

She *promised*.

This fight was never hers, and she fucking promised me.

# CHAPTER 32

# Emiliya

Even through closed eyelids, the light is too damn bright. It feels like there's a dull spoon carving a hole through the back of my skull, and every incessant beep next to my head only drives it even further.

I lift an arm to cover my eyes, but something in my hand pulls, a piercing pain shooting through me. Resigned, I move away from the source of the light, but it only makes the beeping even faster.

Is that my alarm?

When I try to slam my hand to the side, hoping to turn it off, it's like my limbs aren't listening. Everything feels sluggish and muted. My muscles aren't cooperating, and when I try to focus, my head only throbs harder.

I want the sound to stop. I bury my face in the scratchy pillow, but it doesn't help, and the pain in my head is only getting worse with every passing second.

Something touches my hand. I try to jerk back from it, and finally my arm cooperates, sliding over rough sheets.

God, what happened? With every breath, more and more pain filters past the fog of sleep until it's demanding my attention.

My whole body feels like I was run over by a truck. My back. My head. Even my shoulder feels like it's been run through with a knife. No matter how I shift to get away from it, there's only pain.

I whimper, the pounding behind my eyes only growing in intensity when I try to remember what happened. I went to Savage with Alexei and then... nothing. Just a blank void where memories should be.

The beeping sound only gets faster the more I struggle to get away from it, and the thing on my hand holds me even tighter. Against my better judgment, I crack open an eye so I can see what I'm fighting against, but the bright lights pierce my vision until I cringe away with a groan.

Shit, even my throat hurts.

"You're alright," a deep voice soothes, the sound like weathered rocks under calm waters. As it washes over me, the beeping slows to something less piercing. "You're okay, sweetheart. Can you open your eyes for me?"

Reluctantly, I try again, and it's only marginally less painful.

I blink slowly, trying to ignore the throbbing ache behind my eyes as I look around. Everything's so fucking bright, and turning my head away from the window makes me dizzy, but I've spent enough time in hospitals to recognize one.

That explains the beeping.

It takes several painful moments before I'm able to focus my gaze on Alexei. He watches me like he's worried I'm going to disappear. "There you are," he says with a sigh, hands clasped tightly over mine.

"You look like shit," I mutter through dry, cracked lips.

There are massive bags under his eyes, his hair is a disaster, and his shirt is covered in dust and what looks like dried blood. Butterfly stitches cover a jagged gash across his forehead that matches the scar on the other side.

"Hate to break it to you, but you don't look much better."

I laugh, the sound breaking off into a cough. He's quick to offer me a cup of water, tucking a lock of hair behind my ear.

The water is heaven on my dry throat, and I protest weakly when he pulls the cup away, but even that much effort has my eyelids ready to flutter shut again.

"I don't know what you're talking about." I try to smile, but it hurts so much that I give up almost immediately. "I always look fantastic."

"You do. But you also look like you're about to hurl." Alexei shrugs. I let my eyes close, and he moves his hand to my cheek, tapping until I open them again. "Time to stay awake now. At least until the doctor comes to check on you."

"Let me sleep."

"I'd love to," Alexei replies, "but the doctor said you have a concussion."

I try to roll my eyes, but he doesn't relent. Probably because I have to take deep breaths to stop the room from spinning afterward.

"Why'd you lie to me, Emiliya?"

"I didn't," I reply on instinct, though I still don't know what the hell he's talking about.

"You said you'd stay out of the way, and you did the opposite." His words tickle something at the back of my head, but before I can figure out what, he shakes his head. "So, now, I'm rescinding my offer to take you home. You're stuck with me."

"What happened?"

He frowns. "You don't remember?"

"We went to Savage, but I don't remember anything after that."

Alexei hums, stroking his finger over my cheekbone.

His phone rings, making me jump. Alexei curses under his breath as he looks at the screen, shooting me a concerned glance.

"I need to answer this," he mutters, waiting for me to nod before he answers. *"Da?"*

His free hand rests on the thin blankets tucked around my legs while I pick at the IV in my other hand, doing my best to pretend I'm not listening. There's a voice in the back of my head screaming that I need to tell him something, but I can't remember *what*.

The urgency in my blood makes me antsy, makes me want to demand to know what happened, but I can't seem to find my voice.

"No, he's outside. Why?" he asks whoever he's talking to.

Alexei's face is blank as he listens to whatever the other person's saying before fire flashes behind his eyes. He opens his mouth to reply, and his face contorts with anger as he's interrupted. I flinch, but he strokes my leg as he turns away, glaring at the door.

"Bring him here. I'll handle it." His jaw is tense, and his eyes glance briefly at the heart rate monitor when it reflects the way

my stomach twists with his mood swing. If I could tear the
sensor off my finger without risking nurses and doctors rushing
in and fussing over me, I would.

"Everything okay?"

"No," he bites out, grinding his teeth. "But it will be." He
pockets his phone and stands, pressing a gentle kiss against my
brow. He prowls toward the door like it's personally offended
him, tearing it open.

"Lev!" he calls, voice tight. A moment later, Lev's shaved
head appears in the doorway and my lungs forget how to func-
tion.

All at once, I remember.

Seeing Lev behind the bar.

The look on his face as he focused on whatever he was doing.

The way he winked at me before he turned away, stalking
toward the emergency exit and out of the club.

Trying to keep Alexei from getting any closer to whatever Lev
put there.

The heat, the pain, the screams before I lost consciousness.

I remember the defeat when I thought it was all over.

I remember *everything*.

"I need you to swing by Morning Star," Alexei tells him.

"Seriously? That's all the way across town."

"The manager's having an issue with one of the members
of security, and I'm a little preoccupied right now." There's no
room for argument in Alexei's tone, a deadly undercurrent to
every word. Lev's eyes cut to me, a look so scathing I cringe.

Alexei *needs* to know about Lev.

I should have told him as soon as I knew Lev was working with Father. But Father still has all the power over Mom. He's tied my tongue without being anywhere near me, bound me to silence without even needing to be in the same room.

"Who's going to watch your back while I'm gone?" Lev asks Alexei.

"I can handle myself. Go make yourself useful."

Alexei glances from me back to Lev, snarling when he sees he hasn't moved an inch.

I wish I could turn off the heart monitor so it will stop echoing my inner turmoil for all to hear.

There's a defiant tilt to Lev's chin, and he only backs down when Alexei narrows his glare. Menace pours off him in waves until Lev retreats, his tail tucked between his legs as he scurries back into the hallway. Even then, Alexei waits until my heart rate returns to normal before he closes the door, pulling out his phone and shooting off a text.

"I think we need to talk," he says. His gentle words are completely at odds with the harsh, commanding tone he used with Lev, and I swallow thickly.

Alexei's still alive, which means I failed.

And Father's going to make Mom pay the price.

As soon as Lev's gone, he's probably going to be calling Father, telling him exactly what a fuckup I am.

I grab my hair at the root, pulling it tight until the last of the fog wrapped around my brain clears.

Alexei crosses the room, prying my fingers loose. The heart rate monitor slips free in the struggle. A flat drone whines from the machine.

With one hand, Alexei grabs my chin, tilting it up until I have no choice but to look at him. Concern dances in his eyes, but it hardly touches the edges of the darkness crashing down around me.

"My mom," I gasp. "She needs to get out of that house. Alexei, *please,* get her out of there." My chin trembles as I claw at his wrist, ready to throw myself at his feet and beg if I have to. I'll put myself through anything, I'll let him humiliate and hurt me.

I'm so desperate it feels like there isn't enough oxygen in my lungs to keep up with my thoughts.

I need to move. I need to do *something*. But when I shift, my arms feel like they're going to give out. I can't even get out of this bed, much less put up a fight. I'm entirely at Alexei's mercy.

"Take a deep breath," Alexei urges as the door flies open, a team of nurses taking in the scene. "Get the fuck out," he snarls over his shoulder.

I make eye contact with one of them, a woman I've come to know in passing.

Her eyes are narrowed in concern, but when I nod, she swallows before urging everyone out of the room, eyeing Alexei warily.

When the door shuts behind them, a fierce determination steels Alexei's face. Resting his forehead against mine, he stays until my breaths slow down and my chest is no longer heaving.

"I just talked to Andrei, and your mom is fine. She's safe."

"She is?" I ask shakily as I lean against Alexei like he's the only thing keeping me from collapsing.

"Yeah. You can see her in a bit."

There's a loud knock at the door, but this time Alexei doesn't seem irritated by the interruption. Unhurried, he presses his lips against mine, his touch so gentle and purifying it nearly brings tears to my eyes.

"Come in," Alexei calls, rising while I stare at my trembling hands. He turns around, blocking my view of whoever just walked into the room. "This him?" he asks.

"Yeah."

"Fantastic," Alexei sighs, sounding drained. I risk a glance around him, and scramble backward until I'm pressed against the pillows, creeping as far as I can until I feel the cool wall against my shoulders.

Yan is standing next to Andrei, his hands in his pockets as he takes me in with a solemn expression.

"What are you doing here?" I ask, my voice trembling.

Why is he here? With Andrei? With *Alexei*?

I didn't even realize how terrified I was of seeing Yan again until now, when I have no way to escape him. My heart throbs like a hummingbird's wings, fluttering faster than I can handle.

"Hey, hot stuff."

His greeting sets off something in Alexei, his face contorting in a mask of rage that makes my shoulders creep toward my ears.

"Don't talk to her," Alexei barks, snapping his fingers in Yan's face. "Focus on me."

Yan's entire body tenses, a barely contained snarl erasing all traces of his usually playful expression.

He's always been the first person to throw out a joke and make me laugh when things looked bleak before, but right now, he looks fucking lethal.

As he stares down Alexei, Yan might as well be a stranger.

"I've known her since she was a kid. Who are you to tell me I can't talk to her?"

Andrei closes the door and leans against it with his arms folded over his chest, watching them with a bland expression. "If he doesn't kill you first, he's going to be your boss," he says, sounding bored. "I'd suggest you listen to him."

Yan's hands flex at his sides. He's a stubborn man with a mind of his own who's never quite learned to bite his tongue. It makes him an excellent guard, but when he has to take direct orders, it's a disaster.

I always thought he knew that about himself, and that's why he never aspired to more under Father's command. Apparently, he was just waiting for an opportunity.

One I handed to him on a silver platter when I left.

"After all this time, *this* is the best you could find?" Alexei growls at Andrei before he looks Yan up and down, apparently finding him lacking.

"Hear him out," Andrei shrugs. "He's the one who has info on your cousin."

"Is that why you told me to send my best man away? Because this *mudak* had something to say?"

"Lev's your best?" Yan snorts, apparently content to ignore Alexei's boiling contempt. "Really? And here I was, thinking you might be able to lead this fucking brotherhood. But if he's your best, we're all fucked."

Pulling my knees to my chest is agonizing, but I ignore the pain, working to make myself as unnoticeable as possible.

"And why's that?"

Yan's gaze flashes to me, his jaw working as he swallows.

"I don't know how much Emiliya's told you, but Nikita's a heavy-handed son of a bitch. He does whatever it takes to get what he wants, even if that means he has to beat and manipulate his own family. And when you hid Emiliya away, you took away his favorite tool." There's a look of remorse on his face I'm not prepared to deal with, and I look away from it, closing my eyes when the room spins around me.

I want to tell him to shut up, that Alexei doesn't need to know all the details of my manipulation and betrayal, but I'm too busy focusing on not puking.

"You did a good thing when you got her out of there. It was more than I had the guts to do." Yan pauses until Alexei lifts his chin in silent acknowledgment. "So, imagine my surprise when your supposed *best man* showed up at the house last month saying he wanted to talk to Nikita. Lev refused to leave until the boss told us to let him in."

I can't decipher the look on Alexei's face, but there are only lingering traces of surprise. I bury my head in my knees.

If they have to do this now, do they have to do it so loudly?

"I didn't see him again until a few days ago, when he hand-delivered Emiliya to Nikita at the hospital. He even waited outside the room while Nikita threatened her mom. Told her that if she didn't get you to your club last night, he wouldn't just kill Irina, he'd make her suffer for it." He shrugs, a rueful tilt to his chin.

"And why should I believe you?"

"You could ask Emiliya, but from the look of it, she's still fucking terrified." There's a pause, and I wait for the ground to open up and swallow me whole. "But from what I can tell, you're a decent man. You got Emiliya out, and that meant I could focus on Irina." He clears his throat. "Neither of them deserves Nikita's abuse."

There's a fraught pause before Alexei nods.

"Andrei?"

"I already have someone tailing him. Lev won't get far."

He and Alexei start talking in hushed voices, their expressions intense.

Yan doesn't wait for permission before striding toward me until he can take the seat where Alexei was holding his vigil.

"You okay?"

I nod slowly, keeping my eyes closed as another wave of dizziness consumes me.

"No, you're not." He rubs a hand up and down my arm, making soothing sounds until I stop trembling.

"Irina's safe," he tells me. "I took her to my place yesterday, and she's with Dr. Bonilla right now. He even came in on his day off to make up for the other day." His words are quiet, but it feels like he's yanked apart the massive knot in my chest, tearing each thread that squeezes my lungs to shreds.

"Promise?"

"I promise," he vows. "Now, seriously, are you alright? Because you don't look like your normal, gorgeous self."

Despite myself, a shaky laugh bubbles out of my chest.

"She has a concussion," Alexei says, closer than I was expecting. "Bruised lung, a fractured rib, and she needed stitches on her shoulder, but the doctor said she'll recover."

Yan hisses sympathetically. With careful movements, he helps me resettle on the bed, taking his time when bile burns in the back of my throat. "You think you can talk Alexei into getting your mom so she can see you?"

"What, your legs don't work?" Alexei asks.

Yan glares, but stands, giving my hand a final squeeze.

"Fine. I'll go get the doctor, and then I'll stop by with your mom."

Andrei follows him into the hall, leaving Alexei and me alone. When he touches my hand, I practically melt into the small comfort.

The tiny gesture settles me, lets me know he's here because he wants to be.

*Everything's okay.* My mom's safe, and Alexei won't let Father anywhere near me. If he were going to blow up at me over Lev, he'd already be yelling, right?

But he isn't.

Instead, he's looking at me like he's worried. About *me.*

"I love you," he says, the corner of his mouth twitching upward. My heart stutters in my chest, both from the words and from his smile. Hope fills my chest until I feel like I could float.

"You do?"

"Yeah, Emiliya, I do. And when you look at me like that, I think you might love me, too."

I do. Fuck, I do. But when I try to tell him, my mouth is dry. As if Alexei can read my mind, he smiles, a brilliant sun coming out from behind a thick layer of clouds.

"When I get back, I want to hear you say the words, okay?"

My gut clenches. "Where are you going?"

"I need to see an old friend, but Andrei will stay here and look after you and your mom until I get back. It'll probably be a few hours." He pauses, waiting.

It takes longer than it should for me to realize he's waiting for my approval, but when I do, it slams straight into my chest.

Alexei doesn't need to ask anyone for permission, but he wants mine.

Because, my opinion matters to him.

My head swims as I nod.

"I'll come back to you as soon as I can, and the moment the doctor says you're good to go, we're going home," he says before kissing me like I'm precious.

# CHAPTER 33

# Alexei

L ike an old scar, the drive to Terre Haute, Indiana, is familiar and unpleasant. Even though I haven't been here in five years, the path is burned into my memory, refusing to let me forget it, no matter how hard I try.

Nadya and I haven't tried to keep up with Dad since he was thrown behind bars.

What's the point? He threw his life away in the pursuit of glory, and he happily ignored the two children who needed him. He left us behind like we were nothing.

For as often as he'd preach that our decisions don't exist in a vacuum, he managed to forget it as soon as it really mattered.

The last time I visited Dad was after my twenty-first birthday, when I thought I might be willing to forgive him. But the only thing he gave a shit about was the Bratva. He didn't ask about me, and he didn't even mention Nadya.

As far as I'm concerned, that was the end of our relationship. But I need advice.

And suddenly, I can't count on anyone else to give me perspective. Lev's not an option, Andrei has to look out for his own family, and I can't turn to Nadya on this.

My dad's a shit father, but he knows what it means to be committed to the Bratva. If nothing else, I can trust him to guide me to do the right thing for them.

The three-hour drive flies by, though every mile scrapes like sandpaper along my spine as I get further and further from the people I need to be with.

By the time I've gone through every checkpoint and metal detector, I'm more than ready to turn around and go back to Emiliya, where I can watch her and assure myself she's still alive and mostly unharmed.

The image of her limp body at Savage is going to haunt me for the rest of my life.

I wait at a metal table in a room made entirely of solid stone. The bright lights don't offer a single shadow that could conceal anything, and I'm acutely aware of the camera in the corner recording my every move.

Not a single word said in this room will remain private.

I focus on the door, waiting until a pair of guards lead my father into the room.

His arms and legs are shackled together. His shoulders are thinner than I remember in his orange jumpsuit. His hair has gone gray. The strain of living in prison aged him more than I was expecting.

I wait to feel a flicker of pity, but it doesn't come.

"Hey, Dad."

The guards secure his handcuffs to the table before positioning themselves next to the door like silent sentinels.

I could have set up bribes to give him more leeway in here, but
Dad isn't worth it. From the look of things, Maksim agreed.

Good. Then he won't notice anything different when either
Nikita or I take over and shake things up.

"Alexei." He nods. "It's been a while." His face is set in stone,
guarding his thoughts as carefully as he taught me to.

There's so much I need to catch him up on, but I'm distinctly
aware that everything I say will end up in the laps of the feds.

They've been around, and other than an occasional appearance at my clubs, they've kept their distance. But after Nikita
escalated things by setting off a fucking bomb in a crowded
nightclub, I have a feeling that's going to change.

It's only luck that's kept them off my ass, demanding state-
ments about what happened and full access to the wreckage.

Hell, I wouldn't be surprised if they've already taken the
liberty.

"I wanted to let you know that Maksim passed away," I say.

Dad leans as far back as he's able to in the unforgiving metal
chair, his face contemplative. His gray brows are drawn together; his hands interlaced on top of the table.

"I take it his son has stepped up in his place?"

I shake my head. "No. He was found dead in his apartment
weeks before his father died."

"Ah." Dad smiles, looking more like the man I remember
him as, quick on his feet and full of energy. "Nikita, then?"
Before I'm able to snarl out a denial, he's already grinning,

opportunity shining in his eyes. "You know, he has a daughter about your age. Has he married her off yet?"

"No."

Even the thought of marriage makes me queasy. Between the shit with Konstantin and Dad's obvious desire to see me rise through the ranks at any cost, it's going to be awhile before I even *think* about broaching the subject with Emiliya.

"But Emiliya *is* mine."

As I sat at her side in the hospital room, holding her hand and waiting impatiently for her to wake up, I decided the matter is settled. Nikita can threaten whatever he wants, but I'm not going to let him steal her away from me.

No amount of violence or threats will ever separate her from my side.

I love her, and she's going to be with me until she decides she doesn't want to be.

"Does Nikita know that?" Dad smiles conspiratorially, and it makes me feel like a child all over again, sharing a secret from Mom and Nadya.

I have a sinking feeling that no matter what I do or how much money I earn, he'll always view me as the little boy who depended on him for guidance. He'll never view me as the man I am because he'll never get the chance to know me.

In his mind, I'm still frozen in childhood, unchanged by time or experience.

"He knows enough to know I won't let her go," I answer honestly. Dad rubs his chin, and I decide to toss him a bone. "And if I have my way, it won't be Nikita who takes over Maksim's role." I shoot a glance at the guards and offer no more than that.

Dad's forehead wrinkles as he raises his brows, a small smile lighting him up from within.

And, fuck, maybe I should have tried to pull some strings to ensure this conversation was private. If I have to speak in half-truths and dance around it, he'll never be able to tell me exactly what he's thinking, but I don't want Dad to think things are going to change.

When I take over the Bratva, I have no intention of making things easier for him.

He made his bed, and now he has to lie in it.

"Well, that warms my heart, son."

To my surprise, the flicker of pride in his eyes does nothing for me. I don't care how he feels about me one way or another.

Everything I have, I've built without him. And nothing will change that.

"And how's your sister?"

I exhale slowly. My seat is just as uncomfortable as his, and the stone walls echo every sound in the room, from each word he says, to the guard's nylon uniform rustling as he shifts from foot to foot.

"That's why I'm here, actually."

"Is she in trouble?"

"No," I assure him. "But someone's reached out to ask for her hand in marriage."

Dad's brows pinch together as he leans forward, his hand-cuffs clanging against the table. For a moment—so fast I'm not sure I didn't imagine it—he looks distraught.

Surely he's always known it would happen, eventually. Nadya was always going to fall in love and marry someone, but maybe it never hit him that he wouldn't get to see it. That he was going to spend her wedding day the same way he's spent more than a decade. Alone, with only the bars of his cell for company.

Good.

I hope his regret is the kind of pain that keeps him up at night. It's the least he deserves for abandoning us.

When he clears his throat, a vindictive sense of justice makes me sit up even straighter.

"Does she love him?"

"No."

"And does he love her?"

"No."

There's no missing the disappointment in his eyes when he looks away, blinking rapidly.

"Who is he?" he asks, his voice distant.

"Konstantin Lavrov."

Dad's loud, despondent bark of laughter rings off the walls, grating on my already strained nerves. "That little fool hasn't managed to get himself killed yet?" It takes him a moment to settle, looking mildly interested when I don't share his amusement.

I don't know what Konstantin was like when Dad was locked away, but he's more than made a name for himself in the time since. He's single-handedly managed to seize control of the west coast, ruthlessly stomping out any competition.

"He's willing to mediate conversations between Nikita and I so long as I allow him to marry Nadya."

And, unfortunately, I need his help if I want to settle the score without more unnecessary bloodshed. The Bratva has lost too many men as it stands. Between The Outfit, the bombing, and the inevitable unrest when I take over, there aren't many men left to lose.

I'll kill Nikita. With Konstantin's help, the stubborn fools that hesitate to back me will either figure out the error of their ways, or they'll meet the same fate. He can provide more men and extra guns to keep me from being backed into another corner.

Konstantin wouldn't just be providing assistance, he'd be throwing me a life vest.

Especially when I don't know if Lev is the only traitor I have in my ranks.

And that's not even mentioning any help Konstantin could extend where The Outfit is concerned.

"In all the chaos of the past few months, I haven't had a chance to take care of my little pest control problem. I've allowed things to slip through the cracks, and now I may need to clean the whole house." I shrug as Dad sits up straighter.

"Is it fair to assume your cousin's looking into it?"

The bitter sting of betrayal burns just as much as it at the hospital, but what Yan said makes sense.

Lev was supposed to give me the all-clear at Savage, and he was nowhere to be seen. He knew when I was at Underground, and he made sure he wasn't in the building when the shooting started. He knew I was going to be at the park when Nikita caught me unaware.

In retrospect, it was only through pure idiocy that I never even considered him. Then again, I've always had a blind spot when it comes to family.

Andrei texted me while I was still driving here, and now Lev's in Virgo's basement, waiting for me to deal with him.

There's no way around it. If I'm going to rule, I need to make sure everyone else understands the cost of going behind my back.

It'll be a lesson born of blood, whether I like it or not.

"No. I have someone else handling it," I answer.

Dad hums, tilting his head from side to side. "I think you should talk to Nadya. She's a stubborn girl, but she's always had a soft spot for you. You can talk her into making a sacrifice for her family. If you play your cards right, she'll be invaluable."

That's what I was afraid he'd say.

I can't afford to make an enemy of Konstantin, but I can't sacrifice Nadya's happiness for my own, either.

"I can't do that."

"I know you care about her," Dad says, eyeing me seriously. "But Nadya knows what this life entails. She'll come to understand."

"She deserves more than that."

"She does," he concedes. "But if you want to make sure Nikita doesn't have the chance to fight you for his daughter, you might not have another choice." He clears his throat, closing his eyes for a long moment. "Talk to her, son. Your sister might surprise you."

***

If the three-hour drive away from Chicago was agonizing, then the drive back is nothing short of tortuous.

More than anything, I want to check on Emiliya and try to figure out how to broach a conversation with my sister, but instead I turn toward the opposite side of town.

Despite leaving later than I would have liked to this morning, it's only a little after sunset. Too early for most of the regulars who linger at Virgo, but that's fine by me. It's less people I have to worry about hearing something and getting spooked enough to call the cops.

While I make my way to the basement, I swallow down any lingering doubt or regret.

I don't have room for them anymore. I need to be sure of myself. I need to prove I can do what needs to be done.

I key in the code for the door, expression set in stone before I come face-to-face with Lev. He's tied to a chair that's been bolted to the ground.

He snarls around a wadded-up cloth, one eye swollen shut. Of course, he wouldn't lie down and accept his fate with grace. No, Lev has always been the kind of man to put up a fight, even when it was clear he'd already lost.

I wouldn't expect anything less.

He may be a traitor, but he's still a Trenin.

Several men are lined around the room, including Philipp, who looks as pissed as I've ever seen him. He's recovered from his surgery well, and I can't help but hope he's the one who gave Lev that black eye. It's less than he deserves for putting his life on the line for me, but it would have been a small measure toward justice.

Lev glares at me as I rip out the makeshift gag, spitting out a mouthful of blood at my feet.

"I think we need to have a chat, don't we?" I ask, conscious of all the eyes in the room eagerly watching my every move.

I can't blend into the background anymore. If I'm going to throw myself into this role, then I'm going to have to get comfortable being in the spotlight in a fucking hurry.

"I'd love to," Lev drawls, his voice ragged. "But I'm a little tied up at the moment."

"I'm glad you're keeping your sense of humor." I drag a chair from the corner of the room, putting it in front of him before sitting down. With my elbows braced on my knees, I'm able to take in every enraged line on his face. "It won't do you any good, but still"—I shrug—"I'm glad to see it.

Ironically, if he were confused, or surprised, I might have listened to him plead his case. But his anger is as good as a confession right now, and whatever he said when he was dragged in here will all eventually filter back to me.

For once, Lev doesn't have any secrets.

"So, why'd you do it?"

I don't elaborate.

From the simmering resentment that's pouring off the men who've pledged their loyalty to me, Andrei let just enough detail slip to whoever he had grab Lev. We're all on the same page, and we all know the price a turncoat is expected to pay.

"You're going to get us all killed, you know that?" Lev's voice is like acid, but it has no impact.

"Is that so?"

"You're so fucked up over that piece of ass you can't even tell who's playing you. I've been by your side since we were children, and instead of questioning her, you've got *me* in this fucking chair?" He scoffs, a sound I've only heard from him when he's on the edge of his control. "You're a fucking moron."

I wait a moment, watching his chest heave. His nostrils flare with each breath.

"We're remembering our childhoods very differently. I remember you whining whenever Nadya and I stayed with your family. And if I recall, you only tried to ingratiate yourself to me after I started making money."

I allowed him to, and for a while, he proved to be helpful. Lev would do the things I didn't have time for, and in exchange, he got to be closer to the action than he was otherwise able to.

Until now, I thought he was happy with our setup.

What did Nikita offer him? Was it more power? More wealth? If Lev thought Nikita would ever allow him to have more than an illusion, he's an even bigger sucker than I thought he was.

"Did Emiliya tell you I betrayed you? Are you really so willing to throw away your own *family* over the word of that *suka*?"

"If you really want to know, no, Emiliya was not the one who informed me of your betrayal. Now, if you're done with this little show, it'd be a great time for you to answer the original question. *Why*?"

There's no give in my voice, just pure ice as I meet his glare.

Lev's lip curls into a smirk that has me grinding my teeth.

"I'm not going to absolve you of this," he hisses, setting his shoulders with resolve. "If you're going to make the tough calls, you're going to have to live with them. I'm not giving you an excuse so you can use it to keep the guilt at bay."

I hate him. I hate how easily he can see through me, but I'll be damned if I let him know it.

"You're going to drag this whole Bratva into the ground. Nikita will do what needs to be done. He won't waffle back and forth and get distracted by a tight body. I did what I needed to do. That's more than you have the guts for."

I hum, pulling my gun out of my waistband. I flick the safety and press the barrel right against his forehead.

To his credit, Lev doesn't flinch or waver. Instead, he leans into it.

"Too bad your opinion doesn't count for anything anymore."

He holds my eyes as I pull the trigger with a deafening bang.

For a single moment—a single heartbeat—I let my grief crush me. I let the full weight of my actions scream through me, destroying a part of myself I didn't even know I was still clinging to until it was gone.

As soon as I blink, I push it aside, turning to make eye contact with Artyom as he leans against the wall.

"Have someone clean the mess and drop his body at his mother's house."

She deserves to know what happened to her son.

"Sure thing, Pakhan."

When I pass, Artyom holds out a hand.

"He was wearing this when we found him," he says, holding out a watch. The gilded crystal of the face is cracked, but the workmanship is unmistakable.

*Blancpain.*

Is that all it took? A fancy watch and Lev threw away a lifetime of blood.

"Leave it with the body. He can be buried with it."

I leave the building without looking back, waiting for the weight of my guilt and new responsibility to devastate me. But, somehow, I stay standing.

# CHAPTER 34

# Emiliya

Andrei is shitty company.

In the hours Alexei's been gone, he's hardly said a word to me. I don't know if it's because he's generally a miserable asshole, or because he really, *really* doesn't want to talk to me.

"Any chance I can talk you into leaving? Or stepping into the hallway?"

Even waiting for Alexei to come back in total isolation would be better than this stoney silence.

"Not likely," Andrei replies, sounding annoyed as he leans against the door like a statue.

"Perfect," I mutter sarcastically. "That's exactly what I wanted to hear."

I turn to face the window. The sunset is painting the sky in brilliant purples and blues, and it's more entertaining than anything else has been since the nausea faded away a couple hours ago.

I have no clue what happened to my phone. Maybe it was destroyed in the explosion, or maybe Alexei just forgot to give it to me before he left, but I'm so bored I'm tempted to get off this bed and waltz out of the room, just to see what Andrei will do.

I've already counted the ceiling tiles, and after the doctor came by with a round of pain meds, I was able to sit up and count the floor tiles, too. But I fell asleep halfway through, so if I get really desperate, I can try again.

Maybe that will distract me from thoughts of Alexei, and of how the longer I sit here waiting for him, the more worried I get.

"Do you have any clue when Alexei's coming back?" There's no disguising the whine in my voice, but if it really bothers Andrei, he's free to step into the hall.

God, I wish he'd leave me alone. As far as I can tell, Andrei's only saving grace is his ability to ignore me. But even in silence, he's annoying. And even if I wasn't pissed off about what he said the other day, judgment pours off him in waves, making the room feel almost suffocating.

"No." Andrei stares straight ahead, only moving to check his watch. From the way he's been doing it with more and more frequency, I'm under the impression he wants to leave just as much as I want to see him gone.

"At least tell me he's alright."

Finally, he gives me an exasperated look. "As far as I know, he's fine."

I want to scream my frustration in his face, but how the hell do I really expect him to know? Andrei's phone has been silent, and other than the doctor, the only person he's let into the room has been Mom.

Fortunately, Andrei waited in the hallway while she was here. I don't know if I would've been able to look him in the eye if he'd borne witness to the way I ugly-cried when she told me how Yan snuck her out of the house and made her comfortable in his apartment.

Mom left with Yan ages ago, and every time the doctor's stopped by, he's left as soon as he could, Andrei's impassive glare chasing him away.

Doesn't he understand I'm on the edge of losing my shit?

If something's happened to Alexei, Andrei's phone would be blowing up, right? He'd be doing something other than using his silent presence like an intimidating space heater.

That doesn't stop me from wondering *what if*.

What if Father found him?

What if Lev ambushed him as soon as he left the hospital?

What if he's been shot... or worse?

I spiral, unable to relax until the door finally, *finally* opens and Alexei steps through. He looks exhausted and worn down, but still so beautiful I could cry with relief.

He must have changed out of his dirty, bloodied outfit at some point. The only sign he was caught up in the blast is the cut on his forehead, and as I look at him, it all hits me again.

I love him.

I love him, and I nearly lost him. If I were in any state for it, I'd tear out of here and hunt Father down.

How dare he try to kill someone so good, someone so perfect he might as well be made for me?

Alexei said I'm stuck with him, but if anything, it's the opposite. He just doesn't know it yet.

He's across the room in a flash, pulling me into his arms.

"Don't cry." The way he strokes my hair makes me think he's trying to comfort me, but his words come out like an order, and I can't help but choke on a sound that's caught between a laugh and a sob.

"I love you," I lament, pressing my tear-soaked face against his shirt.

Alexei goes rigid as I wrap my arms around him.

"Say it again," he commands.

This time, I laugh. "I love you." He pulls back far enough for me to see his breathtaking smile. He's stunning when he smiles, lit up from the inside, but still...

He looks like shit. Even worse than he did this morning.

His hair looks like he's been running his hands through it all day, his stubble is out of control, and the bags under his eyes make him look far older than he is.

"Rough day?"

He chuckles, shaking his head like none of it matters. "I love you, too."

"If loving me makes you look like this, maybe you should reconsider."

"Never," Alexei sighs as he presses his lips against mine, stealing the air from my lungs. As naturally as breathing, his kiss calms me, erasing all the stress and doubt I've been dodging for days. With his body pressed against mine, I feel free. "There's no point. You're stuck with me, remember?"

I've never wanted anyone to have the power to destroy me the way Father has, but Alexei? He could destroy me with just a few words or a single careless action. He could ruin me, and I've given him everything he needs.

But I trust him not to.

Because he. Loves. Me.

"Please tell me the doctor said you can go home. I'm sick of not having you in my bed."

I laugh, immediately regretting it when my ribs scream in agony.

"Last time I saw him, he said he was going to get my discharge papers."

"How long ago was that?"

"An hour," I say as I raise my uninjured shoulder in a half-hearted shrug. "I think he's scared of Andrei, though. You might have to track him down."

Alexei glares at Andrei over his shoulder, but it rolls right off him.

Forty minutes later, Alexei's carrying me out of the elevator and down the hall to his condo, ignoring my protests that I am, in fact, able to walk. The old woman at the end of the hall sticks her head out, glaring at us like we're nothing but a couple of degenerates.

"Mrs. Sullivan thinks you're a brute," I tell him as he opens the door, fumbling with the keys without letting me go. I might as well be arguing with a brick wall for all the good it does me.

"Mrs. Sullivan needs to mind her own business," Alexei mutters as he finally gets the door open. He stops dead as soon as he's past the entryway. I follow his gaze to figure out why and see Nadya sitting at the island.

Her whole body sags when she looks at us, not even trying to hide the relief on her face as she guns toward us.

"You're okay," she breathes. "I've been calling you since last night, and…" Her eyes flicker from Alexei's face to me, her features hardening. Fixing her shoulders back, she points at the living room.

"Go put her down. Right now," Nadya orders, her voice harsh and uncompromising. Alexei shifts me in his arms, and when I look at his face, I can't tell if he wants to move me out of the line of fire or use me as a human shield.

"I'm—"

"Now, Alexei."

The way she snaps at him makes me feel like I'm back in school, waiting to get scolded by the principal, and apparently, he feels the same way. His already tired face is pale, his eyes scanning the room for an escape.

"Put her down, or I will make you."

Alexei swallows, maneuvering around his sister until he can lay me on the couch. I've never seen him look scared before, and I don't like it. He grabs a throw pillow off of an armchair and tucks it behind my head before he yanks the blanket off the back of the couch, keeping an eye on Nadya.

As soon as he backs away from me, Nadya launches herself at him, pulling him into a hug so tight I wonder if he's able to breathe.

"Learn to answer your phone," she snarls, her face red and eyes wet as she buries her face in Alexei's shoulder. "I was scared to death, you fucking asshole."

Slowly, like he's dealing with a feral animal, Alexei hugs her back, graciously ignoring the way her shoulders tremble.

"I'm sorry. You're right, I should have called. I was..." His voice trails off. "Busy."

"I was right?" She sniffs, her expression anguished. "Care to put that in writing?"

"Not a chance."

She searches his face, lingering on the cut on his forehead.

"Did you hear about Lev?"

Alexei doesn't answer for a long moment, and when he does, he clears his throat. My stomach drops, but his posture is resolute. I don't know what happened to Lev, but whatever it was, Alexei knows exactly how it happened.

He just doesn't want Nadya to know it.

"Yeah. I heard."

"I was terrified you were with him. That I'd leave my apartment and find you the same way Aunt Vera found him. I was so scared I'd never get to yell at you for pissing me off again." Nadya looks torn between hugging him again and punching him in the face. Her eyes dart to me, and something shatters behind her expression.

"Were... were you two at the club when the explosion happened?"

"We were," I answer before Alexei can try to pretend otherwise. His sister deserves the truth, no matter how much he wants to protect her from it.

A silent conversation takes place while they look at each other, one I don't want to be privy to.

"We need to talk," they say at the same time. If I didn't feel like I'd just been caught up in a bomb, I'd try to slip away to give them privacy, but I'm not sure I can. For all my protests about being able to walk when Alexei carried me from the car, I'm exhausted, and I definitely can't walk to my room on my own.

"Before you say anything, I need you to know what kind of man Konstantin Lavrov is," Alexei rushes to say.

Nadya shakes her head, stepping back as she folds her arms over her chest. "I don't care. Call him. If it keeps you safe, I'll do whatever the hell he wants." Her voice is determined, even as Alexei's shoulders slump. He runs a hand through his hair.

"He isn't a good man, Nadya. He'll do anything if it'll make him a little bit richer or more powerful. If you marry him, you'll be nothing but another one of his pawns. I don't want to see you getting hurt by any man, but especially not him."

Unable to look at her, Alexei flops into an armchair, his elbows resting heavily on his knees. Nadya smiles sadly and sits on the coffee table in front of him. She looks at me, and I can't meet her gaze for long.

I shouldn't be here for this.

"I don't want you to get hurt, either," she says softly. "And despite what you think, I'm not oblivious to the kind of life you lead. I know Konstantin isn't a good man." She folds her hands over his, silently begging him to meet her imploring gaze. "But I've handled bad men before. And I've always been able to make my own choices. So let me choose this. Let me protect you."

Alexei's expression is tortured when he says, "I'm not sure I can."

"If it helps, if you don't call him, I'll track him down and propose to him myself." The protest in the back of his throat cuts itself off when she shakes her head. "You've done your best to let me ignore the Bratva, and I'm grateful for it, but I don't need your permission, Alexei. Not on this. Not when you've finally found someone who makes you happy."

She nods her head in my direction, smiling when I lay a hand on his arm.

"You finally found something that doesn't belong to the Bratva. If Emiliya makes you happy, then she's worth the sacrifice. Let me do this for you."

When he nods, Alexei's shoulders sag under the weight.

\*\*\*

No matter how soft Alexei's bed is, every time he shifts the pillows around me, I have to bite my tongue to hold back a whimper. But as painful as it is to adjust, lying down flat is even worse.

I've never been more grateful for painkillers in my life. Without them, I'd be nothing but a sobbing, agonized mess, and that's something neither Alexei nor Nadya to witness. Though from the way Alexei grimaces, murmuring soft apologies under his breath, I'm doing a terrible job of hiding my pain.

"Alexei?" I ask, if only to distract him from how much it hurts just to find a comfortable position.

"Yeah?"

"Are you going to kill my father?"

He goes so still I wonder if he's even breathing. I can hear Nadya puttering around in the other room, trying to stay out of the way but still terrified to let her brother out of her sight.

I can't say I blame her. So am I.

"I am," Alexei answers after a long beat, refusing to look at me.

"Good." His eyes snap to mine, and I let him feel every ounce of hate I have for that man. "If I didn't feel like a walking bruise, I'd ask to come along."

"Yeah?"

"Can you make me a promise?"

"Anything."

"Make him suffer. He doesn't deserve an easy death."

With such tenderness that it makes me ache, Alexei brushes a thumb over my cheek. He doesn't need to say it for me to know what he's thinking. Not when he's smiling like he's glad I'm still here, when his eyes are bright with regret for everything that's happened.

"I promise," he whispers, leaning forward to rest his forehead against mine. "He'll feel every moment."

Even though there isn't a part of my body that isn't screaming in agony, while we're in this little bubble, nothing can touch me. Not my father, not the dread plaguing Alexei. Nothing. It's just the two of us.

As long as we have each other, that's more than enough.

# CHAPTER 35

# Alexei

Even though I had hours to brace myself before Konstantin arrived, it wasn't enough. Before I can compose myself, he's in my office, an infuriating grin in place while I remind myself how much I need him.

To his credit, he didn't gloat when I called him. He just said he'd prep his private jet and have his lawyer draw up the paperwork.

I reread the contract again. On paper, this is nothing but a business arrangement. There's nothing to be found here about weapons or an arranged marriage. Nothing about murder and power struggles. No, it's all about revenue streams and controlling stakes.

The lump in my throat feels like a cancer that refuses to die.

"Nadya deserves better than this."

I don't realize I've said that aloud until Konstantin leans back in his chair, hands fisted in his lap. "And what does she deserve?"

"Someone who loves her. She threw her entire youth away trying to keep me on the straight and narrow. She hates the

Bratva for the way it took our father away from us, for the way it ruined her life, and for all the ways it keeps her from knowing who I really am."

I clear my throat, working my jaw as I look at him.

"If she marries you, Nadya won't be able to hide from it anymore. She'll be just as entrenched in this life as you and me."

And if she hates it, there's no divorce. Not when Konstantin's position requires strength and stability. If I go through with this, Nadya is going to be stuck for the rest of her life.

"You want her to be happy."

"Yeah. More than anything."

He tilts his head to the side as he thinks, and for once, I hate this life as much as Nadya. I have more money than I could ever need, men look to me for direction, and I'm able to inspire fear with no effort, but none of it will revoke the damage we're about to unleash.

I can't fix it if Nadya wants to sacrifice herself any more than I can undo what Nikita's done to Emiliya.

They're both in my bedroom, doing their best to keep each other distracted while I'm in here. For as much as I expected Nadya to keep holding a grudge, she let it go and embraced Emiliya as easily as she's forgiven me.

How am I supposed to get Konstantin to understand that Nadya is more than my sister? I've never had to exist without her, and sending her to him feels like carving half of my soul from my body.

"I've heard you're taken with Nikita's daughter," Konstantin says, watching me with a knowing gaze. "I've also heard you've been having issues knowing who to trust. Am I right?"

I bite back my instinctive anger.

"You know it is."

He hums. I want to punch the look of pity off his face.

"I can't promise your sister will be happy with me, but I can promise you I won't hurt her. She won't want for anything, and I'm not going to try to keep her from you. If you agree to this, you'll be able to focus on Emiliya while I take care of Nadya. You'll have my aid in dealing with Nikita. Even if you delay and ask around, you won't find anyone else who can offer you what I can."

There's a stone on my chest, slowly crushing me.

I hate that he's right.

With my attention split between Nikita, Emiliya, Nadya, and The Outfit, things are falling through the cracks.

Add on the additional focus I'll have to put into cleaning up Savage, and I can't protect everyone at once.

I can't keep Nadya safe *and* let her live the life she wants. I can't explore the feelings growing between Emiliya and me while I constantly have to keep an eye out for another attack from her father. I can't ask Andrei to leave his pregnant wife to watch my back all the time. I can't pull Artyom away from his regular duties. And without Lev, I have a gap I'm not sure how to fill.

I have no one else to turn to.

Can I trust Konstantin to make Nadya happy? Fuck no, but I don't have any other options. I don't know how he'll treat her, or even why he's insisting on marrying her in the first place, but I'll have to find a way to live with my choices.

Even if they aren't really mine.

They're hers.

Nadya will sell her soul to the devil as long as it protects me.

"I need your word," I tell him. I'd rather be anywhere else. That I'm even considering this is a testament to how far off the rails my life has gone since. "I need you to swear to me that you'll keep her safe."

"I swear." Konstantin nods, his face as solemn as I've ever seen. I search for any signs of deceit, but either he's telling the truth, or he's expertly mastered controlling his expressions.

The latter wouldn't surprise me, but instinct tells me he's being sincere.

Fuck, I hope he is.

With a pit in my gut, I sign the contract and push it across the desk before I can change my mind.

"Wonderful," Konstantin says with a grin. "Now that's handled, what do you need to handle your little problem with Nikita?" I refuse to look at him as he folds the contact and slips it into the pocket of his suit jacket.

"I need to find a way to kill him, but getting access to him is challenging, at best."

"You literally have a key to his home hiding in the other room with my fiancée," he says smugly, his face lit up with a smirk that makes me want to punch him in the face.

I cut him a glare, but I'm not so far gone as to delude myself into thinking he wouldn't know they were here. I just hoped he'd be gracious enough not to point it out.

I should have known better. Konstantin Lavrov doesn't know the definition of the word.

And once again, he's right. All I need is a way to get past Nikita's guards, and Emiliya can give me the keys and all the codes I need to get inside his home.

"Once I get into his home, I need to make a show of force. Something that will cut down the men who have pledged their support to him. If it were just a few unknowns, I wouldn't give a fuck, but he has connections to men with money, men who command respect in their own right."

Konstantin raises a single brow.

"I don't want to deal with infighting until the end of time. I need everyone to understand I am their pakhan, and that to deny it will mean death. And I need to do all of that without making even more enemies or giving The Outfit another opportunity to exploit our weaknesses."

"You're aware that's virtually impossible, right?"

"I'm not stupid. But you asked what I needed."

"Well," Konstantin sighs, looking up at the ceiling. "I can deal with Nikita's allies. But if you want them to fall in line, you'll have to prove you're strong enough to control them. Kill him yourself, and make sure you have a reputable witness or two…" He shrugs as he trails off. "It's one way of showing them you're fully capable of handling yourself. Like you did with your cousin."

My lip curls knowing he had spies in that room.

"Word travels fast."

"I didn't stumble into the position I'm in by mistake." Konstantin smirks. "If you want the crown, you'll have to be smart. Kill Nikita. Then we can give some of his supporters a little visit.

When you tell them you're taking over, I'll make sure they know to keep their mouths shut."

\*\*\*

I twist a sculpture of a bird in my hand, running my thumb over the detailed feathers and painted beak. Tiny chips and painstaking lines of dried glue mar the surface.

It's a tiny thing, but it clearly is important to Emiliya if she went through all the work of putting it back together. I glance around the rest of the room. The decorations are far and few between. Plants are lined up on every surface. Most of them are wilted, but some still show signs of life.

A few leaves have fallen to the floor, a distraction from how clean everything else is.

It isn't what I was expecting when Emiliya described her room. She told me about knickknacks and decorations, but this little bird seems to be the only thing left.

What did Nikita do with the rest of it?

I tuck the tiny bird into my coat pocket. Emiliya can add it to the chaos she's made of the rest of my condo. Even though she's only really had full reign over the kitchen and her room, there are signs of her everywhere.

All the drawers and cabinets have been reorganized, making it impossible for me to navigate my own kitchen without getting lost. All my books are out of order. Her dresses are mixed in with my suits in my closet, a chaotic blend of colors and fabrics that drive me up a wall every time I get dressed almost as much as it makes me smile whenever I see it.

But she moves around with ease, not bogged down by fear or concern.

I watch as a cherry-red Bentley pulls into the driveway, and I wonder if it would be worth bringing any of the plants home for Emiliya, but something tells me she'd scream at me if I so much as touched them.

Hell, she practically bit my head off when I tried to water the one in my room this afternoon.

Considering she's still struggling to get out of bed, it was more impressive than it should have been. And maybe I should be concerned by how hot it was to see her all worked up, her eyes spitting fire until I backed down, but that's an issue for another day.

As soon as Emiliya figures out the power she holds over me, I am beyond fucked.

A guard opens the Bentley's door and Nikita steps out, not bothering to look up at the dark, empty house. Neither does Yan, following hot on Nikita's heels. He only stops when Nikita turns around, tossing him a glare.

I roll my eyes.

Of course, Nikita's the type of person who won't let his guards into the house. At least it works in my favor.

For now, anyway. Like Konstantin said, I'll need a witness, eventually. I can claim credit for Nikita's death all I want, but without someone willing to verify it, there will always be whispers.

I refuse to tolerate doubt.

For all the shit he put Emiliya and her mom through, for all the damages he caused at Savage, for all the stress he's caused me, I'm going to end this.

Tonight.

If Nikita's too blind to notice someone watching him from the shadows, then it's his own fucking fault.

The front door slams shut, the sound echoing throughout the house, and only then does Yan look up, seeming to know exactly where I'm waiting. Between him and Emiliya, getting into this house was a breeze.

I'd offer him a reward for everything he's done in the short time I've known him, but something tells me that as long as Irina's safe and he's allowed to stay by her side, he doesn't want anything else.

Not when he looks at her the same way I look at Emiliya.

I wait until Yan turns away, walking down the driveway, toward the car waiting down the road. As far as I'm concerned, as long as Irina's happy with him, they can have each other.

I wait long enough to ensure Nikita has moved through the house, settling into his comfortable routine, and oblivious to the fact that his house should be completely devoid of life. Waiting until I'm positive he's ignorant that anything is out of place.

He's a nightmare to everyone around him, but now he's bereft of anyone to terrorize. I take no small amount of pleasure in knowing he'll die exactly how he should: entirely alone.

If I make a noise as I stalk through the halls, Nikita will assume I'm a member of the household staff, or, if he remembers he has one, maybe even his wife. Either way, it doesn't matter.

My gun is secure in my waistband, but I make no move to grab it.

Ending Nikita with a quick bullet to the head is a mercy he doesn't deserve. It's not what I promised Emiliya, and that woman has faced more than enough disappointment in her life.

I'm not going to add to it if it's the last thing I do.

When I find Nikita, he's stabbing a fork into a plate of re-heated leftovers as if they've committed a grave offense. His tie is loose at his collar, his jacket tossed away. Stripped of the gravitas he usually carries like a coat of arms.

He jumps when I clear my throat, holding his fork like a weapon.

"How'd you get in here?" he demands, his rage a thin veneer over his sudden fear.

"It turns out it's not difficult when you have the right connections," I shrug. "We have a few things to discuss, don't we?"

"What's there to discuss? There was an explosion, people died, and you're still standing. It's the cost of war with the Italians." Subtly, Nikita glances around, looking for either a weapon or a way out. When he spots Konstantin standing in the other doorway, casually adjusting his cufflinks, Nikita freezes.

"It might have been. If The Outfit had any part in it." I shrug. "But you're the one who had your daughter bring me there, so you'll forgive me if I doubt their involvement. Did you know that little stunt nearly got Emiliya killed?"

For a split second, something like regret flashes in Nikita's eyes, but just as fast, it's gone. My blood boils when he keeps his focus on Konstantin.

Konstantin looks up, seeming surprised to find the attention on him. Nikita empties his hands, abandoning any hope of using a fucking *fork* as a weapon.

"If you're looking at me because you think I'm going to help you, you're out of luck." Konstantin shrugs. "I'm just here to observe, like someone who films nature documentaries." I almost, *almost* roll my eyes as Nikita's gaze darts back and forth, calculating the odds.

I might not know much about numbers, but even I can see that, on the surface, they look about even. We're on his turf, he knows where the weapons are, and, presumably, he thinks if he calls for help, someone will come running to his aid.

All his guards are out in the cold, right where he left them.

Nikita is all alone, and it's his own damn fault.

He sets his shoulders, lunges, and it's exactly the opportunity I've been waiting for. Nikita rushes at me, his fists clenched. He leaves himself wide open, allowing me to duck out of his path and grab his collar.

When he swings his fist toward my face, I use the momentum to swing him around, pressing him forward until his face slams into the cabinet in front of him. The door bangs as he struggles to get free, driving his elbows back until he's able to catch me in the ribs.

The blow winds me.

It's enough of a distraction to loosen my grip, and Nikita takes full advantage, throwing himself back until I have to choose between keeping my hold on him and falling backward. My hip slams against the stone of the island while he whirls around, using all his strength to go straight for my face.

Nikita has more bulk, but I have the advantage of both height and speed, and when he hits my chin, I move with it, pushing forward with my legs while he's on the backswing.

My foot hooks around the back of his knee, and I'm filled with a sense of satisfaction when it buckles under him, giving me the room I need to give him a little taste of everything he's done to Emiliya.

I force my weight onto Nikita's chest, pinning him in place while he howls and struggles beneath me.

The skin on my knuckles bruises and splits as I throw every ounce of my burning, boiling anger behind my hits.

I pound my fists into his face until Nikita is no longer recognizable, until he's no longer trying to fight back, only holding his hands up to try to protect himself from further blows.

I hit him until he passes out, his body limp and defenseless.

Even then, I don't stop.

Grabbing his head by his hair, I slam him into the cold tiles under us until his blood splashes over the floor with every new blow.

I hit him for every bruise he's ever laid on Emiliya, for every moment of terror he inspired in her and Irina.

When his breaths are nothing but wheezing gasps, I smile, remembering how bloodshot Emiliya's eyes were after he tried to kill her. Her broken chuckle when she said it was the only time he'd tried, like she wasn't sure if it was the truth or not.

The only reason I stop is because I have a promise to keep.

Nikita needs to know exactly what this is about. It's no longer about the Bratva, or power, or even revenge.

He's dying at my hands because he dared touch Emiliya. Because he treated her like someone who isn't worthy of every ounce of kindness and respect his pathetic existence could have conjured up.

He should have cherished her and loved her with everything he had, but he didn't, and his loss is my gain.

Every breath is poisoned with the taste of blood as I shake out my hand. Pain filters in past my rage, and I'm pretty sure I've broken something, but it was fucking worth it. I sit back on my heels just as Konstantin leans around me, taking a look at the mangled mess that was Nikita's face.

"You really don't half-ass things, do you?" Konstantin asks with a shit-eating grin. "If your sister's anything like you, I've got my work cut out for me."

"You have no fucking clue," I say, wiping my face against my sleeve. The fabric comes away stained red. "Did you do what I asked?"

He nods, plucking a matchbook out of his pocket and tossing it in my direction. "Gas has been running since we got here, and there's fuel all over the upper floors. All it needs is a spark."

I look around the kitchen, ignoring the blood and the cabinets that broke in our fight.

Every part of this mansion is gleaming and perfect. Not a home, but a beautiful prison that's kept everyone inside it miserable, trapped under Nikita's thumb.

He groans, starting to stir.

Perfect.

"Then it's time for us to leave," I say as I light the matches, flipping them toward the gasoline-soaked rags Konstantin dropped in the corner. Instantly, they light up, fire licking along the walls and gliding over the hardwood.

By the time we're outside, the whole building is damned to the same fate as its owner.

And when I close my eyes, I can just make out Nikita's screams over the groan of a structure ready to collapse.

# CHAPTER 36

# Alexei

With every tiny bump in the road, the throbbing pain in my hand gets worse, until I'm swallowing curses and squeezing my eyes shut to block out the pain. I shouldn't be surprised that Nikita's hard head managed to break my hand.

"You good?" Yan asks, giving me a wary look when he runs over a pothole.

"He's fine," Konstantin drawls before I can tell Yan exactly how much his driving is exacerbating the pain. Konstantin rolls his shoulders and stares into the side of my face with a weight that's impossible to ignore. "Right, Alexei?"

I know why he's covering up my injury, and maybe somewhere down the line, I'll appreciate it. But right now, I'd rather rip his head off.

This is an injury that can be exploited, and until my position is rock solid, it's something I can't afford to let become common knowledge. Not even to Yan, who has nothing to gain by exposing me.

I only have to keep myself together for one more fight. After this, I can pop some pills, have a doctor set the shifting bones in my hand, and go home to Emiliya.

I can bury the pain long enough to go home to her.

"Yep," I grit out. "I'm fucking peachy."

Keeping my expression as neutral as I can, I nod at him. I don't so much as blink before he turns his attention back to the road.

By the time he pulls in front of Mikhail's house, I've found a second wind, letting certainty wash over me. Mikhail is far from the final obstacle I'll have to face if I want to be pakhan, but if I can convince him to drop his pride, the path will be far easier.

The trouble lies in convincing him he's already been beaten.

"Wait here," I tell Yan as I get out of the car.

In a moment, Konstantin's at my side, eyeing Mikhail's house with a blend of curiosity and boredom. All traces of his earlier amusement are washed away, replaced with a cold intensity I don't want to find myself on the wrong end of.

"No matter what goes on in there," he says, nodding toward the house, "you can't show him how much you're hurting. If you do, you'll be dead before my wedding."

"If I'm dead, you'll never see my sister again."

He hums.

"We'll see about that."

With my good hand, I knock.

"What the hell do you think you're doing here, Trenin?" Mikhail snarls, his expression twisted in a furious snarl as he rips open the door. His eyes flick to Konstantin, and something akin to worry flashes for just a moment before he's able to smother it.

Not giving him a chance to compose himself, I stroll into his home like I've been invited, checking his shoulder with mine as I pass. He whirls around to watch me incredulously, barely even noticing when Konstantin steps inside, flicking the lock behind him.

Mikhail rushes to reach for a weapon, and I tense before he freezes, his hand hovering over his hip. His glare disappears as panic takes over.

I click my tongue.

"Don't tell me you left yourself unarmed," I chide.

"I'm in my own home."

"And maybe if you hadn't opened the door, that might have meant something." I shrug. "But here we are. Don't feel too bad about it, though. Nikita made the same mistake earlier."

Mikhail's expression flares with a flash of doubt before he contains himself, falling into the same cocky attitude he's had my entire life.

"Get the fuck out of my house." He glances at Konstantin, his jaw flexing. "Both of you."

"We will, but you and I need to have a little chat first." I face him head-on, hiding my hands in my pockets before he's able to notice the swelling and rapidly darkening bruises. "I wanted to give you the courtesy of letting you know in person that Nikita is dead."

"Bullshit."

He looks at Konstantin like he expects him to contradict me, but he finds nothing. Moment by moment, uncertainty washes over Mikhail until, finally, he blanches, his skin growing deathly pale.

"It doesn't matter. Get the hell out of here."

Despite how sure he sounds, his hands are trembling even as he clenches them into fists.

"If you're trying to impress your new boss, you're doing a shit job," Konstantin warns, raising a single brow.

"Good thing Trenin isn't my boss."

Konstantin sighs in disappointment, pulling his phone out of his pocket. Moments later, he shoves it in Mikhail's face, grabbing the back of his head with his other hand and forcing him to look at a photo of Nikita's burning mansion. Mikhail snatches it away so he can take a closer look, not even seeming to notice when Konstantin lets go of him.

By the time Konstantin slips his phone out of his limp grip, Mikhail's swaying on his feet.

"That doesn't mean anything. Anyone could have torched his house."

"But they didn't," I say calmly, keeping my eyes glued to a portrait of Mikhail and his family hanging on the wall. "I did, which I'm sure Nikita would tell you himself, but"—I shrug, giving him a brief glance—"his charred corpse is likely being discovered by firefighters as we speak."

"And why the hell should I believe you?"

I lift a single shoulder, wishing he'd put up more of a fight. The adrenaline that fueled me when I stormed inside is quickly fading, and the throbbing pain in my hand is refusing to be ignored. It takes effort not to scream on every exhale.

"Because it's the truth. But if you'd rather wait for the coroner to confirm it, feel free. I'm sure it will be a fun report to read."

"That's even if they find a corpse," he scoffs. "For all you know, Nikita's fine and well."

"Oh, I assure you, he is very dead," Konstantin interrupts, chuckling darkly. "You should've been there. It turns out Alexei can put on one hell of a show when he wants to. But if you don't believe me, Yan's waiting out front. He'll tell you the same thing."

He rolls his neck as he grins.

"I have no dog in this fight," he continues, "but if you ask me, it'd be smart so shut the fuck up and listen to your pakhan."

Mikhail meets his glare while tension brews between them, his disbelief and fear tearing each other apart.

I clear my throat, stealing his attention while I point at the portrait.

"Mikhail, how old is your son now? Sixteen, seventeen?" He stiffens to the point I wonder if his spine will snap. "Old enough to be involved in the family business, I'm sure. Definitely old enough that you're training him to follow in your footsteps, right?"

As much as I hate to admit it, Mikhail holds his own power. If he wants to, he could prove to be a real problem down the line.

When I call a meeting and throw my name forward as pakhan, anyone can challenge me for the title. Whether it's a battle of wills or a physical fight depends on who opposes me.

If I can't get him to back down tonight, I'll have to find a way to compensate not just for my hand, but for every weakness in my life, and I'll have to do it in a fucking hurry.

I might have cut the head off the beast, but Nikita's generation will be a hydra if I'm not careful, and Mikhail can stand his own ground while he guns for my head. If he thinks I'll give him any room to breathe, he'll take every inch until he's standing on my neck.

"You don't like me, do you, Mikhail?"

"That's one way of putting it," he seethes.

I hum.

That Nikiya even tried to bypass formally being named pakhan is a testament to how little he and his ilk care about what really matters. They only care about power and the wealth the Bratva is able to give them. Not the brotherhood, not the hard work, not the comradery.

If it doesn't make their lives easier, then it's as useless as dirt.

If things don't change, their corruption and greed will topple everything we've fought for. The Outfit will find every weak spot, the cops will dig into our damaged foundation, and the rot will consume us all until there's nothing left to rule over.

I won't let that happen. Not after everything we've been through.

"While you've been busy doing everything in your power to prop up Nikita, I've been making my own friends. Ones who don't particularly care about you. Or your family." I tilt my head in Konstantin's direction. "I'm going to call a meeting as soon as news of Nikita's death goes public. We can't keep skating through a war without a pakhan."

Mikhail opens his mouth to argue, but I silence him with a sharp look.

"When I put myself forward, you won't challenge me. In fact, you'll sit on your ass, smile, and endorse me wholeheartedly."

"No one will accept you," he hisses, lip curled back in a snarl.

"Take a look around you. Nikita's guard is waiting outside. Men have put their lives on the line because I asked them to. Even when Nikita did everything in his power to have me killed, they focused on getting me out of an explosion before they focused on themselves."

I raise a brow, daring him to disagree.

He doesn't.

"They've already accepted me. You're being left behind, and you're too blind to even realize it."

"If you think I'll ever look at you as a ruler, you're out of your fucking mind."

Konstantin laughs, the sound loud and harsh. It's so late that the volume feels almost vulgar.

"You should consider yourself lucky, Mikhail," he says with a grin. "Alexei seems to think that more death will only lead to your lot eating yourselves alive, but if you ask me, when a tool refuses to do its job, you have no choice but to force it into submission. And I don't have the same qualms about spilling a little blood."

"You don't scare me, Lavrov"

Konstantin's grin turns vicious, the promise of violence bright in his eyes as he says, "I love that confidence. Is your son just as fearless?"

He leans down until he's level with Mikhail, his expression just as cruel as it is excited.

"Is your wife? Or will they fold as soon as I get ahold of them?"

Mikhail jolts as if he's been slapped, wide-eyed as he looks to me. I'm not going to offer him an out. If casual cruelty is how Konstantin wants to secure my position, then fine.

It's not often someone can challenge a man of Konstantin's caliber and walk away from it unscathed.

As long as Mikhail's blood is on his hands, I'll be able to shrug and pass the blame.

The fear in his eyes is exactly why I need Konstantin, even if I have to sell half of my soul to get it.

"Call off your guard dog, Alexei," he mutters with a note of defeat in his voice.

"I don't control him any more than you do. But like I said, I've been making friends. If you want Lavrov to back off, then pull your head out of your ass and realize I'm going to take over whether you agree to it or not. It's only a matter of how much you need to lose before you fall in line."

His jaw flexes, but Konstantin is the type of man who won't stop at threats. He'll salt the earth if it'll get him what he wants.

And he wants whatever will let him have Nadya.

There's a reason he's been pakhan for as long as he has, and it isn't because of his gentle, empathetic nature. The only way out of his web is to give in and give him whatever he demands.

Mikhail's shoulder slump as he closes his eyes against resignation and a warring resentment as he comes to terms with the gravity of his situation.

His chosen leader is dead. Even though he put his time and money into keeping Nikita in power, he has nothing to show for it, and I won't pull my punches to make sure it stays that way.

But if he gives in, the Bratva will have some semblance of peace for the first time in months, if not years.

"Leave my family out of it," he eventually says with a sigh. "They've done nothing wrong."

"Then fix your attitude and show your pakhan the respect he deserves," Konstantin pushes.

His nostrils flare as he looks at me.

I'm not foolish enough to think he won't push me and see exactly how much I'll let him get away with for the rest of time, but we both know I already won. No matter how hard he fights, Konstantin will always be in the back of his mind, a threat that's always waiting in the shadows.

"I won't challenge you," he mutters bitterly, his jaw grinding over the words like glass. "But when you collapse under the weight, I'll be first in line to pick over your corpse."

He can't hide the way he flinches when I walk toward him, meeting every hateful thought and word he's barely holding back with a steady look.

"Get off your high horse or we'll see just how long you can last when no one's there to cut you slack because you're too much of a coward to do what needs to be done. I won't let you hide behind your own incompetence the way Maksim did."

Konstantin opens the door, letting in a rush of cold air that barely registers over the ice in my tone.

"Oh, and Mikhail?" I call as I step onto his porch. "Your actions reflect on your son. You should consider that when you decide how you want to behave in the future."

# CHAPTER 37

# Alexei

As soon as I find Emiliya scrolling on her phone, curled up on the couch, I come to an abrupt stop.

I should've known something was off as soon as I stepped out of the elevator.

Instead of being greeted by Emiliya's blaring music or Mrs. Sullivan banging on my door, there was silence. I'd like to think my neighbor gave up or moved out, but I'm willing to bet she's hiding out in her condo, drafting yet another complaint to the owners of the building.

Unfortunately for her, the owner now works for me. The only one that sees her complaints is a trash can.

Though for all I know, she's given up and moved out rather than continuing to put up with us.

It's no longer in question who's in charge of the Chicago Bratva, but I've still had to spend far more time away from home than I'd like, getting everything in line and making sure our operations are running like fucking clockwork, no matter how much Mikhail grumbles when he thinks I can't hear him.

If I've learned anything from Konstantin, it's that a well-placed spy is as valuable as gold.

I hear every word he says, and he's going to figure it out sooner rather than later.

Since I left this morning, the only thing I've wanted was to crawl back into bed with Emiliya and show her exactly how much I've regretted getting home so late over the past three weeks.

At this point, I don't even care if I have to do that by holding her as she sleeps. I just want to be with her while she's still awake. Not a passing moment here and there or a quicky before I leave in the morning, but actual time with her.

"Is everything alright?" I ask.

For an agonizing moment, Emiliya doesn't answer. She just freezes in place, like she's waiting for something to ruin the delicate peace she's found in our condo.

"Are we dating?"

Instantly, I breathe a little easier, shrugging my jacket off my shoulders and tossing it over the back of one of the armchairs.

"Since I know what it feels like when you come on my tongue, I'd say we're doing a whole lot more than dating."

When she doesn't answer with her normal snark, I pause to really look at her.

She's uncharacteristically hesitant as she drops her hands to her lap, her spine ramrod straight.

"What happened?" My voice is harsher than I intend, and the way she flinches makes me feel like a monster for it.

"Mom called you my boyfriend earlier." She looks anywhere but at me as she shrugs. "And I realized we skipped right over the part where we talk about that sort of thing and jumped straight into moving in together."

I squint. I never thought we needed to define our relationship.

But I'm helpless to deny Emiliya anything, and if this is all it takes to reassure her, I'll gladly tell her exactly what she is to me.

Despite the doubt on her face, the label isn't what matters to her, and we both know it.

"You're mine, Emiliya. And I'm yours." Her shoulders fall a fraction of an inch, no longer bunched around her ears. "If that means I'm your boyfriend, then I'm your boyfriend. Your partner, your lover, I don't care. I'm yours."

I stalk across the room until I'm standing over her, setting my phone down on the coffee table before I use my uninjured hand to pluck hers from her hand and drop it next to mine. They can stay there for the rest of the night.

Whatever anyone else needs, they can wait.

Emiliya is far more important.

"And in case I haven't made myself clear," I say as I sit down, pulling her into my lap so her back is pressed against my chest, "I love you. I don't care what you call me, but when other people ask about you, I tell them you're mine. Nothing less."

She melts against me, warm and so fucking strong. Does Emiliya know how much I admire her strength? She carries the weight of everything on her shoulders with such apparent ease, that when she does need rest, when she needs reassurance, when she needs *me*, I'll happily give her everything I have.

She reaches behind me until she's able to scrape her nails against the back of my head. A shiver wracks down the length of my spine.

"Is that something that happens often? People asking about me?"

"Are you really surprised my men ask about the beautiful woman on my arm?"

Her hair is silky as I push it over one shoulder so I can trace my lips over the skin exposed by her simple tank top.

If Lev hadn't tried to use my relationship with her to rile me up, I don't think anyone would've said a fucking thing, but he opened a door I've struggled to close. My men may have doubts, but everyone knows better than to voice them in my presence.

Not that I'll ever tell Emiliya that. Their opinions of her and our relationship are worthless to anyone except themselves.

Something anyone who's dared open their mouth has learned in a hurry.

"I can't let them think they'll ever have a chance with you, can I?"

Emiliya feels like home as she leans against me, like everything I've ever wanted and so much more.

She shifts her hips, turning to press a kiss against my cheek while I run my hands over her arms, practically groaning from just feeling her in my arms. Despite all my best intentions of letting her lead tonight, my cock stirs when she shifts, grinding her ass against me.

She chuckles, missing nothing.

Mentally, I curse the cast on my hand, keeping me from touching her as gently as I want to.

I can't wait to get the damn thing taken off in a couple of weeks.

"Is that all they say?" she asks. "That I'm beautiful?"

There's an undercurrent of insecurity in her voice, one that makes me want to hunt down every man that's ever made her feel less than perfect. Nikita, Daniil, hell, even me.

She's a fucking gift; one I'll never take for granted again.

"Sweetheart, if anyone tries to say anything different, I'll cut out their tongues and make sure they're kept alive to serve as a warning for everyone else. You're mine. That means you're worthy of just as much respect as I am, if not more."

She swallows thickly, and I shift my hands to her torso, playing with the hem of her shirt.

"Because I put up with you?"

"Yes," I agree, my thumbs brushing over the underside of her breasts. "But mostly because you're *you*. You have more worth and pride than most of those men combined, and if they don't recognize it, that's their problem. Not yours."

She taps my cheek, and when I meet her eyes, her smile is as brilliant as the sun. I bask in its warmth before she pulls away, twisting around so she's straddling my hips.

How anyone could ever look at this woman and focus on her past, on their own misconceptions of her, and happily ignore everything she has to offer is beyond me. Then again, their loss is my gain.

Especially when she pulls her shirt over her head, tosses it aside, and wraps her arms around my shoulders. Her cheeks are flushed and her pupils blown out, making my blood thrum under my skin.

"I love you, too," she whispers against my lips as she presses her chest against mine. Not for the first time, I curse how many layers I'm wearing. "Take me to bed and let me show you exactly how much."

I don't need to be told twice.

I scoop her into my arms, holding most of her weight with my left arm and crossing the condo in quick strides while she traces her lips over my jaw.

When she takes my earlobe between her teeth, I'm as hard as a fucking stone. All the tension I've been carrying around fades away as I lay her on the bed, her hair spreading around her like a fucking painting, designed to tempt and enchant.

For a moment, I'm not worried about The Outfit and the way they've been keeping their distance. I'm not thinking about Konstantin and all the text messages and phone calls he's been making. I'm not looking over my shoulder like I've been doing every time I step outside. The exhaustion from all the late nights and endless meetings is gone, and all it takes is a flutter of her lashes.

"You're so fucking beautiful," I tell her.

I toss aside my vest, wishing I had the words to tell her exactly how perfect she is in my eyes. When I throw my tie away to join it, Emiliya's whole face is soft.

"You know, you don't have to charm me." She sits up enough to start undoing the buttons of my shirt. "I'm going to sleep with you, anyway."

"I don't waste my time saying things I don't mean." I shrug, covering her hands with mine until she meets my eyes. "And we both know I've never needed charm to get you naked."

"No," she concedes, working until my shirt is completely undone. "But here I am, still half-dressed." She lies back down, hooking her thumbs under the waistband of her sweats for emphasis as I shrug off my shirt. "Maybe you're losing your edge."

I laugh, a dark sound that has her breaking out in goosebumps.

"Don't tempt me, Emiliya. I want you far too much to play games, but if you force my hand, I may change my mind."

I lean forward, scraping my teeth over her throat, letting the threat sink in.

In answer, Emiliya lifts her hips, giving me room to slip my hands under her and pull down her pants with no effort at all.

"Wise choice," I murmur before pressing a kiss against her breastbone, trailing kisses down her body and spreading her thighs until they're resting over my shoulders on either side of my head.

"Now, stay quiet and let me kiss you."

Her eyes flare, bright and fiery as I seal my lips over her clit, flicking my tongue like I've been starved for a taste, even though I had her like this earlier this morning. After so many long days and even longer nights, I'm not sure I'll ever get enough of her again.

As soon as she threads her fingers through my hair, I pull away, smirking at the way she whines.

"I want to feel you come. I want you to come so hard you won't even complain when you remember me fucking you every time you move tomorrow morning. Think you can do that for me, sweetheart?"

Dazed, Emiliya nods. The unfocused look in her eyes sends a bolt of lust down my spine, shooting straight to my aching dick, still trapped in my slacks.

I work her with my tongue until her thighs clamp around my head, her fingers so tight in my hair it's bordering on painful as she cries out, a needy sound that rips through the room and sets my blood on fire.

My self-control is hanging by a thread as I lap at her release, torn between grinding my hips against the mattress and ripping off my belt and ridding myself of my pants as quickly as humanly possible.

The instant she falls limp, I sit up, stripping my pants off, then slamming my mouth against hers, plunging my tongue past her lips until she has no choice but to taste herself on me. She doesn't hesitate, and, fuck, if the way she returns the kiss isn't hot as hell.

Passionate and ferocious, Emiliya acts like she needs this just as much as I do, like she's missed me just as much as I've missed her.

"Fuck me," she pants against my mouth. "Please, Alexei, I need you to fuck me."

Goddamn, she's perfect.

I slide into her in one hard thrust. When she arches her hips, I slide just that much deeper as I groan against her throat.

Bone-deep satisfaction cuts through me as we move together, the urgency I was expecting to find completely absent.

Emiliya's still here. Not because I'm forcing her, or because Nikita's told her to, but because she wants me. She's still scared, but she isn't running away. She's choosing to stay, and I'll spend every minute of the rest of my life making sure she doesn't regret it.

Our orgasms build like a fire until she pulls on my hair and forces me to look at her, to take in the flush on her cheeks, the way her tongue traces her bottom lip, leaving a slick trail I want to chase.

"I love you," I can't resist telling her.

"Love you, too."

She pulls me in for a kiss, our bodies moving as one until the fire consumes us both, scorching any traces of who I thought I was before I knew her.

Emiliya came into my life like a storm, shaking up everything. But among the debris and wreckage, she helped me find myself again, and I wouldn't trade that for anything.

# CHAPTER 38
# Emiliya

"You know..." I say, drawing out the sound as Yan leaves Mom and me alone in the exam room. I watch as she turns her head to follow every movement, her eyes lingering on his ass until the door shuts behind him. "I didn't think you were into younger men."

She can pretend all she wants, but I'd have to be blind to miss the way she was blushing when they got here, leaning into him more than she needed to as he helped her into the exam room.

I can't say I blame her. If I were into older guys, and weren't completely head over heels for Alexei, I'd probably be crushing on Yan too. He's a decade younger than her, but he has a silver fox thing working for him, with gray strands weaving their way through his dark hair.

Mom's cheeks burn bright. I hide my laugh behind a cough.

"I don't know what you're talking about," she says tightly, averting her gaze.

"Sure, you don't," I say breezily, resting my head against her shoulder.

Without Father, Mom's so much lighter. Happier. She's spent more time smiling in the month since Father's funeral than she has in the past three years.

She's still conflicted when we talk about him, and she probably will be for some time, but without his influence, she's starting to see exactly how much damage he caused her.

There was a moment at his funeral when there was a lull from people pretending to wish us well, when she took my hand in hers and smiled at me like the weight of the world had been lifted from her shoulders.

For the most part, people were gracious enough not to point out how happy she looked at her husband's funeral. Everyone except for Yan.

He was just as happy that day as I was.

He's been glued to Mom's side since the explosion, going so far as to move into the cozy townhouse she bought with the insurance money from the fire.

If there's something growing between them, she's refused to say, but from the way they look at each other when they think no one's paying attention, I wouldn't be surprised.

"I just want to make it clear that if you wanted to, I wouldn't be upset about having a stepdad," I say with a smile.

Her head whips toward me so fast I have to lift my head from her shoulder, her expression incredulous. My face hurts with the effort it takes to conceal my grin.

"*Lastochka,*" she scolds, "it's only been a little over a month. It's far too soon for me to be thinking about marriage again."

If she'd been in a loving marriage, sure. But Father hadn't given a shit about either of us for so long I don't even remember what his affection looked like. Now that we're free of him, I'm finally able to see a future worth fighting for instead of from.

I'm no longer scraping by, waiting for another opportunity to make things a little easier. I don't wake up every morning with a lead weight pressing down on my chest. I'm excited to see another day, and Alexei's been with me every step of the way.

But if Mom isn't there yet, I'm not going to push her. I'll gladly sit by her side until she lets go of all the baggage he thrust upon her.

Even if I have to wait the rest of her life.

But no matter how much she denies it, she's doing so much better since Father died. She's still sick, and she always will be, but she isn't nearly as depressed. Her mood swings aren't as dramatic. She's laughing more easily, and she's far more gracious with herself when she struggles.

If underneath all that there's still part of her that feels conflicted and misses him, then I'll let her. She can take her time letting go and finding her own happiness.

"I'm just saying, if you decide you want to date someone else, don't use me as an excuse to hold back."

"Even if I wanted to be with Yan—and I'm *not* saying I do—I don't think he's going to be interested in someone like me."

"Someone like you?" I ask incredulously. "You mean someone funny, well-read, and interesting? You mean the best mom anyone could ever ask for?" She won't meet my eyes, and I can't help but sigh. What I wouldn't give for her to let go of all the crap Father filled her head with over the years and see herself the way I do.

"Would you change your mind if I told you Yan always asked about you before? Or how whenever he compliments me, it's always in relation to how pretty *you* are?"

For a long moment, she's quiet. Eventually, she murmurs, "He does?"

"Every time. He's never stopped seeing you."

Mom smiles to herself, picking at her nails.

"I don't know if I'd consider listening to smut as being well read," she says sheepishly.

I throw my head back with a laugh. By the time Dr. Bonilla walks in, his round face curving up with a smile when he spots us, we're both laughing, and I've never felt so free.

***

None of the security guards give me so much as a second look as I make my way through the construction zone that used to be known as Savage. Alexei must have half of the city's police force in his pocket with how quickly he got them to chase away the feds and wrap up their investigation so he could start working on repairs.

Crews started working around the clock before Father's body was released for burial.

But even if one threat has been taken care of, The Outfit's still around, waiting to take another bite out of Alexei's Bratva as soon as they get an opportunity.

As a precaution, Alexei's keeping a rotating schedule of security around the clock, monitoring everyone and everything that comes in or out of any of his businesses, but especially Savage.

The whirring of power tools chases me all the way to Alexei's office, nearly drowning out the sound when I knock on the door.

"Is there any chance you could pick somewhere quieter to work?" I call out as I open the door.

In an instant, all his attention is on me, his smile lighting up the room as I make my way to his desk. His work is abandoned without a second thought, ready and waiting for him whenever he's ready to return to it.

As soon as I close the door, the sound returns to a more bearable level, and I blow out a sigh of relief.

"Why would I want to do that?"

"So you can hear yourself think," I suggest with a shrug. I plop myself on the corner of his desk, looking over the scribbled notes in front of him. "How long have you been here, anyway?"

I woke up briefly when he slipped out of bed this morning, but that was before sunrise. He's been leaving early most days, and lately, I'm lucky if he's home before I've already crawled into bed for the night.

Not that I can blame him for it. He's been working his ass off to put out all the fires that sprung up after Father appointed himself as pakhan, and getting a handle on everything that fell to the wayside since Maksim's death has been more of a challenge than I think he was anticipating.

There are only so many hours in a day, but I'll always be waiting for him once he has everything under control.

"How was your mom's appointment?" Alexei asks instead of answering my question.

"Fine. When are you going to find someone to help you with all of this?" I wave a hand at the mess on his desk. There isn't a single inch of the glass desk visible under all the paper and notes. I don't know how he's able to keep track of all of it.

"As soon as I figure out why running a criminal outfit requires so much fucking paperwork."

"I think that's the *organized* part of organized crime," I tease. To Alexei's credit, he huffs a breath that could generously be interpreted as a laugh. "And if you ever want to see me during daylight hours, you're going to have to find someone to help you."

"Last time I checked, it was still daylight. And here you are." His gaze is warm as he rubs circles against my knee with the thumb of his uninjured hand, the other still wrapped in a cast. "But maybe you have a point."

As he sighs, he leans back in his chair like a king surveying his kingdom. Despite the bags under his eyes, the traces of dust from the main room still dirtying his shoes, and the mess of paperwork around him, he still manages to look regal and in control.

"I'll ask Andrei if he'd be willing to take some of this off my plate, and I'll tell the club managers to figure out their own shit."

Even knowing what a struggle it is for Alexei to let go of his tightly held control, I won't deny that I'm selfishly glad to know there's a light at the end of the tunnel. I want to have him back to myself. But I'll wait as long as I have to.

Alexei's worth it.

His hands glide up my legs, settling on my hips as I move to straddle his lap, his arms sheltering me from everything outside of the two of us.

"I've missed you," I confess.

"I've missed you, too," he says softly, resting his forehead against mine. "I'll make it up to you."

"You don't have to," I say out of instinct. "I know you're busy. Just... try to find some time for me when you can, alright?"

Alexei sighs, pulling me closer to his chest. "How about we go out tonight? I can show you off, and I'll let you know exactly how important you are to me."

"I'd like that," I whisper with a shy smile.

As he presses his lips against my forehead, I close my eyes, grateful Alexei's given me a life where I'm not just surviving, but I'm able to live for the first time.

# Epilogue

## EMILIYA

"You're going to kill me," Alexei pants, throwing an arm over his eyes as his chest heaves to catch his breath. I giggle, while I kiss my way up his abs. My scalp buzzes from where his other hand is still fisted in my hair, holding me close.

I nip gently against his pec, and he gets the message, loosening his grip enough to let me pull myself up so I can press an obnoxious kiss against his cheek.

"But wouldn't it be a great way to go?"

Alexei hauls me into a kiss while his chest vibrates with a growl.

I'm a gross, sweaty mess, but in his arms, it doesn't matter. He looks at me like I'm the most beautiful thing he's ever seen, no matter how disgusting I feel. His lips move against mine in a slow, indulgent rhythm, and I love it. He's everything I want and so much more.

But we don't have time for this right now.

Alexei already turned off two alarms, and as much as I want to spend all day with him, he'll never forgive himself if he's late to Nadya's wedding.

I pull away regretfully, a move that takes all my willpower.

"Are you ready to let me out of bed yet?"

Immediately, any good resulting from our enthusiastic morning sex is undone. Alexei's back to the same stiff, stressed-out mess he's been for weeks, and I almost regret saying anything at all. We flew to California on Konstantin's private jet yesterday, and not even the warm weather has successfully thawed Alexei out.

In fact, with every hour drawing us closer to the wedding, he only gets worse.

He's been snapping at anyone and everything, constantly on edge. The only time he's even marginally relaxed is when we're alone together.

Switching gears, I pull the luxuriously soft sheets up until we're both wrapped up in them, safe and isolated from the rest of the world in a cozy cocoon.

"Have you ever thought about having kids?" Impossibly, he grows even stiffer. "Not now, obviously," I backtrack, swallowing down an instinctive wave of anxiety. Shit, could I have chosen a *worse* change of topic?

"In the future, I mean. Or, if you don't want any, never works, too. I was just curious."

"Is that something you want?" Alexei asks. "Kids?"

I pause. Do I?

"I never really thought about it." I always figured that whoever Father arranged for me to marry would be the one in charge of that decision, and I'd have to go along with what they wanted.

Closing my eyes, I rest my head against Alexei's chest, listening to his heartbeat. I can picture it. Alexei chasing down a toddler, smiling like they're the center of his universe. Giving us a home where we all know we're safe and loved.

My heart squeezes in my chest.

"I might not mind having a couple. Maybe in a few years," I admit.

"With me?" Alexei's wide-eyed, pulling his arm away just enough to make eye contact. I almost laugh.

"I mean, you'd do. We could make some good-looking babies, but maybe I should shop around a little, see what other options are out there."

"That's not going to happen," he mutters into the crook of his arm. "You're not going to make babies with anyone but me."

"Is that so?"

His arm tightens around my shoulders, fingers digging into me hard enough that I know he doesn't want to be pushed on this. I settle in, tracing over his collarbones, following the lines to his shoulders. He moves his other arm, using his bicep as a pillow beneath his head.

"I don't know if I'd be a good dad," he eventually admits. "If we're going to have kids, I don't want to fuck them up, you know?"

"You won't."

If I know anything, it's that.

Alexei cares too much about the people he loves to be anything but an incredible father. He'd take care of our kids with
the same intensity he has with everything else. He'd guide them
through life and make sure they know to take no shit, and he'd
defend them as fiercely as he does me.

Especially if we ever had a daughter.

"You'd be a great dad. If, you know, that was something you
ever wanted."

He sighs a long breath, idly twirling a lock of my hair around
his finger.

I sit up, patting a hand against his sternum while he eyes me.

"We don't have to figure that out today, but I *do* have to
shower. Up to you if you want to join me or not," I announce as
I extract myself from his arms. I can feel his gaze lingering on the
sway of my hips as I saunter into the bathroom, and I can't hold
back a smirk when I hear him climbing out of bed to follow me.

He catches me before I even reach the door, and I laugh as
he pulls me into a kiss, suddenly far less concerned about how
much time we have to get ready.

***

We've been sitting outside the gorgeous wedding venue for a
half an hour, and I'm starting to wonder if Alexei's having some
sort of silent panic attack. He's staring out the windshield, his
hands braced against the steering wheel. His face has been wiped
clean of any emotion.

I reach across the center console of this stupid rental car and lay a hand on his thigh, offering him support the only way I can.

Alexei hasn't wanted to talk about his arrangement with Konstantin, and he's been avoiding Nadya since the night he brought me home from the hospital, so I have no way of knowing what's going through his mind right now.

But shocking him back to reality got him moving when we were at the hotel, so it's worth trying again, right?

"What do you think about getting married?" For the first time in what feels like ages, he blinks, eyeing me curiously. "Not today, but once things are a little more settled. When you have more free time."

True to his word, Alexei is slowly learning to give up control. Andrei stepped up to take on some of the work, and Alexei's learning how to delegate tasks and trust his men to get the job done without him being there to micromanage them, but there's still plenty of things that need his attention.

It'll take time, but he's made a point of being with me when I wake up every morning. For now, that's enough.

"If you bring up looking for other options again, we're going to have problems."

"Well, obviously not." I grin. Like he's emerging from a melting block of ice, he flexes his hands, making sure they still work. "I live with you. I sleep in your bed. If I tried to marry someone else, it would get awkward."

There's a glint in his eye that makes me laugh.

"Maybe it's just all of this," I say, pointing at the wedding venue, decorated with pink lilies and delicate white flowers. "But I'd be down to marry you. When the time's right."

Alexei hums under his breath, looking more like himself with each passing minute.

With a knowing look, he lays his hand over mine, stroking his thumb over my bare ring finger.

"I'll keep that in mind. But if you so much as look at another man while you're talking about getting married and having babies, you know it won't end well for him, right?"

He's smiling, but his tone is deadly serious. Luckily for him, I'm as much his as he is mine, and even if an attractive naked man was in front of me doing a little dance, I'm not sure I'd notice.

I only have eyes for Alexei.

"Yes," I say indulgently as I press a kiss against his cheek. "You're a vicious killer, and I love you."

"I love you, too," he says as he finally reaches for the door handle to get out of the car.

Immediately, I'm slapped in the face by a wave of oppressive humidity. If I didn't already feel bad for Nadya, the weather would do it for me.

Alexei crosses over to my side of the car and takes my hand in his.

"Being a man in my position comes with certain expectations," he says gravely, not meeting my eyes. "If you don't want to deal with that, I'd prefer you tell me now. I won't force you to stay with me, but I don't know if I'll always be able to offer you that option."

I pull his hand, trying to urge him to look at me.

"If you stay with me, you'll always have security. You can still live your life, but you'll have guards whenever you go out. And if we end up having kids, they'd be stuck in this life, especially any sons. They'd be expected to follow in my footsteps." His throat bobs as he swallows. "I understand if you don't want that. For them or for you."

I caress his cheek, forcing him to meet my eyes. He leans into the touch, and it warms me more than the oppressive sun and suffocating humidity ever could.

"You said I'm stuck with you, right? Well, that goes both ways. I'm not going anywhere."

He nods, the corner of his lip twitching

"Good."

Finally, he moves toward the venue.

"By the way, how do you feel about alexandrite?" he asks casually.

I freeze, my hand jerking in his when he doesn't stop with me.

"Alexandrite? Like, the gem?" He nods. "I love it. But is that just a general question? Or are you asking for a reason?"

He moves his head from side to side, not confirming either way, but he doesn't fool me.

"If you don't want to ruin the surprise, I recommend you stay out of my office."

I perk up, but his face still reveals nothing.

"Which office? The one at home, or one of the clubs?"

"If I refuse to answer that, you're going to ransack every one until you find something, aren't you?"

"Only one way to find out."

I smile noncommittally, following him inside. If he didn't want me to poke through his office, he wouldn't have said anything, and we both know it.

I can't wait to see what I find.

# Want more?

If you want more of Alexei and Emiliya, get the free bonus epilogue here: https://BookHip.com/KHBLNPX

Thank you so much for taking the time to read Sacred Bond! If you want to help me out, please consider leaving a review on Goodreads and Amazon.

# About the author

Erin Robinson writes dark romance for readers who like complicated men and the women who make them fall to their knees.

When she isn't writing, she can be found digging around in her garden, herding her ridiculous cat, or curled up with a book in hand. She hopes that in time, she'll be able to pursue writing full time.

For updates on future releases, including sneak peeks, sign up for her newsletter on her website, authorerinrobinson.com.